CONCRETE RAINBOW

CONCRETE RAINBOW

A Novel in Two Parts

BOOK I: Forever Beach

BOOK II: Crystal City

by Jason Quinn

For Ziya.
Without you
I would forever
stumble
in darkness.

FOREWORD
BY LEE CATALUNA

Jason Quinn has worked in theaters such as Kumu Kahua, the venerable home for original work by Hawaii playwrights for half a century, and Honolulu Theatre for Youth, Hawaii's only professional theater company that has, since its early years in the 1950s, championed new work. Both these theater groups have been creative incubators for generations of storytellers who bounce ideas off one another, work on each other's plays, inspire excellence and continually expand and redefine what makes a Hawaii story. This novel and this writer were forged in that creative fire.

Quinn's work on stage and screen is familiar to audiences, and his years as an actor are reflected in his writing. His story has the cadence and color of the spoken word and is written with so much voice, the experience of reading it is almost like listening to the tale being told in a moment of unguarded honesty by the man who lived it.

The pace of the novel and the trials of the central character are relentless. It is an action-packed tale that doesn't let up much until its well-earned ending. However, Byron, the protagonist, is relentless, too, and that's what makes him so compelling. We always see the hopeful boy slugging it out through life, and even in his darkest hours, refusing to totally give up on himself.

Concrete Rainbow plays with scale in many ways. It is an epic story of one boy's life in a small town. It is violence and beauty occupying the same small space. It is a story as much about words as it is about imagery. In many ways, it is cinematic.

In the great Maori film *Once Were Warriors*, the story opens on a tranquil image of Aotearoa (also called New Zealand). There is a glass-like lake, snow-capped mountains, an unspoiled meadow. That image holds for only a few seconds before the camera pulls out to reveal that it's a billboard along a gritty highway. In less than a minute, we're transported from the idyllic image of island life to the brutal reality of one family's existence, battered by poverty, drug and alcohol use, domestic violence, and a kind of brutality that one would never imagine existed if you only believe the postcard images. That movie is a classic for the unflinching depiction of one family's struggle stuck in the storm drain of societal ills.

Concrete Rainbow is that kind of powerful revelatory look at a Hawaii that is hidden from the tourist gaze. It is a story of survival in an island urban jungle. Ultimately, what survives is a young man's dream.

There is no Chapter 7 in Book II. This is intentional.

BOOK I

FOREVER BEACH

"There is a monster that lives in between who you are and who you think you are."

~Kimo~

CHAPTER 1

DIRTY Q-TIP

THERE WAS A BEACH. There was that. It was about a hundred yards away. I could follow a little sandy path between four other houses and there it was. A beach.

But it was Ewa Beach. It was an oven. A cauldron of white-hot, two-inch-thick boiler plate steel. A simmering cesspool.

My sweat was sweating.

It was just before 10 a.m. and the heat was amazing. I was standing on Ewa Beach Road and I could see the heat waves shimmering off the pavement. I never wanted to live here.

I stood on the road in front of my new home. It was a two-bedroom shack, basically.

My new home. My new brother. My new sister. My new dad.

"I live in Ewa Beach…" I whispered to myself. Maybe if I said it out loud I could believe it.

"Ewa…Ewa…Ewa…" I trailed off. What I heard under my breath sounded like:

"Ever…and ever…and ever…"

Shit.

"Ewa Beach… forever, bitch…" I chuckled.

***

How did I not see this coming?

It was the beach.

It was the beach that allowed this whole thing to happen. It was the beach that made me tell my mom, "Yeah, your new boyfriend is cool!"

It was the beach that made me say "okay" to moving into the Fireman's little shack with his little kids in those little rooms with their little toys and their little voices. The voices that said "mine!"

The screams that said "I'm telling!"

It was the beach.

I know that it was the beach. I know it was the buzz of the foaming ocean as it slowly sifted itself though the sand. I know that it was the smell of the seaweed that tickled above my cheek and behind my nose. The prickly feeling of the salt drying on my sunburnt skin. I know it was that. The beach drowned out the little voices in the little house. The little kisses my mother would give her new boyfriend, the Fireman. The little moans from the Fireman's little room while his little kids slept soundlessly. It was the beach that whispered loud in my ear. I could not hear my mother say, "The Fireman is going to be your new father."

That was covered by the curling waves rolling themselves over the jagged reef.

One of my mother's boyfriends had ridden motorcycles. In return for bangin' my mom, he would take me to ride dirt bikes. Another one of my mom's boyfriends had owned a sailboat, and in return for bangin' my mom he would take me sailing. How was this time different?

This would be a few months. I could come down to Death Valley and swim in the ocean until the Fireman was done.

The beach tricked me.

The beach distracted me and I didn't realize the Firemen and his two kids were here to stay. Or no—my mom and her kid were here to stay. In Ewa Beach. In this fucking heat. In this little fucking house.

Forever, bitch.

***

"Eh!" There was a voice.

It came from the house next door. All of these houses had been built between 1950 and 1970. Simple single-walled houses with jalousie windows. They all sat on stilts about four feet off the sandy dirt. The boy was yelling from one of the windows. I tried to look through the louvers to see him but the east sun was still angled behind the house and in my eyes. I smushed my face and squinted. I could feel my nose was starting to burn. It must have looked red.

"Try wait, I stay coming out," instructed the boy.

In the time it took him to walk through his tiny house, I tried to figure out what he had said. I had been living in California for the past five years. I couldn't understand Pidgin anymore. Whoever this boy was, he spoke it thick.

"Brah, why you stay standing in da middle a da road? You trying for come *make*?" he said.

I stared at him. He was big. Maybe fifteen or sixteen years old, same as me but he had me by about eighty pounds. He stared back waiting for me to answer. I couldn't. I wasn't sure what he had said. He was big and I think I was scared.

A bigger voice came from my new house. It was my new dad. He was speaking Pidgin now.

"Eh, Maka, dis Byron," he said.

He came out to the road and put his huge arm around me. He stood over six feet tall and I looked up and saw his fireman mustache move when he talked.

"Dis is my new stepson. Member I was tellin you? I was tinkin you guys could jus da'kine, eh? Surf an fish an whatevas," he said.

He continued on, telling Maka that I used to live here but up in the mountains, in Makakilo. How I used to surf and spearfish but I moved to the Bay Area. "Where dat stay?… Oh da Bay Area is da'kine, California… Oh like L.A.?" No, the Fireman told him, more like San Francisco.

"Oh so what? You only speak haole now?" The boy who was almost as big as my new dad was talking to me now.

"Um yeah, sorta. I kinda lost the Pidgin. Everyone made fun of me when I talked so…" I trailed off.

"Whoa! You get one deep voice eh? You sound like da'kine, what is dat? Darth Vader!" The huge boy laughed. "So then you wen start talking haole? Brah! They make fun a you, just choke'em with the force… YOU

UNDA ESTIMAT DA POWER!" He laughed again at his own Darth Vader impersonation then got serious.

"Or betta yet, for real kine… You shoulda wen give'em one false crack right in da mouth," he said, and he clapped his hands together as he said it.

It was loud and it made me flinch. They both laughed. I was really making a good first impression here.

"Shoots brah, I was going surf right now, cuz. You like go?" the boy said.

He was smiling now. He looked like a big smiling brown teddy bear. I smiled back and he took that as a yes. The Fireman said nothing and walked to the carport area where his old Ford Bronco was. He pulled out a huge surfboard that looked like it hadn't been used in years and began looking for a leash. When he found it, he laid everything in the grass and sprayed it down with the hose. He looked at me as he washed everything. He wanted to say something. He wanted to tell me that he knew. He knew I didn't want to be here. He wanted to tell me that over time things wouldn't seem so…

But he didn't. Or couldn't. Just like he couldn't be my dad. It was too late. My dad couldn't be my dad. My dad was in jail and I was too old. I was almost sixteen. He would have to just be Johnny. He would have to just be my mom's new husband. He would have to just be the Fireman.

"Later we should talk?" he said. The Pidgin was toned way down. He could do that. "Okay," I mumbled as I grabbed the surfboard.

The huge boy was at the end of a sandy path that led to the beach sitting on his surfboard with two other boys. One was even bigger and his legs looked kinda funny. His calf muscles were huge. He looked like Popeye but the leg version. I wondered if it made him run faster or kick down doors better. I started thinking up nicknames. Spinach legs? Calf razor? Supercalves? The other was smaller than me and super skinny. Skeletor? Bonez? They were all smoking cigarettes.

The path was bordered on both sides by the wooden fences of the houses. The boys all sat except the skinny one, who leaned against the wooden barrier.

"You smoke?" said the teddy bear as he offered me the pack.

"Yeah," I lied and took one.

I tried to remember his name and I tried not to cough. I failed at both.

I coughed so hard I thought I was going to throw up and almost did. I dropped the cig in the sand by accident. They all laughed. I was looking like the toughest kid in the world. I got myself under control just in time to see the Teddy Bear light another cigarette and pass it to me. But this one didn't have the brown filter part or the printed letters on it like Kool or Marlboro. In fact, this one was hand rolled and much fatter. I took it. My eyes were watery and my hands were shaking. I knew it was weed when I smelled it. My real dad used to smoke it. I never had before but I wanted to look like I did. I tried to be casual.

The skinny one finally spoke. "Eh, you never wen smoke bud before? No need if you no like."

He reached over and yanked the joint from my hand. I guess I had stood there looking scared for too long. The Teddy Bear stood up and brushed himself off. He took the joint when it made its way to him.

"Ya name is Byron, eh?" he asked.

"Yeah," I said.

I still couldn't remember his name but I didn't wanna ask.

"You no need smoke, bumbai I no like you get busted by Johnny."

The other boys began tying their leashes to their boards as the joint made its third pass around the circle.

Busted by Johnny? The thought rolled through me. If he was gonna try to be my new dad, then he would try to change all the rules and tell me what and when? And if I didn't listen… what then? He would ground me? He would spank me? What could he do? I'd like to see him try. I had to play along with this whole thing because it stopped Mom from laying on the living room floor crying, but I didn't have to believe the bullshit fantasy that my life was going to be better. My life had already been good. I'd had shit poppin' in Cali.

I held out my hand this time as it came by. The Teddy Bear raised his eyebrow. They all stood still and waited for my next coughing fit.

This was nothing like the cigarette.

It was sweet and thick. It tasted like green tea with brown sugar. It eased its way down my chest. I held it in until it tickled. As it came out it looked like the smoke machine at the junior high dance.

"*Whooooaaa!*" The Teddy Bear laughed and slapped me on the back. The other boys smiled too.

"He wen suck down the whole ting in one hit!" said the skinny one. They all laughed and shook my hand. Pounds, fives, hugs and congrats like I had just won the gold medal in something.

As I looked down at my surfboard I thought, "How the hell am I ever going to reach all the way down there and pick up that surfboard?"

It was so far down. No, I was so high up. Everything was so far and so spaced out. I was so comfortable. The Teddy Bear handed me some wax. I waxed my board. The water kissed my legs as I strapped the leash to my ankle. I began to paddle out and the water washed over me. The wind and the sun took turns cooling me off and warming me up like it was a game that they played with each other.

I got to the lineup and rested my shoulders. They didn't hurt. They tickled. I stretched them out and it felt so good I got goosebumps. I watched the clouds. I watched the wind carry the birds in circles over the water.

"Eh, super lungs," shouted Teddy Bear. "That's your wave brah, get'em, get'em."

He was right. I had daydreamed myself into the perfect spot. The swell rolled up, slowly building to a peak as it got closer to me. I spun around and began to paddle swiftly but not too fast, making my way to the apex. The wave was on me. It started to lift me up from the back of the board. I stopped paddling and began to do a push-up, sliding my left foot up to my hands while leaning with my body to the right. As I stood up, my board slid down the wave to the bottom with so much speed. There was so much wind. I was falling out of the sky. Falling, rushing towards the crystal clear shallow water. I could see the reef fish swimming for a split second before me and the wave came crashing down on top of them. The sound was loud. The crashing water was behind me. The shoulder of the wave was in front. It told me to lean right and push my toes down. It told me to lean left and put all my weight on my back foot. I went up and came flying down only to turn and shoot right back up again. On my way back down I saw the Teddy Bear. He was smiling and yelling. They all were. So was I. I was flying. I opened my arms and closed my eyes.

The wave smashed into me with all of its spirit and ripped the air from my lungs. It held me underwater and twisted my body. Twice I felt my calf kicking my head. I flipped over and over until I could not tell which way was up. I opened my eyes and saw bubbles and sand. Bubbles and sand. I had to breathe. I did. I took a huge breath of bubbles and sand. I coughed and breathed again. My head broke the surface. I threw up bubbles and sand.

I took one breath of stinging air. Then the next wave smashed down on me. I was plunged deep into the violent churning of thousands of pounds of water. The ocean whipped my body around like an old plastic bag. I stopped fighting because I was beaten. I let it do with me what it willed. The crashing and the churning mixed with the ringing in my ears and grew louder and louder. My chest burned and my head throbbed as my heart began to explode.

And then it didn't.

***

The pain disappears and the bubbles slowly fade away until everything is quiet and clear. The water is dark blue and I can see off into nothing in every direction. Dark glowing endless blue. It is everywhere. Above and below me. I am no longer sure which is which. I am sure that I am moving with the water. A fast and persistent pressure is all around me. I can feel it with my skin. I can hear it rushing by my ears. I can hear a yawning rumble from far away followed by clicks.

I begin to see a light that is different from the dark bluish glow. It is a gold shimmer. As the current brings me closer I can see the light is framed by a huge valley. Underwater mountains that reach up higher than I can see. Littered across the valley floor are sunken ships. Hundreds of them. From old Spanish Galleons to modern military battleships. All of them broken to pieces with rolling hills of gold spilling out of them. There are shadows floating above them. Small shadows floating from ropes like balloons floating from strings. They are bodies. Swollen corpses attached to the sunken ships like upside down strange fruit. As I float closer I see the bloated faces of men, women and children with small fishes biting at the dark purple flesh. I wave my hands to try to keep from rubbing against one of them as I pass.

At the very center of the valley floating just above the corpses, bathing in the golden glow, is a man who is not tied to a rope. He has his eyes closed and isn't moving with the current. I float by closer and closer. I am going to hit him. I start swimming but my arms do nothing to change my direction. His eyes open and he reaches out and grabs my leg. I yell nothing into the rushing water around me. He pulls off my leash. Suddenly a shark the size of a sixteen wheel semi-truck bursts up from the golden glow. It opens its bloody corpse-strewn mouth and I watch as the entire lower half of my body slides into it. Its teeth clamp down and my hips and spine crack like microwave popcorn. Dark purple foam wraps around my body and sparkling explosions fill my eyes.

I reach my arms up in one last ditch effort.

***

My hands slammed into the bottom of my surfboard. There it was! I pulled my head up. I gagged and spit. I laid half on my board unable to do any more. There were no waves. The set had passed and the water looked like a lake of fizzing root beer. Fizzzzzzzz.

It was flat and calm. After a moment I could lift my head up and look around. I saw the Teddy Bear.

"Eh you almost when DIE yeah?!" he said.

I could only nod yes.

"*CHEEEEEHUUUU!* Right on brah, right on! Dat was one big set!! Eh you betta start paddling—here comes one nodda one!"

I turned to see the watery mountains building and rolling and coming towards us. I pulled the rest of myself onto the board and paddled towards the oncoming set, hoping to get over them before they broke.

I would not live in that little house in those little rooms.

I would live in these watery mountains. I would live high above the sea and ride the water like these birds ride the wind. I would fly and I would never land. I would live like this.

Forever.

***

It was easy to do.

Between the four of us, Maka (Teddy Bear), Opele (Bonez), Lyle

10

(Supercalves) and me, we only needed twenty bucks. That was enough for a dub-sack. Maka's older brother Kaipo sold weed around the neighborhood and would always cut us a break if we were short, or stuff it when we were not. With that, we could roll about two or three bombs or four or five pinners, based on the occasion.

I told Maka he looked like a Teddy Bear and he didn't really like it. He said I looked like a dirty Q-tip. That was because of my hair. I told him my hair was kinky cuz I was half black and half white. He said God was unfair to me.

"Brah dats junk. God wen give you black people hair and a white people boto!"

That got a big laugh. I told him my dick was black. And, he should not be racist. Especially since his own mom had some black in her.

"Huh, my modda no more black in her?" he said.

"Well, maybe not now," I stood up and grabbed my crotch, "but last night she did!"

Maka stared at me with a blank look on his face. I laughed at my own joke but I was alone. Bonez and Supercalves stared at the sand sensing an argument. I was just playin' dozens but Maka took it wrong. Maybe it was a lost in translation thing. Pidgin or no Pidgin, I should take it easy with the "Yo Mama" jokes… But it was fine.

We spent pretty much every day getting high at the end of the sandy path and then surfing, spearfishing, or banging on rocks and trees and sticks and coconuts making music. I would rap about the day's events and say stupid stuff to try to make them laugh. Once, I rhymed Maka's name with the Hawaiian word for weed. Pakalolo. I said,

> *I always roll with my crew*
> *so I'm never going solo*
> *I take a hit of Pakalolo*
> *and surf with Makalolo*

That was a nickname he liked. From that point on he was Makalolo. I was hoping I would get Superlungs because of that first day, but since my last name started with a Q… I unfortunately got stuck with Dirty Q-Tip. It was fine.

We would sit and talk. They would ask me about the mainland and I would tell them stories. Stories about Oakland and Montalvin. About Crips and Bloods. Rap battles and girls. They would tell me of older uncles and cousins who had surfed huge winter waves on the North Shore or been in huge fights downtown or in Waianae. Stories of dads and older friends who had caught huge fish after amazing struggles. We would sometimes sit together not talking. We would just listen to the ocean and the wind. We would get lost alone together. Until the sound of the manapua man would come riding on the breeze. It was like an ice cream truck with the jack-in-the-box song except it was an old beat up van and there was no ice cream. There was fried or steamed pork buns and fried noodles with pork hash. There was rice cake and Hawaiian Sun juices. There was Laughy Taffy and Skittles and Snickers and all the things that made the four of us dig in our pockets for our salty, damp one-dollar bills.

I always had to remember not to go in the house when I was too stoned, especially every other day. That was the Fireman's schedule. Twenty-four hours on, twenty-four hours off. When he was home he would eat dinner in front of the T.V. and then wrestle his two kids. There would be tickling and head locks and laughing and crying. My mom would be fussing around, straightening up the kitchen pretending to be mad at the noise they were making.

It was fine.

CHAPTER 2

THE BIG BAD WOLF

I SAT IN THE tiny little room. Little kids' toys all around me. My little stepsister's favorite stuffed animal was a fish. I sat on it. When I leaned back something sharp jammed into my spine. It was my little stepbrother's toy fire truck. I tossed it hard against the wall. It didn't break and I wasn't sure if I had wanted it to or not.

It was hot in this room. The early morning sun was already beating down on Ewa Beach and I could barely breathe. The whole family was out there eating breakfast, talking loud and fast, bowls banging, cabinets opening and shutting. It was the big day. The first day of school.

Summer was over.

My endless days of smoking weed and surfing were done. I was sober now. This was real. I really lived here.

And I was going to James Campbell High School. The place had a reputation. I dug around and found a brand new black-and-white marble ninety-nine-cent composition book my mom had bought along with all the school supplies. I wrote "Back in Hawaii" on the cover then immediately crossed it out and wrote "4 Ewa Beach." Then I opened it to the first page and wrote "The Westside's Eastside High" then I crossed it out. "Outta the frying pan, into the Campbell's soup." I laughed and crossed it out and then just started scribbling words…

#

13

Under funded,
Under staffed,
Under review,
Underachievers,
Under the stairs smoking on Kools.
Understanding that long standing political grandstanding
Has undercut planning for this school.
Preteen mothers,
Used rubbers,
Crack pipes,
Slap fights under the track and field lights.
Slim chances on hot nights.
Only left turns and big bags of not rights...
Frozen in search lights...
The first fights...
Were lost...
9 years old...
My Pops told
Me...
The only way for you to lose
Is to not fight back
Now you go right back
Kick
And spit
Talk shit
Until the end
It don't matter if you win
He ain't fightin you again...

#

Before me and my mom moved to California I had gone to a super small elementary school up on a mountain called Mauka Lani. The best thing about living up on the mountain had been the hills. Me and my friends would push our bikes up countless hills talking about which path we were gonna take, which bump we were gonna jump. Then ride down them at crazy speeds. There were hundreds of paths and we had names for all of them. I would always try to talk my friends into the biggest ones with the biggest jumps. Eventually we started to cross paths with the biggest boys.

At first they would just try to scare us to make us scream or cry. One time, when we rode by them, they all spit gum at us and our friend Lucy got it so bad her dad had to cut her hair. She was happy though because she was a tomboy and loved having short hair. I was mad though. Why did they always scare us? I couldn't understand. I thought if they wanted to play with us why not just ask. I told them that. They laughed at me.

"Whoa you one nice guy yeah? You like let us play with you guys?" said the one they called Kevin.

I was happy to actually talk to Kevin. He didn't seem so bad. Maybe they always teased us cuz they didn't know any of the games we played. How could they? I was the one who made them up and being scared and selfish I never told the big boys. "What game you guys is playing?" asked Kevin.

He was smiling. The big mean Kevin was actually smiling, and so were his friends.

"We're riding the Big Bad Wolf!" I said proudly.

"Big Bad Wolf? What is dat?" he said.

Of course! How would he know?

"It's a path! You start at the colored mountains way up there past the construction site, then you ride to the left of the dumpster, though the parking lot, down the steep grass hill over the buffalo jump, past the mango tree through the bushes, then to the right of the swimming pool and end at the fire grass at the end of the houses!!" I said.

I was very proud of it. It was one of the coolest paths I had come up with. Kevin made a sad face.

"Oh shucks, we like come wit you guys but then we no more bikes."

See, I was right. They weren't bad kids or mean. They were just mad that they couldn't play with us. They always had to sit behind Mauka Lani Elementary coughing and bored because they didn't know my games and they didn't have bikes.

"My name is Byron. This is Danny and Robby, they're brothers, and this is Lucy. You should say sorry to Lucy cuz she had to cut her hair when you guys threw gum in it," I said.

Kevin looked at his friends. They all had strange looks on their faces. Maybe no kids had ever been nice to them before.

"Oh wow," said Kevin, "Sorry yeah? We was just trying for scare you guys. Like one joke, you know? We was trying for make you tink we was going for spit at you but then the wind wen take our spit and gum and push it more further yeah? We never mean for really hit you guys."

At this, one of the big kids laughed. It is kinda funny, I thought.

"Maybe we all take turns," I said. "There are four of us and four of you. We can all take turns with our bikes. It's super rad!"

"Dat's one good idea, brah," said Kevin.

"No!" said Lucy.

She stood behind me with her bike between her legs and her fingers turning white as she gripped her handlebars. Her eyes were locked on Kevin.

She saw something.

I looked back at him. He was still smiling but something was strange. His eyes were sparkling. No not sparkling. His eyes were hiding a sparkle. Or a spark. His eyelids were trying to cover a spark. The same type of spark I would see when my dad would light an empty cigarette lighter. A constant small sparkle. His whole face was trying to hide it. My stomach dropped beneath me. We were in trouble.

"I guess we can't share. Sorry," I said.

Kevin put one hand on my handlebars.

"Nah, we go take turns, like you said."

Lucy started to peddle and one of Kevin's friends, the short chubby one with bushy hair, grabbed her and started to pull her off the bike with one arm and pry her fingers loose with his other hand. The other two boys quickly ripped Danny and Robby off their bikes. Kevin grabbed me by my afro and lifted me into the air. I would not let go of the bike until he punched me twice in the stomach. I dropped to the ground heaving. He had knocked the air out of me. The big boys rode off.

"CHEEEEEHUUUUU!" It echoed through the hills.

I watched them ride away and my first thought was, "They're going the wrong way. The Big Bad Wolf is the other way."

***

The four of us sat there for over an hour. Maybe we thought they would come back? Maybe if I tell my dad he'll go and get all the bikes back.

I had seen him fight a few times. I sat there in the grass imagining my dad picking Kevin up by his hair and smacking him around like a little bitch. I played it over at least six times before a sinking feeling wouldn't let me imagine it again.

Lucy stood up and threw a handful of dirt and rocks at me. "I'm not your friend anymore." She walked away.

Danny and Robby started to leave. Danny turned around and said, "Tomorrow we go look for da bikes yeah? They probably just going ride'em little bit then leave'em somewhere."

Robby was still sniffling as they walked away.

I walked into my house and could smell pakalolo. My dad was a very dark-skinned black man. He sometimes rocked a jerry curl but today his hair was in a mini fro with an afro pick sticking outta the top. He was sitting on the floor next to the record player. Parliament Funkadelic was blasting. He didn't notice me come in.

"Dad!" I shouted.

He turned, and then seeing me, he scrunched his face. He pulled the needle off the record. "What happened?"

"Big kids beat us up and took our bikes," I said.

Okay, Dad. Pick me up and give me a hug. Put your boots on and go beat the shit outta Kevin and all of those kids. Then go beat the shit outta Kevin's dad. Walk up to his house and kick down the whole door. Beat them down till they start crying and saying sorry for everything.

"Go get your bike!" he said and turned back to his record collection.

"But Dad… they're big kids. They'll beat me up," I said.

Then, finally, after holding it for over an hour, I started crying.

What! Now? Now I'm going to cry in front of my dad? Why didn't I cry when I was walking home, then no one would have seen me and all my tears would've been gone. This sucks. My dad looked at me. He was thinking something. I took his pause for a good omen and stopped trying to fight back the tears. I began to sob. My head lit up as the back of his hand smacked me across the face. I fell down and my face started to glow warm. I stopped crying and was frozen in shock. My dad had whooped me many times. But usually it was with a belt. He would sometimes smack me on the back of the head but never had he smacked that hard and *never* had he smacked me in the face.

"It's time to start growing up, Son! Stand up and wipe off your damn face! *Shiiit!* Standing there crying like a little baby. What you expect *me* to do? Go out there and smack around a bunch of little kids? Have you lost your goddamn mind? Your Momma too soft on you. She got you acting like a little bitch. Got it twisted up in her head like she ain't know who she is, where the money come from, who you goan need to be."

He turned his head and looked at the towel rack. He was mumbling now and it seemed like he was talking to the towel.

"She acting sideways, talkin out the side of her mouth. Talkin bout hoppin out the stable. Got me worried… Got me thinkin bout… *shiiiit*… thinkin bout coppin a plea. She ain't goan hold it down for no two to five. That bitch be in the wind anything more than six months. I betcha she try to take my son with her. What kinda faggot he goan be afta that?"

He turned and stared at me. "Fuckin baby… C'mere."

I slowly walked up to him. He put his hand on my face where he had struck me. Then he began to wipe the tears off my face with his thumbs. "I'm not going to be around for a while… no matter what, I'm gonna have to do at least six months… you know… like last time, you member. Shit happens. But look here little man, I care what happens to you if I ain't around. It's simple: you grow into a man or you grow into a bitch. You let people step on you, take things, disrespect you—you wind up being a bitch. It don't matter if these kids are bigger than you. There's always gonna be assholes who are bigger than you. Just cuz someone is stronger than you, does that mean they can have all your shit?"

He waited for an answer. I shook my head no.

"No. I ain't goan be here. You gotta start being a man. You hear me? You go out there and you get your bike back."

"But…" I started.

My dad smacked me again. This time tears rolled down my face but I didn't make a sound. I held my breath to keep the crying sounds from coming out.

"It don't matter if you fight and you lose. When two people fight, two people lose. You just have to make him not want to fight you again. You punch and kick and you don't stop! You bite and you scratch and you grab onto his fucking ears and you rip them off! You bite and you rip the hair until it tears out of his head. You hear me? He knows then. 'Naw I'm sayin? He knows he can win if he fights you, but he's still gonna have to go to the hospital. And he might lose an eye or a cheek or a chunk of his arm. I promise you Byron, word will get out and no one will take you for a bitch and steal your shit. You hear me?"

I did not hear him. He did not know who Kevin McKenzie was. He had not seen the spark in Kevin's eye.

"Son, if you don't come back here with your bike, I will whoop your ass harder than any of those kids ever will!"

He pulled out the record he was looking for and placed it in the record player. He looked at me. His expression said, "What the fuck are you still standing there for?"

I turned around and he put the needle on the record. "Voodoo Child" started and the sound of an electric guitar followed me out of the house. I turned back as I walked up the hill and I could still see my dad through the open door sitting on the floor lighting another joint.

***

I heard them before I saw them.

It was dusk and the light breeze carried their echoing voices down from the colored mountains to the edge of Panana Street just past the construction site. They were dragging the bikes up the powdery colored-gravel hills right to the spot that I had told them about. I was surprised that they were doing the Big Bad Wolf. But after a few moments of watching them, it was clear that only Kevin wanted to do it.

He was in front of the other three, who were complaining. He yelled cuss words and insults to keep them moving. At one point the bushy-haired chubby kid jumped on a bike and said he was going home. Kevin threw down my bike and ran with superhuman speed to the back of Chubby's bike, which was really Lucy's. He grabbed the whole back tire while it was spinning and pulled the entire bike into the air. Chubby fell forward over the handlebars smack onto his face in the colored dirt. The other two kids laughed nervously like hyenas. Kevin went back to my bike and continued to drag it up the hill.

The others followed much more obediently now.

Kevin was a freak of nature and he would kill me. My father was thinking I had a problem with regular bullies. Kevin was not a regular bully. Kevin was the bully of bullies. He was that bully that bullies have nightmares about. I had to do something, though. I knew my dad was not bluffing.

I sprinted behind the bushes past the mango tree and around to the wall behind the swimming pool. I crouched down and I waited. I was crying. Not with tears but just a quiet wailing like when you blow over a Coke bottle. When I tried to stop doing it I felt sick, like I was gonna throw up. I held my breath until I got dizzy and that helped. Then I heard my bike. One of the screws on the chain guard was loose and it made an unmistakable *clang clang clang* as it went over the bumps.

"CHEEEEEHUUUUUU!"

I got up on my hands and knees. Kevin flew by going faster than I thought my bike was capable of. I let him go. Then went two more. The chubby one—I want the chubby one. He came by much slower than the others. I jumped and tried to clothesline him off of the bike. His legs got tangled and then me, him, and the bike rolled end-over-end down the left side of the embankment. As we rolled, the handle bars acted like two spinning baseball bats smacking both of us in the head, ribs and back.

We finally came to a stop at the bottom and he was pinned, completely wrapped up in the bike. It took me a second to get my left leg free and then I jumped on him. I punched him over and over in the face. His nose started bleeding but I didn't stop.

"Help! Help, Chad! Get this kid off of me!" he screamed.

I heard the two other kids run up behind me. I stood up to face them and squared off. There was blood all over me and I was yelling.

"C'mon you fuckin bitches!" I said over and over again.

They helped the chubby kid out from under Lucy's bike and walked down in the direction Kevin had gone, looking back a few times over their shoulders. The whole time, I was yelling at them.

When they were out of sight, I sat down with all three bikes around me and tried to catch my breath. Then I ran up to Lucy's house. Danny and Robby were there playing Super Mario Bros. They saw all the blood and stopped.

"I got your bikes back. They're down by the pool. Now I gotta get mine back. I need your baseball bat."

***

I watched Lucy, Danny and Robby push their bikes back up the hill towards Lucy's house. It would be dark soon. The wind was picking up as the sun fell behind the mountain, casting a shadow all the way down to the sugarcane fields. All the hills and mountains on the west side of O'ahu are covered with long, dry grass mixed with Keawe trees and jagged, pokey plants that, if left natural, grow up to about shoulder-height. When the wind blew through like it was now, it sounded like waves rolling.

I sat on the wall next to the pool. Kevin would come soon. He had to. It was like some sorta law or something. I started to feel sick again. The sun was setting and I was shaking. I had on surf shorts and a t-shirt. I had lost my slippers somewhere along the way. I was now sticking my toes behind my knees to try to keep them warm. The blood all over my hands and arms was sticky and starting to dry. It looked like giant scabs. Part of the wall was breaking apart and I was sitting on sharp pieces of brick. It hurt but I didn't move.

I didn't even want my bike anymore. I didn't care if I got a whooping. My dad could use the big belt with the buckle. I didn't care. At least I would be home. Maybe Mommy would stop him. Maybe she would sleep with me in my bed and keep me from thinking. Maybe she would rub my head and tell me it was time for a new bike anyway. Maybe Daddy was wrong. She told me that sometimes.

The first time she said it I couldn't understand what she meant. How can Daddy be wrong? Daddy is a finite thing. It is limited to the center of what is right. Inside the very core of what it is right, there is Daddy. Outside of right, Daddy does not exist. Therefore, no words or actions that are brought forth from Daddy can be wrong.

But I watched very close after she said it. After she whispered it in my ear when we were huddled together in the dark. Daddy had whooped me with the belt and I had blocked too many of the blows with my hands. Daddy had told me many times not to play outside with my socks on, putting holes in all my socks, and I kept forgetting. Well, today I would learn. He threw me up the stairs. My arm got caught in the handrail and he almost broke it. He took off his belt and beat me with the buckle side. Mommy tried to stop it and he spanked her with the belt too. Mommy wasn't listening to Daddy either. This time he put us both in the closet. We laid there together afterwards, locked behind the closet door in the dark. We were both crying and sniffling.

"Just look at the waves…" I whispered.

"Shhh… Be quiet sweety… try to sleep…" I could feel her shaky hand rub my head.

"When he takes you to the room… just look at the curtains. The fan is on and it looks just like the ocean…" I told her.

"Daddy is wrong sometimes. You have to be careful when he is drinking and smoking," she whispered.

What if he was wrong now? What if Mommy was already home and she made him dinner and he was sleeping? She could be waiting for me. She could tell me he was wrong and it's fine. That bike was old and too small anyway and she will find me a new bike. My birthday is coming soon.

"What you fucka!" Kevin was yelling from way down the hill.

He was carrying my bike over his shoulder like it was a baby's toy. The other three boys fanned out reluctantly behind him. Chubby was walking slowly, looking at the ground. He had washed his face but his shirt still had blood on it. Both of his eyes were puffy and swollen and starting to turn black. I stood up but I left the bat on the ground by the wall.

"What brah?! Why you like scrap for?" said Kevin as he got closer. "You said we can use you guy's bikes and then, what?"

He was about ten feet from me. Chubby's eyes never left the ground.

"Gimme my bike back," I said.

I tried to say it loud and tough but it came out as almost a whisper.

"Try take'em," he said and held my bike out with one hand.

I can't even lift my bike all the way off the ground with both hands and he's holding the entire thing up in the air with one arm. How strong is he? Is he as strong as my dad? Nobody is stronger than my dad. My dad would beat the shit outta Kevin. I'm going to beat the shit outta Kevin! I picked up the baseball bat gently and whispered again, "Gimme my bike back."

Kevin's eyes got wide and his head shook like he tasted something bad. The other boys backed up slowly all looking from me to Kevin and back again. Kevin made a weird sound and spit flew out of his mouth.

"Brah! I was coming for give you your bike back! You like scrap brah we GO! Up and up you FUCKA! Why you get one bat for?!"

He threw my bike into the deep grass and rushed me. I stepped forward and swung the bat just like I would for a low pitch and caught him right on the shin. It made a low thump sound as it struck the muscle on the side of his calf. He jumped back yelling cuss words. I leaped at the tall skinny one and swung for his head. He ducked and lifted his arm up. The bat struck him across his shoulder and back. Chubby and the other kid started to run away. The skinny one ran behind them holding his arm. I squared back off with Kevin, who had tried to circle around me. I was screaming and crying and snot was coming out of my nose. "Gimme my bike back!" I wasn't whispering anymore.

Kevin jumped forward again and this time tried to grab the bat as I swung. He missed and I hit his forearm. This time the bat made a high pitched *bing* as it hit the bone.

"Aaaaagh!" he yelled but he tried again.

I swung and missed but he was starting to time my swings. A chill ran through me. The longer we circled he would eventually get it right and grab the bat.

I started backing up but the wall was behind me. He jumped forward and I swung. He caught the bat with one hand with so much strength and speed that it lifted me up. I let go and fell on the ground. He lifted the bat over his head and brought it crashing down.

Ping! It hit bricks and rocks.

I had rolled to the side and grabbed a piece of broken brick that was laying on the ground. He was still bent over the wall, just starting to turn and lift the bat again. I smashed the brick into the side of his head and he dropped the bat and staggered back. I picked the bat up and swung for his head. He turned and I hit him in the back. I swung again and hit him in the thigh. I swung again but he was running backwards now and I didn't follow.

He stood away from me breathing hard. His head was bleeding badly and he had to keep wiping blood out of his eyes. I stood ready to swing again. My heart was beating hard and my head was ringing. He spit blood and I looked at his eyes. I should have never looked into his eyes.

That spark was now a roaring fire. Bright green crackling flames. He was smiling. Somewhere in there was something very bad. He turned and ran up the hill towards the colored mountains. I couldn't let go of the bat and I just sat down. I let my eyes close tight and tried to breathe without throwing up. Bile edged its way up my throat but I couldn't spit because I was breathing so hard.

It was dark.

The light from the nearest parking lot reflected off the pedals of my bike that was laying on its side in the deep grass. I started to crawl over to it when I heard a loud banging sound from the colored mountains. I couldn't see anything. It was too dark and the sound was too far away. Maybe as far away as the construction site. Again, banging and wood breaking. Then came Kevin running back down the hill towards the pool. Running towards me. He was carrying a broken two by four about six feet long with nails in it.

No way!

He was laughing and screaming in a high pitched voice.

"Now we go! You fucka!"

I was frozen. He came straight at me and swung it. But the wooden beam was so long and heavy that the swing was slow. I ducked and it hit the wall behind me. I swung the bat and it cracked him right in the face. He fell backwards, dragging the wooden beam with him. He stood up quick but I stayed right up on him and he couldn't really hit me with the beam. It just kept sorta pushing me from side to side. He dropped the beam and picked me up over his head and slammed me down on the ground. All the wind was knocked out of me and I could not move. I saw little flashes of light around the corners of my eyes. He picked up the wooden beam and brought it over his head. The flashes turned red and blue. Then I heard a loud sound.

Burp-burp.

It was a police car. Kevin disappeared. I heard keys clanging and radio chatter as the cop walked down the hill towards me.

"Ey… kid, you okay or what?" said the cop.

He was shining a flashlight in my eyes. I sat up.

"Ey… that was Kevin McKenzie, yeah?" he asked.

I didn't say anything. I stood up and walked over and got my bike. I tried to walk by him and he stopped me.

"What's your name, brah?" he asked.

I looked up at the cop's friendly round face.

"Byron."

"You okay, Byron?"

"Yeah."

"You do yourself one favor. Stay away from Kevin. That kid is psycho!" said the cop.

No shit.

I pushed my bike up the hill to my house. I went in and went straight to the bathroom and threw up in the sink. I looked at it and I was mad I didn't make it to the toilet. My dad opened the door and looked at the sink. I closed my eyes and waited for the slap. He picked me up and hugged me so hard I almost threw up again. His eyes were watery and he smelled like beer and weed.

"I love you, Son. I'm so proud of you. You stood up for yourself. Those kids ain't gonna fuck with you again. Remember dat lil'man! Nobody can fuck with you. Ya dig? Don't let nobody treat you like shit," he said.

I took the hug. I needed the hug.

That was his last piece of fatherly advice before he went back to jail.

And he was right, mostly. Those kids never messed with me again. But Kevin beat the shit outta me every single time I saw him. I fought till I could not fight anymore every single time. At least four times that year before he went to juvenile hall for putting some other kid in the hospital. But all the other big boys knew I would fight. They would tease me if Kevin was around, but on their own they simply nodded and kept walking. Lucy and Danny and Robby drifted away. I just couldn't come up with any cool games anymore and they didn't wanna be around just in case we ran into Kevin. And then we moved and I rushed to shove any memory of him into the outgoing current.

***

But now we were back and the memories of him scattered the shoreline like my new little brother's broken toys.

Where was Kevin now? Juvenile hall? Prison? Was he dead? No. I knew the answer was no. Deep down in my gut I knew the answer was no. How could he be anywhere else than James Campbell High? Kevin McKenzie doesn't die. He doesn't go to prison. He doesn't exist outside the nightmares of misguided children like me.

Going to James Campbell High School was my nightmare.

Kevin McKenzie would be there with his burnt Indiana Jones hat, tattered black and red sweater and bladed glove saying, "Welcome to high school, bitch!"

CHAPTER 3

WET CINNAMON NOODLE

"Quoooooooow!" YELLED MAKALOLO FROM outside my window.

Bonez and Supercalves were with him outside ready to go. Fuck it. I grabbed my backpack and ditched the tiny ass house without saying goodbye. Not like anyone would have heard. The living room was complete chaos with everyone getting ready for the first day of school.

"What is that?" asked Maka looking at my backpack.

"It's this crazy new invention dude, check it out. It's a bag with straps so you can put it on your back. I'm gonna call it a backpack," I said.

The other boys laughed.

"No stupid! Why you bringin'em for? No need, bradduh!" said Maka.

I looked at the boys and no one had bags or anything. I tossed my bag under the house and tucked my new rhyme book into the back of my shorts.

Maka lit a pre-walk-to-school joint. Along the way he explained our schedule:

"I get'em set cuz, try check'em! Soon as we hit campus we go to da O-Building restroom and spark a fatty, afta dat we go first period and second period. Boom, first recess we reconvene in da restroom and smoke a bomb. Den we go turd an fort period. Lunch time we ditch school and torch one nodda one on da way to da Manapua Truck. Den if we like come back, we come back. If no like den whatevas."

You had to give it to him, the guy could plan.

I was really high by the time we got to school. We passed through the parking lot where all the rich kids (that's a relative term—it's still Campbell

High) were parking their Toyota trucks and lowered Honda Accords. Beautiful little Filipino girls everywhere. My chest was pounding thinking about every single one of them. It was tight spandex and lace bras covered with a loose "localz only" tank top or daisy duke cut-off jean shorts with a tight wife beater.

I didn't wanna smoke again. I suggested we do a lap around the whole school before the bell rang. I wanted to see as many girls as possible. The school had five main three-story buildings surrounding a big lawn with an outdoor stage. Each building had its own clique.

Jocks by the weight room.

Cheerleaders close by the gymnasium.

The S.O.S. (Sons of Samoa) by D-Building.

Military bratz by C-Building.

E.B.B. (Ewa Beach Boys soon to be Ewa Beach Bloods) far side of O-Building.

Makakilo Boys (soon to be M-Town Crips) on the campus side corner of H-Building.

Random other groups broken down even further: nerds, theater kids, stoners, etcetera.

It was a definition. Each group was a definition that the people in it could share. Each group had a paragraph's worth of ideas that they attached themselves to. It was written all over them. How they dressed, how they talked, what music they listened to. For some it was actually written on their clothes in big logos. If you confirmed that paragraph, they were cool as hell to you. Which then made everyone know *you* were cool. It was like feedback on a microphone.

Maka's older brother Kaipo sold weed so everyone knew him. That meant everyone knew Maka. As we passed by the different cliques, we shook hands with all the boys while the girls smiled and whispered to each other wondering who I was. I smiled and wished I wasn't so high so I could start remembering names and, more importantly, which girl belonged to who.

As we toured, little fights broke out here and there. You would see everyone start running towards one and circle it until it was over. I watched the swarms of kids moving back and forth across the campus, the red dirt clouds being kicked up as hundreds of little feet stampeded in this direction or that, and imagined herds of zebra moving back and forth across the plains of Africa whenever a lion attacked. Mostly, military kids were being jumped by local kids cuz they talked big or talked different or wore overalls with spray paint or talked to the wrong girl or—the most common reason to get beat up in Ewa Beach—for being white. Blonde hair, blue eyes and freckles? There is nothing you can do.

You are a haole.

You are going to get beat up on the first day of school.

If you listen close you can actually hear Malcolm X chuckling in his grave.

***

I sat in the back of first period with my hat pulled down and my sunglasses on. I ripped out a page of the textbook and wrote "let's go get high" then I threw it at the prettiest girl. She cut her eyes at me like she was mad. Then she picked up the paper and read it. She looked back at me and smiled, shaking her head no, but it wasn't *no*. It was *not now*.

In second period I did the same thing. This girl was prettier. She had daisy dukes and a tight wife beater. Her long jet-black hair spilled down her back and all over the chair and empty desk behind her. The paper actually made a *thump* sound when it hit her in the back of the head. She turned around mad and was gonna cuss me out right then and there.

"Read it!" I whispered.

The teacher heard and looked up.

"Eh, can use the restroom?" I said in thick Pidgin.

The teacher was haole and was obviously scared. He said yes right away. I waited outside the classroom door for so long I forgot what I was waiting for. Then I heard the cute little voice with a Pidgin accent ask if she could use the restroom. She came out with a nervous smile. She held my hand and we walked to the boys room. I pulled her inside and lit a joint. We smoked together in silence. The joint went back and forth until it was gone. Her eyes got so red. She was looking at me and I could tell her heart was beating so fast. There were wooden jalousie windows all along the top of the restroom. They split the sunlight onto her long dark hair and it actually shined black. I touched it and she giggled.

"Whoa... your eyes is so red!" she said.

"I'm really, really stoned," I said laughing.

"Whoa… your voice is so deep! I can feel 'em shaking my chest… try say sumting?"

"Sum ting," I said.

"Eh! No make! Why you like tease me?"

She pushed out her beautiful lower lip pretending to pout.

"I'm just fucking with you," I said.

I went to pinch her in the ribs. As soon as I touched her she pushed herself up against me and put her hand on my shoulder.

"How come you talk popolo, you not popolo yeah?" she asked.

"My dad is popolo. I just came back from the mainland that's why. Sometimes I talk like—"

"Oh yeah," she cut me off. "My aunty is like that. She goes mainland and comes back talking all funny kine."

She reached in the front pocket of her cut-off shorts and pulled out a smashed up stick of Big Red chewing gum. It was hot from being against her leg.

"We no like smell like weed, ah?!" she said.

She split it in half and then passed me some. We both chewed for a while, amazed by the taste. I wanted to kiss her but I couldn't move. I didn't want to fuck up how she looked standing there.

She kissed me. Her breath was cinnamon.

"Eh! You guys finish up da pakalolo and go back to class!" came a huge voice from outside.

We both snapped apart and answered in unison: "Okay!"

"Eh!" The security guy sounded surprised. "You guys not making babies, ah?! Get outta there!" he said playfully.

She giggled and started to leave, then turned back.

"No say nahting yeah?" she put her finger to her lips and made a shushing sound. "I get one boyfriend…"

I smiled and said, "Not a word."

That happened three times that week with three different girls and three different flavors of gum.

In California I had made out with two girls total, in my life!

***

Following Maka's meticulous schedule had made life at Campbell High a soft summer breeze.

After a few weeks I started to realize that my fear of this school was unwarranted. This school was great. If you had a problem with someone you could settle it. Right then and there. Just fight. After a handful of scuffles, it was clear that I could scrap.

The security guard would let it go as long as it was fair. Even if you didn't have a problem with someone in particular, you could find someone with a problem. If you just didn't feel good that day, don't try to hide it. Let it out. Pick someone about your size or bigger. Stare at them in the eye. Chances are they would love to fight also. Win or lose, whatever that shitty burning feeling you had in your stomach was, it will come out in your fists. After the fight, you feel better.

It was exciting. If someone said something wrong, looked at me wrong, or was just wrong to begin with, I could go up to them and ask them to stop being wrong. We could fight about it. If they won, we could fight again. If they lost, we could fight again. Eventually, no one wanted to fight. I was strong now. Working out with the jocks and the wrestlers. I could bang out twenty reps of two hundred and twenty-five pounds on the bench press. Military press one-hundred-pound dumbbells over my head. I had a lighting fast jab and a couple of pretty sick combos. If the fight went to the dirt, which it almost always did, I had a "go to sleep" head lock and a solid arm bar that would separate your elbow. I could get my ass beat and did, but I wasn't really someone to fuck with.

We kept asking Maka's older brother to sell us more weed, but he said we shouldn't get caught holding more than he was selling us. I think he was embarrassed about not having much to begin with. We usually had a few extra joints. I would make the rounds with all my boys shaking hands and selling whatever I didn't want to smoke. No matter what clique you were in, everybody loved weed. Sometimes I would give it away to some cute girls and realize after I didn't have any money to buy more. That's when we would walk over to the haoles and ask for a few dollars. My voice was so deep it scared the military kids and they would just give us money without a fight. I could spot the ones that would just hand it over. The goal then became to flip it. Flip the whole thing. So they give you the money willingly. Then nobody feels any kind of way about it. If I was bored sometimes I would see how far I could take it. This one kid caught me on the wrong day.

"Hey wassup guys? How ya doin?" I asked a group of H-Building kids. They were military nerds who tried to dress up like rocker kids hoping it would make them look tougher.

"We're okay…" the bravest one said.

"Hey man, the water fountain is broken where we hang out. Can I have a sip of your soda?" I asked.

"Uh… yeah, sure," said Braveheart.

I drank the whole thing then spit the last of it out and looked at the can in disgust.

"Oh shit dude… did you spit in this?"

"What? No!"

"Why did you make that face then?"

"What face?"

"That face you made when I took a sip?"

"I didn't make a face!"

"You made a face! You made a face then you looked at your little friends and they made the same face!"

"What face?!"

"Don't fuck around! I saw you looking like 'Ha ha, look guys, I spit in this, now the dumb local guy gonna drink it.' I saw you, bitch!"

"Why would I spit in it when I'm drinking it?"

"If you didn't wanna share just say, 'Brah! I no like share!'"

"I'm cool with you bro! We're cool! I—"

"Say it! Say, 'Brah! I no like share!'"

"No! You can have the soda! Please… just—"

"Say it. Say how you feel! So I don't walk around thinking we're friends and we're not!"

"We're… sure… okay, we're friends. You can have it!"

"Say 'Brah! I no like share!'"

"Okay!" he yelled at his shoes. "Brah I no like share!"

"Are you fucking teasing the way locals talk?"

"You told me to say it!"

"I told *you* to say it. Say it the way you would say it, not mock the way I said it."

"I thought you meant verbatim!"

"What the fuck is vertebrae? Now you teasing locals! Using crazy vocab an' shit. What's that mean? Huh? You thought I meant vertebrae?! You thought I meant for you to tease locals?"

"It means word for word—"

"I know what it means! Why would I mean that?! Are you trying to say I want haoles to tease locals?! Why would I tell you to tease locals? What the fuck?! Could you imagine what would happen if all my friends think I go around telling haoles to tease locals? I'd get my ass beat! Why would I want to get my ass kicked? You sound fucking crazy! I'm fucking local! You're fucking haole! Are you trying to get my ass kicked? What? Did you think I was popolo? Huh?!"

"Wha… what's popolo?"

"Black! What, do blacks and locals look the same to you? Did you think I was a black kid?"

"No, NO!! Of course not!"

"What do you mean 'of course not!'? What's… what's wrong with black kids? Are you fucking racist?! Huh? You fuckin haole! Huh?! White boy, are you KKK? I'll beat your fuckin ass, say some racist shit, I fucking dare you!!"

"I'm not racist!"

"I was fuckin thirsty, water fountain's broke, I ask someone who I thought I was cool with for a sip of a fucking soda! You spit in it! It gets all over my only good tank top, you tease me for being local, but then you say that's not as bad as being black. How can I not beat the fuck out you? On behalf of my community, my heritage and all black muthafuckas on this planet, how can I not accept my duty to right this wrong?!"

"Please… *Please!!*"

"Are… are you smiling? Is this funny?"

I grabbed him by the shirt and spoke in my best James Earl Jones impression.

"All I wanted was a Pepsi, ya dig? All I want is a muthafucking Pepsi. Buy me and my friends a muthafucking Pepsi."

"Whoa brah, look his pants!" yelled Maka.

You could see the wet spot growing between the kid's legs.

"Don't piss on my money, white boy!" I said.

The money was in his wallet. A black leather wallet like the ones you see in those glass boxes in a store you walk through on your way to the

99 Cent Store or Ross. The kind of wallet that makes you think, "Why would anyone pay eighty dollars for a fucking wallet?" Those haole kids always had at least forty to a hundred dollars on them. It made me sick to my stomach. My friends and I would scrape up two or three dollars each to try to come up with twenty dollars to buy weed. Then piece together another two dollars out of dimes and nickels to buy some fried noodles off the Manapua Truck. The bedwetter had one hundred and twenty-three dollars in his eighty-dollar wallet.

Why is he here? Why did his parents throw him to the wolves? Why not bus that Pee Wee Herman up to Radford High School? What would I do with that kind of money in my pocket every day? Buy more noodles? Buy more weed? I definitely wouldn't buy an eighty-dollar wallet. I definitely wouldn't let some punk kids walk up to me and take it!

"Throw the kid back his wallet," I said to Maka.

"Brah! Dis one good wallet!" he pleaded.

"What the fuck you goin do with a wallet? You don't even have pockets!" I said.

Maka looked over his surf shorts and discovered he was wearing a pair that didn't have the side pocket. Bonez and Supercalves laughed. Supercalves started poking at Maka's legs where the pockets would've been. Bonez, who never said more then twenty words a day, was holding his own face with both hands. From between his fingers came a high-pitched laughing sound that was almost words: "*Youuunoooomooore even pockets!*" Supercalves started slapping Maka's legs and Bonez gave up trying to contain the laugh and joined in the slapping. Maka was laughing also, but he was playing at being mad at them and started smacking them in the head. They were circling around and around trying to slap and grab each other laughing and squealing. They sounded like hyenas.

I grabbed the wallet and pitched it back across the field to where the military kids were. They were standing in front of their friend who had peed his pants so no one could see and slowly walking towards the restroom. The kid dashed out of the circle to grab his wallet and a few other kids saw that he had pissed his pants and started laughing and pointing. He abandoned the wallet and ran to the restroom but it was too late. Everyone within eye shot saw and was teasing. Another local kid picked up the wallet and started to walk away.

I felt weird. My stomach felt weird. Empty. Not hungry empty. A heavy hole pulling everything around it empty. Parts of me tore off and started swirling towards the center of the empty hole.

That kid is gonna be the kid who pissed his pants forever. I knew he was an easy five bucks but did I need to squeeze him so hard? Did I need to make him piss his pants? Was I that scary? What did I look like to him? I was just fucking with him. Was I just fucking with him? I thought I was just fucking with him. Did I think I was just fucking with him? Maybe I was trying to teach him something? Trying to show him the rules? Maybe next time he'll be smarter? Tougher? Maybe he'll snap and finally stand up for himself? Or is he just weak? A weak little bitch. Maybe I'm a weak little bitch for even thinking this dumb ass shit…

Maka ran across the field yelling at the local kid who had grabbed the wallet.

"Brah, das my wallet you fucka!"

"Not even cuz, I jus wen drop'em!" said the local boy.

Maka punched the kid in the face and they started scraping. One of the local kid's friends took off his shirt to join in. I took off my shirt and started slowly walking towards the fight. With each step I felt better. The empty feeling couldn't survive the fire. The questions couldn't survive the fire. I could breath. I could think. My hands tingled as I shook out my fingers and arms to loosen them up. Fuck that kid. And fuck these guys for trying to steal Maka's wallet!

***

"Eh Byron, try come around the back real quick?" said the Fireman.

Shit. Did I mix up my days again?

He wasn't supposed to be home today.

I was really, really stoned.

In the last couple of months I had gotten into a rhythm. On the nights when the Fireman was home I wouldn't come home from school until six-thirty right as dinner was being scooped out of the trof. The kids would be fighting and playing and getting scolded. Complete mayhem. I would show face and scarf down some food, then say I was going "right outside." I would disappear and not return home until after 10 p.m. My mom would come out of the room all sleepy-eyed and messy-haired saying we would have to talk tomorrow about what my punishment would be for staying out so late. Then tomorrow I would come home right after school and listen to the talk, which consisted of me saying I'm sorry and her saying we'll talk about it tomorrow when the Fireman is home.

Rinse, repeat. As long as I came home at some point we could keep kicking the can down the road.

I went around the back of the tiny shack taking deep breaths to try to breathe myself sober. The Fireman was standing next to a beat-up car. He had a big smile on his face. Before I could put together what was going on, he tossed me the keys.

"Happy birthday," he said.

"It's not my Birthday..." I said flatly.

He shrugged his shoulders grinning under his mustache. "What... you no like'em?"

I could only think of one thing. I couldn't think about him maybe getting me a car to try to get closer to me. I couldn't think about how old and beat up the thing was. I couldn't think, this doesn't make up for stealing my mom and my life in California. All I could think was how many girls I could make out with in this piece of shit car. He was saying something about responsibility and testing myself, but all I could see was Malia, Liz, Jessica, Katey, Maria, Marianne... *Lisa, Angela, Pamela, Renee I love you, you're from around the way...*

"Byron, you hear me or what?" The Fireman stood blank. He had been saying something about my learner's permit and only using the car around the neighborhood until I got my real license.

"Can I drive right now?" I said.

He had obviously not gotten the response he'd expected. "Yeah, go," he said dismissively. "Be back before it gets dark."

I looked at the sky: 10 a.m.ish. Before it gets dark? Yeah, right. I hopped in and started it. It sounded like a moped. It was a 1983 four-door Mazda GLC hatchback. It was rusted so bad you could see through the floorboards to the road. The seats were falling apart. The back windows were stuck shut and the cheap tint was peeling off of them. But for me the only big flaw was the stereo. There was none. I didn't care about anything else.

I stopped by Supercalves' house. He was half in, half out of his car working on something. He smiled when he saw me pull up and pointed at the car laughing.

"Eh Q! What, you get one car now? You fucka!"

"Need sounds though!" I yelled, revving the engine, laughing with him.

He nodded and motioned for me to come sit in his car. I parked on the road and hopped in the passenger side of Supercalves' Monte Carlo. He was putting electrical tape on some wires under the dash. I lit a joint while he worked.

"Brah, two thousand watts to the subs in the trunk, for the two eighteens. One thousand watts split between the two six-by-nines and the two eights and the deck running the four twitters, two right there by your head. Try check'em…" he said.

Some of it was gibberish to me. But I knew it meant it was about to hit harder than Ike Turner. I passed him the joint while he looked for the perfect song to show off with. I read the titles in his ridiculously huge tape case. Bob Marley, Michigan & Smiley, Dennis Brown, Yellow Man, Big Youth, NWA, DJ Quik…

I looked back to the house and I watched his dog. It was chained to the backyard stairs sniffing the air. That dog loved smoking weed and in a second or two he would start barking because we weren't sharing. Then it hit me. "Oh Shit! Hold on." I rushed back to my car and grabbed my Walkman. I had the perfect song. I cued it up with the headphones then passed him the tape. You could hear the popping sound of the tape for a couple seconds and then… a high-pitched voice said, "Just kick a little something for them cars that be bumpin…"

The bass was loud!

LL Cool J's voice came through: "Cars ride by with the boomin systems…"

And then we smelled smoke…

"Shut it off!" I yelled.

He started hitting buttons but the damage was done. He laughed. We got out and walked back to the trunk and looked at the smoking subwoofer in silence.

"Eh, I saw that girl you was making out wit on the first week of school," he said.

I was thinking how happy I would be with a sound system like that and how sick I would be if it just blew up. But here he was smiling like nothing happened.

"Which one?"

He re-lit the joint and said, "The one you said you wen make out wit in the bathrooms on the first day of school."

He passed me the joint and I took a hit. "Yeah… which one?"

He punched me on the arm, smiling as usual. "Filipino, long black hair… thick thighs."

I felt my stomach do a flip. I had been looking for her. Cinnamon Girl. She switched classes or something and I hadn't seen her since.

"She get one boyfriend you know!" he said.

I nodded like, "So…?"

The dog started barking and Supercalves walked over and cupped his hands around the dog's nose and blew weed smoke softly into its mouth and nose. The dog wagged its tail happily and started licking its whole face.

"On the weekends she stays at his house on da odda side of Fort Weaver Road. Brah, I tink so he stay pretty old, cuz… like twenty years old or something… haole guy." We were both watching the dog who was rolling around on his back making weird sounds.

"I think she goes over there and just sits around, cooking and waiting for him for come home from work," said Supercalves.

He was rubbing the dog's belly and suddenly its dick started getting hard.

"Eh Brah! No do that! Jackson, what?!"

We both laughed and Supercalves grabbed the water hose and sprayed the dog. He jumped up taking chomps of the water like it was food. I watched for a few minutes getting a kick out of how much fun they were having. Then I shook hands with Supercalves and drove off. Two blocks away I remembered what I had gone there to ask him. I needed some old car stereo stuff but what was I doing now? Damn. I was really high. I looked out the window and saw that I was on the other side of Fort Weaver Road.

Okay. I guess I'm looking for Cinnamon Girl. Which house could it be? If her boyfriend was twenty-ish and had his own place he was probably military. Those guys don't give a fuck. They come down to Hawaii and bang all the little girls and then leave. But then again… why wouldn't you?

I was looking for a sign that said: "Young White Military Guy Lives Here"

There were seven houses on that street. Three of them had at least four cars in the driveway and on the lawn. Nope. Two of them had borderline hoarder amounts of shit in the carports and front and back yards. Nope. One had curtains from the 1970's. Nope.

One had no curtains, no cars, but a crotch rocket CRX 1100 chained in the side lawn area, dead grass, a pair of dirty combat boots, some Nike house shoes and a tiny pair of dainty sandals in front of the door. Bingo.

I knocked on the door. She answered. I took a breath like I was going to say something, watching her eyes go from surprised to… something else. She walked back into the house but left the door open. I went in and watched her thighs rub against each other in the tiny gray cut-off sweatpants. She had the waistband folded up so tight the crotch seam went right up her ass. I followed her into the kitchen and the smell of boiling chicken adobo and rice hit me like a wall. She turned and looked at me like, "Well?"

"I smelled the food…" I said.

She reached up in a cabinet and grabbed a bowl.

"It will taste better in an hour but you can have if you want."

I started to say I was joking, but then thought, fuck it, it smells good. I ate and she sat on a stool, staring at me, slowly running her fingers through her hair. It was so long it took almost five seconds for her fingers to go from her head to the end.

"Can you get me some water?" I asked.

She walked to the fridge and said, "Do you want a beer?" I said yes right away.

I didn't want a beer. The chicken was hot and I had cotton mouth from the joint I smoked earlier. As the food hit my stomach, I started to realize I was sitting in a full-grown man's house, eating his food, about to mess with his girl. "What time is he coming home?" I asked.

"I don't know. He said they had something about rotation swaps or training or I don't know. This whole week is not a set schedule."

My last bite got stuck in my throat. She looked like she wanted to smile. She passed me the beer and I chugged it.

"Are you trying to get caught?" I said.

"Caught doing what? I just stay talking to a friend from school. What? I no can have friends?"

I finished the beer and looked at the empty bottle.

"You make out with all your friends from school?"

She took the bottle and dropped it in an empty trash bin. It made a loud *thump*.

"Why? You like me?" She leaned dramatically against the wall. Her hair sprawled out behind her. "You ask everybody at school where I stay and then you drive around looking for me. You get one crush on me, yeah? You love me? All we wen do was kiss! You love me?" She was teasing me and I couldn't tell if it was playful. It felt mean.

"I was bored. My friend said he saw you here. I thought maybe we could fuck…" When in doubt, open your mouth and let the truth fall out. But that wasn't the whole truth. I didn't want to fuck. I wanted to get high with her again and watch her hair glow black in the sun. I wanted to kiss her and listen to her giggle when I bit her lip again. This, whatever this was that was happening right now, this was not that. This was something different. She stood there maybe thinking the same thing I was thinking.

"Okay, but not here. He might come home soon," she said.

***

The car made struggling sounds as I drove. I struggled to think of where to take her. Again, we didn't talk. We just smoked and drove. If she was from Ewa Beach, I could just take her to Hau Bush. Where was she from again? Waipahu? If she was from any further east than that, she would not want to go to Hau Bush. Everyone thinks that beach and the surrounding trees are haunted or some shit. She was probably from Waipahu, but it seemed like she didn't care where we were going. She pulled out a fresh pack of cinnamon Big Red gum and passed me a piece. She had changed into a little sundress and the bubbles in the tinted windows were making weird shapes on her legs when the sun would hit them. It was almost high noon and it was hot. Her neck was sweating from where her hair was resting on it.

I drove deep into Hau Bush past where the road ended and parked in the sand under some trees and we started kissing. I reached right into her panties. Her lips spread apart and she was wet. She smelled like the ocean on a hot day. I stopped. My ears started ringing. My heart was beating so fast that I couldn't relax enough to figure anything out. I slowly began to realize that through all the big talk and swagger, I actually had no idea what to do.

I mean, I knew.

I put what I have into what she has.

But… I had never… I couldn't…

"What's wrong?" she said softly.

My mind scrambled. I was looking for anything to say besides, "I'm a virgin and I'm so nervous that my dick won't get hard."

I'm a virgin and I'm so nervous that my dick won't get hard.

The words exploded in my head.

Virgin, nervous, dick, hard.
Version, sick, retard
Urgent, time, tick-tick, Freon
Peon
Not the Don
Not the Bomb
Just a con—a con Don…

A condom!

Yeah, that's it. "Shouldn't we have a condom?"

"Oh… yeah… but we no need do all kine… I could just…" she said as she reached between my legs. I let her. She rubbed me and then started untying my surf shorts. She leaned over and put her head between my legs and started to kiss me but it did nothing.

She sat up.

"What, you no like me?" she asked.

I didn't know what to do. I was thinking about telling her the truth. She obviously knew what she was doing. Maybe if I told her, she could slow things down so I could breathe.

She started crying.

"I'm sorry… I just…" I said.

She yelled at me, "Just do it already!"

She wiped her tears away and looked at me. Her mascara was smeared all over her face and her hair was all frizzed out.

"That's what you guys do, ah?! You guys just fuck us all, right?" she said quietly.

"What?"

"Just do it! I just like for him to know how it feels," she said.

"What? Wait… you want me to know how it feels?"

"No. I want *him* to know how it feels."

I still wasn't getting it.

"My boyfriend, stupid. He wen cheat on me." She started crying again. "Why he wen do that?!"

I just sat there with my limp dick hanging out.

Smelling like cinnamon.

CHAPTER 4

TEACH A BOY TO FISH

THE BEAUTY OF WHAT I had created was breathtaking.

Before me, spread over four plates, were five overstuffed, meticulously handcrafted peanut butter and jelly sandwiches. Two of them were toasted, but I had decided the toaster popping was too loud and might wake my mom up. It was three-thirty in the morning and the munchies had me hypnotized. I tried to carefully lift the toaster lever manually right before it would pop but kept forgetting what I was doing until—*POP!* So I abandoned toasting the last three sandwiches and told myself that soft PBJs had their place in the world too.

Now, standing here relishing in my achievement, I couldn't decide which one to take a bite out of first. Toasted? Yes, most definitely toasted. I picked it up and it was still warm.

As I slowly sank my ravenous teeth into the crispy glorious manifestation of my covert labor, I immediately encountered a devastating design flaw. I had misjudged the peanut-butter-to-jelly ratio. Way too much peanut butter! I reached for my glass of milk and discovered my second mistake. Always check for milk before deciding on PBJ. There was no milk in the fridge. As I closed the refrigerator door, I was met with my third and most crucial mistake. I had mixed up my days again and the Fireman was home.

He was standing in the kitchen fourteen inches from my face.

I stood there with a mouth full of peanut butter unable to move my

43

tongue. He didn't say anything. I tried to chew but my mouth was so dry that I thought I might gag.

"No milk?" said the Fireman.

He walked outside. The screen door slammed behind him. I could hear my mom's groggy voice coming from the bedroom.

"What are you guys doin?" she was asking.

I leaned over the trash can and half gagged, half spit a baseball sized lump of peanut butter into the trash then put my face under the faucet and rinsed my mouth.

The Fireman came back into the house with a half gallon of frozen milk he had grabbed from the outdoor freezer. The door slammed again and this was too much for my mom. She came into the kitchen wearing a short silk bathrobe I had never seen before and wished I still hadn't.

She yell-whispered, "What are you guys doing?! It's the middle of the night!"

I motioned to the sandwiches and began to try to come up with something when the Fireman said, "I had him get up early to start making sandwiches. We're gonna lay net."

My mom's face twisted. Her eyesight was really bad and although I'm pretty sure she could make out the sandwiches, I know she couldn't see how red my eyes were. She looked at the Fireman and she put her hand on his chest.

"Oh… well… this early?" she said.

She wasn't whispering now. She was happy and seemed excited.

"It's almost four." The Fireman started explaining: "First light is five-fifteen. We gotta walk the net and the inner tube all the way to the gate and stuff. Come Byron, wrap those up and fill two jugs with water and finish making the coffee."

He walked back outside, slamming the door again. My mom looked at me smiling. She put her hand on my face. "I'm glad you two are doing stuff together." She looked like she was gonna hug me. "Mom! Your robe…" She realized how revealing it was and walked back into the room. We must have woken the little kids up. I could hear them fighting already.

***

The sand was cold.

The warm water splashed against my feet as we dragged a huge inner tube with a circle of plywood tied to the bottom. It looked like a huge black donut with a coffee-cup saucer stuck to the bottom of it. It was filled with a hundred and fifty feet of net, our fins and masks on top. It felt like it weighed a hundred pounds. The net was carefully layered into the tube with floaters on one end and weights on the other. Once we paddled out to where we wanted to start, we would be able to slowly drop it in the water as we swam, stretching it out over an area of a hundred and fifty feet.

I felt pretty good. The coffee I drank was kicking in and I had been able to choke down a sandwich. The sun was still under the horizon, but the sky was turning fire red and orange. The mist from the ocean gave everything a hazy dream feel. The Fireman gave short instructions that were mostly grunts accompanied by waving gestures from his free hand.

"Let's kinda head…" he said, pointing with all his fingers up into the soft sand and out of the wet-packed sand we had been walking in.

We dropped the tube and he tossed me some fins and a mask. I fumbled around with the snorkel while he looked at the water. He was thinking about the wind, the tide, the current and the swell. When I looked at the water, it didn't look right, but what did I know?

"The water's not right," he said.

I looked up at him.

"It's a shitty morning to do this…" He mumbled the rest of the sentence while he messed with his gear.

I put my fins on and he used his hands to tell me to put them back in the tube. We dragged it down into the water and it almost flipped over twice before we were even waist deep.

"Don't let it roll over!" he yelled.

I jammed my hand into the yellow nylon rope that held the plywood to the tube. The rocks and dead coral banged against my ankles and toes. I used my legs to jump my body onto the front of the tube to push it into the waves so it wouldn't be rolled over.

"Aw, shit!" I yelled.

"What, wana?!" yelled the Fireman.

"Yep…" I said, trying to sound tough. I had stepped on a spiny sea urchin. It felt like some deranged doctor had just shoved a hand full of syringes into my heel.

"Yeah… get choke wana on this part of the reef. Try not for step on'em!" he said between mouthfuls of water he was spitting out.

What the hell did that mean?

It meant he was swimming and my dumbass was trying to walk on a reef filled with Hawaiian spiny sea urchins. We continued straight offshore right through the wave break, getting smashed by a wind-blown two-to-three-foot white wash. I knew it would get easier once we got past the break, so I focused on the goal, swallowing about three gulps of ocean in the process. Finally, the waves were rolling under us instead of breaking on our heads.

"Kay! Just hold'em for a sec," he said.

I stretched my arms out as far as I could and grabbed the nylon on either side trying to hold it steady. He reached into the tube and grabbed his fins. I couldn't see him but I could hear him go under to put them on. He popped up about thirty seconds later.

"Go put your stuff on," he yelled.

I grabbed my fins and mask and let myself slide completely under water. The sounds instantly changed from wind and crash and foam to the rolling of rocks and sand. I winced when I squeezed my fin over my left foot. I must have had a lot of wana in that foot. I put my mask on underwater and blew through my nose to clear it and came up. I was greeted by the howling wind and a mouth full of water.

"Eh… Byron… can you hear me?" yelled the Fireman.

"Yeah!"

"Try look at where we came in. Brah, the current is rippin!" he shouted.

I looked back but I hadn't taken note of where we got into the water. As if reading my mind, he said, "The green house, right next to the long rock wall!"

I saw it. We were two or three hundred yards to the left of it. We were supposed to be headed four or five hundred yards to the right of that green house. Damn!

"We gotta bust ass, brah!" he yelled and I felt his side of the tube pull to the right. He was swimming head down breathing through his snorkel. I shoved the snorkel in mouth and blew the water out with my first exhale and started kicking. The wind blew over the water, making tiny little waves on the surface called chop. That's exactly what it looks like. Some ocean god taking a giant clever to the ocean and chop-chop-chop! This chop loves to jump off the top of the water and dive right into your snorkel, but only if you are about to take a really big inhalation.

For the next forty-five minutes to an hour, all I could hear was the sound of both of us kicking and choking. Every five minutes or so I would hear him yell "more right" or "go left" because we had drifted too shallow or too deep. The water was cloudy and I couldn't see the bottom. Every once in a while I would see a small reef fish desperately swim by. It seemed they were getting their asses kicked just like us.

Suddenly a huge wave lifted the entire inner tube up over our heads. I hung on as best as I could as the nylon rope rubbed away my skin. Up and up it went to the top of the wave. It was an outside set. The first one nearly flipped everything over. The second was right behind it.

We went up and the tube flipped.

The Fireman hung on to the nylon rope with one hand and held almost all hundred and fifty feet of net into the upside down tube with his other. He was not human.

"Try flip'em back! Quick! Try flip'em back!" he yelled.

I grabbed the plywood and pushed all my weight down on one side and it went under. Then the both of us pushed up on the other side. It happened just as a smaller wave rolled under us and actually helped it turn back over. Only about twenty feet of net had spilled out and I began to try to gather it back in the tube.

"Leave'em! We gotta beat the set!" he yelled.

I looked towards the horizon and saw another outside set forming. We both put our heads down and kicked towards it with everything we had. My legs were burning and my right thigh kept trying to cramp. Each time, before it did, I stopped kicking with it and only used my left for two or three kicks until the feeling faded and then pumped with both legs again. It was a sprint and we made it.

"Kay, rest," he said as he layered the spilled net back into the tube.

I floated on my back trying to catch my breath. My stomach was burning from drinking too much salt water. I half coughed, half vomited into the water.

"Eh, you okay or what?" asked the Fireman.

"Yeah… I'm cool…"

"What? Was drinking'em?"

"Yep," I said between spits.

"Me too… Kay. You ready?"

We kicked right for another twenty minutes or so, past the military fence that separates Ewa Beach from Iroquois Point military base. They own the land, not the water. We began slowly dropping the net into the ocean while swimming towards the beach. As the inner tube got light the wind kept pushing it towards Ewa and we had to kick against it. When we finished, the net looked like a big question mark with the top of it towards the horizon. From the surface, all you saw was the Fireman's makeshift floater (milk jugs, water bottles, syrup containers) bobbing up and down in the waves. When a fish swims by and sees the net, it instinctively swims straight off shore along it, eventually hitting the semicircle at the top and getting stuck.

We both hung on to the empty tube and let the wind and current carry us back to where we had started. We dragged the tube up the beach and lay in the sun that was now about a quarter of the way up the sky. It was warm. Ewa Beach warm, but right now it felt amazing.

***

Sand in my face.

The Fireman's little girl just threw sand in my face. I sat up and she was smiling at me. It didn't get in my eyes. She's kinda cute. Okay. I guess my little sister just threw sand in my face. I looked at the sun. It was noon. I heard the Fireman yell from out in the water with my brother.

"Shiloh, c'mon!"

They were swimming around the military fence in waist-high water towards the net we had laid. I was salty and sunburnt. I walked into the water and it cooled my face and chest.

"Hey!" my mom said.

She was wearing a bikini with a flowy kinda wrap thing that was flapping in the wind. She had this big sun hat on that was doing everything it could to take flight. She was carrying something. Food!

We sat on the beach eating spam and egg musubi. She was talking about something, but I was chewing so aggressively I couldn't make it out. She was happy. Everything was working out. I watched the Fireman with his daughter on his shoulders and his son splashing the water to scare the fish towards the net. They were all laughing. I smiled.

"I know things have been hard for you, Byron," my mom said while she rubbed my shoulder. My mouth had suddenly gone dry. I put my head down and tried to swallow my last bite.

"I know you feel like we left a lot behind, but as a family, I know we can make a good life here. We can all be happy together?" She left the end hanging like a question.

I couldn't say anything.

I nodded yes.

"I think we might buy a house in Makakilo, four bedrooms. If it works out, you can have your own room!" She said this with the brightest face I had ever seen. She was expecting me to smile and laugh and be happy.

This was what she thought I had been disconnected about? This was what she thought the problem was? I didn't have my own room?

No, Mom. The problem is not that I have a new dad who doesn't know the first thing about me and a brother and a sister who… whatever. It's not that. It's not that I'm in a school that has textbooks from 1973 being used by teachers who can't speak standard English. A school where you can get in a full-blown fist fight in the middle of class and not even get a pink slip. What am I doing here? Who am I here? I don't look or sound or think like anybody here anymore because you moved me away! I didn't want to leave Hawaii! But I did. You said we had to. We had to get away from him. We had to hide like fucking bitches. So we went! And I adapted. I changed the way I talk and dress and think. I found something I really love. I start growing and getting a dream and then you bring me back here?! Dad's safely behind bars serving fifteen to life, so let's go back? I don't fit here anymore! I don't want to live here! I don't want to grow up here! I want to go back. In fact, I never wanted to leave Cali in the first place, but I did for you, Mom.

You guys are going to pull out of Ewa Beach now?! Now that I've made new friends and protected and proved myself in this hot box. You gonna move me again?!

I spit a mouth full of dry spam musubi into the sand.

I took a deep breath.

My eyes were watery.

Here we go.

Time to tell the truth about how I feel. This is it. No more Fireman. No more new little brothers and sisters. No more! If we move, we move back and pick up where I left off!

"I'm not feeling very good… Mom…" was all I managed.

"Oooh, why don't you go take a cool shower and lay down for a while, sweety?" she said, worried.

"I don't want you to be with Johnny," I said and looked her in the eyes.

She was stunned for a second and looked away. I watched her regroup and turn to face me again.

"I understand you feel uncomfortable. It's a natural feeling, but—"

"I'm not uncomfortable. I'm serious. I'm not cool with this shit," I said.

"Don't talk to me that way."

"Does it matter how I talk to you?"

"If you want me to listen?"

"You don't listen to me anyway."

"That's not fair and that's not true."

"What do you know about fair?"

"Byron!"

"What's not fair is, I don't have any say in all of this! My life goes this way and that way and I don't have any say! This is supposed to be my new neighborhood? This is supposed to be my new friends? Over and over again? This is bullshit. This is supposed to be my new dad?!"

"This time will be different."

"Why? Because he's a good father?"

"He is."

"How do you know?"

"I don't like how you're talking to me."

"How do you know?! Because he's your high school sweetheart?"

"You need to change your tone."

"Did he show a certificate?"

"Okay… we're not doing this."

"Or you know it in your gut?"

"Byron, I think you're angry and scared. I think it's time we got you someone to talk to about your anger. About what happened—"

"Because your gut is never wrong, right? It's never wrong when it comes to picking fathers—"

The smack came with a spray of sand.

She had been leaning on the hand she smacked me with and now both of my eyes were filled with sand. I didn't move or make a sound. I sat with my head between my legs and tried to blink the sand out.

"Here, use the water," she said calmly.

She passed me a thermos filled with water and I tilted my head back and started to rinse my eyes. I blinked out enough to see she was looking at me. She was set. She was waiting for me to see she was set. Firm. She wasn't gonna let me go that way. She slowly and deliberately dusted the sand off of her hands. Then she very slowly reached for the cheek she had slapped. I looked at her. I didn't want her to touch me and say sorry. I didn't want her to touch me at all. As her hand inched closer, my heart began to pound in my ears. The beach began to narrow and morph. It stretched out before me like looking through a telescope. She got further and further away from me but her arm kept stretching out. I had to breathe hard and deep to keep my body still and not jump out of it. I wanted to smack her hand away before it touched me. She looked into my eyes and became unsure of what she was seeing. Her hand stopped short of touching my cheek and it was shaking. When she spoke it was a whisper and she was crying.

"You are so angry. I know you're hiding in there somewhere. I know why you're hiding. I would, too. But you have to know it's better now. I want you to come back out here, with us. I am so sorry, Byron. I am so, so sorry."

I could hear a deep rumbling sound. I realized it was coming from me. I was growling. I was crying and I was growling. Her eyebrows scrunched together and she pushed herself to touch me. I slapped her hand away and stood up, flying sand everywhere. She covered her face and yelled, "Byron! Wait!"

The Fireman's voice came from out on the water. "What you guys doing!"

He was standing in chest-high water out on the reef about a football field out. He was concerned.

My mother stood to face me, blinking sand out of her eyes.

"I'm sorry I hit your hand, Mom," I said.

I sounded like a robot. It felt like I yelled it from far away, somewhere deep inside of me, just hoping that my mouth would repeat it. She stared at me. She didn't look scared anymore. She looked angry.

"You are my son. I am your mother. You will not hit me. You will not cuss at me. You will climb up out of whatever this is and you will talk to me and let me help you."

"Everything okay or what?" called the Fireman.

He was moving as fast as he could to get to us. I turned and looked at him.

Then I walked away.

CHAPTER 5

TWISTY TIED DREAMS

My nose was getting sunburnt.

I was riding in the back of Bonez's Toyota pickup truck with Makalolo. Bob Marley was singing "Exodus" but all we could hear in the back was the rumbling bass. Supercalves was in the front with Bonez. We were going up the Pali Highway trying find a waterfall called Ice Ponds. I guess it was supposed to be cold.

As the truck climbed the mountain, we could feel the temperature change. It was a relief. I put my shirt back on as Maka continued his story. "She tell me she no like bone cuz I wen bone her cuzin. I wen tell her, 'Eh, dat was like, summertime already.' Brah, no matter, she no like. Brah, I telling you, lose money already. I no like keep trying, she's fat anyway." He busted up laughing and he slapped me on the arm. I smiled and watched the puffy clouds drag themselves over the top of the mountain. The tops of the trees scraped the bottom of the bloated sky animals, spilling their guts all over the plush mountain forest.

"Brah, you wen stay the night at that haole chic's house, yeah?" said Maka.

The haole chic? My first thought was the cinnamon chic in my car, but I had told no one about that. Oh shit, Blondy from the military base! That's right!

"Dude! YO! That chic was crazy!" I said, sitting up straight. "She tells me on Friday at school she's gonna be babysitting so, you know, come through. Okay. Keep in mind I just met the chic about thirty minutes before. I met her walking through the hall in second period and before the bell rings I got her pressed up against the wall with my hand up her skirt. So, blah blah blah, I go over and she's watchin some four-year-old kid or some shit. I never see him, he's asleep by the time I get there—"

"Eh, she stay da'kine eh? Military? How you wen get on base?"

"That's why it took me so long to get there. I walked from Ewa Beach Road to just outside the back gate at Iroquois and walked along that path to the left, you know—"

"Ho! You wen jump'em?" he said.

"Yep, not a scratch. Fuck barbed wire! I get to her house, and now she's frontin, 'Oh do you really like me?' I'm like 'Bitch, I just snuck into a military installation for you! Ha! I just jumped barbed wire! That shit could've Freddy Kruggered my whole stomach!' Anyway, finally panties come off, and I'm trying to get the condom on and she's all nervous and shit. Like, before she was flirtin mad hard, now she's all frozen. She starts talking about her uncle or some shit, touchin her. She starts crying. I'm like, bent all weird half on, half off the couch with my pants down with a soft dick, condom all hangin off it like a shriveled elephant trunk or some shit!" I finished, laughing.

I got up on my knees in the back of the truck and put my arm in front of my nose like an elephant and made the elephant noise, *pheeeeeaw*!

Maka lost his shit, laughing and coughing, tears wetting his cheeks as the truck down shifted up the steep incline. The wind was cold now. The sweet smell of the damp rain forest tingled in my nose. The wind was musky and full of energy, full of life.

"So what? You wen leave or what?" asked Maka.

"Yo!" I said. "I turn around to maybe get her some water or something. I'm tryin to be, ya know, supportive an shit, and there's the little kid standing there the whole time!"

"No!" yelled Maka.

He got up on his knees and started making the elephant trunk *pheeeeaw*.

Supercalves stuck his head out the window of the front cabin and yelled, "Eh, what you guys doing?"

We just kept laughing.

Bonez pulled off the Pali Highway to the right and stopped the truck.

The music kept playing: "Sun is shining, the weather is sweet yeah… Makes ya wanna move ya dancing feet…"

Supercalves handed the joint out the window and Maka took it. I turned it down. I was still high from the last joint. I could feel the cold breeze carrying the mana of the mountain. It blew right through my skin and chilled an empty part of me.

I could see her blond hair in the morning light after we had tried to have sex. We sat on a bench in the shady doorway outside while inside the little kid ate cereal and watched cartoons. She was embarrassed. So was I. We were both little kids. Both virgins. Sort of. She had told me a secret. A dark secret about her uncle she probably had never told anybody. And now, in the doorway she was back peddling. She was nervously pulling at her hair, which was draped over her shoulder. Pulling it so hard strands of it were ripping out. I lit a joint and told her to smoke it because it would make her feel better. She said she always pulls out her hair. Mostly the split ends. She took my lighter to show me how she burns the ends sometimes. A big chunk of her hair caught fire and I grabbed at it and started slapping it out. We both sat quietly for a moment. She was looking at me and I was looking at her. Most of the front left section of her beautiful hair was short and blackened. It smelled bad. She started laughing a horrible laugh. She flicked the lighter crazily and started trying to light the rest of her hair. I grabbed the lighter and walked away. She yelled from the doorway. I didn't hear her words.

"That sucks…" I mumbled.

"What?" said Supercalves. I shook my head and turned down the last pass of the J.

All of us put our rubber slippers in our pockets and walked barefoot through the narrow path. I felt the wet mud and fallen guava fruit squish through my toes. The occasional rock or exposed root would press the bottom of my feet reminding me to step lightly so I didn't bruise them. The wet leaves and underbrush slid against my skin. The fresh and cold water drops eventually soaked my shirt and surf shorts.

Off the path about a hundred yards away, I saw a twisty tie wrapped around the branch of a ti tree. I almost missed it because it was a green twisty tie. Strange.

We made it to the waterfall. The name fit perfectly. There was no ice but you couldn't tell us that. Compared to the lukewarm ocean we swam in every day, Ice Ponds was the Arctic Circle. Maka was the first to suicide splash off the top rock almost two stories high. Then we were all trying to outdo each other. I did a back gainer into a can opener from the same spot. Bonez climbed a tree that was growing from the top of the ledge, almost ten feet higher than where we were. He hung there for a moment. Nobody said a word. It was very high and the water was pretty shallow. He jumped, legs spread, hands over his nuts.

"Cheeeeehuuuuu!"

Splash!

He popped up instantly with blood all over his face. He had hit his head on the rocks below.

We all jumped in and pulled him up on the rocks. He was laughing as the blood gushed out of his head.

"Eh, I wen crack my head open or what?" he said.

"Bonez, stay still, brah!" said Maka.

We each made cups with our hands and poured water onto his head. There was a lot of blood but the cut wasn't really that bad, about a three-inch gouge above his left eye. I was about to tell him so but Maka kept shouting, "Brah, don't move. Just breathe, Bonez. Oh cuz, no die on me brah!"

Bonez began to cry.

"I wen crack my head! No! I no like die! Brah, help me you fucka! Help me!" Bonez pleaded.

Maka smacked Bonez in the face hard.

"Brah, stay still. I gotta look inside your head. You wen crack your head, Bonez. No move. I going look inside for see how bad!" yelled Maka.

Bonez got quiet. We all did. Maybe Maka saw something I didn't. I was on the wrong side. Maybe he could see chunks of brain or something. Shit. Maka held Bonez's face gently in his hands and looked super close into the cut. So close their noses were almost touching.

"Bonez…" whispered Maka. "There's nothing but air inside your head…"

I lost my shit! I fell backwards and I couldn't breathe. Supercalves smacked the water with both hands shouting and laughing. Bonez punched Maka in the face and he playfully fell in the water.

"Fuck you guys! I wen crack my head and you guys like make one joke!" said Bonez.

He tackled me in the water and put me in a headlock, then Maka picked us both up and body slammed us into the water.

***

We walked back through the path quietly, cold, tired and hungry. Bonez had my shirt wrapped around his head to try to keep the skin from flapping. Then I saw it again. A little green twisty tie wrapped around a branch of a ti tree. It was maybe two-ish in the afternoon and the sun was different. The green tie really stood out now. In another hundred yards or so, I could see another one. Why? There was no trail so it wasn't marking a path.

"Hold up a second," I said.

I walked through the high grass all the way up to the second twisty tie. The boys hung back, standing there completely uninterested. From where I now stood I could see a third twisty tie. This one was yellow and stood out a little more, but it was completely out of sight from the path. "There's another twisty tie over there, a yellow one," I yelled back.

"So what?" yelled Maka "We go, brah. I'm hungry!"

"I tired. I like go sleep," said Supercalves.

"My head stay cracked open!" yelled Bonez.

Everyone yelled, "No, it's not."

I pushed on, crawling through ever thickening rain forest. The canopy became a ceiling, casting shade downhill over the valley I was slowly making my way though. I could hear the boys behind me cursing and shouting at me to stop and turn around, but I wanted to know why someone would mark a path without making a path. What the hell? After almost an hour, with both my feet now bleeding and bruised, I found my answer.

In front of me for almost the width and length of a football field was a sea of five-foot-high marijuana plants.

***

I wanted to hear what Maka was saying.

We were haphazardly parked just off the road in a gravel patch that served as a parking lot for a small Korean mini-mart at the bottom of the Pali Highway. The sun was about an hour from setting and I couldn't imagine driving back up there and trying to hike back to the spot in the dark. Maka had his back to us about fifty feet away talking on a pay phone. Bonez was pacing back and forth rapping his knuckles on the door to the truck bed. He spoke to Supercalves and me in a whispering growl.

"Brah, we just should go back and grab as many plants as we could carry. We just go grab'em! Put em in the oven on little bit heat, four hours, bang, she go cuz! You seen'em, those plants stay ready! Get plenty buds on top'em!" he explained. Supercalves was agreeing, but I wanted to hear what Maka's older brother had to say.

It was true the plants were ready to harvest. The fan leaves were all purple and yellow. The buds were all crusted in white powder. It looked like they were dipped in shaved ice. Walking through the plants, I had felt like I was on the cover of the Peter Tosh album. Bonez continued to push the two of us on his plan. His voice was cracking more as the sun started to disappear.

"I tellin you guys! We only get little bit time left. What Kaipo going tell us? Go get the plants. Then what? He going take'em! Probably just give us like, one ounce for share. Brah! Get pounds out there! We go get'em, we no tell nobody!" yelled Bonez. He was right. Maka's older brother would take a lion's share, but I couldn't think straight. I wasn't sure putting weed in the oven to dry it was the best way to go. I had a feeling that none of us had any idea what to do with an actual plant. Considering everything we knew about weed had been passed down from Kaipo to Maka to us, I figured calling him was the right move. I just wished I could hear what Kaipo was saying. I could tell Maka was just saying "yes," "no," and "okay."

Maka hung up the phone and walked up to the back of the truck. Supercalves and I slid up to the tailgate and Bonez walked up close.

"Kay. We go back to Ewa Beach and grab money from my braddah. He like us go buy trash bags and da'kine, garden scissors, and gloves. He said we go come back ass crack early in the morning. We all going bring cars. He gotta call his friend," Maka finished. He was almost whispering.

"What friend brah? See! Now get one more person who going know!" yelled Bonez.

"Shut UP!" yelled Maka. "Why! What you like do?"

"We go grab'em now, keep'em for ourselves. The more people we tell the less we get and den!" said Bonez.

"And what? We go cook fuckin pounds of pakalolo in your oven? Stupid!" said Maka.

"I never wen say dat!" said Bonez, backpedaling.

"What den? Tell me what for do!" Maka said, putting his head down against the truck. He was breathing hard. For a moment I thought he was crying.

"Yo… we don't have to do nothing," I said. Everyone was quiet. "Ya know. Go to Zippys, buy a few zip packs, hamburger steak with brown gravy all over. Go home, climb in bed. Go to sleep," I said.

No one made eye contact with me. It was too much weed. We couldn't begin to understand how big of a thing this was. Maka began to make wheezing sounds. I thought maybe he was finally breaking down. Then I realized he was laughing. Then Bonez and Supercalves started laughing too. They were laughing at me.

"Fuck that!" laughed Maka.

***

Who was this guy?

He looked like a forty-year-old chubby Mr. Flanders from the Simpsons. He talked like it too. Except he said "dude" almost every fourth word. He wore a faded aloha shirt that looked like it was stolen from the wardrobe of the original *Hawaii 5-0* T.V. show. He had a super short pair of cut off jean shorts that were borderline daisy dukes and the actual pair of sandals that Julius Caesar was wearing when he was murdered.

He walked through the five-foot-high weed plants with his arms outstretched like Moses parting the Red Sea. The sun had just risen and the light was cutting through the trees sideways. Rays of golden light beamed out from behind him as he floated clumsily over the uneven dirt.

"Dude, this is like… dude… the most reefer I've ever… dude… look at this… brother it's fucking radical… I'm so humbled… that you would call me, dude. That I can have this experience! To have my eyes behold such a… dude… such a site. Dude, this is awesome! It tickles! Dude, it tickles my nose and my tummy! My tummy is tingling, dude!" said the old man.

"Brah, I no care about your fuckin tummy you fucka. Who's evers this pakalolo, they goin be comin back soon brah. Tell us how for cut'em or I just going start rippin'em out da ground!" said Maka's older brother Kiapo.

He was scary. Not quite six feet tall but all muscle. His head was shaved all except the top, which was thick and long down to his shoulders. His skin was so dark you couldn't make out the hand-poked prison tattoos all over his chest and neck. He was standing in the middle of the field with his arms filled with trash bags and stuff.

"Okay, dude, just let me feel the vibe. I know there's pressure but just breathe for a second…" said the old man.

Kaipo dropped all the stuff he had in his hands and commenced to ripping out one of the plants from the root.

"Dude!! Okay, wait!" yelled the old man.

Kiapo stood waiting. The old man took a few steps backwards then fell on his ass. He couldn't stand back up. He had to roll over on his tingling tummy and slowly stand up one leg at a time. He dusted himself off and looked at all of us. We couldn't help it. We all started laughing. Even Kaipo started to smile.

"Okay… okay… first of all, brother, we need to begin with those plants over there, dude. These here need another month… okay? The owner of this marvelous production is rotating by section, month by month. So, it appears they will have a crop every month. It only makes sense to take this month and next—"

"We takin'em all!" said Kaipo.

"Dude, that's a waste of a beautiful life," said the old man.

"Mr. Mervin! How you like me cut'em or do I just rip'em?!" yelled Kaipo.

"Okay, Kaipo! If you destroy these plants for no reason, I will turn around a walk away! Dude… I'm not doing this! You called me! Dude!! Okay! I will not help you dry! I will not help you cure and you'll be left with shitty molded pounds of shitty shit! Do you understand me, dude?!" yelled the old man.

He was breathing hard and his face was bright red.

Kaipo stood there. I could tell he was thinking about beating the old man. We could all tell. So could the old man.

But then Kaipo changed his whole tone and spoke in almost a whiny voice. "Okay, Mr. Mervin, but da'kine already, we go! It's dangerous for be standin round here. You know whose plants dis is?! If they come back they not goin be happy… you know what I saying right?"

"Yes, Kaipo," said the old man.

He walked over to Kaipo and patted his shoulder. "We are all a little freaked out bro. Nothing to it but to do it, brother!" he said.

He looked at the field and took a deep breath. "Okay… don't rip them out. Cut them the best you can from them bottom, okay kids? Lie it down gently and wrap branches with string, like this, okay, like when they pack a Christmas tree. Okay? Put it in the trash bag bottom first then gently take all the air outta the bags before you tie it, okay? Start from here and go all the way to the edge of that corner. We'll be lucky if we can get this all done today—but slow is pro… and use your gloves!"

***

I could see the old man through his living room window. He was backlit again but this time from inside his house. It was almost midnight. His wife was crying and yelling and he was talking and soothing. Sometimes they raised their voices and you could hear them.

"I no like dat kine drugs in my home!" she yelled in a heavy Filipino accent.

"It's not drugs! Sugar, it's just reefer, okay, and it's only for ten days, okay, just to dry it out. Then we'll put it in ziplock bags and move it somewhere else! Okay?" he pleaded.

She disappeared from the living room, then reappeared in the kitchen window.

"What are you teaching them? What kine role model you? You drug dealer!" she screamed.

"That's not fair, baby muffin! These kids aren't my students, okay, and besides it's just reefer!" he said.

She stormed out of the little house and jumped in her car. My car was blocking hers in their driveway. She backed up and almost hit it, her tires screeching and engine reving. She leaned on the horn the whole time while I started my car and backed out of the way.

The old man casually walked out as I was pulling back into the driveway. He had both hands in the pockets of his ridiculously tight shorts. All of us sort of gathered around him.

"Okay, looks like she's on board," he said with no sarcasm at all. "I'm going to put up some rows of string across the garage and the living room, while you kids bring all the bags inside, okay? Kaipo, I need you to go to Home Depot and pick up ten three-by-four window screens, twenty-five relative humidity gauges, the small ones, okay, six temperature gauges, ten boxes of gallon-size ziplock bags, and two industrial fans, okay?" said the old man.

"What is that?" asked Kaipo.

"That's those big ass fans they use in warehouses," I said.

"What, brah! I was talking to you or what?" said Kaipo.

His eye's locked on mine for a moment until I looked down and almost pissed my pants. Kaipo looked back to the old man.

"It's the big ass fans they use at warehouses," said the old man looking at me with a grin.

"So what? I paying for all this?" said Kaipo.

"In about three weeks none of us are going to be having money problems, okay, but I can spare a few dollars if you ask me nicely, dude," said the old man with a smile. Kaipo put his hand out and the old man gave him what looked like a few hundred dollars. Kaipo grabbed bags out of his truck and began gently laying them on the ground. We all started to help but the old man stopped me.

He said, "What's your name?"

"Q," I said. "Um, Byron Quintis—" I almost said sir but stopped myself.

"I've seen you around the school. I'm Mr. Mervin. I teach drama and video production at your school, okay. You four are going to be very active and creative members of my program, okay. Tomorrow you four will go to homeroom and say you're going to be working on a project for me and we will rotate the days so there's always someone here checking the temp and humidity," said Mr. Mervin.

He took his hands out of his pockets and rubbed them together. "Okay, nothing to it but to do it, okay. Let's get moving so we're not here all night!"

CHAPTER 6

SIN

WE WERE AT MR. Mervin's all night.

Gently unwrapping the plants and hanging them upside down on the strings Mr. Mervin had crossed from wall to wall. There were over a hundred and sixty plants. Some of them were bigger than others and some were just too young and hadn't even budded yet. Mr. Mervin looked like he was going to cry when he threw those away. He said in two days we would cut all the fan leaves off and let them stay like that until the stems got brittle enough to break if you tried to bend them.

In the morning I got the permission slip from homeroom and walked the long way to J building. I was tired. I knew damn well there was no way my friends would be up this early but I couldn't stay home. This was the day the Fireman was home.

I walked into the unfamiliar classroom. It was dark and it took a few seconds for my eyes to adjust. Then I realized there was a movie playing on a pull down screen hanging over a stage in the back of the room. I could hear whispers as I came in. "Who's that?!"

Then someone made a joke and a corner of the room busted out laughing.

I sat down at the closest empty chair to me and scanned the room as my vision got clear. About twenty kids all dressed weird: long pants and boots, flannel shirts, one kid was wearing a trench coat.

The movie was something a student had made. On the screen there was a teenager sitting in the kitchen with a pile of white powder on the counter in front of him. The kid put his face in the pile. Then we heard the ridiculously loud sound of sniffing and some sort of heavy metal began to play. The door of the kitchen busted open and two other teenagers came in with toy guns. The first kid picked his head up off the table, his face covered in powder, and stood up with an enormous dildo in his hand. "Let me introduce you to my little friend!!" He started rubbing the dildo back and forth. The whole classroom busted out laughing and cheering. It cut back to the two kids, who then got a bucket of what I hoped was milk thrown on them. The class lost their shit. One kid stood up and then fell down laughing. The screen went black and the classroom lights came on. A girl stood up on a table and started swinging a black and red flannel over her head while everyone cheered and chanted her name. "Cindy! Cindy! Cindy!"

She put her hands up to quiet the applause.

"Thank you! Thank you! I just want to say that when I signed on to direct this masterpiece, I knew it was gonna be hard"—she motioned like she was stroking a dick between her legs—"I knew it was gonna be rock hard, which is how I like it!"

Everyone laughed.

"But wait, wait, I need to thank the wonderful actors, especially Tim and Craig," she said. Everyone applauded.

"Let's face it, they are the best at taking it in the face!" she said looking at them. "Next time though guys, open your mouth!" She laughed while the whole room made an *ewww* sound.

She got down off the chair and walked past me into a small room behind me.

I had to run it back three times in my head.

She had a white wife beater tank top on with a black lace bra underneath, and black jean shorts so short you could see the bottom of her amazing ass. It shook as she stomped by me in huge black untied steel toe construction boots. She had a black and red flannel in one hand and a lolly pop in the other. She stuck the lollipop in her mouth as she passed by and actually winked and smiled.

Who does that?

She went in the room and shut the door.

"Hey!" said some dorky white kid. "Are you Q?" It was the trench coat kid.

"Yeah," I said.

He passed me a small piece of paper. It was the class pass. With this piece of paper all my other classes were to look at their schedules, and if I had completed all my assignments and was on good standing, I could be excused from that class and come here. Basically, no teachers really cared enough to go through their schedules. It would be a win for them to get a smart mouth pothead out of their class. Cha-Ching!

"Ayo," I said. "Who's that chic?"

I pointed to the door she had just closed. He looked at the door like it was the most beautiful door he had ever seen.

"That was Cynthia," he said.

***

It sounded like a large animal slowly dying. It echoed horribly through Bonez's run-down house. I kept my eyes on the window. Across the street I could see the Fireman going in and out of his soon-to-be-old house, slowly loading all of our stuff into his truck to move to our new house in Makakilo. I knew he couldn't hear us. We were far enough away, but I could hear us. I could hear it. The sound of a fifteen-year-old boy laying in a ball on the hardwood floor of his house crying the cry you cry when you cannot cry anymore.

"*Sahu, sahu, sahu, uuuuwwww… sahu, sahu, sahu, uuuuuwwww…*"

Over and over again until I thought I was going to go insane. Maka, Supercalves and I were against the wall in the corner pretending to be invisible.

"*…ahu, sahu, sahu, uuuuuwwww… sahu, sahu, sahu, uuuuuuwwww…*"

The "uuuuuwww" part was like when you blow over the top of a bottle. Blood and spit would slowly pour out of his mouth onto the floor making a puddle that he would roll his face in as he rocked back and forth. His left eye was swelling up bad and you could barely make out the eyelashes though the puffy lid. His right eye was open looking far off.

I stood as still as possible, smoking my eighth cigarette in row. Kaipo was in Bonez's bedroom flipping over the bed, emptying out the dresser, digging through the closet. "Brah! If I no find'em I going come back inside dere and drag you outside, put your feet up on the stairs and stomp on your legs!!" Kaipo yelled as he stormed back into the living room and jumped up and down to illustrate his point.

"You know what that means you fucka?!"

Bonez just lay there rocking back and forth. Kaipo got right down in his face and yelled, "It means I going *snap your fucking legs*!"

He jumped again and this time his bare feet slammed down right in front of Bonez's face. Bonez squealed like a pig and scurried back to the foot of the couch. He grabbed the throw rug and hugged it like a little blanky. Bonez didn't look like the tough fifteen-year-old badass that I knew. He looked like a scared little boy.

A vision of my mother rippled across my mind. I could see my father standing over us yelling and snapping his belt like a bullwhip… me squealing in fear trying to burrow into my mother's armpit to hide from the next wave of blows that were sure to come crashing down on us… her screaming and crying trying to take the blows… the smell of whiskey…

"Eh Kaipo, leave'em alone already," said a voice.

I looked at Maka and Supercalves to see who said it. They looked at me with sheer horror. My right hand burned. I looked down to see that I had balled my fist over the lit cigarette I was holding.

Kaipo turned slowly towards me. "What… you fucka? You like say sumting?" He was almost whispering.

I guess the voice had been me.

He punched me in stomach, knocking the wind out of me. I fell to the floor. I gagged and almost threw up, then stood back up. I took a deep breath and said it again. "Leave'em alone already."

He went to punch me again but I moved and swung for his face.

It felt like I was swinging through jello.

The fear that had paralyzed us for the last hour of Kaipo's rage had not worn off. I was too scared to give it my all. He was older, bigger, stronger, and fucking scary.

He grabbed me by my hair, slammed his fist into my face a few times and then dropped me on the floor next to Bonez. I lay there for a few seconds trying to blink away the stars. I realized my face was in the puddle of Bonez's blood and spit and I started gagging.

Kaipo was laughing. "You guyz is tough now eh? You tink you can talk to me wit chour deep voice n' I goin get scared?! You guys like scrap wit me?! I lick all you guys one time! You guyz is babies still yet! You guyz like steal from me? Who wen take care of everything? Was me eh!? What? You tink I wasn't going be fair?" said Kaipo in a surprisingly reasonable tone to Maka and Supercalves.

"We never when steal nothing Kaipo. Q told Bonez just wait. I when tell'em too!" said Maka.

"We all when tell'em!" said Supercalves.

"You tink I was going steal from my little braddah and his friends?" pleaded Kaipo. "What kine is dat?"

I turned my head and looked up at Kaipo. The rage was gone and he looked deflated and scared. Here was a twenty-two-year-old man who had just beat the shit out of two teenage boys and trashed a family house.

"We never thought that, Kaipo," said Maka, taking a step closer to his older brother. "You know Bonez, he gets funny sometimes…"

Kaipo turned and kneeled down towards Bonez and me.

"I was going be fair. I was brah! You know what? I never even when tink was you guys, in fact, I know you guys is solid. I knew was Bonez. Dis fucka! What an den? You like fight me for this fuckin fagget." He flicked Bonez on his swollen eye and Bonez squealed. "Tell me where the weed stay and we call'em fair." I opened my mouth to say I didn't know where it was but then I saw the trash bag under the couch.

Kaipo saw it too.

***

"C'mon boyz, we can do it!" yelled Kaipo clapping his hands like a sixth-grade football coach. We were all busy putting the house back together while Kaipo walked from room to room rallying us in the fourth quarter. As we passed him he would pat us on the back or mess our hair.

"Can! Brah!! We can! We can put'em back. This that Risky Bizness movie brah! Put'em all back perfect. Nobody going know. We work to-gether, one team. You guyz is my star players!" he shouted like a loving coach. "Can brah! Hustle, hustle!"

Bonez was still on the floor, leaning against the couch holding ice in a plastic Safeway bag wrapped in a dish rag up to his eye. Every now and then Kaipo would walk over and speak softly to him.

We got everything pretty much done in about twenty minutes and Coach Kaipo had us huddle up over by where Bonez was sitting. He sat on the couch with Bonez by his feet like a little puppy. He even rubbed his head while he made sure we all had the story straight.

"K'den, this was messed up cuz… I not going lie. I wen lose my temper. But you guys can not be stealing from me! We gotta be one team. All this fighting for just this little bit weed?" He held up the trash bag that Bonez had taken. "This is small kine! I was going give even more than this, you bugga." He rubbed bonez's head. "You guys trust me yeah?"

We all nodded yes. I grinded my teeth. I could see another reason for this kindness. What would happen if one of us told our parents? What if our parents told the police? I couldn't see it playing out very well for Kaipo. I searched Maka's eyes trying to see if he was thinking what I was thinking. It didn't look like it. He just looked happy Kaipo's rage was over.

"What you thinking Q?" said Kaipo. There was a flicker in his eye. "I looking at you and you stay looking all around. What? You like more lickings? You going try tell on me?"

Oh shit. How did he know what I was thinking?

I stood there still. I noticed my fists were clenched again. This time I would fight my hardest. Kaipo was not Kevin McKenzie. I could fight back. The last bit of fear was leaving me and it was being replaced with fire. The last thing my dad taught me, it don't matter if you win, just—

"What?! You going tell your dad I wen give you dirty hurts brah?" said Kaipo.

My *dad*? Can Kaipo fuckin read minds?! My dad…?

Wait… the Fireman? That's not my dad! Telling the Fireman had never crossed my mind. I don't need him to help me. I don't need anybody! What I need is to get out of this house.

"I need you to stop acting like a fucking psychopath and let us out of this fucking house!"

I had yelled as loud as I could and was standing with my fists clenched ready for another beat down. My voice had not cracked. In fact, it had come from deep in my chest and echoed off the walls with a power I had never heard before. It shocked me. It shocked Kaipo. He had stood up but wasn't sure what to do.

"Byron, what you guys doing?" said the Fireman.

He was standing outside the screen door.

No one answered. He opened the door slowly and it creaked. He stepped in and we could feel his weight in the room. Kaipo looked small compared to the Fireman. Here was a fully grown man standing amongst children. He scanned the room and walked slowly over to Kaipo.

"Kaipo, what are you doing?" he said softly.

Kaipo's shoulders fell and he looked down to study the hardwood floor.

"You a big man, eh Kaipo? Slapping around little boys?" said the Fireman.

"I'm okay—" I tried to say.

"Shut up, Byron!" said the Fireman.

I shut up. The Fireman looked at Bonez and then looked at me.

"You always liked to push around the younger kids, even from keiki days," said the Fireman.

He reached down and picked up the trash bag full of weed. Kaipo reached out to grab it but the Fireman slapped his hand.

Kaipo stood shocked for a second. His chest puffed up and his arms got wide. The Fireman slapped him in the face. Kaipo stood there with a twisted look, unable to move.

The Fireman slapped him again and said, "What?! You like do something?"

SLAP

"Do something! You like scrap eh, you like scrap?"

SLAP

"What?! Punk!"

SLAP

"You only like scrapping kids?" said the Fireman as he pushed Kaipo backwards onto the couch. Then he opened the trash bag.

He stood there quietly staring into it. I could hear a dog barking a few houses down. I was holding my breath until I saw little sparkles in the corners of my eyes. I slowly took some air trying not to make any noise. The sound of the trash bag closing and being tied in a knot was loud.

"Maka, go home. Lyle, you too. Opele, go in your room and shut the door. Byron, go wait for me by the truck," said the Fireman.

No one moved.

"GO!"

We all moved.

Maka and Supercalves flew out the door without looking backwards at me. I stopped on the stairs and kneeled down looking through the jalousie window by the door.

As soon as the screen door had shut behind me, the Fireman leaned over and grabbed Kaipo by the throat. Kaipo didn't even try to fight back. He just sank deeper into the couch making a dry gurgling sound. The Fireman's face was almost touching Kaipo's.

"You got these boys selling weed for you? You like them get kicked outta school like you? You feel like a big man eh! I promise you Kaipo, I'll kick your ass! If I see or hear… I fucking promise! Even if I think your talking to my son I will fucking put you in the hospital!" whispered the Fireman.

He let go of Kaipo's throat and stood up. I walked fast across the street to the truck. My head was swimming. I went behind the truck and threw up.

***

The Fireman walked up to the truck, got in and started it. I didn't get in. My chest was pounding. I started walking up and down the length of the truck. The Fireman turned the truck off, got out and stood looking at me from across the truck bed.

"You alright or what?" he said gently.

"I can't go with you!" I said angrily, panting.

"Get in the truck. You don't have to talk to me. You can talk to your mom when she gets home," he said.

"I'm not getting in the truck!" I said.

"Get in the truck," he said again.

"No!" I yelled

"Byron, get in the truck!" he said and started to walk around it.

"What are you going to do, choke me?!" I yelled.

He stopped. The look on his face was strange. He was studying. He looked like he wanted to hug me. He started to say something then stopped.

"I have to go get my car," I said.

"We'll take care of that later. Right now I want to get you home."

"I want to get my car!"

I was trying to calm myself down but it wasn't working.

"I think we're going to rethink the whole car thing for awhile," he said.

"Who's we?" I asked.

"Me and your mom. She said it was too soon to give you a car and I think she was right. I think you need to spend some time at home."

"What?! You mean like, what? I'm grounded?!"

"Hey… call it what you want. Get in the truck!" he said, getting frustrated.

"I'm not getting in the truck! I'm not getting grounded. I'm walking across the street and getting my car!" I yelled.

I started to walk. He stepped towards me and grabbed my arm. I spun around swinging and he stopped me like you would a toddler throwing a tantrum. He easily put me in a headlock and reached into my pocket and took the car keys. He let me go and I spun around to try to punch him but I slipped on the gravel, fell down and scrambled back up. He backed away with his hands up.

"Get in the truck, Byron," he said gently.

"No…" I whispered.

"Your mom told me what happened to you… about your dad… I'm sorry… You know it's not your fault… I think…"

He took a step closer to me.

"I'm not getting in the fucking truck!" I screamed. I was crying. "You're not my dad! This is not my house. You ain't my fucking superman! What was that? I don't need you! I can handle Kaipo! I can fight my own fights! I can handle my own beatings. You gonna make me get in the fucking truck?! You gonna beat me?! I can handle it! Go! C'mon! You can't beat me worse than my real dad! You never gonna be real! You're just pretending so you can fuck my mom! You just want my mom, you don't want me! So stop pretending! The jig is up! You win! You got her! I'm on my own now. Fuck you!"

We both stood there still. I wiped the tears from my eyes and spit a bunch of snot into the dirt. He stepped forward and I yelled as loud as I could.

"I'M NOT GETTING IN THE FUCKING TRUCK!!"

He got in the truck, started it and drove away.

***

I sat in the cafeteria at the farthest table in the back. I was eating the worst possible imitation of lasagna that ever existed. I had never been in the cafeteria. No cool kids ever ate lunch on campus. I thought it mostly had to do with the stigma behind not being cool enough to break the rules and walk off campus or whatever, but no. Mainly it was because the food was gag inducing. It was also seventy-five cents. The doors of my car didn't lock so I had dug through the ash tray and found three decent sized roaches to smoke and a dollar eighty-three.

I figured the school lunch was the best bargain. I figured wrong. My nose kept bleeding so I had a pile of bloody tissue around me and every time I swallowed a bite I thought I was going to barf. I was so hungry my hands were shaking. My head was pounding and if I let my thoughts drift tears started rolling down my cheeks. So I sat there by myself trying to keep it together. Every two minutes groups of kids would come by to shake my hand so that other kids would see that they were cool enough to shake my hand. Finally some kid in a fucking trench coat tried to shake my hand right as I was blowing my nose.

"Wassup Q," he squeaked.

"Can you see what I'm doing right now!" I yelled. "Dog! I don't even know you! Fuckin bounce!"

He reeled back like I had hit him. Then turned and actually ran away.

Maybe I should try the orange juice. I chugged it and started to feel better. I was just about to stand up and trash the rest of the food when I saw the hot Filipino chic from the video room stomping towards me. She stood right over me and pointed her finger in my face.

"What's your fucking problem?! Yelling at my fucking friends. I'll kick your ass!" she said.

I wanted to laugh. I wanted to tell her how cute she looked all worked up like that. I wanted to say sorry for whatever she wanted me to say sorry for. I wanted to yell back and tell her she needed to check her tone. But I had nothing. I had no fight left. I sat there with my eyes full of water. I was scared that if I talked the tears would spill so I said nothing. I just stared at her.

"Are you okay?" she said so softly.

She sat down and grabbed my hand like she knew me. The touch sent a spark up my arm and started a warmth that loosened everything inside of me. I shuddered and tried to speak.

"Did you drink your orange juice?" I said with an awkward laugh as tears started running down my face. I had no clean napkins left and was desperately wiping my face with the bloody ones. She took the black and red flannel that was wrapped around her waist and threw it at me while she went to the next table. She started smacking little freshman boys on the head and stealing their orange juice. She grabbed my arm and pulled me outside.

We stood alone against the wall behind the cafeteria. It was shady. The line between the shade and the sun was so defined it looked painted. If you watched it a full minute without blinking, you could see it move.

"Strange to see someone like you cry like a baby in front of the whole school," she said.

She talked fast. It took me a minute to figure out what she had said.

"I wasn't fuckin crying. I got a bloody nose. It makes your eyes water."

I was starting to get a hold of myself.

"So you weren't crying, your eyes were watering? Got it," she said.

Without thinking I blew my bloody, snotty nose into her flannel.

"Hey what the fuck!" she yelled.

"Sorry, I wasn't thinking," I said.

I went to hand it back to her and she made a disgusted face and passed me a cigarette. I put the flannel on the ground between us. She flipped open a Hello Kitty Zippo and lit mine, then hers.

"Hello Kitty makes lighters?"

"Fucking cool, right?" she said flipping it open and shut.

One of the kitchen staff came back and threw a trash bag into the dumpster and went back inside.

"So…" I said, trying to think what to say next.

"A needle pulling thread."

"What?"

"Nevermind. Who beat your ass?" she asked.

"Nobody. Let's talk about something else."

"It's a warm day today, don't you think? They say this heat is supposed to last a while. This being a tropical island and all," she said in a mocking tone.

"What the fuck are you talking about?"

"Something else," she said with over dramatic honesty.

And then I finally caught up.

"I see… she's wit-tee in a white tee," I mumbled.

It took a second and then she looked down at her white tank top and smiled.

"Orange juice?" she said, picking up the four juice cups.

I took one and she took one and put the other two on the ground.

We drank the juice and smoked. After a while I got lost in my thoughts while watching the sun make its way towards us. In twenty minutes, there would be no shade here anymore.

She giggled.

"Your eyebrows furrow so hard," she said softly and reached up to touch my forehead. I smiled and pushed her hand away.

"In twenty minutes there ain't gonna be no shade here," I said.

"So we have twenty minutes of top-notch stimulating conversation to continue." She furrowed her brow and imitated me staring at the grass. I smiled and shook my head.

"Who are you?" I asked.

"Finally, a proper introduction," she said in a fake British accent. She put her hand out for a handshake. I gave her a "you're weird" look and shook her hand.

"I'm Q," I said.

"Yeah, I know, you're the drug dealer," she said all matter of fact.

She pulled out two more cigarettes and tried to pass me one. I turned it down. I think I had smoked enough cigarettes for a week. She put them both back in the pack.

"I'm not a drug dealer. I just sell a couple joints here and there."

"Of course! I was just teasing you. You're Q the kissing bandit. You kiss the girls and make them cry," she said smiling to see how this landed. I laughed out loud.

"What?" I said. "I kissed a couple a girls, but it wasn't me who made them cry."

"Of course not!"

She flicked the pack of cigarettes a couple times and pulled two out then remembered I didn't want one and put them both back again.

"So mister 'I'm not a drug dealer.' Do you have any weed for us to smoke?" she said with a smile.

I grabbed another orange juice and opened it.

"No… sorry… I'm having a rough week," I said.

"I'll say," she said with some weird accent that I guess was supposed to be an imitation of some chic from the 1920s while poking at her snotty flannel on the ground between us.

Weird. This chic was so weird.

"So I'm Cynthia. My friends call me Cyn," she said putting her hand out again. I shook it again.

"Cyn as in Sin. Like against God?" I said looking her over.

She had multiple piercings in her ears as well as one on her nose and tongue, long jet black hair, unlaced combat boots, cut off jean shorts, wife beater, black lace bra, silver jewelry with skulls. She looked like a porn star dressed as a Goth chic.

"No," she said.

"Just short for Cynthia?" I asked.

"If you're not my friend, yes."

"And if I am your friend?"

"No."

"What?"

"C'mon, keep up."

"I bet it's short for cynical."

"Of course I'll make out with you!"

"What?"

"Too slow on both topics. Just Cynthia for now till you can pick up the pace," she said and winked.

She grabbed the last juice and opened it.

"You can't just say all kinds of wild shit and act like it's clever. It's just wild shit!" I said.

I was embarrassed that she was running circles around me.

"Oh my god! So sensitive. Am I being too wild?"

She whipped her hair back and then into her face and made a tiger growling sound. Then she poured the juice into her mouth and gurgled it.

"What the fuck!"

I busted out laughing. Then she laughed and spit juice on both of us.

"Sorry! Sorry, I got carried away!" she said, still laughing and wiping juice off her face.

She reached for the flannel.

"Don't use that!" I said.

"Oh shit! That was close."

I kicked it away from us. She was looking at her hair in front of her face and squeezing out juice from it.

"So… anyway, the trench coat mafia leader told me your name. I think he's in love with you," I said.

"Oh yeah, the boring conversation about my name. No. He's my friend. People always tease him but I'll kick their ass if they touch him. He is an artist and he draws these amazing comics."

I made a face.

"Not comics like what you're thinking!"

"How do you know what I'm thinking?"

"You're thinking like regular comic books, like for kids," she said.

"That's exactly what I'm thinking!"

"See, that's so ignorant to be closed minded about something you know nothing about."

"Don't call me ignorant!"

"Don't be ignorant!"

"Don't push me," I said, raising my voice.

"Or what? You gonna beat me up?" she said, raising her voice.

"You're one of those chics who thinks they're tough by pickin fights with guys cuz the guys won't hit back, right?"

"Are you one of those guys who thinks they're tough cuz they do hit chics back?"

I stopped.

She was not someone to talk to when only half your head was in the game.

She sat there with her head cocked, chest out, arms wide, ready for war. Her cute little nose was flaring as she breathed. I smiled.

"No. I am not," I said slowly like a white flag being raised by a tired infantry soldier. "So…" I said after a few seconds.

"A needle pulling thread," she said again with a smile.

"Sewing needle… haha," I said with a sarcastic laugh.

"It only took him twice! Yea for the gansta in the back of the class!"

She clapped a couple times and then noticed the pack of cigarettes in her hand and pulled one out and lit it.

"Can you take the sarcasm down like one or two notches," I asked.

"Okay," she smiled. "Deal. It seems like you're having a rough patch. You're probably not always this sensitive."

"What? See that's what I'm talking about. Chill for a minute."

"I was being sincere."

"Whatever, it's all good. You got that phat ass, so you can get away with a little more," I said smiling.

She ignored the comment about her ass and put her lighter back in her little Hello Kitty pouch. As she was zipping it back up I saw rolling papers.

"Oh wait, we can still get high if you don't mind being a little ghetto," I said.

"I live in Ewa Beach, I'm a lot ghetto."

"Pass me your rolling papers."

I took one and rolled the three fat roaches I had found in my ashtray. She lit it and we passed it back and forth. It burned all uneven and twice I spit on it to keep it from running too bad. I could tell she had never smoked a roach joint before but she caught on quick. Watching her spit on her finger and rub it into the side of the joint made my stomach flip. It was kinda sexy. Now I was being weird.

We sat. The sun was on our feet now.

"Cyn," I said.

"Yes."

"Your friends call you Cyn?" I asked.

"Oh my God! Beating horses with sticks doesn't make them die more—" she started.

"Wait a minute… Give me a second… Wait, what?" I said.

"You have said 'wait, what?' like thirty times since we met," she said, sighing through the whole sentence.

"It's 'beating a dead horse,'" I said.

"Exactly."

"There's no stick."

"You don't have a stick?" she asked.

She looked down between my legs with a concerned look.

"The phrase! The saying!" I started yelling.

"No wonder you're so angry all the time."

She was very proud of herself. I took a deep breath and tried to speak evenly and without pauses so she wouldn't jump in with a wisecrack and throw me off.

"Naw yo, whatever! Listen, okay? Just check it! If you haven't thought of it already this can be your new spin on your name! Cyn could be short for Cynthia, but you want it to mean more. And it ain't like a sin against God cuz blasphemy for blashemy's sake is dumb. You're not dumb. You said your friends call you Cyn? Right? It should mean sin as in honest. Like the apple of truth. You're honest, brutally so. *So* honest, it's like sin, boom! It's 'Sin-cere.' That's clever!"

"Winner, winner, chicken dinner!" she said with a smile.

I had actually stopped her for a second. Her eyes were turning red as the weed kicked in. As she thought about it, I could tell she was working it into her own words in her head. She gave a slight nod to herself when she finished and I could see the gears change on her eyebrows.

"What's up with yours? Q." She said the Q with a deep voice and then giggled because she was stoned.

"It's not as cool as yours. Just short for Quintis," I said.

"But Quintis is already short."

"I'm actually pretty tall."

"Oh my god, that's lame!" she said, but she was laughing her ass off.

She looked amazing when she laughed. Her whole face opened up and her eyes danced. The sound of it came from deep in her belly and echoed in her chest. I wanted to be inside of that laugh.

"You shouldn't come around Mr. Mervin's class anymore," she said wiping tears away from her eyes.

"What?"

I was waiting for a punchline.

"That room is for artists. It's a safe place for weirdos and kids in trench coats who draw beautiful pictures, and future directors and poets. Not for drug dealers and bad boys like you."

It was hard for her to say, at least. She couldn't look me in the eye when she mumbled it.

"I… um… that's fucked up," I said.

"What are you gonna do in there besides tease people for not being cool?" she asked.

I started to say all the things I could do and realized I couldn't think of one thing that she would call art.

"I don't know… I could learn how to make movies and shit like you did," I said softly.

"You could, but that takes a lot of patience and planning. There's a lot to it. More than you think. I could teach you but…" She shrugged her shoulders.

Then it hit me.

"Rap is art!" I blurted out.

"Poetry is art!" she said. "I doubt what you do is poetry."

"How can you even say that? Didn't you say some shit about being ignorant but still talking!" I was starting to yell now.

"Okay. Spit some shit! Homey! That's what you say right? Drop that flow son." She was laughing now. She was very high.

I yanked my beat up rhyme book out of my shorts and looked for something that she might give me a little credit for. A half of a Campbell soup rhyme? A song about Peter Tosh wearing posh Oshkosh b'gosh?! There was nothing. I had written nothing but trash since I got to Hawaii. As I flipped through the pages all I saw was half ideas in crude scribbles with lines through them. Some of them completely inked out. Vulgar poems that belonged scratched on the inside of a bathroom stall. I searched my mind for some thought of mine that had substance. Maybe I could put it together right here on the spot…

I found nothing. There were no actual thoughts in my head. It was just a raging symphony of static. A waterfall of white noise and busy signals going over a cliff to the broken concrete and shattered television sets below.

She jumped up and stood there in an animated b-boy stance saying, "Yeah G, word, bust it dog, lace dat shit God…"

I had no choice. I spit my most recent thing.

#

I take a hit of Pakalolo
and Jam with Makalolo
I always got a crew so I'm never going solo
The main reason I suppose
That my legend grows

I'll stick my foot up your ass
And tie my shoe through your nose
I can strike a pose
And I don't fuck hoes…

#

I stopped. I could not continue with the look she was making. Her face was contorted like she was eating a moldy lemon. It took almost ten seconds of silence for her to regain her composure.

"Remember our deal about being all sensitive. I'm being 'Sincere,'" she said with a straight face.

"Fuck you! I don't need to be in your stupid little art room!"

My voice cracked and my eyes started watering again. God dammit! This was not the day to run into her.

"I'm sorry."

She stood up and started to walk away but then turned back.

"I'm sorry. That's what I came to talk to you about to begin with. It's not about your rapping thing. I'm sorry about whatever is going on with you, but you can't come in there. I'm sorry," she said.

"Fuck you bitch, I ain't trying to hear whatever it is you yappin about. I was just mindin my own bizness till you came here with your weird ass. I was just tryin to be cool," I said.

"That's the problem, you're trying to be cool."

"Bitch, get to steppin," I said and turned towards the dumpster.

Cynthia walked away.

I sat there letting the sun burn me. Only my face was in the shade now. What the fuck had just happened?

I walked over to the big tree just off campus and lay down in the shade. The grass was long and I completely disappeared in it. I watched it lean back and forth over me.

Maybe I could just go…

I could just exhale and let my soul out of my body. It would move through the grass. Maybe the grass would breathe me in. I had read some-where that we breathe out Co2 and then the grass breathes it in. The grass breathes out oxygen and then we breathe it in. Through it all, the molecules themselves separate and come back together but remain the same. So that the air we breathe today is the same air that my ancestors exhaled hundreds or even thousands of years ago. The same air passing through an African man standing in a field somewhere passes through the African grass and up into the clouds then down into the ocean. It evaporates back up into the clouds and blows across the planet for years until I breathe it in. If I could breathe out my soul the grass would breathe it in. I was sure of it. The air was here before me. It will be here after me. My soul just used it for a small moment. The things that make up my body will return to the Earth. I just use them for a moment. When the moment is over, does my soul stay on the breath and in the air?

I jumped up from the grass. The school bus was in the parking lot and kids were starting to gather. I must have been asleep for over an hour. My thoughts were starting to fade. I lay back down for a moment and went around my head picking up pieces of a cloud. Scooping chunks of ideas and questions and putting them together until they sat nicely one on top of the other. Then I ran it through three times until the pattern of words were familiar by sound.

#

Where does your soul go?
Does the grass from graveyards breathe
exhaled air from those buried underneath?
Does the past pass when you pass away?
Or is it something that couldn't have been any other way?
Is there nothing new?
Our irrelevance is puzzling,
The puzzle being
That just because we are beings
It doesn't mean we are free from the obscene
Fact that we are nothing
But dust and wind
Lust and sin
Can a heartbeat find some kind of rhythm
To a song that belonged

To long forgottens
I wonder when the breeze blows
Do these flows
Sound similar to an enslaved negroe
With green toes
on the middle passage
To being sold when he froze
Did his lips taste love?
Did he know then that his blood
Would be generations later locked up as a thug
That would see the same sun
And breathe the same air
I tussle with these images
We are limited
By our belief of what the limit is
Can we stand up?
Can we unlatch the shackles of these handcuffs
That were wrapped around the soul of what this man was
His hopes, his dreams, they don't die, they pass on
through song
through those who experienced the essence of his charm
Choose to be strong
Choose to laugh at
what can't be changed
and change what can't be laughed at
I pass that, through Hip Hop
through breakbeats and poetry
Exactly the way the wind told it to me
Word for word
As I heard it in meditation
And hopefully the meaning wasn't lost in translation

#

I thought about what weird chic would say when I dropped this on her.
Is this art?

I pulled out my rhyme book and realized the pen I had shoved in it was gone.

Then I heard a slapping thump sound. Unmistakable. It was a solid punch. The sound of a fist landing square between the cheekbone and Jaw. It was followed by the sound of the eighty or so kids going "*Oooooooooooow.*"

I stood up and looked into the parking lot. Kids were swarming towards the school bus. I started making my way over.

I could hear the security guard yelling over the crowd noise. "Nuff already, get in the bus, calm down already!"

I jumped a small fence and reached the outside of the crowd and could hear kids yelling: "Crack'em already!"

"Lick dat fucka."

"Knock'em out."

"Fuck dat popolo."

"Please just leave him alone," screamed some little white girl dressed like she was in the movie *The Breakfast Club.*

A tall, skinny black kid pushed his way out of the circle with his chest puffed up, swinging his shirt over his head. He was impressive. He sounded like he was from some tough ghetto hood on the mainland. A group of about ten other popolo kids fanned out around him. They looked like a Wu-Tang album cover photo.

"Fuck this muthafucka! I'll bust his ass. You fucking mokes! I'm Suga-C, nigga! I don't give a fuck. You flip flop wearing muthafuckas!" he shouted as he swaggered around.

I couldn't see who he was going to fight. The huge Samoan security guard was desperately grabbing and pushing kids, trying to get to the military popolo kid. The guard looked like he was scared.

"Get in the bus you fucka! Dis guy goin kill you!" screamed the security guard.

I searched the crowd. The popolo kid looked pretty solid. At least he talked a good game. Whoever he was going to fight would have to be pretty big and scary. I started scrolling through my mental list trying to figure out who it could be.

CRACK!!!

The sound of another punch! The circle split open as a big chubby popolo kid in a basketball jersey fell limply to the pavement.

Some popolo girl screamed, "Oh shit! D-40!"

She tried to run to him but her friends held her back as the circle widened like the ocean going around a rock.

There, standing in the center of the circle with a psycho smile that almost made me piss my pants, was Kevin McKenzie.

He shuffled his feet like a boxer. He was sliding his head from side to side. He was barefoot in a pair of faded, dirty surf shorts with a torn and tattered old t-shirt. Two of the black kids rushed Kevin and tackled him to the ground. One held Kevin in a sloppy choke hold. He was on his back with Kevin on top of him like two spoons. The other popolo was on one knee landing blows to Kevin's head and face. Most of the blows landed but he was also hitting his friend in the back of the head. The tall skinny popolo who called himself Suga-C ran over and started kicking Kevin but he also wound up kicking his friend. Kevin was rolling over and over while whiplashing his head forward and back. He was trying to head butt the kid holding him. The back of Kevin's head finally smashed right into the black kid's nose, sending the poor kid's head slamming into the pavement. The kid went limp and Kevin was up before the other kid who was on one knee could figure out what happened. Kevin field-goal punted the one-knee kid's head, his shin making direct contact with the one-knee kid's jaw.

He dropped like a bag of books.

Now it was Kevin and Suga-C.

The bus driver yelled to the security guard, "Brah, get the other kids on the bus!"

The security guard started grabbing kids and squishing them into the bus. They didn't give much resistance. They rushed to their seats so they could still watch from their windows. Suga-C could dance. He bobbed and weaved, slid from side to side, ran forward and shuffled back, never even throwing a punch. He was trying to tire Kevin out. He didn't know that Kevin McKenzie's instincts were developed from over a thousand years of evolution. Passed down from sacred cannibal tribes of South Pacific indigenous warriors. He didn't know about the midnight ceremonies with clay pots filled with the boiling blood of sharks, grizzly bears, mountain lions and black panthers. Kevin McKenzie stopped moving all together and stood with his hands to his sides. He stepped closer, whispering…

"C'mon you fucka… go… hit me you fucka… try knock me out brah… I bet you no can… I bet you… what?! You scared?"

Suga-C took the bait.

He jumped in and swung a haymaker. Kevin took the punch square in the jaw, then he wrapped his arms around Suga-C, lifted him up into the air WWF style, brought him over his head and dropped him down on the pavement behind him. The sharp sound of bones breaking snapped through the air a second before everyone gasped. The other black kids abandoned Suga-C and leapt onto the bus. The bus driver closed the door and the security guard stood in front of it as the driver put the bus in gear. Kevin ran up to the security guard and tagged him with a three-punch combo, dropping him to his knees, holding his mouth. Kevin put his fingers through the rubber on the collapsible doors. The bus was rolling forward with the bus driver screaming at Kevin.

"Let go, you fucka! *Let go!*"

Kevin was banging his knee on one of the doors at the hinge that bends inward while pulling his arms outward. He was able to open them enough to squeeze through.

He ran straight to the back of the bus and started smashing his fist into the face of one of the popolos. The other remaining four black kids opened the emergency door and jumped out the back. The alarm went off. It mixed with the sound of police sirens coming from way up Fort Weaver Road.

Kevin jumped from the back of the bus in slow motion, looking like the Incredible Hulk. His rice bowl haircut was frizzed out and splotched with blood. Just as he was about to chase the popolo kids, he turned back. His face was mangled with blood and rage as he scanned the crowd of kids, looking to see if one of the popolos was hiding there.

His eyes caught mine.

He tilted his head to the side like a dog recognizing a familiar word. Then he smiled. The moment slowed and smudged like holding a record in place with your finger as the feeling of every black eye and every bloody nose and every busted lip and every broken rib rushed back onto my body. Then the fingers came off of the record and the phantom pain disappeared. He turned back and ran after the popolos.

CHAPTER 7

SEXY AS FUCK

THE SMELL WAS TYING my stomach into knots, but in a good way.

Pinakbet, a Filipino vegetable stew. I loved it. It was boiling on the stove in Mr. Mervin's kitchen. I was sitting at the kitchen counter while his wife was in the living room watching a Filipino soap opera. I had tried to make small talk but she pretended she couldn't understand English and kept her back to me. There was no way she was going to offer me some. I sat there like a trained dog with a treat on his nose. I was thinking about what exactly would happen if I just took some.

I hadn't eaten very well over the last three days. I broke into a couple of cars looking for loose change and got a few dollars. Bullied some smaller kids out of their lunch money. I couldn't go to Maka's house because it was next door to the Fireman's old house. They would find me there. I couldn't go around the school because I was afraid of Kevin McKenzie. Mostly I walked around until I got tired then sat on the beach hoping to fall asleep. I couldn't sleep. One thought would lead to another and they all lead to my mom crying. I would have to stand up and walk somewhere else. The only thing that would stop my thoughts was my stomach. Sometimes it would ache. Sometimes it would burn. One time it rolled into a knot and I had to hold my knees until it stopped. Two things I had learned that are rock solid facts:

Sleeping on the beach with no sleeping bag or blanket is fucking freezing, and…

Three days with no vegetables will make you constipated until you eventually shit water.

This morning I walked into the 7-11 and made myself a chili cheese hot dog with everything, put three musubi and a bag of seven pork hash into my shirt and walked out. That made my stomach scream. I was gonna swim out as far as I could and take a shit because there was no toilet paper in the public bathroom at Haubush. I was standing in the sand trying to talk myself into it when I heard super loud music. I turned just in time to see Bonez hanging out the window of his truck.

"Everybody gon be at Mr. Mervin's house tonight for talk about the stuffs. Seven turdy!"

I was about to ask him to shit at his house but I was too embarrassed. Plus the feeling went away. He peeled out and spun around in a dusty donut throwing sand in a giant circle and was gone.

I stood up and grabbed a bowl from the cabinet.

"Thank you for dinner, Mrs. Mervin. It smells really good. I am starving!" I said as sweetly as I could.

As soon as it touched my mouth the salt and the pork and bitter melon almost made me cry. It was so good. Through my misty eyes I could see Mrs. Mervin turn her head and give me a look. She didn't say anything. Her face turned soft when she finally saw me. I must have looked pretty bad.

"Get some rice in the cooker. Wash your bowl afta!" she said as mean as she could and turned back to the T.V. and turned it up super loud.

"Hey Q," said Mr. Mervin poking his head in from the garage. "Why don'tcha c'mon inside here."

I shoveled a few more bites into my mouth and put my bowl down.

Then I picked it back up, scooped some rice into it and walked towards the garage. Then I turned back around and scooped some more pinakbet into the bowl, spilling some on the counter.

I wiped it with my hand then licked my hand.

My hand was nasty.

I put the bowl down and started washing my hands.

"Now, please!" said Mr. Mervin.

I grabbed the bowl and went in.

Maka, Kaipo, Bonez and Supercalves were sitting on the floor in a half circle. There were stacks of cardboard boxes that you use to carry four six packs of soda in. Each one had stacks of weed in gallon-sized ziplock bags. It was so much weed. Each stack had little color-coded stickers on them.

I sat down on the floor. Mr. Mervin was humming some gay-ass song. He sounded like Popeye. He kept half humming, half sing-mumbling, and then he would switch to whistling like he couldn't decide which one made him seem less nervous. It made him seem very nervous.

"Now boys, let's figure this out," he said in a cheerful tone.

"I already wen figure'em out, Mr. Mervin," interrupted Kaipo. "I going take'em all and give some to all the boyz, they going sell'em, and I going give you da'kine. Fair amount for all your hard work."

We all sat with our heads down.

Mr. Mervin took it in stride. He must have figured it would go down this way.

"Well, Kaipo, I must say, that sure sounds fair, but…" said Mr. Mervin. "I've known you a long time, and, I gotta tell you son, you're not very trustworthy when it comes to this kinda stuff."

I knew things were going to get thick but I was hungry. I was taking huge bites trying to finish before Kaipo beat everyone up and took all the weed.

"Neh, Mr. Mervin, you trust me brah. Plus, you no like have all dis stuffs in your house yeah?" said Kaipo.

"In for a penny, in for a pound, or sixty pounds, I should say," he said, laughing at his own joke. He looked at me and I chuckled with my mouth full. Then a second later it hit me: sixty pounds.

What?!

"Listen Kaipo, you're not walking outta here with all of this. You will fuck this up and go to jail for twenty years. Or worse, someone will kill you and rob you," said Mr. Mervin. He spoke slow and condescending. Kaipo stood up and the boys kept their heads down. I put the bowl down and scanned the room. Two steps to my right was a huge mesh bag with baseball gloves and helmets for little league. There were baseball bats. I was dangerous with a baseball bat.

"Mr. Mervin, I no like argue wit you brah, but I not working for you! I wen bring all dis to you. All of dis is mine," said Kaipo. He was talking in an almost whinny pleading tone. "What you going do wit all of dis wit out me? You no can sell'em! I get friends, cuz, they know people. It's all set up already. Dis ain't small time no more. Dis is big boy stuff. I going sell'em by the pound! I going have all of this gone by two months in fact. I cut you in. I give da'kine percentage of the whole ting. What you like, ten percent?"

I was having a hard time being scared of him after seeing the way my stepdad punked him. I kept imagining how it would feel to take that baseball bat to his knee. What would it sound like? It's hard to hit the knee. I would probably just catch the thigh. Then it would be a soft sound, like hitting a mattress or something. What if I got lucky? It would make a high-pitched ping, like hitting a rock covered in a towel.

"What you doing you fucka!" yelled Kaipo.

He was talking to me. Mr. Mervin was standing there with his hands up and a shocked look on his face.

I was standing by the wall with a baseball bat in my hands.

Oh… okay… I guess so.

I was not scared. I felt warm and excited. I felt calm. I wanted to see if I could make his knee go *ping!*

"Brah, put the bat down you panty. Your daddy not going save you dis time!" said Kaipo with a mocking grin.

"He's not my dad," I mumbled.

I stepped forward and swung the bat high to let him gauge the swing. He leaned back dodging it easily. Mr. Mervin dove out of the way so dramatically I almost laughed. Boxes of weed fell over like buildings collapsing. The boys crawled out of the way and stood up behind me. I swung again making it look at first like it was going to be the same swing, then I brought it down. *PING!* Kaipo fell to the floor. I brought it down again, swinging for his head, but he put his hands up and the bat hit his arms. I swung again. This time I heard another ping. It must have been a bone in his forearm. I swung again, and again. Maka grabbed the bat out of my hands and Supercalves tackled me to the floor. Kaipo was crying and for the first time I realized I was yelling.

"He didn't save me! Nobody can save me!! Fuck you! I'll fucking kill you!"

"Nah Q! Stop brah, dats my brother!! Q, stop! That's my brother. It's done already, stop brah!" Maka was yelling in my ear while he held me to the floor.

His breath stank and he was spitting all over the side of my face.

I stopped yelling and moving and the only sound was Kaipo whimpering like a hurt dog.

"Now boys we need to stop. Everybody be calm, okay!" said Mr. Mervin.

His wife opened the door to the garage.

"I'm calling the police!" she screamed as she slammed the door.

"No more fighting! I'll be right back!" said Mr. Mervin.

He ran towards the door then stopped, went back to the wall with the sports gear and grabbed all the baseball bats. He hurried after his wife.

"Get the fuck off of me!" I said to Maka.

"You not going do nothing yeah?!" he asked.

"I'm cool, I'm cool!" I said.

Yeah, I was cool, I thought as I stood up and looked down at Kaipo. He was laying on the floor holding his knee with his face in the smooth cement so we couldn't see his tears.

"I going kill you, I going kill you…" said Kaipo over and over in a whisper.

"Come kill me, bitch, I'm right here," I said.

Maka looked down at his brother then up at me and his face was all twisted up. Then he punched me in the face. It knocked me back and I tripped over some boxes. He tried to grab my shirt and swing again but he fell, too. Supercalves and Bonez ran over to break us up.

"Stop!" yelled Mr. Mervin's wife.

We stopped. She was standing in the doorway of the garage. She looked at all of us. She looked so small. Her eyes were wide as she looked around the room as though she had never seen it before. Each stack of marijuana made her take a pronounced inhale. It was obvious this had been hidden from her. Mr. Mervin quietly appeared in the doorway with his head down. When it seemed she had taken a full tally, she started hyperventilating.

"Aye! Aye! Aye! Aye Dios ko!" she said breathlessly.

"Now pumpkin… now listen…"

"Putang ina mo!! Ikaw tumahimik! Walang hiya ka!" she screamed at Mr. Mervin.

He tried to move towards her and she lunged for a basket of dirty clothes and flung it at him. He caught it and began putting the clothes back, all the while shooting us looks of embarrassment. She fast-waddled to a lock box behind the dryer and punched a six digit code.

"NO, NO, NO! Pumpkin, *don't*!" yelled Mr. Mervin.

She swung back around with a ridiculously huge 357 revolver.

"Mga walang hiya kayo! Ang kapal ng mga mukha nyo! Dito sa bahay ko nyo gingawan ito?! Lumayas kayo!" She was screaming and mumbling breathlessly in Tagalog.

"Sweety, put the gun down…" said Mr. Mervin soothingly.

He took a few steps into the room then put his hands on his hips and took a deep breath.

"PUT THE FUCKING GUN DOWN!"

She swung around pointing the gun at him and he put his hands up.

"Papatayin ko kayo!" she said. Spit and tears were flying from her face.

"Ooh… ooh, tita, kukunin kong lahat, dadalhin ko nang lahat," said Kaipo softly.

"Ngayon na?" she said.

"Pasensya na… tita?" said Kaipo gently.

"Itapon nyo yan! Ang lahat na ito yan! Ayokong makakita sa bahay ko ang mga iyan!!" she said.

"Pasensya na, tita," he answered.

Kaipo got up and began stacking the boxes the best he could while limping and favoring one arm.

"No! This is not what we agreed. Sweety this is a lot of money! We can have everything we ever wanted. This is real. This is everything!" pleaded Mr. Mervin. "If you give it to him, it's gone. All of our dreams! Gone! If you—"

"SHUT UP!" she yelled, finally in English. Kiapo stopped stacking and sat on a five gallon bucket and rubbed his knee. I realized my hands were up. So were everyone else's. I slowly brought mine down as she waddled back and forth wiping her face with her sleeve.

"Alam mong mahal kita? And I trust you. I follow you, always. But dis one is mga Demonyo! I will tell you and you will listen. I don't blame you. How could you know. All of you, how could you know. But I know. I know this boy is Aswang!" she yelled. She pointed the gun at me.

Kaipo's eyes widened and he stared at me.

"How do you know?" asked Kaipo.

"Basta alam ko! Titingin ko lang sa kaniyang mga mata nya, maraming tinatagong kadiliman yan. Wala kong tiwala sa lalaking yan. Tingnan mo yung mga mata nya. Makikita mo kung gaanong karaming kadiliman meron sa mga mata nya!" she said without missing a beat.

Kaipo looked at my eyes. His face changed. He looked like he was seeing a monster.

"Go now!" she yelled.

Everyone started stacking boxes into the truck while she held the gun on me. I made like I was going to help and she almost shot me so I stayed still.

Kiapo was ready to close the garage door from the outside. Maka and Bonez were sitting in his truck. Supercalves walked by me without looking at me. I started toward the truck and Supercalves stopped me. He finally looked at me. He shook his head no. I understood. The baseball bat had changed things. My stepdad grabbing Kiapo's throat had changed things. This crazy Filipino lady calling me Aswang changed things.

I leaned against the wall. Stacking the boxes into Kaipo's truck would have been too much for me anyway. My head was swimming. I leaned over and put my hands on my knees. I caught a whiff of myself and it made me gag. I didn't want to throw up. Who knows when I would eat again. Mr. Mervin tried to whisper something to his wife and she stormed back into the house. He came and rubbed my back and I stood up and pushed his hand away.

"I know it's a lot to take right now, but trust me young man, this is the best-case scenario," said Mr. Mervin.

I didn't know what "scenario" meant. There was a dope-ass song called "The Scenario" with a Tribe Called Quest.

I was tired and sick.

"Hey, Mr. Mervin, I hate to ask this… but, I don't feel so good and I don't really have a place to sleep. Can I just crash on the floor here?" I asked, trying my most charming smile.

It came out weird. Mr. Mervin looked like I had punched him in the stomach. He looked at the door as if his wife was going to come busting back though it just for considering letting me stay. I stopped him before he could come up with an excuse.

"Hey, you know what? After all that drama, I think I should go for a quick swim anyway, and I don't wanna wake y'all up when I come back so don't sweat it. There's this girl I know. I could crash at her spot," I said finally, mustering up another smile.

He saw right through it. He took a long look at me with his eyebrows scrunched and his lips smushed together. Then his face lit up.

***

I was tired.

I could feel little prickles on my hands and feet. I saw tiny flashes of light dancing around the edges of my eyes if I walked too fast. I had to stop every block or so just to catch my breath. Mr. Mervin had called one of his students. She was having a big party for her sixteenth birthday because her parents were away. He gave me directions and his wife packed me a bag with a toothbrush and stuff. I was holding a Tupperware of pinakbet and it felt like it weighed a hundred pounds.

I stopped on the corner of a cul-de-sac. The house was right next to the back end of a golf course. At night the golf course was pitch black. The kind of dark that seems to spread. It was trying to slowly seep through the chain link fence that separated the houses from the empty space. I could hear the music coming from the house. It was metal. In fact, it was Metallica's "Enter Sandman." I knew it because there was no way to get away from that song for the past year. As soon as I had that thought, the song stopped and I heard a house full of drunk teenagers divided.

"Fuck that, it's my party and I'll play what I want!" yelled a voice I recognized.

"C'mon, that song is so played out, dude!" yelled some dorky kid.

"Why not just stick sharp objects into my ears!" yelled another.

"Please murder me!" said some chic.

"Can we compromise? Play something from their first album!" said another chic.

"How bout you sing that rooster song!" squeaked a voice.

That had to be the trench coat kid. That was the winner. There was a unanimous sound of dozens of voices cheering "Yeah" and "Woooooo!"

"Hey! There's some weirdo homeless dude outside staring at your house!" said a girl.

What? Wait… I'm the weirdo?

I took stock of myself for the first time in days. My hair was nappy. My tank top was dirty and stained. So were my shorts. My slipper was broken and being held together with safety pins. I was Parliament Funk, The Bomb, like a sweaty dumpster, standing outside her house with a pink backpack and a Tupperware from the 1970s in my hand.

Cynthia came outside by herself. Stone Temple Pilots started playing in the house and everyone inside went back to arguing about music. She was dressed in some kinda skimpy lace white wedding dress with combat boots and a sash that read "Sweet 16."

"Wassup, Sin?" I said trying out my smile again.

"Sup Q?" she said in a fake deep voice, mocking me.

"Are you like, a Filipino Madonna?" I said.

"Are you like, Kid n' Play after their second album flopped?" she said without missing a beat.

Her smile was better than mine.

Out of habit she stepped forward to hug me but thought better of it. She looked me over again and her tipsy smile turned to a look of pity. A wash of embarrassment surged through me and my hands and feet tingled.

"Why don't you come through the back and use my shower?" she said.

My eyes started to water. I'll die before I cry in front of this chic again.

She opened a six-foot wooden fence on the side of her house and I followed her though a little alleyway. It was dark but I could see other kids in little groups smoking cigarettes and talking over the music. She opened a side door to the house and then another door into what must have been her parents' bedroom. She turned the lights on, started going through the dresser, and pulled out a pair of cargo shorts and a faded black t-shirt.

"For after, you can have these," she said tossing them on the bed.

She stood with her hand on the doorknob just about to leave the room.

"Come hang for a little while when you're finished, if you feel up to it," she said.

"Yeah cool…"

"And, hey, if you can… don't look at me like that. My boyfriend gets jealous easy," she said with a grin.

She shut the door before I could say "what the fuck?"

I looked in the mirror and quickly looked away. Maybe I *was* looking at her funny. I felt like a lost dog who just got petted and given a home. I took a shower and almost had to rip the hair outta my head to get the knots out. After I got dressed, I went through the bag Mr. Mervin gave me looking for a toothbrush and stopped.

At the bottom of the backpack was a gallon-sized ziplock bag filled with smaller ziplock bags. Sixteen small ziplocks with what looked like an ounce each—a pound total. I opened one and smelled it. It tickled the back of my head between my ears. I found the toothbrush and stuffed the ounce in my pocket. I shoved my dirty clothes on top of the rest of the weed (ain't nobody touching that!) and shoved the whole bag under the bed.

I brushed my teeth and walked out to the backyard. There were about forty kids spread out all over the yard. In the back left corner was a giant avocado tree with a hammock. Some kids were leaning against the tree. A big popolo kid was in the hammock. Other kids were sitting and leaning along the rock wall and fence. Cynthia was sitting on the back of a chair surrounded by some older rocker-looking men who looked like they were auditioning to be in a Nirvana video. They sat around an old metal-framed glass patio table looking at Cynthia like a pack of grungy wolves. Kirk Cobain's ugly stunt double sat the closest to her, tuning a guitar.

This was not my scene. A whole bunch of drama room weirdos and some mainland rocker haole's trying to fuck a sixteen-year-old little Filipino girl. I just needed to crash. Get some sleep and get my head together and move on.

"Ayo," I said loud enough so everyone could hear me, "anyone got some rolling papers or something?"

The dopest thing in the world is walking into a party with enough weed for everyone. You can keep your golden chariot. Nobody makes an entrance like the dopeman.

Everyone stopped whatever they were doing. I tossed the ziplock down on the table.

"I come bearing gifts!" I said as Shakespearean as possible. "A small token of my appreciation for letting me crash the party."

Everyone was very happy.

The guitar guy immediately grabbed the bag and smelled it. He made a face and started emptying out a cigarette. Almost all the kids were around the table now fawning over me and the weed. Cynthia cut her eyes at me. I ignored her and walked over to the hammock. The big black kid was still in it, slowly swinging back and forth smoking a cigarette. It wasn't until I got right up to him that I noticed he was wearing a Walkman. I grabbed the earphones off his ear.

"Ayo, this is my seat! Beat it!" I said.

He jumped up quick and almost fell out of the hammock. He stood up and opened his mouth as if to say "Who the fuck are you?" He was almost a foot taller than me and had me by at least fifty pounds. He was used to bossing around these nerds.

It took him a few seconds to fold. He looked me in the eye and then his shoulders slumped forward. He looked down and then noticed everyone crowded around the table.

"Oh shit, smokey smokey!" he said jogging over.

I climbed into the hammock and as soon as I got settled in, a wave of tired hit me like I had never felt. The thought of fighting the sleep added to its strength. I wanted to check the Walkman and see what tape was in there. The kid was black, maybe it was something good. I could turn it up loud so I wouldn't have to hear the rock shit these kids kept playing. I just couldn't muster the strength to roll around and grab the Walkman from the grass. I could see the avocados hanging above me. I could smell calamansi but I couldn't turn my head to see it. The citrusy sour smell was suddenly lifted up with the smell of thick green mountainy guava smoke. For the first time, I smelled our weed.

Finally, it burns.

Finally, the smell of the gold that ripped apart my summer friendships. It carried with it my memory of fighting with my stepdad. The wispy scent brought with it the cold of sleeping on the beach. What was my mother going through right now? Could I go home now? Where was home? What did the new house look like? It was some happy picture that I couldn't see. It wasn't mine.

"Hey, you gonna smoke with us?" asked Cynthia.

She was standing over me slowly rocking the hammock back and forth with one hand. She had a fat joint in the other.

"Yeah…" I said.

I reached for the joint but she put it to her lips and took a long pull.

"This is way better than the bullshit you had the other day," she said passing it to me.

"Yeah…" I said taking a hit. It was strong and wet. I started coughing horribly.

"Bitch…" she said laughing.

"Fuck you…" I said between coughs.

"I just don't get it," she said.

I took a long, slow, tentative breath through my nose to try to keep my lungs from spasming.

"Get what?" I said weakly.

"Ask everyone about you and they're like 'Q this' and 'Q that.' Everyone's got a Q story and they talk like you're this mythical person, like some superman shit, flying through the air. But every time I see you… you look like you're falling…"

She plucked the joint out of my hand and skipped back to the table.

"I'm ready!" she shouted.

Everyone cheered and the wax-museum Curt Cobain began playing some rock shit. I thought again of trying to get to the Walkman but now I was stoned. All I could do was turn my head to the table. Cynthia was back up on the chair facing my direction. Everyone was circled around her with their backs to me. Her voice came out like wind blowing over a bottle. Thin and hollow. It rode above the chords and over the three rocker kids who harmonized with her.

"*Oooooouuuuuooooouu…*"

It was haunting.

The harmony stopped and she took a long pull of the joint and passed the roach to someone on the left. Her face was serious. She looked like something else had taken over her body and was using it to say something that words couldn't say.

#

Ain't found a way to kill me yet
Eye's burn with stinging sweat
Seems every path leads me to nowhere
Wife and kids household pet
Army green was no safe bet
The bullets scream to me from somewhere

#

Here they come to snuff the rooster

#

Something was coming through this girl. She started screaming the song and rocking back and forth. Her voice grinded and grated before suddenly spinning into a lifted smooth arc over a peak, only to crash back down with a chord change.

I watched as the porch light sparkled off little beads of sweat forming on her face and shoulders. Everyone swayed back and forth like they were hypnotized.

They were.

So was I.

I felt like I was somewhere else. I knew that I was here, in her backyard. My body was here. My eyes and ears were here, but I was not here. She had taken me without eyes and ears and body. The me without the thoughts and words. She had released that part and placed it elsewhere. Where was this place that she had taken me? Can I get here on my own? How can I stay here? This place is magic. It is free of normal shit. Some notes on a guitar. A girl singing. Put it together and it's more. Much more, but not like,

1+1=3

more like,

1+1= some other shit we can't comprehend with our prehistoric point of reference. My stoney self tried to do the math as I tumbled down the rabbit hole of her music. My thoughts got loose and pretty soon, my eyes closed with the image of Cynthia riding the sound of the guitar down the current with her lace-gloved hands gently putting ripples in the dark walls of my sleep.

***

Heat.

Hot.

I was sweating.

I could hear birds. I could hear an industrial sprinkler far off some-where. I peeled my eyes open. I saw the sun chopping through the branches of the avocado tree. It was noon. I was covered in a thick blanket. I pushed it off me and almost fell out of the hammock. My mouth was dry and I was super thirsty. I turned on the outside faucet and drank out of the water hose. The lever squeeked with a vengeance when I turned it on and it was only a few moments till Cynthia slid open the glass door and popped her head out.

Her hair was matted and puffy and she squinted with one eye com-pletely shut.

"You can come inside and drink water, stupid," she said as she disappeared.

I pushed between the thick vertical blinds and stepped inside. It was dark. It was nighttime dark. I walked into the kitchen and grabbed a cup from the dish drainer. I filled it with water and started gulping. I turned around expecting a wisecrack but she wasn't there. Then I heard her throwing up in the bathroom. I stood there realizing it might be hotter in here than outside.

She came out of the bathroom with a toothbrush in her mouth and a look of disgust on her face. She was still wearing the same clothes from last night minus one lace sleeve. She walked up to me and grabbed the glass out of my hand and splashed the water in the sink.

"There's cold water in the fridge, stupid."

She opened the freezer and frosty air poured out towards the floor as she scooped some ice and put it in two glasses.

"And ice..." she said.

She poured us both some iced tea and squeezed fresh calamansi in it.

"Are you hungry?" she asked.

"Yeah." I shrugged like, "not really," but I was starving.

She turned back around and opened the fridge wide. She pointed at a box of leftover pizza.

"Barf," she said.

She opened the Tupperware that I had brought.

"Barf," she said.

A plate with pancit covered in tinfoil.

"Barf, barf, barf... Let's go smoke a cigarette," she said, giving up.

We went to the side of the house and sat on broken beach chairs in the shade. It was still hot. She lit two cigarettes, passed me one, and began rolling a joint. I didn't really want to get high but I knew she was hungover and I didn't want her to not smoke because of me. Plus, I was feeling much better. If she wanted to get high and do that weird verbal sparring thing, I could show her I could hang.

She didn't say anything, just lit it and passed it to me. She slouched in the chair with her legs open and her head back, facing up. She blew smoke up into the overhang that was giving us our shade. It billowed out of her lips and stayed there like a thought cloud. She had cute little beads of sweat like see-through dots sitting cautiously just above her upper lip. She hawked up flem and spit it like a construction worker. I laughed and she looked at me like she had forgotten that I was there. She ran her hands through her sweat-soaked hair.

"I'm sexy as fuck, huh?!" she said then laughed.

"I was just thinking that," I said sarcastically.

I could see the outline of her lips and hair through the lace of her panties. I could smell her sweat through the cigarette smoke. I could see her chest moving up and down whenever she took a pull of the joint.

Yes, sexy as fuck.

"Ayo, do you know what ashwanga means, or ass wong or ass hang or some shit—"

"Aswang?"

"Yeah, what is that?"

"Why?"

"Why?"

"Yeah, why?"

"That's what I said, too."

"What?"

"I said why, as in why do you want to know why I want to know? If I give the wrong answer are you gonna not tell me?"

"Whatever…"

"Mr. Mervin's wife called me that."

Cynthia laughed and then shook her head. Then she looked at me again. This time she looked at me like she was looking for something.

"She could be right."

"Is that like, asshole in Filipino or something?" I said with a smile.

"It's like a shape-shifting vampire thing. It feeds on like, the souls of a community. It comes out at night to hunt but during the day it can look perfectly human. It's a monster. It comes up out of the dark, splits you open, eats your insides, then fills you with banana-tree husks."

"Dang…"

"Are you going to eat me?"

"If you ask nicely…"

She opened her legs slowly.

"Are you going to eat me…?"

I didn't know what to do. Was she serious? I hesitated and then started to lean forward. She snapped her legs shut.

"Psyche!" she said and laughed.

We finished smoking and went back in.

She put a pot of water on the stove, grabbed two bowls, cracked an egg in each of them, then threw in a pile of kimchi, a few drops of sesame oil and sriracha sauce.

She grabbed four bags of Ramen noodles and put two flavor packs into each bowl, boiled the noodles, then poured the noodles and water into the bowls.

We were both stoned and starving. We stood in the dark kitchen at the counter slurping away without talking. After we were done, she grabbed both bowls and slammed them into the sink with a loud crash. She walked by me and went back into her room and slammed the door. I could hear the loud *click* as she locked it.

Then she came back out of her room with my backpack and a handful of cash.

"Everybody loved your weed. A couple of my friends wanted to buy from you but you were asleep so I went through your shit and sold them some. I figured a hundred for each baggy?"

I was about to say "cool" but she pushed the money into my hand without waiting for an answer, then stomped back to her room.

"I threw those stinky clothes away!" she yelled and shut the door. This time there was no click.

I stood there in the dark heat.

Did she forget to lock it this time? Why did she lock it the first time?

Is she afraid of me? No. I wasn't sure if she was afraid of anyone. Did she lock it loud on purpose last time and then not lock it on purpose this time so I would notice it wasn't locked and go in after her? That would be interesting. Or, was I just really stoned and gassed off myself thinking she wanted me to go in there?

I opened the door to her room and stood in the doorway with a grin. She was sitting up in her bed leaning on the wall wearing the same grin.

"Took you long enough."

"I'm a little shy…" I said as a joke.

"I know," she said not as a joke.

And here I was again. Reality came rushing through my high. She knew what she was doing. I knew nothing about anything I was doing. Was I supposed to fuck her? How was I supposed to start? What if what happened before happened this time. This girl would be mean. If I ever did have sex with this girl, I wanted her to know who I was. I am the shit. I am the best. I am the man. But she knows who I am. She has seen me cry because I ran away from home. She has seen me with my hand out because I'm tired and hungry with nowhere to go. Now, just in case there was any doubt, she would see that I was scared because I have never really been with a girl before.

"Hey, are you okay?" she said.

"Yeah…"

"I'm not going to fuck you, you know…" she said.

She unconsciously pulled the comforter over her thighs.

"What are you talking about? I don't want to fuck you! You're like some weird rocker chic. And didn't you fuck your boyfriend a few hours ago? I ain't seen you take a shower or nothing, throwin up an shit. That's some ill sloppy seconds!"

She put her head into her hands and rubbed her scalp through her hair then screamed. She picked up a porcelain Hello Kitty doll and threw it at the wall. It shattered and a puff of dust just hung in the stale air.

"First of all, I didn't fuck my boyfriend last night, we broke up! Which is none of your business! You're only here because Mr. Mervin gave me your sob story and I have a heart. You're a fucking loser. A nickel-bag drug-dealer high-school dropout. Take your shit and go. I tried to be nice!" she shouted.

She was panting. Sweat was dripping down her arms and some of her hair was stuck to her face. Her little nostrils were flaring and her eyes were on fire.

Okay.

Whatever it was that happened to me before with those other girls was not going to be a problem here. Whatever this is? This works. My stomach was burning and all the pores on my skin were breathing. I stood in the doorway. She threw another porcelain doll and this one hit me. It bounced off my head but I didn't move and it fell on the floor in two pieces.

"Get out! Get the fuck OUT!!" she yelled over and over.

She got up and started punching and pushing me out the door. I grabbed her arms and held them out. She was strong. She kept pulling and pushing, trying to get some leverage. After a few seconds, her arms slowed and her voice went low. She was up against me. She was breathing hard. I let go of her arms and she gently started punching my chest. She wouldn't look at me. She just rubbed her face back and forth in my chest mumbling cuss words. I reached under her arms and behind her back and gently pulled her hair so her head would tilt back. She looked up at me, her face soft, and her eyes were far off. Her right hand reached down and grabbed my dick. It was so hard I thought it would break. She squeezed it.

"He doesn't love me…" she said.

"Okay…"

"Pull my hair harder," she whispered.

I did.

We kissed and she bit my lip hard. I had to yank her head back and squeeze her face to make her let go. She ripped off my shorts and pulled me down on the bed. It felt hot. Her smell suffocated me and held me under like a giant wave crashing around me. I could not see her. I saw hair and lips and sweat. I was aching in the salty tingle of every move. I could not breathe. We gasped at each other. We were banging our teeth together, biting and scratching each other. I was drowning but I couldn't reach for the surface. Instead I swam down. I lost sight of myself, of her, of us. I swam down and down and down into the heat and the truth of what is and found nothing.

I busted through the surface only to find that I was in a room with a girl and we both stank.

CHAPTER 8

MONEY, CLOTHES AND HOES

It had been over a month since I was with her.

After we had sex I put my clothes on and left. I had said nothing. I was suffocating in that heat. The same smells and feelings that had drove me crazy for her before we had sex then drove me crazy from her. I couldn't breathe in that room. I stepped outside of her house that day and felt a breeze that picked me up and hadn't put me down until now.

Until I had run out of weed.

I had spent the last month hustling the rest of the weed in the backpack. I had made over two thousand dollars and had spent almost all of it. Sometimes the money came and went so fast I didn't even count it…

> *I kept my profit in my left pocket,*
> *what I owe below my nutsack.*
> *Right next to my ass crack*
> *The drug game is shitty, gritty, pity it's all we know.*
> *I braided my fro…*

I had to buy small gram-sized baggies and rolling papers because most kids I was dealing with couldn't spend more than twenty bucks. I met this old biker dude, leather vest and everything. He traded me three eight balls for four ounces. I sniffed some off the back of my hand in a seven eleven parking lot. It just felt like a super strong cup of coffee but the buzz was gone in less than a half hour.

I smoked joints like cigarettes. In fact, I kept empty cigarette packs and filled them with joints. I could go through a half a pack of joints in a day all by myself. If I was at a bus stop and the bus came before I finished or if I just didn't feel like smoking anymore, I would give it to a bum or someone or just flick it into the grass. Why smoke a half-smoked roach when I have twenty fat fresh ones ready to burn?

I had meant to stop by her house or stop by the school and talk to her. I told myself I couldn't go by the school because I didn't want to run into Kevin McKenzie or I didn't want my mom to find me or I didn't want to bump into Maka. Those were all true, but mostly I didn't want to see her. I didn't want her to see me. I didn't like her seeing so much of me. She saw things. When she looked at me I felt naked. Not confident, walking around, "Haha, look at me, I'm so strong and handsome!" naked. More like Adam and Eve trying to cover up with some fig leaves naked.

So I stayed away from my school and her house. I caught the bus to Waipahu, Pearl City and Mililani. I walked around those high schools making friends and selling weed. Pearl City High School had a lot of popolos. When I walked up, there were about twelve of them sitting and standing in the lunchroom banging on the table. A tall skinny popolo kid was rapping and a huge chubby popolo kid in a basketball jersey was dancing. D-40! I remembered his name from the popolo girl screaming it when Kevin dropped him in the parking lot. The one rapping had a cast on his left arm. I recognized that kid too. It was Suga-C!

#

Tall Chocolate Butter
Go tell ya mother
It's me Suga-C
They all shook of me
The Pimp with the Capitol P
Immaculately
Flowin, no M.I.C.
R.I.P.
To fake hardcore
No encore
It's curtains for your dumbass

I'm sharp as cut glass
I cut class
Grab your girl and cut ass
In a Cutlass
Supreme
Nah mean!
Now your girl can't walk
She hobble-ing
Five days ago she was
Model-ing
Five minute ago she was on her knees
Gobble-ing
Five days from now she's on the phone
ring-ring
But I aaaiiiint eveeeerr
Aaansweeering
Cuz it's me Suga-C straight Pimp
OG
Ooohh weeeeee

#

Everyone who was hanging out in the room jumped up and down with "Ooohh shiiit" and "Hell yeah!" I looked around the table and saw a few of those kids from the parking lot that day. I walked right up to Suga-C.

"Wassup, Suga-C?"

I put my hand up but he left me hanging.

"I don't know you local boy," he said.

He turned his back on me

"It's like that? That's some rude shit," I said with a smile. "I'm tryin to be friendly… I heard you spittin some dope shit. I come over to tell you that and you turn your back."

"I don't want no trouble with you fuckin makahawkins!" he said.

A couple guys on the table chuckled.

"What the fuck is a makahawkin?!"

"You, nigga!" said Suga–C.

D-40 stood up and Suga-C turned around to face me. A few kids grabbed their stuff and walked away fast. There were nine of them now. Everyone else in the lunchroom started walking closer, sensing a fight.

Okay.

I didn't want to fight him. I thought he was talented and I wanted to meet him and his friends. Plus he already had a broken arm. On the other hand, I liked to fight. I saw Kevin take these guys apart. It would be fun to see if I could also.

"Okay. Not here," I said, thinking about getting in trouble with a backpack full of weed. "How about we take a little walk down to the parking lot?"

I was still smiling.

"Yo Suga-C! Fuck this flip flop wearing makahawkin up!" said D-40.

"D-40, chill dog. Member I promised ya pops!" Suga-C said to the chubby kid. Then he turned back to me. "Don't think I won't fuck you up with this cast on. The shit is already healed. They taking the cast off tomorrow muthafucka! I'll beat you in the face wit dis shit!"

***

We headed out toward the parking lot. It seemed like the whole school followed us down. I started doing the math in my head. I wondered if I beat suga-C's ass, if his friends would jump in. They should, he already had a broken arm. If so, how many? When I showed up at the parking lot that day there were four guys on Kevin. I didn't have any real friends here today. If the cops come, I'm losing everything in my backpack, best case scenario. Worst case scenario, I go to jail.

We got to the parking lot and Suga-C took off his shirt and addressed the crowd with the gravitas of a Shakespearean actor.

"Ayo! I ain't walkin round here pickin fights with y'all muthafuckas, an yet y'all muthafuckas keep pickin fights with me! I ain't choose to be here with you fuckin Hawaiians! I'm tired of fightin with y'all! Let me be! I'm Suga-C! Bitch! I ain't goan back down! I ain't goan get put down! Recognize *muthafuckas!*"

He had his arms way out and his chest puffed up.

I looked around. There were a lot of local kids here for him to be putting it that way.

"Ayo!" I yelled, doing my best Suga-C impression. "Why y'all Hawaiians keep on a'pickin on me? Shucks gosh darn it. I ain't never done nothin ta nobody. I'm Suga-C, the C stands for Cunt, but you can call me sweet pussy if ya like." I sounded like an old black man with a heavy southern accent.

I don't have a dick so I'm a dyke,
I take the seat off when I ride a bike,
Suckin big dicks is what I like. Ahuh, ahuh.

Everybody started laughing. I started laughing.

I had my hands out and my chest puffed like Suga-C walking back and forth. For a second we were standing side by side like two peacocks. He quickly put his arms down.

#

Is everyone in Pearl City
convinced that this dude's gangsta
Walkin around with his chest out
Like "I'm Suga-C, I'm gansta"
You being gansta is like Hawaiians getting their land back
You keep sayin it, and we just keep watching lips flap.
I can't stand too close cuz I'm paranoid
You look like Chris Rock on steroids
Am I talkin to your ass? Cuz your lips
Look like hemorrhoids.
I thought your school respected you?
But they're all laughing their asses off
Cuz your chest hair looks like you swallowed
David Hasselhoff…
David Hasselhoff, David Hasselhoff
Your lips look like your
constantly swallowing David Hasselhoff
Actin like nobody done told you
Ewa Beach smacked the shit out your whole crew
And that means you,
You and Suga-Cunt ring

You all got your ass beat harder than Rodney King.

\#

The crowd of kids around us exploded with laughter and cheers. I was smiling so hard I had to put my hand over my mouth because I felt like I looked silly.

"I saw that shit! I saw that shit in Ewa Beach! You got your ass beat!" yelled some black chic.

There was more laughter and lots of pushing as the people in the back tried to squish forward. Suga-C looked around worried. Then he brushed his hair with what looked like a little doggy brush. He was trying to appear disinterested.

"Man… fuck dis shit… I thought we was going to straight squab. I ain't no fuckin rapper, I just be freestylin' sometimes."

He put his hand up towards me like he wanted to shake hands.

"Brah if you like scrap, we go cuz!" I said in full blown pidgin. All the local kids in the crowd started yelling and pushing when they heard that.

"Who is dat?" yelled some local dude.

"Dats Q! From Ewa Beach!" answered someone else.

"Dat fucka can scrap brah!"

"Give dat popolo cracks brah!"

"Ayo where's Moon Dog?!" yelled the chubby black dude.

Suga-C's face lit up.

"D-40 my nigga! You right!"

He turned and scanned the crowd.

"Ayo Moon Dog! Where you at nigga?! Moon Dog!" he yelled. There was commotion in the back of the crowd as people were being pushed aside to let someone through. People started yelling and shoving and then someone punched someone and a girl screamed. Finally a skinny black kid about my height was standing right in front of me. The middle of the circle was small now because everyone was pushing.

He didn't look like something I should be afraid of. He wore a black Nike hoodie with a blue backpack, a pair of baggy jeans and some beat up Timberland boots.

He spoke with his head down almost at a mumble.

"We on some battling shit? Freestyle or written?" he said.

"Freestyle…" I said.

"Ayo… nothing personal dog, but you about to get murdered," he whispered.

#

Nothin's gonna stop me from doing
Just what I want to do
So please stay out the way, okay?
Yes, I'm warning you.
Won't be no prelude or hollarin
Bout what I'm gonna do.
I'm eatin fire, I'll spit it out
Right in front of you.
So run to the pay phone, go hit a pager
Go head, call your crew
There's gonna be a fall out
Pearl City crew is fallin through
Biting off limbs, the venom
Is gettin all in you
We on the come up, suckas
Ain't nothin really that ya'll can do
To you new faces,
Our tribe is called
"Who the fuck are you?"
To you "Mo tea sir?"
Is who we bringin the ruckus to
So what the fuck are you sayin
And who the fuck could you say it to
That might believe you
And stand there tryin to humor you
We ain't playin with you
And pain is stayin with you
If you decide and don't watch out
Who the fuck you steppin to

Cuz still waters run deep
And quiet people creep
And you don't know how deep I'm rollin
Or who's reppin who
Or who's weapon will bust
Injectin the fuss
Into the place and trust
If it's one of us
His targets hit
Time to dip
Fully equipt
Of the brain
And of the lip
And of the hip
Trip
And stumble fall on the spot
That you stand
Forever disrespecting Moon-Dog
As a man
Laid back and humble dude,
Flip out? Yes I can
It takes a lot to ever trouble
This man
So if you did?
You definitely mistook Kindness
For a weakness…
That is a violation that cannot be
Tolerated…

#

The bell rang and kids started disappearing.

Moon-Dog didn't stop rapping or even open his eyes until Suga-C grabbed him by his backpack and started dragging him down the hall.

"Ayo Q, we should link up nigga! Not on some battling shit but on some cypher shit, ya know? Where you be at?" Moon-Dog asked.

"Ewa Beach! Front parking lot by the pay phone after school, most times," I yelled as Suga-C dragged him around a corner. I hadn't been there in weeks but it was the only place I could think of that they would know. I felt an icy fire in my stomach. Going there would mean I could run into weird chic. It would mean I could run into Kevin. But before I could think of a better place, they were gone.

I started walking off campus, working the word cypher around in my head. At the last pillar before the end of the parking lot I saw a little hapa Japanese girl holding a folder in front of her. She was standing with her head down looking up at me. Her right foot was nervously grinding into the cement like she was putting out a cigarette. I walked up and gently touched her face. She closed her eyes and tilted her head back waiting. I chuckled to myself, put my hand around her neck, and kissed her. Her body went soft like a bag of laundry and I put my other hand under her arm and held her up. After a moment she pulled away breathing hard and fast. Her face was scared and she kept looking down the parking lot.

"You wanna get outta here?" I said.

She nodded yes.

"You have a car?" I asked.

Most Japanese girls do.

She nodded yes.

She walked me to a brand new 1992 Honda Acura. The inside smelled like plumeria. She didn't talk. I spent the whole ride wondering what it would feel like to own a brand-new car like this. I wondered if she was smarter than me or better than me. I wondered if her parents were better people. I wondered what was the real difference between us that she should have this car and I should have…

I pushed a button and the window came down. Shit… that was cool. I lit a cigarette. She drove us up to the entrance of Aiea Loop Trail. She parked the car and held on to the steering wheel staring out the windshield. She was breathing fast.

"Are you okay?" I whispered.

"Yes…"

She didn't look at me. Her voice was so small. It sounded like a cartoon character for a little kitten or something. Her light skin looked like powder. Her cheeks were bright red like they had been rubbed raw. I reached up and touched them with the back of my hand. They were hot. I leaned over to try to kiss her and the car started rolling backwards. She screamed and slammed back on the brakes. I pulled up the emergency brake between us.

"Oh my god! I one lolo! I never wen put the car in da'kine," she said.

She laughed and put her hands over her face.

"We don't have to do anything," I said.

I gently pulled her hands down from her face and saw that she was crying.

I kissed the tears on her cheek.

"Hey, stop… stop crying. It's okay. We can just go back to the school and chill," I said softly.

"No… no… I like do'em. I just… I don't know…"

She tried to laugh but it came out weird so she just sighed instead. Then she grabbed the wheel again and pulled at it back and forth making a cute little growling sound.

"I never wen do this before. I like you. When we was kissing… I don't know… I feel all da'kine inside," she said finally looking at me.

"Yeah. I feel that too," I lied.

I leaned over and kissed her softly.

I didn't feel anything. I kept thinking that any minute now all those waves that I had felt with weird chic would start crashing into me. Everything about this girl was different. Her lips were small. Her hair was thin and delicate. She smelled like soap and perfume. I tasted the cherry lip gloss as I backed away. A panic started to wash over me. What if weird chic is the only way for me to get that feeling? I started to get mad. Somewhere in the background kitten girl was talking about her boyfriend.

"But every time is like… it's like that. I no feel na'ting when we kiss and then… he just da'kine… put inside and it's done. But everyone stay happy I get one boyfriend! My mudda say he one good boy. My fadda drink wit him and talk about all kine stuffs. Like 'When we going get married?' and 'When we going have kids li'dat.' I like him too but den you wen kiss me and I wen feel so much stuffs and now… whoa my god!"

She started crying again.

"I one slut… I'm sorry! I no can do this! I no like be one slut!"

She started to fumble with her keys and I let her. She wasn't a slut. She was a sweet girl and I was in my own hell. I was thinking how many times was I going to have to sit in a car with a beautiful girl and have my dick just shriveled there like a second belly button.

***

She dropped me off at Pearlridge Mall. I walked down to the bus stop completely confused with myself. I lit a joint and a little Mexican girl shot me a look. She looked like she was straight out of the movie *Colors*. She had been waiting for the bus in the sun wearing a black sweater and a black miniskirt. Her sweater fell down off her shoulder showing that she wasn't wearing a bra. Her eyeliner was so thick it looked like she used a Sharpie. Underneath all that makeup she was cute. She chewed her gum loud and rolled her eyes.

"You wanna smoke with me?" I asked.

I held the joint out. There were four other people at the bus stop—an old Filipino lady and three construction workers in yellow shirts. They pretended not to notice the smell. She held out her hand trying to make me walk over to her. I didn't so she rolled her eyes and looked away. I stood there smoking for about a minute until she got up and walked over to me.

"What's your problem?" she said.

She took the joint and hit it hard then coughed until her eyes watered.

"That's really good shit!" she said passing it back.

"Word…" I mumbled.

"You're not from here?"

She took the joint again and hit gently.

"I am. I'm from Ewa Beach," I said.

"No, silly boy. I mean like from here."

"Yes, silly girl, from here," I said.

She rolled her eyes and my bus came.

"Keep the rest. This is my bus."

"This is me too," she said.

I took the joint and got one the construction worker's attention.

"Ho, brah! You guys like da rest?"

One came over and took it.

"Tanks eh cuz!" he said.

"So you are from here," she said when we sat down next to each other.

She smelled like Aquanet, cheap perfume, cigarettes and sweat. My dick was rock hard from the bus stop all the way to her house. She talked the whole way about how she hated it here, she hated her friends, she hated her school, she hated her slutty mom, and most of all, she hated her dad. The bus got to the guard gate at Iroquois Point and the popolo MP got on the bus to check everyone's ID. I started to say I didn't have a military I.D. but she held my arm and said, "You're fine!"

"Wassup sweetheart, why you don't be callin a nigga?" said the MP.

"Hey T! My dad took the phone out of the wall and locked the window in my room. Sorry... but I have been thinking about you!" she said.

She touched his arm and he smiled.

"You got I.D.?" he said to me.

"He got jumped by some local kids at school today. They took his wallet. Fuckin animals..."

He looked at me closer. He looked at the way I was dressed and made a face. He looked back at her and made a different face. Almost sad or embarrassed or... sickened.

"Can you please just let him on, T? *Pleeeease!*"

She put her hand on his chest. He looked out the window at the guard shack then back towards the bus driver and everyone else to see who was listening.

"Have fun... *brah!*" he said to me.

We got off and walked to her house. It was hot. We were both drenched with sweat by the time we got to her door.

"Whose truck is this?" I said, pointing at the driveway.

"It's my dad's... Nice, huh?" she said.

"Is he home?"

"Yeah... but he's up in his room with the A.C. on full blast. We can do whatever we want."

She opened her door and we walked in.

It was freezing in her house.

"You got any coke?" she asked bluntly.

"Yeah, a little bit."

I took out a baggie and shook a little coke onto the back of my hand between my thumb and pointer finger. I held it up and looked at her.

"You're handsome..."

She put her bag on the floor, slinked over to me and grabbed my dick. Then she pulled at my shorts so she could look at it.

"Oh, hell yeah," she whispered to herself and bit her lip. She grabbed my hand and sniffed up the coke. I shook out a little more and took a bump.

"Let's go outside at least, so if your dad wakes up—"

"Fuck my dad!"

She was pulling me to the couch.

"I'll fuck you but I ain't fucking your dad," I said opening the sliding door to the patio.

"It's too hot out there!"

"I like it hot…"

"You so fucking cheesy!" she said giggling and rolling her eyes.

She stepped through the door and sat down in the patio chair. Then she lifted her legs and pulled off her panties. She leaned back and spread her legs.

"C'mon!" she blurted out impatiently.

I had to put my hand over her mouth to keep her quiet. She kept yelling shit in Spanish. The metal legs of the patio chair kept scraping on the cement. I stopped looking at her because she kept looking at the patio door. Instead, I buried my face in her neck and shoulder, the sweat and hairspray and cheap perfume pulling me down like a dirty brick tied to my belly button.

She wouldn't look at me when we were done. I pulled my shorts up and she stared at the patio door like she was trying to open it with her mind.

"Hey, did I hurt you?" I asked, wondering why she was being cold.

"I know he fucking heard us!" she whispered.

"You think he's pissed?"

"I think he doesn't care…" Her voice trailed off.

I walked away and forgot her name.

***

When I was hungry, I ate whatever I wanted. Plate lunches with fried ahi tuna and mac salad, shoyu chicken, fried shrimp tempura. No more Manapua Truck! McDonalds, Jack in the Box, Taco Bell, Burger King—it all made me sick if I ate there more than once a day. Pizza Hut had a lunch salad bar that I would raid the fuck out of. When my shirt and shorts got dirty I threw them away and bought more. Finding a place to sleep was still a problem. If I could turn it into a party it was nothing to crash on someone's couch. I picked up coke here and there when I could. I wasn't really into it but coke goes a long way when you're trying to make a party happen. I would make friends and then buy beer and pizza and Barry Whitestuff, but more than two days in a row of that would get my stomach horribly mad.

Then I met this cute thick-slash-chubby Filipino girl from Pearl City. She had come to pick up her younger brother from a house party in Mililani. She gave me a look then quickly caught herself and looked away while she was scolding her brother for drinking and smoking pakalolo. I walked over and apologized to her. I told her I didn't know he was only fourteen. I asked if she could give me a ride back to Pearl City. She dropped off her little brother at her parents' house.

"Okay," she said getting back in the car. "Where do your parents live?"

"So listen, I promise to never sell or give your little brother any weed… or drugs… or anything… but… do you… wanna smoke with me?"

I watched the gears turn in her head and I sat there with a "why not?" smile on my face.

She was twenty years old and worked as a bank teller. She and her husband had a place. He was away at basic training. After our first night together, she said I could just come over and stay the night if I wanted. For the next five nights I would just show up at around midnight, eat whatever she had made, wake her up, smoke her out, and do whatever she asked in bed. Speed up, slow down, harder, softer, in a circle, to the right, to the left—it was basic training, she was my drill sergeant. In the morning when I would wake up she would already be at work. I would walk around her place looking at the pictures of her and her husband in perfect poses with perfect smiles on their faces. They were hiking with matching water bottles. They were at the beach with sunburned noses. They were dressed up at some military ball. Their wedding picture was beautiful. I didn't see any pictures that said she didn't love him. Was she pulling a cinnamon girl and fucking me to get back at him? Was she lonely with him away and just needed something? Was it something that had nothing to do with me?

Was it something that I couldn't understand like explaining Rakim's lyrics to an eight year old white boy? Or… was I just too fucking handsome and irresistible that she lost all control? Gassed off myself, I would leave the thoughts in her place and lock the door behind me.

It felt like the world was a big fat ass in the palm of my hand.

Until I ran out of weed.

CHAPTER 9

SUNGLASSES MAN

"Wow brah, I stay looking for you all ova!" said Kevin.

I was sitting on a little chain-link fence that covered an electrical meter on the corner of O Building. There was mud all around it. The sky was a dark grey and drizzling off and on.

"Where all your friends stay?" he said.

He was talking nice, like he was not a mutant killing machine.

"I don't know. This is my first day back at school," I said.

I was trying to look him in the eye enough to not be a bitch, but not so much that we'd start fighting. My heart was pounding. I tried to focus on not breathing too fast. My hands and legs wanted to shake. I gripped the fence with both hands and swung my legs casually. Up close like this, he wasn't that much bigger than me. I had grown. He was about an inch taller and maybe ten or fifteen pounds heavier: six-one and two hundred pounds. As I was sizing him up I noticed he was doing the same thing. His eyes scanned me and his prehistoric instincts calculated the outcome.

I slowly slid down off the fence. If I jumped down we would throw down. I leaned against the pillar and lit a cigarette. He smacked the cigarette out of my mouth. My lighter fell on the ground.

"Brah! No smoke, you can get cancer!" he said.

We both put up our hands and slowly danced around each other. A couple other kids took notice of this and started walking over to see a fight. Kevin picked up the lighter and held it out to me.

"We not fighting!" he said to me and to the kids gathering around.

"Dis is my friend from hanabata days cuz. We not fighting, mine your own bizness you fuckaz!" he yelled.

Everyone acted like they were leaving but only took a few steps away. Like when you swat at flies. Kevin stood there with that psycho smile on his face holding my lighter out in front of him. He looked like a Spanish sword fighter with one hand behind his back, legs together with his chest out. I put my hands down, stepped right up to him and casually took the lighter.

"Yeah, I have been trying to quit," I said.

I leaned back up against the pillar and lit another cigarette. I noticed a few drops of rain land on the cigarette before I felt it on my skin. I put the lighter in my pocket and looked him in the eye. The green fire danced. He smiled at me.

"Where your friends stay?" he asked again.

"I don't know, this is my first day back…" I said again.

"Where you was?"

"I was sick at home."

"No lie, you was all over. Pearl City, Aiea, Waipahu…"

He studied my eyes.

"I was looking for your girl's house. She said she would make me soup," I said.

"I no more girlfriend," he said.

"I'm joking. Why do you wanna know where I was, Kevin? Did you miss me?"

My chest was pounding. This was the longest conversation I'd had with him since I was nine years old. The bell rang, followed by a loud thunder roll. Kids began coming out of class. It would only be a minute or two before this standoff was noticed and a crowd would form around us pushing us to fight.

"My friends was looking for your friends. Maka, Lyle, Opele… where they stay?"

He lost his smile and was now pacing back and forth. My stomach was sinking. Something was not right.

"Today, which is the day after yesterday, and the one before tomorrow, is the first day that I have been back to this school. I don't know where my friends are because they ain't my friends no more. Do you know where they are, Kevin?"

"I wen go to da'kine, Maka's house but then, after Kaipo went to jail, no one knows where Maka stay. I wen go to Lyle's house same ting, I wen go to—"

"Wait, what?! Kaipo's in Jail? For what?"

"Drugs! You never wen know? You lie. Cops wen find like twenty pounds of chronic buds!" he said.

"Shit, that's fucked up! Maka must be fucked up…" I looked at the ground.

Kevin was looking at me. He stopped pacing and stepped closer.

"For real kine you never wen know?" he asked softly.

"No…" I mumbled.

Kevin tilted his head to the side and looked at me. He looked like he was sad that I was sad. He put his hand on my shoulder.

"Sorry eh? If you see Maka dem, call dis number. Uncle stay looking for dem."

He passed me a torn piece of paper with a number on it written in pencil.

"Who's uncle?" I asked.

"I thought you was one drug dealer now? You don't know who's Uncle? Brah! You better wen ask somebody, before you get major kine lickings!"

"I'm not a drug dealer. I just sell a few joints here and…" I stopped myself. I was selling more than a few joints now. Maybe I should find out who Uncle was.

"Brah, we friends and den you keep lying to me!" he yelled.

He smacked me in the face. I slid sideways off the pillar as he was throwing a jab. He cracked the pillar with his fist. I danced off the sidewalk and into the grass. He shook his right hand and put his fist up.

Here we go.

"Kevin!" yelled someone from the parking lot behind O-Building.

Kevin didn't turn. He was focused on me. He was smiling and trying to close the distance carefully. A horn blared. In the parking lot was a huge black lifted Ford F-250 on gigantic swamp tires. In the driver's seat was a late-thirties dark-skinned local man with a full sleeve of tribal tattoos around a massive arm hanging out the window. He wore dark shades on his scruffy face. There were three other huge-looking men in the back of the pickup that made the driver look small. If you drove a truck up to the gate at Halawa prison and honked the horn, these would be the four guys to make it over the fence.

"Kevin you fucka! Stop scrapping the popolo guy an get in the truck!" yelled sunglasses man.

"We not scrapping cuz! We just playin! Dis is my friend!" yelled Kevin.

Sunglasses Man took off his sunglasses and his green eyes burned through me. He was searching me.

"Your name is Q-tip or some dumb shit like that, right?"

"Yeah" was all I could get out.

"You the new weed guy in Pearl City, Waipahu and Ewa Beach."

He wasn't asking and I couldn't talk with those eyes checking my answers.

"Where are you getting your shit from?"

"My dad," I said.

It just flew out of my mouth and I froze after I said it because it made no sense. It was such a weird lie.

"From your dad?" he was surprised by the answer, too. His eyes suspended their full-cavity search of my soul and his face scrunched up.

"Your dad is selling weed again?" he asked.

"No, he gave it to me to sell," I said.

"That sucks. He got fired or what?" He sounded concerned.

"What?"

"Your dad. He was working at Fire Station 11, right?"

"No! I mean yes. That's my stepdad. My real dad lives on the Big Island and I fly over there. He gives me shit to sell and I fly back."

I watched his face. He looked into each of my eyes, one at a time, and then his focus drifted away. It looked like he was remembering something. I didn't move at all. It was long and uncomfortable. I tried to keep my eyes somewhere vaguely around his forehead and not breathe too hard. I could hear my heartbeat in my ears. I flinched when he snapped back and looked at me again. He picked up right where he had left off as if nothing happened.

"So you fly over to the Big Island, get weed from your biological father and come back here and sell it," he said plainly. His Pidgin accent had disappeared. He was speaking slow and clear. It left no room for "oh no, that's not what I said, I meant this not that…" It was nerve racking.

"Yes," I lied.

"Where?"

"Huh?"

"Where on the Big Island."

"Kona…"

"He lives in Kona?"

"Yeah."

"Who does he get his weed from?"

"I'm not supposed to go around spreading that shit… I mean I'm sorry… but I can't…"

"I'm asking because you've been selling a lot for a little bitch ass kid and if he is buying this much in Kona, I probably know who he is buying from."

"No… he grows it…"

"He grows the shit that you've been selling in Kona?"

"Um… Yeah… Kona Gold… but… because he said he was having problems… he actually started growing it in Hilo cuz I don't know exactly but… hey… listen I don't want to have any problems with nobody. I'm just selling a few pounds here and there at parties and to friends, like I can just back off it you know…"

"What's his name?"

"What?"

"What's his name?"

"Who?"

"Your dad."

"J."

"J what?"

"J.W."

"Don't fuck with me…"

"No, I mean, everyone calls him J.W. or J-Dub. His name is James W. Quintis."

"That's… his real name."

I said yes but he wasn't listening to me anymore.

He put his sunglasses back on and looked across the street to the basketball courts.

"Go across the street if you guys like scrap! Or what? You like go back to jail you fuckin dummy?" yelled sunglasses man at Kevin.

"Eh, we go across the street to the park?" Kevin asked me.

He sounded like he was inviting me to a game of cribbage. By this time there was a huge circle around us. He turned and started jogging to the park across the street from the school. The thunder wasn't rolling any more. It was cracking and lighting was flashing every few minutes. The rain would be dumping on us soon. I looked at all the expectant faces. I knew I was about to get my ass beat in front of the whole school and my stomach rolled over into itself. My eyes met with Cynthia's. She had just appeared in the crowd. She looked down at first and then back up with a look that said "walk away."

I started walking towards the park and then stopped. What would happen if I "walk away"?

Everyone knew Kevin was crazy. What would happen if I grabbed Cynthia's hand and we "walk away" from the parking lot and straight to her house. You don't fight Kevin McKenzie one on one. You don't fight Kevin McKenzie four on one! You "walk away" or he puts you in the hospital. He breaks bones. She was right. I stood there trying to catch this thought.

Walk away

It was hard to think it. Like catching a whiff of something on a breeze.

Walk away

What was stopping me?

A gust of wind came through the parking lot, lifting into the air the red dirt kicked up from the flip flops and basketball shoes that were shuffling their way to the fight. It brought with it the words I needed for the thought I could almost have. You don't fight in the conflict… you fight the conflict itself. You rise above violence and the negative metal squeeze chute that leads us like cattle to the soul-slaughtering prison industrial complex. You shake off the blinders and see that the track just goes around and around. You realize that we repeat the same mistakes as those before us and fall victim to the ghetto traps that by design are meant to keep us from realizing our higher selves. I felt the wind lift me and push me free from this spectacle of ignorance. I could walk and keep on walking…

And sometimes when the wind blows

> *I can hear what I'm supposed*
> *To be…*

I watched the gust of wind pass back through the school and disappear.

I walked to where Kevin was waiting for me in the gravelly parking lot. He had taken off his shirt and was jogging in place, moving his arms up and down like jumping jacks. I was thinking I should move around a little too but I felt paralyzed. I felt like I was being remote controlled. I could barely see. The lighting and thunder was on us now but everything sounded far away and echoey. Sunglasses Man pulled the truck up and all the escaped convicts jumped out and started slapping Kevin on the back. I saw Moon-Dog and Suga-C and all the Pearl City popolos. I saw Mr. Mervin and his whole class. I saw three of the school's security guards. I shook my head back and forth and heard all the yelling move through it like molasses. Was I dreaming? Was I about to get jumped by sunglasses man and all those big dudes?

"Up and up!" I yelled in a slow-motion bitch voice.

The rain started to shower us with huge drops just as Kevin took three measured steps towards me. His first swing was so slow I watched his shoulders rotate back and then forward before I realized I should start moving. *CRACK!* Everything snapped back. The crowd let out a huge *"Ooooooo"* as I rolled backwards and tried to get my balance. I fell on my back and he was instantly on me.

This was not a dream.

I am here now.

Fight goddamnit!

I was able to get my legs around his hips and squeeze while leaning back onto my shoulders and he couldn't hit me in the face. I grabbed at his arms but he started hammer punching me in the stomach. It only took two of those before I knew I needed to try something else. I put my lower back down on the ground and when he twisted his shoulders to punch me in the face, I climbed his left arm and hugged him tight. He stood back up, taking me with him, and I let my legs fall back to the ground, let go and shuffled away.

We were back standing toe to toe, squared off again except now I was not paralyzed. My nose was bleeding and I could feel my left eye swelling but I felt good. I shook my arms out and blinked through the raindrops.

A lightning bolt struck so close everyone ducked and looked around. The thunder followed immediately and I yelled. I charged him and as he lunged backwards, I stopped and laughed. So did everyone else. He looked around and then charged me. I shot two jabs and a right hook that landed square. He swallowed it all and smiled. He threw the exact same combo but the hook didn't land. I ducked it and landed a haymaker. His eyes opened wide for a second and he dipped back. He smiled again, but I could see—that shook him.

We spun around and around, our bare feet shuffling over the wet gravelly pavement. He charged again and I hit him with the same combo. He charged again and timed it, then did some weird left hook out of nowhere that rocked me back. I fell into the crowd. They picked me up and threw me back in the circle where he timed a perfect jab that sent me sprawling to the other side. This time I fell into his boys. One of them sucker punched me in the gut. D-40 and Suga-C rushed them and the whole thing erupted for a moment.

Sunglasses Man grabbed Suga-C and literally tossed him back across the circle then yelled at the guy who punched me. The whole circle was pushing and yelling. Sunglasses Man moved to the center.

"Let 'em fucking fight! Fair fucking fight! Up and up!"

Everyone started yelling "Up and up!"

The circle slowly reformed and I was pushed back in. I threw a blow that landed right on Kevin's nose but then I slipped on the speed bump. He grabbed my tank top to pull me into him but it ripped and we both fell awkwardly. I spun around and crawled up but my shirt was now around my legs. He chased me around the circle swinging wildly, trying to land a few while I was stuck tripping in my shirt. He did. My head rang as I fell into the crowd for the third time. It was dark and all I could see were legs and feet all around me. Lightning flashed and I saw Moon-Dog pull the shirt off my feet. Someone else grabbed me and tossed me back in the circle. My head was swimming and my lungs were on fire. My arms felt like water-logged tree trunks. I tried to shuffle my feet but my ankles were cramping so I simply stood in one spot and yelled over the thunder, "Come on, muthafucka!"

Kevin was smiling again. He shook his arms out then slowly swaggered towards me. At first I thought he was savoring the moment but as he got closer I saw his smile was different. His nose was broken and big red snot bubbles were spraying out with each shallow breath. His left eye was swollen shut and something was wrong with his right hand. He wasn't savoring. He was hurt. He was trying to cover it with his psycho smile.

It would be now or it would be never. I ran in swinging wild and screaming. He stood his ground and swung wide, looping, dying-man punches. We stood at arm's length clobbering each other. Lighting flashed over our heads. Kevin backed away, turned to Sunglasses Man, stretched his arms out desperately and collapsed.

The monster fell.

The kid who beat me to a mushy, bloody mess over a dozen times. The boogey monster at the end of almost every nightmare was down. I took a huge breath and yelled from deep in my stomach as the thunder cracked over our heads.

Fights broke out all over the crowd. The whole thing pushed and pulled as kids yelled and threw punches. Kevin started to roll over onto his back and I leaped onto him. I picked up a piece of broken tar from the parking lot and smashed it across his head. The piece flew out of my hand so I balled my fist and slammed it into his face over and over. I was screaming and growling. Both of my eyes were swollen and filled with blood and rain but I could see. I could see his face was broken. It wasn't hard anymore. It was soft like punching a pot roast and it rocked and bounced off the pavement with every blow. Then I heard a deep, gentle voice.

"If you can stop now then you've won. If you keep going, you will lose more than you could ever know."

I felt a hand on my back.

"Trust me, stop now."

It was Sunglasses Man.

He was kneeling beside me. Almost whispering in my ear. I started to hear the rain. Kevin's face looked like a clay model from a straight-to-video horror movie. He was alive. Giant bloody puss bubbles grew and popped around his broken misshapen nose. I looked at my hands. The rain washed the blood from them revealing the clenched, skinless pink knuckles. They were flesh-covered clubs. I tried to open my hands but they were cramped and frozen into fists. Sunglasses Man helped me up and my vision started to widen. The crowd that had only a few moments ago been cheering and laughing and oohing and aahing were standing in complete silence. The teachers and other random adults were trying to turn invisible and slowly walk away. I saw Kevin's boys pick him up and toss him into the truck. I looked at Sunglasses Man. He grinned and took off his sunglasses.

"I see you," he whispered and I shivered.

I looked down. Away from the green fire of his eyes. My hands slowly unclenched and shooting pain raced up my arms. I looked up and he was climbing back into his truck. I stood and my legs felt like they were going to fold. Lighting-hot shocks entered me with every breath. I looked around and saw Cynthia. She was staring at me. She looked like she was either going to scream or run or both.

Then I heard the sirens.

***

Why was he allowed to pick me up from the police station?

That was my question. I didn't know stepdads could do that. I guess it was better than my mom coming in there all wide eyed and loud.

"Where is he?! Where's my son?!" she would be screaming over and over as she ran around the station.

Yeah this, I guess, was the lesser of two evils. Me sitting here in silence in the passenger seat of the Fireman's pickup truck. I was shirtless and my left eye was swollen shut. There was road rash all over me and maybe a few broken ribs. I tried not to fog the window but I was breathing through my mouth because my nose was filled with clotted blood. The Fireman kept rolling his window down because I smelled like sweat and filth but it was still raining so he had to keep rolling it up when the rain blew in. I stared out the window and watched the wind push rain around underneath each street light.

We reached the parking lot of our new house. It was literally down the street from where I grew up. I could see parts of the old bike path we used to ride down when we were kids. The Big Bad Wolf. I smiled. Fuck you Kevin McKenzie. I kicked your ass!

I was about to get out of the truck when the Fireman stopped me.

"I don't want to be your father. You're all fucked up..." he started.

"You can't be my—" I raised my voice but he cut me off.

"Let me finish!" he said firmly.

"I don't want to be your father because your father fucked your head all up. I would hate to be the one who did that. I have a son. I found him an amazing woman who can help me raise him. That's your mom. She's gonna help me. I want to help her. But you're too old for me to be trying to force shit on you. Even if it's for your own good…"

He said this to the windshield. He sounded sorry about it. As if it were a thing that needed to be changed but couldn't be changed. Like he knew the rain that was hitting the windshield would only get worse and there was nothing either of us could do about it.

He placed my car keys on the dashboard.

"Your mom and I had a talk. She can't be here for this conversation and she can't make your decisions for you. There are two other kids we have to think about. You can't be bringing drugs and criminals into the house—"

" I never brought—"

"Please, let me finish," he said quietly.

"I pretty much spent my whole life in Ewa Beach. You think I don't know what you're doing and who you're doing it with? You keep going and you're going to find out how much you really don't know. You'll find out who the real people are real soon here, Byron."

He stopped. He was watching the windshield again as if seeing the real people do real things in the rain drops.

"But, you don't have to. You can come inside right now. You can take a hot shower. Eat some beef stew. Sleep in a warm bed. Go to school everyday all day. Hold hands with that cute Filipina girl. Graduate and be a real part of this real family. Your mother loves you but her love can't go where you're headed because it also has to be here with your brother and sister."

He gently patted the car keys on the dashboard.

"Or you can rip the bandaid off now. All your stuff is in the car. You go and you don't talk to us and jump off that cliff. But I will tell you, there are rocks at the bottom that you hope you land on cuz if you don't… then the sharks will be waiting…"

What the fuck?

We both sat there without moving, like gunslingers at high noon. To move would be to push things forward. I didn't want to turn my head away because he might take that as me wanting to get out of the truck without the car keys. I certainly didn't want to turn towards him, and the last thing I wanted to do was look at the car keys. I stared at the windshield. Deep inside of me I could see what he wanted me to see. I could see how simple the choice was supposed to be. Of course I wanted to be with my mother, eat beef stew, and have a happy Brady Bunch life. Of course I wanted to be a good kid, get good grades, join the football team, graduate and get a good job and… what?

It was a single car key on a faded-red bottle-opener keychain with a broken mountain-climber-type clip. It sat in a sunken section of the dashboard that was black from countless coffee spills. The holding cell coffee and peanut butter and jelly sandwich rolled loudly in my stomach. The sound broke the stand off.

"Alright, why don't we go inside and get some food and we'll talk more later," he said while opening his door.

"Fuck this…"

I grabbed the car keys off the dashboard and jumped out of the truck.

"Wait!"

I walked as fast as I could over to where my car was parked. I was pulling out by the time I saw my mom running from the house into the parking lot. She was barefoot in a super long night shirt with one of the Fireman's jackets hanging on her shoulders. She was yelling my name. I could hear her. The rain was loud but I could hear her. I reached up and turned the rearview sideways so I couldn't see her crying.

#

I hear her though…
and it echoes…
in the giggles…
of coked up hoes…
sometimes when the wind blows…
I can hear what I'm supposed to be…
but mostly…
I cheat life and she cheats me back.

BOOK II
CRYSTAL CITY

"Some wounds never heal. Years go by and it gets covered by thick tough scarred tissue. The muscles grow around it. It becomes hidden, but underneath it's raw and festering. It's pain, red hot pain that is many times worse than on the day it was born. The slightest touch can light your soul on fire. So you protect it. You protect this growing puss-filled hurt. You guard it and you keep it safe. You keep it secret. You will fight for it and you will kill for it."

~Kimo~

CHAPTER 1

WHERE THE SHARKS SWIM

THE LAST WAVE WAS a monster.

A real life manifestation of a bodiless creature that rose underneath me and tried to swallow me in its thirty-foot jaws. Hundreds of thousands of gallons of water being pushed thirty feet into the air and then slamming down all at once. The sound was deafening. I managed to just barely scramble over its teeth and head as it leapt above the water and came crashing down behind me with a sound that shook the beach and echoed off the surrounding mountains. Immediately after it broke, the spray rained down on my back just as angry as the wave had been and lasted for almost ten seconds.

This was a winter swell at Makaha Beach on the west side of Oahu. Every other big-wave surfer would be on the North Shore. Makaha was off limits to anyone who didn't know someone.

I looked back and stole a glance as I paddled for my life. From behind the wave I watched it block out the sliver of sun that was just starting to peek its way over the mountains behind Makaha Beach. The spray filled the whole sky and made rolling rainbows that appeared and disappeared in the wind.

There was one more wave in this set. It was bigger than the last one. I could not be caught in front of it. I paddled my burning arms just trying to keep the strokes long. I was almost completely gripped by panic. I was out of breath and my lungs and heart were about to burst into salty flames. The wave jacked up bigger and bigger. A smooth wall of water building itself up into the sky right in front of me. The sun glittered off the thirty-foot face. I had to get over it before it broke. There was no way I could hold my breath for as long as this monster would hold me down.

As I paddled up the wave, my whole body perfectly vertical, my grunts joined together in my gut and came out as a roar. To my right I watched in panic as it began to break. The top of the wave pitched over and created a barrel big enough to drive a car through. My board broke through the top just as it pitched and rolled underneath me. I had made it over… but the undertow of all that water was pulling me back. I kept paddling hard. The spray rained down on my back.

Then it was quiet.

There were only four other surfers out besides me. I did not stop paddling until I was in line with them. Three of them I didn't know. They were older local men. Two of them had mustaches. Their boards were relics. They looked like they had gone into hibernation in the 1970s and only came out when the waves were bigger than fifteen feet. We had paddled out about an hour before sunrise and they had already been here. This was my first time being in something this big. I was starting to wonder how much piss my body could make because every time a new swell appeared on the horizon I would piss my surf shorts. I hadn't caught one wave in almost two hours. Either I was never in the right spot to catch one, or I was too scared. A fifteen-foot wave with a thirty-foot face is not a wave you just paddle into from anywhere. I didn't want to kook out on the drop early in the set and then be held under by the next four to six waves. This is where you can die no matter how well you read the water. It became very clear to me as soon as we started paddling out that I shouldn't be out here.

The other surfer out today was Sunglasses Man. He sat on the outside of the lineup. He looked back at me for a second to see if I had made it. He was smiling and shaking his head no. He was teaching me a lesson. It was not a surf lesson.

I sat up on my board as close to one of the hapa Tom Selleck's as I could without it being weird. I stretched out my arms and tried to slow my breathing. I stared at Sunglasses Man. He was playfully splashing his hands in the water. Cupping them together making a squirt gun out of his palms. Completely at home and calm.

His name was Kimo.

***

Two days after I had left home for good, he had walked up to my parked car at Haubush Beach Park and knocked on the window. I was sleeping in my car and it was almost noon.

"Brah, you gon die of heatstroke if you stay in deah…"

He was right. It was hot as fuck. I had passed out in my seat as soon as I had parked at dawn and was too hungover to wake up.

I couldn't tell how old he was but he was at least in his late thirties. He stood about six feet tall. He was slimmer than I originally thought but he was ripped. He was standing there with a three prong spear and a bag filled with fish and octopus. He told me to walk with him down the beach. He said he wanted to talk.

He talked with everyone we passed. The old uncles who were fishing. The old aunties who's back lawns spilled onto the beach. The passed-out meth heads. The little kids who were playing in the water. He gave everyone a hug and a huge, genuine smile. He asked about uncles and aunties and kids and parents. He knew details about everyone and if he didn't, he would ask. He interrogated with humor and honest curiosity. He offered patient advice and compared problems he heard with his own or others he knew well. The way he talked would change depending on who he was talking to. He would speak thick Pidgin to the uncles fishing, he spoke Ebonics to the popolo alcoholic, haole English to the white lady in the big yellow house. He even spoke Japanese to the little Japanese kids playing in the water. By the time we had looped back he had given away all of the fish and all of the octopus.

We hadn't talked.

He took me to Barney's to eat. He said we would talk there. I got back in my car and followed him in his truck. As soon as we sat down, an uncle came out of the back to hug and talk to Kimo. By the time we finished eating, over fifteen different people had come to talk to us. He had bought nine plate lunches to share with anyone who didn't adamantly insist on not eating. One auntie with two young kids in tow cried as she explained they had cut off the electricity at her house. He told her to call them and ask for Micah and tell them Kimo said turn it back on. She hugged him and promised to pay him back.

"No worries aunty! You always wen look out for me back hanabata days."

As she was about to leave he called after her. "Oh, you know, Aunty? You still get that empty carport behind your house?"

She nodded yes.

"You know what? I stay working on my friend's car and Uncle giving me hard time for park'em at his house. I can just bring'em by your house and leave'em in the back? I'll put one car cover on top'em?"

"Of course," she said.

He talked to everyone like that. A favor for a favor.

We didn't talk.

He said to follow him back to his house. We would talk there.

I followed him out of Ewa Beach through the back roads towards Makakilo. He took me to a new development of houses at the bottom of the hill. He pulled into the driveway of a brand-new two-story house. It had a front and back yard with a two-car garage in the back. It was surrounded by hundreds of identical houses up and down the block. I pulled up beside him and got out.

He took a call and I stood outside his truck while he talked with his window up. That was the first time I had seen a mobile phone outside of a Big Daddy Kane video. I listened to the sound of his engine running as his air conditioner made a high-pitched whirring. Then his window rolled down and I almost pissed my pants.

"Hey kid, listen, this is one of my houses—well, one of Uncle's houses. Here's the key. There's a garage in the back. I'll try to get the electricity on in the next day or so but some shit is going on with the whole block. None of the houses got electricity yet but the water is on. Just go get a cooler and a grill and some candles or some shit for now. Get yourself cleaned up, man. You look like shit."

He looked me up and down and then took off his sunglasses and looked me in the eye.

"You not smoking ice are you?"

"What's ice?" I honestly didn't know.

"Are you popolo or Dominican or what?"

"What's Dominican?"

"Popolo then. My cellmate was popolo. He looked out for me. In fact the popolos was the only ones that looked for the Hawaiians and Samoans."

"That makes sense,." I blurted out.

"Yeah well, we look out for you guys here."

He put his sunglasses back on.

"Kevin is a fucking psycho but he we love him. That's kinda my fault and I'm sorry. I should've been looking out for him more after I got out. Maybe tightened the rope a little. Marianne spoiled him while I was locked up and he ran around like a fuckin retard beating everyone up, and it was only a matter of time… whatever. What's done is done. He can't work out here no more. He don't scare no one after that fight with you. You said you get your weed from your dad on the Big Island?"

"Yeah," I said quickly, trying not to think of Mr. Mervin and failing. I panicked for a quick second then told myself Mr. Mervin was my dad so if Kimo did his truth probe he wouldn't see it as a lie.

"Aiight, if you need more I got some. Don't push too much coke out here—save it for the Concrete Rainbow, and don't fuckin touch the ice! Don't sell it, don't smoke it, don't even fuckin hang with muthafuckas who doin it, you got that?"

"What's ice?" I asked again.

He laughed and then looked at me dead serious. "It's the shit you don't touch."

"Yeah, but I ain't never heard of that shit. What is it? Like crack?"

"Ice. Batu. Crystal methamphetamine. That shit is fucked up."

He made a face as he studied mine then decided I was being straight up. His window came all the way down and I could smell weed mixed with some kind of lemon car freshener and his cologne. He took a deep breath and broke it down.

"Originally the shit came from a plant, like most drugs. A Chinese plant, like a bush, called Ephedra. They flipped that shit though. This Japanese dude, Ogata or Akira or some shit, figured out how to turn that shit into a crystal. Before you had to shoot that shit up—now you could smoke it. Kamikaze pilots was on that shit and German blitzkrieg muthafuckas too. Shit didn't catch on here though until they started burning down all the marijuana fields. Operation Green Harvest. You wanna talk about fucked up timing. A couple of mainland crime families were trying to see if this meth stuff would sell big in America like crack did, so they talked to Uncle and a few other families to try it out here first. It's fucked up but I was locked down, so… not like I would have had a say about it anyway. Shit took off. Now it's outta hand. It's a real fuckin problem."

He stared at me to see if I was really listening or if my eyes had glazed over. I was listening but barely hanging on to it.

"You owe me two G's by the end of the week and we'll go from there. As far as—"

"I can't—"

"You can. You can and you will. Just move what you can around Pearl City, Ewa Beach, and Waipahu. Don't push Waianae or Town until I can introduce you to a few cats. And stay the fuck away from The Garden and Crystal City."

"What's Crystal City?"

"You're killin me… for real. I thought you were listening?"

"I was listening!"

"Maybe, but you ain't thinking while you're listening. Put two and two together and figure the what-four. If 'ice' is Crystal Methamphetamine and I'm telling you not to go into Crystal City, then what the fuck am I talking about? It must be a place where there's a lot of what?"

"Ice."

"And if you didn't already know, then what?"

"Act like you know…"

"C'mere… stand right here."

I moved a few inches closer and he smacked me in the head. It didn't hurt. It was the way you smack a toddler. Just fingers on the top of the head.

Anger exploded in my stomach and rolled up to my chest like a flash flood down a storm drain. It hit my heart and spread out to my arms and legs. My fists balled up and I had to press my right arm against my leg to keep from smashing it into Kimo face. He stared at my eyes. Reading me.

"You DON'T know. These rap slogans are the dumbest shit! Act like you know is just another way of saying fake it till you make it. Fake muthafuckas never make it…"

"They get raped in jail butt naked!"

"What?"

I put it together for him.

Fake muthafuckas never make it,
they get raped in jail butt naked.

For a second I thought he was gonna slap me again, but he smiled.

"Okay, what the fuck was I talking about?"

"You were gonna explain about Crystal City being a spot where a lot of people go to buy and do ice and shit and never go there cuz it's mad ghetto until you hook me up with the right dude."

"Yeah, for the most part, except Crystal City—you're never gonna have to go there. The kid I got there is… he's got it covered. Alex. He'll meet you in Waipahu or something. We'll work it out, but I don't want you hanging with him or going down to the tents… that's… it's not what it used to be. It used to just be a tough neighborhood. Even with heroin, shit, even with crack. You can't fault somebody for playing the hand they're dealt. All options are on the table when you only got one option. Back in the day, you were still dealing with people. You could keep a handle on it. Keep it contained. You could set it up in a way, kind of cut it off from regular working people… but ice… it's so fast. It spreads so fast… like a fucking plague. These places are starting to look like fucking third world countries…"

He stared off behind me. Up towards the mountains of Makakilo. He didn't say anything. I could hear his air conditioner cut back on. I watched the air-con water slowly make its way down the driveway. I was tempted to turn and see what he was looking at but I knew I wouldn't see it. It was something in his head. He kept talking, his eyes far off in the distance.

"Back in the day, even these poor spots had ʻohana. Families that looked out for each other. Crack and heroin didn't completly fuck these communities. There was still hope. They steal the land, rip out our language, dismantle our religion until our ancient words hold only the smallest fraction of their meaning. They take that fraction and they put it on a poster to sell timeshares. We are the living, breathing leftovers. Just sitting on the counter. They're not allowed to throw us away. They build little boxes to put us in. Set aside little places to put the boxes. So that the smell of us going bad doesn't waft over to the airport where all the money is coming in. But we still had ʻohana. Kapuna could talk to you. Could help steer you back. Could help you learn. Crack can't kill the kapuna. Crack can't kill the ʻohana. Poverty, sickness, oppression, disenfranchisement generation after generation still can't kill our communities. Because the kapuna can always talk. The kapuna can always talk and the keiki can always listen.

But meth. It burns away the ability to listen. The person is right there. Looking right at you. Nodding their head. Repeating your words. But they can't fucking hear you. They turn right around and stab kapuna for ten dollars and fifty cents."

Kimo's eyes came back to me.

"What about you? Can you hear me?"

"Yes." I tried not to look defiant but I felt like I was being challenged.

"I ain't sayin you scared. I know you ain't. I'm sayin it's a waste to put you there. You not made for that. I can use you in the Concrete Rainbow. I could put you at a classy ass party with models from L.A. and like, movie people, and you could sell a shit-ton of coke and party all night. That shit sounds better than smacking around meth heads all night, right?"

He looked at me.

I just nodded.

"Do you know how to pull cars?" he asked.

"If the keys are in it…"

He laughed hard and gave me a big smile.

"Listen kid, I don't know what's going on with you but you ain't alone out here. I'll take care of you. I'll show you some shit and teach you how to make it work. Just show me you can hustle."

He rolled up the window and started to pull out of the driveway then stopped and rolled it back down.

"Hey kid, don't tell your stepdad you working for me yet. We should talk to him together."

He rolled up the window and was gone before I could make any sense of what that meant.

I took my trash bags of clothes up to the master bedroom and lay down on the floor.

I closed my eyes.

I slid down.

Through the floor.

Through the dirt.

Through the lava rock. Into the ocean.

***

I can feel water sliding across the little hairs on my arms and legs. I am under water. I am sliding down underwater. Falling. The blue gets darker and darker but I can still see. I can see the emptiness. It is everywhere. Everywhere is emptiness. I can feel the pressure of the water pushing against my body. Against my skull. It makes a high-pitched squeaking sound. Then I see something. The water is clear forever. Clear dark blue. There is something out there. Its grey body weaving back and forth. It is a shark. It is the size of a city bus. It's teeth are filled with chunks of meat. Filled with chunks of white bloody meat and bone. It swims silently closer. It opens its mouth wide. Its mouth is filled with chunks of people. Arms, legs and faces. Pieces of faces. I recognize one of them. It is my father. His face is split open down the middle but it is him. I try to scream but I have no air. I try to move but my whole body is tingling. The feeling you get before you black out. The shark slowly turns sideways to clamp down on my body.

***

I screamed and opened my eyes. It was dark. It took me a second to put it all together again. My eyes adjusted and I saw there was a little bit of light in the sky outside. I stood up in the empty bedroom and walked over to the window. At first I figured I had slept the whole day and it was just the tail end of dusk. I looked up and down the street at all the cookie cutter houses. Most of them were empty but I could see one haole man in an expensive aloha shirt getting into his car with a briefcase and a cup of coffee. He drove right under my window. I heard a rooster in the distance and could smell the morning. I had slept for over seventeen hours. I laid back down on the floor and watched the light slowly crawl across the ceiling.

This is my bedroom. This is my house. I am lying on my carpet.

The world was moving around me. Slow but unstoppable. Like the light across the ceiling. I watched a fly hanging upside down on the popcorn paint. It was still in the shade but the sunlight was creeping up to it. As the edge of the sun hit the fly, it woke up and flew around the room. It took almost an hour until the room was filled with the hot morning sun. I let it warm up my body and burn away all of the aches. The fly finally found the window and began flying into the screen over and over again.

I stood up and walked downstairs.

Two thousand dollars?

How was I gonna come up with two thousand dollars in just a few days? I hadn't been keeping any real track of how much weed I was selling, who I was selling to, or how much money I was making. Mr. Mervin had only given me a pound. I had smoked, sold and given it all away without any real thought. I would have to get my shit together. I would have to focus and think forward a little. The house felt empty. I suddenly wanted to run out of it. Run out of the house and up the street. Run up Makakilo Drive and across Panana Street… run up to my mom and—

I took a deep breath and pushed my thoughts forward. Two thousand dollars… I would need to talk to Mr. Mervin and force him to give me more. Maybe I could get Moon-Dog and his Pearl City crew to sell some. They must smoke weed. Black dudes in Hawaii who rap? The only reason they wouldn't be smoking weed was if they couldn't find any. I started thinking of all the kids I might be able to trust if I fronted them a few extra grams. Two thousand dollars ain't really shit if I smoked a little less and made each day and night about the hustle. If I didn't just float around aimlessly. Two thousand dollars is easy money. Then keep that hustle up and get some furniture and shit. I could see a leather couch and a huge T.V. slowly appear. Then a leather chair and a pool table. Yeah, easy money. I started to feel better. First things first. Shit, shower, brush teeth, buy a fresh change of clothes, go to the school and talk to Mr. Mervin.

***

Everyone was in class by the time I got to the high school. I walked over to O-Building from the parking lot. I starting to think about Cynthia. I hadn't talked to her since we had been together and I didn't know what I would say to her if I did. I started thinking I should start thinking, at least… I laughed at myself and said the sentence out loud: "I was thinking about you but I didn't know what to think so I didn't for awhile then I decided I should start thinking about thinking about you."

I wondered what kind of snappy comeback she would have for that. I was just about to throw it away when I heard screaming.

The trench coat mafia kid was running down the hallway with an M16 machine gun yelling "Everyone will DIE!" I started to chase him when I heard Cynthia scream "Cut! Goddamnit Q!! Get out of my shot!"

I turned around and saw Cynthia standing with a clipboard and Mr. Mervin holding a camera.

"Lana! Why isn't this hallway clear?!" came Cynthia's voice out of a walkie talkie. It was coming out of a little speaker behind me. Lana, a chubby half-Filipino, half-Japanese girl, came running up to me. She also had a walkie talkie and a clipboard.

"Sorry, Sir, but we need you to clear this hallway. We're shooting a movie here," Lana said apologetically and out of breath.

"It's not a fucking movie! It's a vignette!" said Cynthia's voice through the walkie talkie.

"Sorry! Vignette," said Lana to me, then into the walkie, "Sorry Cindy, vignette…"

She then started gently pushing me. "Sorry, Sir, so sorry, we're filming a vignette here, so if you could just stand on the other side of O-Building, please."

"It's a fucking video vignette mother fucker! It's a think-piece on the trappings of a social structure that isolates and ridicules any consciousness that dares to define itself outside of the predetermined human experience!" yelled Cynthia through the walkie talkie as she stomped up to me in her combat boots. "It's not a movie, it's not a story, it's not a video clip, it's not something you of all people would be able to digest without first labeling it with your regurgitated terms and idea molds!"

She was now standing right in front of me with the radio up to her mouth. She started to say more but stopped. She was breathing hard.

"What's it about?" I said.

"I just told you," she said into the walkie talkie.

"Yeah but I couldn't digest it because I've been brainwashed by society. Please stop talking through the radio."

She clipped the radio to her insanely short shorts without breaking eye contact.

Mr. Mervin was walking over with the camera and the trench coat kid. Cynthia and I kept staring at each other, breathing. Lana looked at us with a "what the fuck" look on her face.

"I'm not mad at you," said Cynthia.

"That's good," I said.

"Well, look who it is, dude. I was wondering what became of our great hero," said Mr. Mervin in his unintentional Ned Flanders impersonation. Lana reached forward and waved her hand in front of our faces. That broke the spell. Cynthia looked down and I looked at Mr. Mervin.

"What is up, dude? You wanna help us shoot our little movie, Q?" said Mr. Mervin.

"It's not a fucking movie," mumbled Cynthia.

"You're right, Cyn. Our video vignette, was it? Our little piece about—"

"Stop calling it little. It's a short. It's not little," said Cynthia with her head down, avoiding eye contact with me.

"Our short piece about school bullying—" started Mr. Mervin.

"Yeah, Q's perspective on the topic would be *so* valuable," Cynthia mumbled.

"My thuggish ruggish bone of a head is too stupid to understand sarcasm," I said, imitating her mumble.

"Or to understand the subtle desperation caused by a life whose sole existence is to be a victim of verbal and physical abuse day in and day out by shitheads like you!" she said at the ground.

"I think I can put it together. Let me guess: The short video vignette is a semi-autobiographical fantasy piece about a trench coat kid who is too much of a bitch to stand up for himself so he gets a gun and shoots all the bullies? What a fucking cop-out."

"The vignette is the character's fantasy revenge against the system that didn't include him!" she said, getting louder.

"But he's not revenging the system, is he? He's shooting innocent kids an shit. Why not fucking grow a pair and go shoot up the police station on some terminator shit, or better yet, walk into the fucking government building with the suit-an-tie dudes…" I snapped my fingers. "What am I tryin to say?" I asked Mr. Mervin.

"Politicians?" he answered.

"Yeah. Politicians, the ones who created an maintain the system. Then he'd be making a statement, but this shit right here…" I said, pointing at trench coat kid. "I don't buy it. It's such a… weird psycho bitch move… even for you, Todd… no offense."

"It's Steve," trench coat kid said.

"Like Steven?" I asked.

"Just Steve…" he whimpered with his head down.

"The day Steven gets even with an M16 leavin no one breathin…" I said in a movie trailer voice.

"Oh, that's good!" said Mr. Mervin chuckling.

"Shut the fuck up!" said Cynthia finally looking up at me.

"It's important for us to have a dialog about these things, Cynthia. Q's feelings on individual responsibility in the face of—"

"Both of you shut the fuck up!" she screamed.

She grabbed the camera and started stomp away but then turned and screamed, "I didn't fucking write this movie anyway!"

"It's a vignette!" I yelled back.

"Fuck you!" she yelled with her beautiful back to me as she disappeared into G-Building.

"Why don't you two go with Cynthia and see if we got all the shots we needed," Mr. Mervin said to trench coat kid and Lana. "Q, you left your bag with me the other day. I have it in my car."

Mr. Mervin walked me to his car. He unlocked the passenger side of his faded-blue 86' VW station wagon. I sat inside and I was enveloped by the smell of our weed.

"You should partner up with Cynthia. I bet with her camera work and your writing you two could win an S.A.V.F.A. award and even be in the Hawaii International Film Festival."

"What the fuck is a *safisfa* award?" I said mockingly with my eyes on an old backpack in the back seat. I was sure that was where the smell was coming from.

"It's an award given to local directors and film producers, students who are trying to make their way in the film business. You should write down some of those things you were saying earlier."

"I don't remember what I said." I reached back and grabbed the backpack. He almost tried to stop me but thought better of it. Instead he looked out the windows around the parking lot.

Inside the backpack was about two pounds all bagged up in quarters. I put my face in the bag and inhaled the smell of the wind picking me back up off the ground and flying me around Ewa Beach, Waipahu, Pearl City, Waianae, the whole westside and beyond. Freedom from whatever.

"I can push more than this," I said.

"You need to come back to school. You can hang out in my class if the rest of school is too much right now. There is a catch, though. You have to make movies. You have to come up with stories and shoot them and make art."

"Do I look like a fucking artist to you?! I'm a homeless kid! I'm a fucking homeless drug dealing kid. I already asked you for help. You just want me to make you money. Fuck it! Bizness is bizness right?! So what are we doing?"

"Q, you've got this all wrong, buddio! I am trying to help. You are talented and I—"

"I'm taking this!" I said and stuck the bag under my arm. I started to open the door but he grabbed my arm.

"Q, we should have a serious discussion about our relationship," Mr. Mervin said with a smile.

"What the fuck are you talking about!" I snapped.

Mr. Mervin sat there stunned with his mouth open.

"What the FUCK are you talking about?!" I yelled again. "I'll break your fuckin face!"

"Q! What's wrong? I don't…" He was scared with his hands up, trying to lean as far away from me as possible.

There was a long pause.

"I swear to god, I'll fuckin smash your teeth through the back of your head!" I growled.

"I… meant… our partnership…" he whispered.

I looked at the bag of weed and tried to find a way to grab myself. My mind was a black sky full of little fireflies. I reached up with my arms slowly and gently tried to push them together until I could see an image in the light they gave off. It was Mr. Mervin's scared face. I started to feel my skin again. I took a deep breath.

"Right… partnership… How much you want?" I mumbled.

"A thousand… for this bag and for the last one," he whispered.

I was trying to do math. To break it all down in my head. To think about how much I should give Moon-Dog and his crew, how much for an ounce, how much for a half, how much for a pound. How much is one thousand dollars when I have to come up with two thousand dollars a few days later. Three thousand dollars? How much can I really sell in a few days? Who do I know who should be running low? Am I gonna have to sell nickel bags? How many in how many hours. Three p.m. to ten p.m. is the hot zone. Is that even possible? The fireflies kept exploding in my head. How was I supposed to keep these numbers straight?

"Alright… How much is left?" I asked.

"Enough to keep this going for a while," he said.

"I can handle more at once. Three, four times this," I said.

"Oh Q, the greedy little mouse never gets the cheese," he said.

"How much is left?" I said again.

"You know Q, if you need someone to talk to, I'm a really good listener…"

He sat there with a concerned look in his eyes. His blonde mustache rebelling against his sunburned face.

"It seems like you're going through something, kiddo. This world is a crazy place. As humans we try to make sense of it, we try to build a narrative that can explain it, make it right or make it wrong. We try to fit it into categories, boxes, files, put things on shelves, but sometimes some things won't fit. Something happens and it doesn't fit anywhere, so it just winds up getting stuck in your belly and it makes you sick. Sometimes talking about it can make it unstuck. Sometimes…"

His nose was so sunburnt. It had probably gotten burnt when he moved here years ago and then each new layer of skin got a new burn every day since. There were divots in it. The cartilage under the skin was probably sunburnt. At this point I was sure I was literally looking at sunburnt cartilage. A skeleton a few weeks into the decaying process. The skin was gone and the cartilage was slowly starting to go. Like drying fish in the sun. It was a dead human face drying in the sun. It was talking. But it was dead all except for the eyes. The eyes were wet. Wet, white eyes in a dead skeleton face. I could see those wet white eyes and that skeleton face stuck in the teeth of a monster. A monster swimming up from the darkness. The eyes were alive and they were looking at me. They were looking at me with concern. Concern and love. The dried skeleton face was looking at me with concern and love. Why would a skeleton face love me? Unless it wanted something from me. It's a skeleton face in the mouth of a monster! What would it want? What the fuck would the dried skeleton face want from me?!

"What the *FUCK* do you want from me?!"

Mr. Mervin immediately stopped talking and threw his hands up to protect his face. It was quiet for a moment. I leaned over and punched him in the face. He let out a sound that was half shock and half pain. It was pitiful. We both paused for a moment, not sure of what was happening. Then a wave of anger rushed through me and out of my arm. I hit him over and over. My elbow broke the rear view mirror and kept hitting the windshield over and over again. He tried to cover up but I grabbed his arms with my left hand and punched until his nose was bloody and the waves subsided.

I sat back in the seat and tried to breathe. He sat with his hands over his bloody face crying.

"Let's go to your house and get all of the weed. Then you stay the fuck away from me," I whispered.

***

Mr. Mervin had said he wanted the duffle bags back.

The thought disappeared in my head somewhere between "of course I'll give your bags back" and "go fuck yourself." I was gonna stop and get something to eat but even with the bricks of weed shrink wrapped, duct taped and zipped inside the duffle bags, it stank up my whole car. I had to get this back to my new house. There was usually a Manapua Truck parked on the corner of Kilaha and Fort Weaver, so I stopped by there to grab some fried noodles to hold me over.

There was some shade behind the Manapua Truck. I sat in the car. I watched an old Hawaiian lady buying something from the Manapua Man. She was very old. She had on a nice pink flower mu'umu'u and she had a matching flower in her long, thick, gray-streaked hair. She had a stroller with her. I wanted to wait until no one was ordering so I wouldn't be away from the car for too long.

Across the street was the Ewa Villa Estates. I remembered that this was one of the places Kimo had been talking about when he was breaking shit down in the driveway the day before. People called it "The Garden" as in "The Garden of E.V.E." It was a group of small cement apartment buildings. If you wanted hard drugs—heroin, crack, ice, whatever—you walked in there. Kimo told me not to go in there alone and I definitely wouldn't leave a car filled with weed on the street outside of it. There were places like The Garden all over the island, he had said. Places that at one time had been just rough neighborhoods. Places that were set up to accept government assistance. Of course that's where people sell drugs.

Kimo had said, "All options fit on the table when there ain't many options." I especially remembered that line.

I tried to remember everything else he had told me: "In just a few years these rough neighborhoods turned into some third world shit. Like for real failed-state type shit. Looking like a ghetto in the Philippines. You don't need to have nothin to do with these places. Especially Crystal City. I got somebody in there. His name is Alex. You meet up with him in Waipahu, don't talk to him, don't hang out with him. He gives you my money and you step. Period. You work with the fun stuff, weed and coke. You work in the fun places with the fun people. You ain't really cut out for the drainage ditch shit."

As I tried to remember Kimo's exact words about the kupunas or some shit, the sound of the old lady who was talking story with the Manapua Man threw me off and the memory faded.

"Bumbai she going learn," said the old lady.

"You gotta tell her now and then, cuz…" said the Manapua Man.

"What I going tell her? She tink she knows, that one! She tell me 'Nanny, I'm a grown woman!' and den she go disappear for two weeks!"

"You think she doing da'kine or what? Batu?" asked the Manapua Man.

"Aye ya! I don't know! I no like tink about it! I just tell her, 'My granddaughter is not my daughter! You gotta take care!' But den what? She like scream at me!" said the old lady.

"What can you do?"

"Nahting! Eh you see her, you tell her for come home yeah?"

"You know I will, Aunty," said the Manapua Man.

The old lady finally turned and began pushing the stroller away. She was singing in Hawaiian to the little baby.

Pûpû hinuhinu
Pûpû Hinuhinu e
O ke kahakai kahakai e
Pûpû hinuhinu e

I was just about to get out of my car when a huge man in a giant ti-leaf sunhat jumped in front of my car door and popped his face right outside of the open window.

"Boo!"

I jumped in my seat and swung instinctively out of the window. My fist hit the hat and the man lost his balance and fell into the dirt by the sidewalk. I heard another voice laughing and spun to see a dark, raggedy looking local man in his late forties, early fifties. The man in the hat got up and started dusting off his surf shorts. He took off his hat and he wasn't a man at all.

It was Makalolo!

Except it wasn't. It was a skinnier version. He looked like he had lost almost twenty pounds. His face was drawn out and you could see his cheekbones. There were huge bags under his eyes and he had little red rashes all over his face and arms. He was smiling and his teeth were yellow. I was hesitant to get out of the car because if I did, I would have to give him a hug and I could smell the both of them from where I was.

"Ho brah! You almost wen crack me!" Maka said laughing.

"You scared the shit outta me. What'd you expect?"

I got out of the car, took a deep breath and hugged him. I could feel his bones.

"Brah you lost choke weight!" I said.

"I'm on a diet!" he said laughing and glanced at his old man friend. His friend had dark Cheapo sunglasses and when he laughed his cheeks went all the way up behind the lens. He had no front teeth. I shook his hand and instantly regretted it. His fingernails were filled with black shit and his hands were sticky.

"I'm Q," I said.

He didn't answer. He just smiled and made a weird nervous chuckle sound. I turned back to Maka.

"Where you been, man?! Everyone is asking about you! What's going on?"

"I just no like talk to nobody, yeah? Everyone like give me shit! I cannot already… I just like relax, you know? I just like no stress!" said Maka.

He looked stressed. He looked fucking freaky. His face was frozen in a permanent smile. His eyes were open wide and were darting back and forth behind me and around me. He saw me looking at his eyes and he put his Cheapo sunglasses on and started fumbling with his hat.

"No stress? Good luck with that shit. But for real, where you at though? What you been doing?" I said.

"Just revving brah!! Vroom-vroom!" he said.

His homeless-looking friend started laughing. "Vroom-*vroooom!*"

They were both laughing uncontrollably and Maka leaned on my car for balance.

He stopped laughing right away. He took a long breath in through his nose.

"Whoa brah, you get the chronic eh?!" he said, reaching for one of the duffle bags.

I pushed him away but he tried to laugh it off like it was a game and he pushed back harder.

"Q, I just like see fast kine!" laughed Maka.

His friend put his nasty-ass hand on my shoulder. I spun around and swung a haymaker. If he would have had teeth they would've been knocked out. He fell backwards onto his ass with his nose and mouth bleeding. I squared off on Maka.

"Brah, what you doing?!" Maka said with his hands up.

"Stay away from the fucking car!" I said.

"Brah, what's your problem!? Dis is why we can not hang out wit you. You always like for beat up everyone!" said Maka.

He walked over to his friend and helped him up.

"I'm sorry," I said softly. "Just don't touch the fucking car… please."

Maka's eyes were all over the place.

"Hey listen, I was gonna get some fried noodles or something. You guys want anything?" I asked.

I held out a twenty dollar bill. Maka's eyes got wide. His friend looked instantly healed. Maka leapt forward and snatched the twenty out of my hand.

"Eh tanks ah?! Brada we was jus playing eh?! We should try hang out."

They both started walking fast. They walked right past the Manapua Truck and into the Ewa Villa Estates.

I got back in my car. I wasn't hungry. Kimo was right. Don't fuck with that ice.

CHAPTER 2

THE BOOK OF KIMO

WEEKS WENT BY LIKE days.

Days went by like hours.

Kimo would pick me up or meet me somewhere. I would usually be in the back of the truck with his boys, Siosi and Sleepy. Unless he would say "we need to talk," then I sat in the front with him. "We need to talk" meant he would talk and I would listen. He had been in jail for a while and had only been back for the better part of a year. He had beat someone to death and had been shipped to the mainland to do his time. I could never get any actual details from him about it or anything about his past for that matter. He would only tell me a story about his past if it related to something he was trying to teach me or show me. He would talk to me like it was important. He would say "This is some shit right here! This is important! Check it…" and what followed would be genius.

He had it all written down in ninety-nine cent black and white composition tablets—just like my rhyme books. There would be some quote on the cover that served as a sort of title.

> Life hits you in waves. Some of them will almost kill you. One of them will. You die either way, might as well surf.

Or

> The best true stories are bullshit
> And the best bullshit stories are true.

Or

There is a monster that lives in the space between who you are and who you think you are.

Or

Fast money stays fast… it ain't gonna slow down just cuz you holding it.

Or

God takes care of Fools and Babies, it's hard heads and bloody knuckles for the rest of us…

Or

Cut corners makes downward spirals

Or

Fuck the world. You can't change the world. You can only change your world. But there is only your world, so change the whole world.

Or

Heaven is order. Hell is Chaos. Life is in the middle.

Some of them just had "Chapter" written on the cover, but they were all out of order. "Chapter 4," "Chapter 2," "Chapter 23," "Chapter 9," "Chapter 31"… "Chapter 7" was my favorite so far.

They were a mess but they were genius. He had started them before he went to jail and continued the whole time he was in. They were written over many years with different pens and pencils. Some pages were stapled in and folded over. Some pages were crammed with tiny writing all up sideways in the margins. Some pages would be crossed out but never so much that you couldn't read them.

He said, "Write your shit down. Never throw a thought away. You might come back to it later and discover the way you thought it up was wack but the seed of it was good. Rethink it and replant it, maybe it grows out different."

Some pages looked like my rhyme book. I memorized some of the poems and spit them over hip hop instrumentals to show him how dope they sounded if they were spit like raps.

He told me if I liked them so much I could just have them. I said I could make a whole series of albums called *Chapters from the Books of Kimo.* He made a sour face and said he didn't want his name out there like that. I said I could turn his name into a symbol or an icon. "It sounds dope just like that: *Chapters from the Book of Icon.*"

"You like to dream big, kid. Most of those poems are gibberish. You think it's deep because you smoke too much," he said and laughed. I recorded a lot of them anyway. This was one of my favorites.

#

If you stick a tiny piece of metal in the small hole of an ant hill
The size of a hand fill
Step away and stand still
Behind underbrush
Tree trunks
Large boulders
Etcetera
Remain hush
Within moments
You'll notice a plethora
Of primates staring intently and tentatively
Reaching through the hole that contains the shiny new Bentley
His hand slides through easy because it's empty
Now he's stuck, he can't let go
He's greedy because it's tempting
Unrelenting.
And now the chosen few who rock the mic
Are saying that they all live like the glossy images
And life is what the gimmick is
The limitless piles of cash
And every minute is
Miles of ass
And if we mimic it fast
Were free at last
Kiss my muthafuckin ass
Life is hard
And in the ghetto it's insanity
I plan to be
One of the few
My man and me

Watts ink
The canopy
Randomly
Tossing thoughts
Like blocks
In preschool
Or the penitentiary
Eventually
Both the same thing
This game won't bring
Bling bling
It ain't real
The jewels
The cars
The cash
It ain't real
We're fools
They're stars
They're cast
It ain't real
It's just a shiny piece of metal in the small hole of an ant hill.

#

Some pages held stories that went on for ten or fifteen pages then would disappear, only to reappear twenty pages later or worse fifty pages earlier or sometimes in a different book altogether. Some of the books had spines duct taped to hold over a hundred more pages than it was made to. It was always *how*. How a person should do this. How a person should think about that.

How you should eat.
Just two meals a day. Fuck Breakfast! That's valuable time, use that time to do shit and let your stomach rest. One hand of meat, Half a hand of rice, two hands of dark green salad. Two times a day. Period.

How you should do drugs.

Never do any drug for more than three days in a row. That's for weed too and drinking. You need to dry out and get crispy.

Don't drink on an empty stomach.

Drink a glass of water between each beer.

Don't sit down after three drinks. Stay standing.

If you're out, don't drink more than six beers until you know where you're going.

Don't drink anything the bartender has to spend time to make.

If you're gonna drink hards, drink hards. Don't switch it up.

Don't drink in the morning. Your stomach should be empty anyway so that's a double rule.

Don't sniff a line fatter than your pinky.

Make sure you use both nostrils.

If you start grinding your teeth chill out for awhile.

If you're gonna drink, smoke and sniff, then space it out. I call it the rollercoaster. Drink until you slur, sniff until your talking straight again. Once you're talking straight, sniff until you start grinding your teeth. Then smoke a joint to relax you back down. Don't ride that rollercoaster for more than three days. Double rule.

Don't cook the coke and smoke it. That's crack. Only bitch ass muthafuckas smoke crack.

Don't use speed or do nothing with needles or pop any pills. Period. And stay away from this new shit. Batu, or Ice. Haoles call it Meth. Don't fuck with it. It's like speed. it's not fun. When you're on it you can't eat, you can't sleep and you can't fuck. That's three of the top top biological goals of any living creature. What's the point?

And every few weeks just don't do anything for 7 days. Nothing. Just eat and sleep and train. Period.

How you should train.

Stretch and run a mile and do thirty squats, thirty push-ups, thirty pull-ups, and thirty sit-ups on days when you ain't goan do shit. That's just like baseline fitness.

Surf at least twice a week.

Box twice a week, Heavy Bag, Speed Bag, Jump rope, spar.
Hit some weights three times a week, Bench, squat, t-bar, pull-downs, curls, tri-extensions.
Hike a mountain once a week.
Oh yeah and fuck like it's an Olympic sport! Like for real, hard!
Like for an hour and a half, five times a week!

How you should dress.

Don't wear trendy brand name shit.
If it's got a logo on it bigger than your fist they should pay you to wear it cuz you advertising for them.
Dress just enough to be in style. In style enough to not be clowned on.
Buy like five nice black shirts, five nice grey shirts, five nice white shirts, three pairs of jeans, ten pairs of shorts, three pairs of shoes, black, white and grey. Two pairs of slippers, one for surfing one for regulars, Couple of high end button downs, one pair of nice slacks. Done. Switch'em all around. Nobody says shit and you don't have to figure out what to wear everyday.
Fashion is wasted focus.

Handle your own shit.

Brush your teeth. Clean your house. Wash your clothes. Fold your clothes. Put your clothes away. Wash your cars. Wash your muthafuckin ass. Nobody cares. Nobody gives a fuck. Nobody. Why would they? Why should they? Handle your own shit. It's easy.
Make a fucking list.
Brush teeth
Drink a glass of water
Stretch
Exercise
Shower
Call Dude about that shit from last week
Wash clothes
Mop floors
Eat lunch
Go see garlic and check on the thing with forehead
Surf

Eat dinner

Drink Beer

Fuck

That way if you smoke a joint, all you have to do is follow the list. Some of the things on the list will have their own list. If getting to the end of a list gets you even one tiny ass notch closer to the shit you want then fuck it. It's a good list. The list is yours. It's a map to the place you wanna be at. Don't matter what map anybody else is following to get where they gotta go. They don't care about you and you don't care about them. They ain;t ahead of you. They are following a different fucking map. One day your map says "Call that chick about that empty warehouse in Kakaako" and six months later your map says "pick up fifty grand from the auto shop in Kakaako". Your map could say "call the Haole guy at the liquor commission for a license" and next year it could say "meet up with leilani at the strip club for a drink". It can, but it won't if you don't. Handle your own shit.

Don't talk shit.

If something is not true don't say it. Shit talkers and liars live in a dark cold lonely hole. The walls are covered with the slippery shit they constantly vomit up every time they try to cry for help. If you get too close to a liar you can fall in the hole with them. Their only hope is time. In time if they close their mouth and don't say shit then all the nasty parasite encrusted excrement will harden. The liar can climb out and take a shower. But as soon as they open their mouth again some shit's gonna fly out and start the whole process again.

Practice truth. What is Truth? It's constantly changing like a hot chick with your credit card. You have to look for the truth. You have to focus on it when you catch a glimpse of it. You have to try to describe what it is to you from where you are with your words. It has to be your truth and your words. It has to be how you understand it. Otherwise keep your mouth shut so shit doesn't fly out of it.

How to pick up girls.

You don't. The whole shit where you're gonna walk up and say something that makes her suddenly want to sleep with you is bullshit. Girls choose who they want. From that point on, you're just trying not to change her mind. It's up to her, then it's up to you. Now, you can trick a girl into sleeping with you. Lie and manipulate a situation and all that, like a pimp. But a Pimp is a liar, the loneliest thing anyone could ever be. A pimp masters one or two buttons of the most basic Human behaviors of the weak and vulnerable. Then just pushes them over and over again. Plus, any girl who falls for that shit you don't want. And if you do want her, if she is dope, she ain't fall for you, she fell for who you were pretending to be, that's lose lose. Get your shit together and the girls will brush their hair to the side and smile and show you their neck. Then you walk over and say Hi. Period.

How to read people.

Most people do the same shit. They are the same. Very few people are different. If you figure out one, you have figured out most. But you can't tell'em. Everyone believes they are different. They are not. They do the same things as everyone else. And they do it over and over and over again. They move in patterns, in circles just like fish or dogs or cats. Try to chase a house cat around the house. It has a bed it always hides under or a t.v. stand it always runs behind. When the cat's not looking, cover all it's hiding spots then chase it again. It goes directly to it's spot then panics, runs around in a scramble and goes back to the same hiding spot again as if it will be open on the second attempt. So if you watched where it went the first time, You know where it will go the second time. People's minds do the same thing.

Put them under a little pressure and watch them close. They will show you who they are when their hiding place is covered. Watch how they walk, how they stand, How they sit. Where do they sit, when they sit? Where do their eyes go when they tell a story? Where do their eyes go when they listen to a story? If you're trying to read someone, tell them a story when their friend walks away. Then, when their friend comes back and sees you two laughing or stunned or sad, tell him to tell his friend the story you just told. What they got from the story and how they say it back is gold. What details do they remember or not remember or add? Then push'em. Pick a very random inconsequential detail (Blue Mustang) (Ordered a Big Mac) and change it and then correct them even though they were right.

What do they do?

Do they fold completely and apologize and stop telling the story? Was it because they doubted themselves instantly? Or knew you were wrong but didn't have the belly to correct you and were now too flustered to just move on. Either way that person would only be good for simple tasks.

Do they argue with you and will not continue until the issue is resolved? Probably more trouble than they're worth. Stuck on random details. Their need to be right outweighs the goal. Sooner or later you will make a mistake or a bad call and they will call it 'slippin' and be stuck on it. Even if they ain't got the balls to confront you they will talk shit about all the little shit you did wrong and it'll spread through your whole crew until it fucks with the bottom line or worse.

Do they pause and study your eyes for a second then correct themselves as if they were wrong and then continue? This is a good sign. That pause meant they knew you were wrong and needed to think and study you to figure it out. They are thinking "Is he bugging? He just told me the story? Is it a bullshit story? Is he fucking with me? Why? That's weird but I should keep going and keep a file on that shit." That is a soldier. That is a fully functioning person that can adjust a plan, see its mistakes and move forward. They will even cut you a little slack for human error.

It went on and on like this.

He would also talk to me this way for hours or for however long he had. He didn't talk like this to everyone. Even if I got bored I had to listen. Not only because he was Kimo and he would fuck me up if I was disrespectful but because he was right. I knew everything he said had been tried many times and then boiled down to the simplest, most efficient way of thinking or doing something. I started to look forward to hearing what he had to say about everything.

He knew about surfing, but not just how to surf. How to catch the waves and the culture and mana behind it. Its history starting with the Hawaiian ali`i. How when Duke Kahanamoku won the Olympic gold medal for swimming he went around the world to Australia, California, and Japan touring with the gold medal and showing them how to choose the trees, cut them and shape them into surf boards. That Duke also was the first to introduce the flutter kick to competitive swimming. No one had even thought of kicking like that!

He knew about religion. All of them. He read all of the bibles. Old Testament, King James and the Bishops' Bible, New Testament. Three different versions. Two different translations of the Qur'an. All five books of the Torah. The Tripitaka and The Pali Canon on the teachings of Buddha. Different spiritual practices from Africa and some oral teachings of the Native Americans. He talked about some dude named Joseph Campbell. He talked about how he was trying to buy original copies of writings from Sumer and some religion called Zoroastrianism.

He talked for hours about politics. But not about politicians. He talked about policies. Mostly on how they were specifically written to keep us in our place. He said getting mad about that was misguided. He said our social structure is based on competition. Always has been since caveman shit. The more you win, the more power you get. The more power you get, the more you win. That power includes being able to change rules. Winners keep winning and losers keep losing. But if the winners change the rules too much and shit is too hard for the losers then the losers kill the winners. There are always more losers than winners and they can always kill the winners. Always.

He knew about relationships, health, or whatever. No matter what it was, his opinion was the right one. But it wasn't smart. It was truth. He was the truth. It was almost like he had a cheat code to Street Fighter or even better Mortal Kombat, "down, up, left, left, right, down, 212, down, up."

He knew when something was about to go down at least five minutes before it was gonna happen and he could tell how it was gonna pop off almost to a tee. So much so that he could outline it, give instructions and say the actual words that would be said, like he went five minutes into the future, took notes then came back.

He would say "Yo Q, put your chain and your watch in your front pocket. The local girl in the daisy dukes is gonna slap that haole marine and his drunk popolo friend is gonna push her. The floor is wet behind her. She's probably gonna fall and her tita friend is gonna go off on the marines and say some shit like "all you faka's is fagats! Dats why you wen join, so you can suck each ottas boto" and make enough of a scene for all the moks in the back to come over. The lights are gonna come on and the four guys working security tonight ain't enough. It's gonna be a crazy stampede of punching and pushing."

In less than five minutes you hear a crash as a cute little hapa girl falls backwards into a table. Her huge Samoan girlfriend starts yelling and slapping a big popolo marine. He is not sure what to do so he tries to hold her arms to keep from getting hit. All her friends start yelling and throwing drinks on him. About twenty local dudes from the V.I.P. start pushing their way through the crowd to get to the local girls. "You fuckin panties like scrap wit chicks?!"

"Give'em cracks!"

"Yo bro, we don't want no trouble!"

"My buddy didn't hit her! She just attacked him!"

Then *CRACK!* Someone gets knocked the fuck out! Drinks are flying. The lights come on and the music stops. People are pushing and shoving. Once we get outside he would look at me and smile.

I would just shake my head.

He taught me how to steal cars. Sounds simple but it's not the same for each car. Ford Mustangs for example have a different steering column lock than Mazda RXZ. In Hawaii you steal Toyota and Nissan. The parts are interchangeable. They are super easy cars to steal, but Kimo didn't like that we locals were stealing each other's cars. He said the Japanese sedans and hatchbacks and coupes, especially the low-end Nissan Sentra or the Toyota Tercel, belong to locals. Their insurance doesn't always cover theft. They use that car to go to work. If it's all tricked out you can steal it, but if it looks like a family car leave it alone. He wanted the convertible Ford Mustangs. He said Uncle had an arrangement with the rental car companies. When a car had more than 60,000 miles on it, they could get more from insurance then they could selling it to the used car dealers. So Kimo walked us through how to steal the Ford Mustang.

Stick a screwdriver in the driver-side door frame until you can get your hands in enough to get a grip. Bend it until you can unlock it. Pry open the steering console and pull out the ignition housing. Pull out the little black spring compartment then push it down with the screwdriver. The steering wheel will still be locked. Put the seat back and use your legs to break the steering wheel lock by turning the wheel to the left. Kimo's friend in Waianae had a chop shop. Bring in a Mustang, leave with five hundred dollars. Simple.

***

The same day I had taken all the weed from Mr. Mervin, I drove to Pearl City High School and parked in the back of the parking lot. I sat on the hood of my car, smoked a cigarette and waited for the bell to ring. I needed Moon-Dog and the Pearl City Crew, but as I sat there waiting for the bell to ring, I started to panic.

I should've stashed the weed at my place first. That had been my original plan, but seeing Maka had shook me and I wound up just driving straight here. It was the dumbest shit ever and I knew it the moment I drove up Waimano Home Road. I pretended holding my breath would turn me invisible while waiting at the light by the Pearl City Police Station in my ghetto Mazda GLC hatchback with no license, an expired registration and no safety check. I thought that turning down the music would be suspicious so I left it bumpin. My whole car smelled like the inside of Snoop Dogg's fingernails. Now, sitting in a high school parking lot didn't feel any better.

I flicked my cigarette and decided that I should leave, get something to eat, sleep and try again tomorrow. Just when I was about to bounce, the bell rang. Hundreds of kids swarmed the parking lot in seconds.

"*Quuuoo!*" Suga-C's voice echoed through the parking lot.

"Whut up, muthagucka!!" yelled Moon-Dog.

"Muthafucking *Quuuooo!*" whooped D-40.

Moon-Dog, Suga-C and D-40 were yelling and throwing punches and jabs in the air and laughing from across the parking lot. They hadn't seen me since I had beat the shit out of Kevin McKenzie and were doing a Shakespearean reenactment. I threw my arms up but stayed sitting. In the time that it took them to get to me, I rehearsed my sales pitch. I would tell them nothing about where the drugs came from but I would give them a fair profit margin. I would incentivize productivity by offering bonuses in the form of reduced-price re-ups and vibrant after-hours company retreats. When they got to my car I was confident that I was ready to convince them.

"Ayo, ya'll wanna sell weed for me? You'll make money and fuck bitches…"

***

We had gotten into a rhythm in just a few weeks.

I would basically get high all day and listen to music and write rhymes and then go into the Concrete Rainbow. That was our name for Waikiki and Downtown Honolulu. Probably because the Hilton Hawaiian Village Resort had a painting of a huge rainbow on the ocean side of the hotel. Me and the Pearl City crew would catch the number 50 city bus into town. We would be in the back of the bus rapping and joking. Me or Moon-Dog or Suga-C would start rapping and D-40, the huge chubby popolo kid, would start dancing. He looked like Biggie Smalls. Especially after that fight with Kevin when I first saw him. Kevin had broken his eye socket when he clocked him so now D-40 had a lazy eye. He always wore the same Hornets basketball jersey. He said he washed it every night. He must've been telling the truth because he sweat like a faucet. He sweat like if a faucet was over his head and pouring water down his face and all over his clothes. Constantly. All day, all night. Water flowing in sheets down to his shoes. What made it worse was he started dancing every single time one of us started rapping. He could really dance too! I said he was born too late cuz if he was a few years earlier when rap groups had dancers he would've killed it. We'd all be in the back of the bus freestylin, boombox blastin, D-40 doing the robot or the wop or whatever the fuck he was doing. Mostly we would laugh. We would laugh so much.

We would walk through Waikiki talking to Japanese tourist girls and selling weed and coke to American and Australian tourist dudes until around midnight. Next we'd make our rounds at a few of the high-end spots like The Wave, Maharaja, Blue Zebra, The Point, Eurasia, Liquids, or college clubs like Moose McGillicuddy's. Once Kimo introduced me to all the bouncers we didn't have to worry about dress codes, lines or cover charge, but I still usually had the crew hang outside. I blended in but all of us together stood out. It wasn't really a problem. Moon-Dog, Suga-C,

D-40 and the rest of the popolo Crew couldn't stand the music and Siosi, Sleepy and the rest of Kimo's muscle didn't like these "fancy kine places" anyway. We sometimes hit the gay bars like Fusions and Hamburger Mary's if we were having a tough time selling, but my crew acted like just going in would turn them gay. They wanted to hit the strip clubs like Femme Nu, Pure Platinum, and Rock-Za. Kimo used to say, "One dollar can put you in her pocket either way. If she gives it to you, you're her pimp; if she takes it from you, you're her trick. She can only see two things. So watch your money."

We would stay at the strip clubs until they closed around four a.m. After that we would follow the strippers to Baby Dolls or Club Alley Cat. Strippers bought so much weed but they were silly. They never bought more than an eighth at a time. They would say, "I don't wanna get too messed up" or "I don't really have to buy weed cuz somebody always just gives it to me" but thirty minutes later they'd come back and buy more. I tried to fuck them all, but local girls were sealed up tight and were usually connected to Maryanne one way or another. Haole, popolo and Latina girls were easy. They were all on a circuit: L.A., Las Vegas, New York and Miami. Every two months they switched out.

Once we were out of drugs, we would steal a few cars (that's why we took the bus—so we could steal cars on the way back) and race back to the westside. Very fast. If we crashed it didn't matter. I swear to god Moon-Dog would crash on purpose. We would bump the cars on the freeway going eighty miles an hour. We would drive so close they would almost be touching, then some of us would climb from one car to another. If we couldn't find enough Mustangs, we would steal whatever and then just set it on fire at Huabush in Ewa Beach or deep on the west side past Third Dips.

Even if on the rare occasion we spent too much in a night and couldn't find a decent car to steal, we could just straight up rob the tourists. Kimo strongly urged us not to, though. "Tourists are gold," he said. "The whole thing is about the tourists." He would start spouting numbers and shit.

He would say: "Coming out of the 1950s, Hawaii's Gross Domestic Product moved from agriculture—sugarcane, pineapple, and whatnot—to tourism. Ain't that some shit. The whole reason Hawaiian's land got stolen, so that the occupiers could sell an agricultural product to the U.S. without paying foreign taxes, disappears in less than thirty years. And now eighty-five percent of Hawaii's G.D.P. is tourism. The land gets stolen and then we gotta bring a towel and pineapple water to the people who stole it… Shit… that's a trip. Don't fuck with those tourists though. You bang'em and it's the wrong one or fuck up and put one in the hospital, they gonna shut down the city lookin for you. Dead serious! This is important! That will fuck up Uncle's real money. You fuck with Uncle's real money, your charred body will be found in a burnt-up car in Waianae."

I got the point. Rob tourists gently, and only when necessary.

When Kimo said I had to meet a few people, a few people meant everyone on the Island. He knew everyone. Everyone was important. Everyone and everyone that everyone knew. He would say: "What if you are talking to an aunty and she is super sad that her sister's daughter's friend is gonna get fired soon. So what? Even if you wanted to help, what could you do? Ask her why and listen. It's because her husband left. Now she gotta work two extra hours a day but her after-school program only goes to four pm. But what if you knew that a friend of yours has a brother whose girlfriend's mom runs a family daycare in her house only about a mile away. How many people get something from you just listening and remembering?"

Shit like that didn't make any sense to me. We sell drugs. We steal cars. We run numbers and we hold dog and cock fights. We are criminals. But I kinda understood how if you do favors for people they are grateful. Maybe he meant they're less likely to tell the cops shit or they can owe you something in the future.

"Remember when we first met? We were eating and Aunty Janice told me they cut off her electricity?" he asked.

"Yeah… sorda," I lied.

He smacked me in the head.

"I asked her if I could park my friend's car in her carport? Remember?" he said patiently.

"Oh yeah!"

"Do you remember where I told you to park the mustang you stole the other night?"

Suddenly it all made sense. A favor for a favor. I knew for a fact it was more than that for him. He made this dorky ass smile when he figured out some clever way to help someone. To me it just seemed like a lot of other people's bullshit to keep in my head. Especially when my head was filled with clouds and clouds of Pali Purple. That's what people were calling my weed. It made me nervous at first. I kept insisting it was from the Big Island and it was called Kona Gold. But it was more purple than yellow and it was more of a functioning-laughing high than Kona Gold. Kimo seemed to buy the whole story about me getting it from my dad on the Big Island. It had been a few months and he never asked me again after I paid him the two thousand dollars, which included me staying at his place with no electricity. I handed him a brown Foodland grocery bag with the cash. All he said was, "You can't put it in an envelope? This is fucking ghetto…"

I wasn't sure how often I would need to do that but I didn't care. I didn't know how much money I was making and I didn't care. Money was not a thing. Even after paying Kimo. There was always more than I was spending. I would buy clothes, wear them and throw them away. I bought two cars in three weeks: a 1988 Toyota Tercel because it was dawn and I was hungover and I didn't want to ride the bus home from Waikiki. It was on the side of the street and the owner was drawing the price on the window. I jumped off the bus and bought it just to drive home. And I bought a brand new Honda Prelude. I bought that one when I had come out of the Zippy's in Waipahu and my hoopty-ass Mazda GLC wouldn't start. I just left the Mazda in the parking lot like "fuck it." As I was walking to the bus stop, I saw the Prelude on the Honda car lot across the street. I walked in and gave them whatever I had in my pocket. It was like three or four grand. I signed a shit ton of paperwork and drove out. I threw the paperwork out the window as I left. Car payment? Yeah right…

I was giving a few ounces a week to Moon-Dog and the Pearl City crew to handle Pearl City High School and the rest of the area. Cynthia's goofy big-for-nothing popolo friend was pushing a few ounces at Campbell High and Ewa Beach. No one fucked with him because he was with me. No one fucked with me because I was with Kimo. No one fucked with Kimo.

***

"Hoy!"

I snapped out of that thought and stared blankly towards whoever had made that sound.

"Wake up…" said the hapa Tom Selleck.

He was pointing towards the horizon. Then I saw all of the surfers lay down on their boards and start paddling as fast as they could. It was a monster outside set. Kimo was already set up and the first wave of the set started to lift him up into the air. He stood up in a super crouch and slid down the wave like a rock skipping over the water. He bottom-turned and curved back up to the top. It was graceful. He cut back just as I was paddling over the top and spayed me. Kimo was playfully riding these waves of death while I was in my final minutes on this Earth.

I saw the next wave in the set and knew instantly. This was the one. I was in the right spot.

I turned around and began paddling. Fear was gripping me. Trying to freeze my arms and back and neck. I forced myself to breathe and measure my strokes so that I would be in the right spot as the wave rolled underneath me. The ocean in front of me began to drop away like I was going up on an elevator.

I was in the perfect spot.

The last jolt of fear sparked in me as I realized if I stopped paddling, maybe it would just pass under me.

That bitch-ass thought was instantly replaced by the knowledge that this was only the second wave in the set. Paddling for this one and not catching it would leave me in the break zone for however many there were behind it. No, the only chance at making it out alive was to commit. I sprint paddled until I was looking down a wall of water that was over thirty feet high.

I felt the moment. It grabbed me and I thought it was going to pitch me over the falls. I stood on the board and crouched just as I went flying down the wave.

I was trying to bottom turn, but I was going so fast. My turn wasn't sharp enough. By the time I was heading back up the wave, I was in the wrong spot and I didn't have enough speed. The wave pitched over my head and I was stalled inside of a massive barrell.

There was a moment. A second of awareness. A second of realizing how beautiful and rare it was to see this amount of power from this perspective and also realizing that there was no way to stop what was about to happen.

In a last ditch effort I tried to dive into the wave, hoping I could punch through the back of it. On smaller waves this works. Instead, the wave simply absorbed me into itself and rolled me up over the top. I felt weightless for three or four seconds as me and thousands of gallons of water flew through the air.

We came crashing down and the impact of my body hitting the rushing water below combined with the pounding of the water from above knocked from me whatever air I had been trying to save for the hold down. The time I would be able to stay underwater just went from three minutes to a mere thirty seconds. I could feel the wave was going to try and send me back over the falls and I knew I wouldn't make it a second time. I pulled and kicked in an effort to punch through the back of the wave, praying that it would have less power after the initial break.

It grabbed me again. This time it folded me backwards and my left heel kicked me hard in the back of the head.

Now I was in the white wash. It was strong and violent. It twisted and bent my body. It pushed me down and down and down. My right leg was still attached to the surfboard and was getting yanked in every direction. It was only a matter of time before the leash snapped or my hip came out of its socket. I reached for my ankle to try and undo the leash or at least hold my leg.

Then something snapped. I felt the energy of the waves disappear. With my last seconds of consciousness, I swam up to the surface. The hiss of the foam dissipating was as loud as that room full of snakes Indiana Jones got trapped in.

But I could breathe.

My leash had not snapped. My board had. All that was still attached to me was about a foot and a half of the tail. With numb and tingly hands I reached down into the water and shakily undid my leash. I saw the next wave in the set less than thirty seconds away, curling and reflecting the rising sun. I also heard yelling.

"Brah I cannot just let the fucka drown!" shouted the lifeguard on a jet ski pulling a floating rescue board with handles.

"He not going drown! Jus wait!" Kimo yelled back.

They were arguing about two hundred feet to my left in the channel while I treaded water as calmly as possible, trying to take slow, measured breaths to get ready for this next wave. The wall of white wash was at least ten feet high. As it reached me I took a deep breath and dove down as far as I could before it began to pull me back up. I fought it with long frog strokes like swimming up a rushing river. Its energy passed and I popped my head back up.

"See brah, what I told you?! Go back inside the tower and finish your breakfast!" yelled Kimo.

"Whatever brah, dis my job, ah? I not disrespecting you Kimo! I no like no trouble but dis my job brah, I cannot jus let dis fucka drown!" lamented the lifeguard.

"Look brada, I stay right here. He not going drown. I just like him swim it out. I stay teaching him sumting!" Kimo said.

"I gonna stay right here too brada, I gotta…"

The next wave was on me and I did the same thing. I repeated this for the next four waves and each time was working myself closer and closer to the shore. Each time I could hear Kimo and the lifeguard arguing.

As I climbed up onto the sand I realized my head was bleeding. I sat down and dug a shallow hole in the sand next to me and started throwing up salt water.

"I no can just let somebody drown, yeah?! You know, ah?" pleaded the lifeguard.

"Yeah, no worries brah," said Kimo

"No disrespect yeah, Kimo?" the lifeguard asked.

"I said no worries," said Kimo dismissively.

He walked up to me and grabbed me by my hair and dragged me up the beach. I stood up the best I could but I was still throwing up and couldn't get my balance.

"How was that?! You faka!" he was saying over and over in my ear till we got to his truck.

He punched me in the stomach and dropped me on the ground. I leaned against his huge right front tire. The sun had fully risen and it was hot. I sat in the shade of the truck on the gravel trying to feel if I had gotten out all the salt water. Kimo slammed his board in the back and then just stood there looking towards the sun and mountains. I watched him out of the corner of my eye and tried to be as quiet as possible.

"I don't know what to do about you," he said in a deep almost-whisper.

His Pidgin accent had disappeared.

He came over to me and sat down in the sand and dirt and leaned back on the car tire opposite me. He wasn't completely in the shade. The sun lit his face and head, giving him a god-like glow. A gangsta god. "Kimo: The God of Gangstas," I chuckled to myself.

"What about this is funny?" he asked softly.

"Nah just, sitting there in the sun like that, you look…" I whimpered.

"What?"

"Like, gangsta… like a gangsta go—"

"This fucking 'gangsta' stuff is ridiculous. It's part of the problem with you. You got this stupid ass fantasy that's like, a frame or a lens you're looking through. It's narrow and it's distorting everything and it's cutting shit off to the point that you really don't see much," he said.

"I don't… under—"

"Stand… right… listen. You almost died. Why?" he asked.

I threw up more salt water and sat hunched over, spitting and drooling for a while, and he sat patiently waiting.

"Because the waves were too big?"

"Why were the waves too big?"

"Cuz the swell—"

"No, the waves weren't too big. Me and Uncle Domino, Kaikani, Petey, we were ripping. Why did *you* almost die?" he asked again.

"I wasn't used to your board. I usually surf on a—"

He leaned forward and smacked me upside the head. Not very hard. He sat back and spoke in the same softness.

"Stop lying. Why did you almost die?"

"The waves were too big because…" I could feel tears starting and I stopped talking. No way I was going to cry in front of him.

"The waves were too big for *you*," he said simply.

I nodded yes.

"Why would you paddle out into waves that were too big for you?"

I couldn't talk. I couldn't shake my head to show "I don't know" because if I did, tears might fall. I forced myself to face him. I forced myself to not look away. To look him in his disapproving eyes.

"Because you had to. Because you lied about being able to surf monster waves to me to everyone who would listen. When I told you it was hard and that it takes many, many years of surfing and knowledge and skills and all that shit, you doubled down and was like 'I don't know maybe it's just that I'm a natural cuz I surfed fifty-foot waves one time in California…' How do you think that sounded now that you been out on a big day?"

He waited for a real answer. I wiped my face and was able to get out one word.

"Stupid…"

"Stupid. Right. And honestly this ain't even that big. This is maybe fifteen feet Hawaiian. Imagine who you would have to be to surf fifty feet. That's twenty-five feet Hawaiian. Do you think the person who can do that is a fifteen-year-old bullshitting runaway from California?" he asked.

"I'm not from California, I'm from Makaki—"

He smacked me in the head again. This time a little harder.

"How do I know what to think of you? How do I know what's true and what's bullshit. If I wanted to show you how to surf big waves or anything, how would I know where to start? I wouldn't. I can't show you anything. You already know everything. All you muthafuckin kids now walkin around talkin this fake gangsta shit. "Act like you know." But if you actually do "act like you know," you never really know! I can't do anything with that. I can't let you hang with us. I can't bring you in. I can't give you a job and a place to sleep and eat. I can't show you how we run this shit. I can't. You're a bullshitter. Bullshitters need to be alone. Or with other bullshitters. They stand around bullshitting each other all day."

"I'm not a bullshitter."

I looked him in the eye. It took everything I had. I was cold by then sitting there in the shade. I was shivering and sick, but I looked him in the eye and repeated it.

"I'm not a bullshitter."

"You are," he said quietly, then he looked away. He watched the waves for a while. I stared at him until my eyes burned. When I blinked, tears rolled down my face. I wiped them off and sneezed. Huge gobs of salt water and snot came out my nose. Kimo got up and grabbed a towel from the back of the truck and handed it to me. He stayed standing looking down at me.

"Come on, I'll take you back to Ewa Beach, get you something to eat and we'll go our separate ways," he said.

I stood up and pushed him hard. He wasn't ready and fell back against the side of the truck, turning sideways to catch his balance.

"I'm not a fucking bullshitter," I said louder.

I had my fists up. He looked at them and smiled a little. He was thinking. He almost looked proud. He put his hands up slightly in surrender and made a reassuring face.

"Hey, you know how this fight would end."

"I am not a fucking bullshitter," I said again.

"It would end the same way you surfing big waves would end." He paused and waited for me to think it through. I did and I kept my hands up.

"Why did you almost die today?" he asked again.

I had never seen the way he was looking at me before. Not on a man. He was pushing me towards something. I couldn't understand why he would call me a liar but then stand there like a loving dad teaching his son to ride a bike. I couldn't understand. I didn't like anything about what was going on. There was a knot in my throat.

Even if I wanted to answer, I couldn't. I just wanted to punch him for making me feel this way. I wanted to punch him. I knew he could demolish me, but I could get one punch. That would be worth it. One punch for thinking he can teach me some bullshit. Some bullshit about bullshitting. Everybody is bullshit. Everyone is a fucking liar. Teachers, politicians, mutherfucking firemen, parents—*everyone*! Who is he to teach me about lying? Who is he to teach me anything about anything? He's not my dad. My stepdad ain't my dad. Even my dad is not my dad. My dad is bullshit. No one can tell me shit.

I swung it as fast as I could to get it in before he knocked me out. It landed square on his left cheekbone. He didn't try to block or move or anything. He just took it. He blinked his eyes a few times and rolled his head around.

That was as far as my anger could take me. I had no more. I put my arms down and waited for him to kill me. This was Kimo. No one wins a fight with Kimo.

"Why did you almost die today?" he asked softly.

I looked at the sand and dirt. He wasn't going to use his fists to beat me. He would use his words to beat me.

"Because the waves were too big… for me."

"Why did you paddle out when you knew you would probably die?"

"I didn't want you to think I was lying."

"But you were lying."

"Yes."

"Did you know you were lying?"

"Yes."

"Well, there you go. You're not so far down the road that you can't even tell if you're lying or not. You got some balls, kid. I'm for real. Paddling into death so that you don't have to be called a liar… that balls."

He took a step closer and he patted my head. I didn't like it. I turned and faced the beach and the cool salty air helped me take a deep breath.

"There is another way to not be called a liar. For you, it will take more balls than paddling out into these waves."

I closed my eyes so that I could roll them and be sure he wouldn't see it even though he was still standing behind me. I couldn't understand or stomach this, but I had nowhere to go and no more fight.

"Why did you lie about this?" he asked.

I didn't answer. He smacked me in the back of the head.

"Why did you lie about this?" he asked again patiently.

"Because… you surf… big waves… and…" I stopped because the truth was pathetic.

"Right," he said. "It's cool man, I already know why. You need to know why. Do you know why?"

"Yes."

"I think your cool as fuck, kid. You're brave, you can fight, and when you're not bullshitting, you're funny as hell, and I haven't met anyone as smart as you since… I don't know—you're smart! If you really do know why you are a fucking liar, then you can stop being a liar. Right?"

"I'm not a fucking—"

I stopped talking.

"Why are you a liar?"

An ocean breeze blew up the sand. I breathed it in deep through my snotty nose. A feeling came over me. *And sometimes when the wind blows…* Goosebumps spread all over my body. Kimo was starting to say something about Native Hawaiians' or Native Americans' hearts being square. I wasn't listening. I could hear the dry grass behind me begin to rustle as the same strange breeze that filled me began to roll through it and up the mountains. I saw my dad kneeling in front of me. Looking me in the eye. Patting me on the head. He was talking softly. He was asking me for something. My babysitter was sitting on the couch naked holding the little blanket my mom would use at night when her feet got cold. She was holding it over her breasts. My dad's breath smelled bad as he was asking me to do something.

He was asking me to lie.

He was telling me what to say to my mom. He was telling me it was up to me. If I didn't lie she would leave and then it would be my fault. The memory swirled and slowly spun around me and my father until he wasn't talking about the babysitter. He was asking me to lie about something else. He was next to me but his voice was far away. It sounded like it was coming through an old shitty speaker. An old shitty drive-in movie speaker that you clip to your door. We were in his room now and he was right next to me but his voice was so strange. I could hear the words. The pauses, the inflections, but they didn't make sense, they didn't form anything in my memory. There was no memory of understanding what was said. I focused on the words. I rewound them and played them again slowly. Syllable by syllable until other pieces of the memory started to slowly take shape. There were curtains. I wasn't looking at my father. I was looking at the curtains. The light breeze was coming in through the window and pushing them slowly up the wall. Brown, sheer, billowing curtains. I rewound the words and played them again. The breeze was pushing the curtains slowly up the wall. Billowing and reaching up the wall. I was afraid they would get caught in the ceiling fan. The bedroom door was slowly being pushed by the wind. I rewound the words and played them. The wind turned into a violent gust carrying sand and dried grass and it pulled the curtains off the wall and slammed the door. Suddenly I was outside of the room. The door was locked. I blinked and saw Kimo still talking.

"...the heart because it's sharp and square, if you lie it turns in your chest just a little. It hurts. That lets you know lying is bad. If you ignore that pain and shit and keep lying, it keeps spinning until it eventually spins all the way around. It tears up your guts until it's able to spin around and around without any problems. And then you can't even tell your lying...

That's some shit right, cuz—"

"I get it!" I said.

"The square heart shit?" he asked.

I turned to face him.

"No, that don't make no fuckin sense. I'm sayin I won't lie to you no more."

"Okay, this is important. Lies have power. They build and they grow and they have children. They are infectious and addicting. Nothing that is built on a lie can stand on its own without more lies. Nothing that grows out of a lie can be healthy. It can only be sick. Lies require constant attention and energy. One lie will grow into a tangled jungle of thorns that you will spend the rest of your life running through blind. Don't lie. Ever. About anything. Once you can do that, then you can start talking and what you say will be the truth. But I think you got a long road for that shit. You lie all the fuckin time. So for now, how about you just shut the fuck up."

"Okay."

"Okay?"

"Okay."

"Okay. Get your crying, snotty nose, bitch ass in the truck."

I got in the truck and chugged hot water from a thermos he had under the seat. Kimo took a second to tie down the board.

"Hey that water might be kinda warm. That thermos is broke."

It didn't matter. I drank it all.

When he got in the truck he looked at me with a huge smile on his face.

"Did you plan this whole shit?" I asked weakly.

"*Whaaat?* I just wanted to take you surfing."

I looked out the window.

"I did plan a little somin-somin for your birthday though…"

"What?"

"A little party, super small. I couldn't go big cuz I figured you were probably gonna drown…"

He patted me on the head again and I looked out the window.

CHAPTER 3

TRUTH VS. TRUTH

My head was filled with Cuervo.

An ocean of it. My thoughts and ideas were scattered across its shore-line. The question of why I was going to Cynthia's house swam in and out of the tequila playfully. I tried to catch it. Maybe grab its ankle or wrist as it dove down. Its giggles made bubbles. Every time I thought about it, more important thoughts distracted me. Thoughts like who the fuck are all those people at my birthday party? How long until the cops shut it down? And, at the moment the most important thought, am I too drunk to be driving this moped?

The headlight was duct taped and bounced every which way except where you needed it. The whole front end had been smashed and then bent and welded back crooked. My legs wouldn't fit behind the handlebars so I had to keep them spread wide open in order to sit on it. And whenever I hit the brakes, the front wheel would pull so hard to the left I'd nearly flip over.

The only way I could keep my balance was to go fast.

I made it to her driveway. I remembered the kid who let me use it had said it was hot wired and not to turn it off. He also said there was no kickstand but don't lay it down or gas would spill out. I thought about balancing it on the side of her house but what if it fell? I honked the little horn and it made the sound of a big bird being raped. I laughed so hard I almost dropped the moped. I started beatboxing, revving the pathetic motor and hitting the horn in rhythm. I didn't notice the lights in the house had turned on and someone was arguing in Tagalog.

Cynthia came out of the house wearing an oversized t-shirt and probably nothing else.

"What the fuck are doing?!" she yelled through her teeth.

"Yo! Listen to this shit," I said laughing.

I started the beat back up and she ran over and grabbed my hand. She was mad. I sat there quietly for a second just taking in how sexy she looked like this.

"Sorry," I said finally.

"Sorry?"

"Yeah… It was a dope beat though."

"Yeah I heard it."

"And it was dope?!" I said smiling.

She didn't say anything. Her face kept changing while she asked and answered questions to herself in her head.

"It's your birthday," she finally said out loud, answering her own question.

"Yeah, there's a party—"

"Yeah, I know."

"Everyone is there."

"Not me!"

"That's why I came to get you."

"Not me on purpose!"

"I came to your birthday party."

"You crashed my birthday party."

"You wanna crash into my birthday party," I said grinning as I slowly patted the broken handlebars.

She laughed. Then she pulled at some of the duct tape. Her head tilted and hair fell over her face.

"You could have asked me before," she said almost in a whisper.

Her shoulders slowly swung from side to side. This was such a different person I almost had the thought that I was at the wrong girl's house.

She went on in an almost shy voice. "It's like you had to check the party first to see if there was any hotter chicks there. Then you're like, 'No hot chicks. Guess I'll just go to Sin's house and beg her to come to my party even though I never asked her in the first place,'" she said to the duct tape.

"First of all, I'm not begging."

Her eyebrows pushed together and her nostrils flared. I changed my tone fast as I reached through her hair and lifted her chin to me. "It was a surprise party. Like I ain't even know people knew I had a birthday…"

"Everybody has a birthday!"

"Listen! I didn't think anyone knew it was *my* birthday and honestly, there is a lot of hotter chicks there—"

"That's not funny!" she said, smiling and playfully hitting me. "Everyone is acting like they know you. Talking about how you beat the shit out of Kevin or all these other guys and how you're fucking this girl or that girl but I know most of it is bullshit and you're like nowhere to be found and most of the people talking are lying! I know you! But I can't tell anybody cuz it will just become a part of all these bullshit stories. It's like folklore or something. I don't want to be a part of that. I'm not one of your hoes. Whatever that was that we did, and I'm gonna go out on a limb here, but that wasn't bullshit to me and you seemed…" She stopped.

She had worked herself up and now I recognized her. Her eyes were watery and she was standing feet apart like she was challenging something. It took me a second to realize she was waiting for me to say something.

"That wasn't bullshit to me," I said.

"I was waiting for you and you never called and all I hear is that you're fucking all these girls."

I was about to tell her some game about the other girls or about how I'm a player and she needs to understand that and get with the program. Then I thought about that breeze that had blown up the beach and through the grass up the mountain and the sound of the monster waves. I thought about the truth.

"I didn't have a phone or even a house. I'm fucking homeless. Kimo lets me crash on the floor of one of his empty houses but there's no electricity or hot water or anything. My stepdad packed all my shit in my bullshit car and kicked me the fuck out. Christmas came and went and I sat in the dark in an empty house with no lights. I dropped out of fucking school. You said it yourself, I'm like a homeless drug dealer bully. When I'm next to you I feel weird shit. Like, you're fucking amazing! You sing and make cool movies an shit. You're fine as fuck! I'm next to you and I can't breathe. I can't talk. I sound like a fucking idiot. You're smarter than me. You talk circles around me. You see right through me or into me or some shit. I can't stand that feeling but I can't stand not having it. But I know… I ain't shit."

My voice cracked and I caught myself. For months I had been either dodging these thoughts or trying to catch them. I had failed at both. Now here I was hearing them for the first time. I wanted to be alone with them. They were embarrassing. I quickly packed them back up and promised myself I would look at them later. Almost under my breath I said "Fuck you… I don't even know why I came here cuz I knew you ain't even wanna fuck with me—"

She kissed me.

I felt like I was falling. She was the only thing to grab onto. I could feel her hot skin through the t-shirt. I let the moped fall over and I squeezed her and kissed her and held on as I dived into the feeling I had been looking for since I left her house so long ago. She ripped herself away.

"Wait, I'm coming with you!"

Then she ran into the house and started screaming at her parents in Tagalog. Other people's house lights started turning on. I stood there for a second going over her lingering smell. Toothpaste, Pantene, Dove and… *gasoline*?

I turned and saw the gas spilling out of the moped onto the driveway. I picked it up and the headlight fell off. I was trying to hold the moped while reaching for the headlight when Cynthia came running out of her house.

"Go! Go!"

Her dad was behind her with machete.

I pulled the moped backwards down the driveway and Cynthia jumped on the back before I could start pushing it forward. Her dad swung the machete and it cut the remaining wires off the headlight. He was yelling in Tagalog and Cynthia was screaming back at him right in my ear. I didn't know how to start the moped. I was fumbling with the duct taped wires when I noticed the screwdriver in the busted ignition switch laying disembodied in the panel pocket. I put them together and twisted just as the second machete blow shattered the plastic on the handle bars. Now she was screaming at me.

"He's gonna fucking kill you! Let's go!"

The moped started and I opened the throttle all the way and it sounded like we were gonna take off but we moved so slow I actually laughed. Her dad was literally walking next to us yelling at me. He finally swung at me and I caught his arm. I held on to him as the moped gathered speed. More house lights had come on and people were coming out of their houses. When he was at a full sprint, I let go of his arm and he almost fell. He was running too fast to swing so he just kept sprinting and yelling. We hit the end of Haiamu Street and I turned wide out to North Road as he drifted into the background. The wind hit us and she squeezed onto me tight. I felt something in the way she held me.

We flew through the broken streets of Ewa Beach.

There was nothing to worry about. No one to answer too. No one could catch us. We were gonna fly away. This moment was ours and no one else's. As long as we never land, this moment could be forever. She was laughing like a little girl on a merry go round.

"I can't go back!" she yelled.

"What?"

"I can never go back," she said as she bit my neck.

Me either, I thought.

"Take me with you," she said in my ear.

"I am," I yelled back.

"No! Like for real! Take me with you!"

"I am! Right off the muthafuckin cliff, baby!"

She put her arms out and her black and red flannel flapped in the wind.

***

You could hear the music from eight blocks away. Disco lights mingled with the leftover Christmas lights colored all the surrounding houses. Cars were parked all over the grass and blocked the streets for almost two blocks back. Some of the cars were lowriders all G'd out with chrome rims and hydraulic suspensions. Kids from the high school and kids I'd never seen before walked around with beer in their hands talking. Some of the people weren't kids at all. There were three barbeque grills going with at least seven huge local guys at the helm. They all nodded or waved or patted me on the shoulder as Cynthia and I pushed the moped up to the party.

I could hear Moon-Dog's voice over the music hyping up the party. We got as close as we could with the moped before the cars were parked too tight to get it through. I was gonna just balance it somewhere when the owner came running through with his arms up.

"Eh, what the fuck brah? You wen crash'em or what?" he lamented with his eyes down making sure not to sound like he wanted to fight.

"Naw man, the headlight got caught in the wind an it flew up and hit the top and the whole shit just shattered… I don't know… it was crazy…" I mumbled.

The poor kid looked at me trying to believe me. Cynthia laughed and pulled her flannel over her face.

"Yo Q!" yelled Moon-Dog over the P.A. system. "Q is back, mutha-fuckas, make some noise!"

The place erupted. Kids started pushing me up towards the garage where the DJ was set up. I wouldn't let go of Cynthia's hand so she got pulled up with me. The music stopped and Moon-Dog put the microphone in my face. I had never touched a microphone before. It had a feeling. A weight to it that didn't make sense.

"Yo wassup!" I said.

My voice sounded so deep and heavy as it went through all the kids and out into the neighborhood. The microphone was getting hot in my hand and energy was flowing up my arm and into my stomach and brain.

"Everybody having a good fucking time?"

The crowd cheered and put their hands up. Again electricity surged through me. No amount of drinking or smoking felt like this. I want more of this. Moon-Dog tried to grab the mic back and he got the Heisman. Someone started yelling "speech" and it caught on.

"*Fuuuck* you, I ain't doin no muthafuckin speech! This is my birth-day party and the last thing I want is some drunk ass muthafucka givin speeches!"

Everyone started laughing and cheering.

"However, I wouldn't mind a drunk ass muthafucka spittin some gangsta shit!"

Only a few people cheered and I realized how local the party was. In fact, except for Moon-Dog and his Pearl City crew I didn't see any popolos. Mostly Hawaiian and Samoan brothers with "localz only" tank tops and surf shorts. Filipino and Japanese girls with their hair all sprayed up in a wave.

"I mean this is Ewa Beach right?"

That got unanimous cheers. I looked behind the DJ set up and saw some guys setting up guitars and drums and stuff. I covered the mic and asked them what the name of the band was.

"Natural Vibrations!" they all yelled.

"You can't have a real party in Ewa Beach without Natural Vibrations puttin it down!"

Unanimous cheers.

I put my hand back over the mic and told the DJ to get a beat ready.

"I got an idea though. Since we waiting for them to get set up, why don't we get ready? Why don't we show these brothas from the eastside how we get down on the westside! Can you dig it? Cuz the westside gets down! You don't wanna get lost out here without a friend. Shit, I don't know about you but I came to get down tonight. Did you come to get down tonight?! If we drop a beat and spit some hardcore westside Ewa Beach gangsta shit, are you gonna be able to handle that shit? Can you dig that? Can you dig it? *Caaaaaann youuuuuu dig it?!*"

The beat dropped and the place went insane!

#

> *Who's the baddest? Who's the sickest?*
> *Who's the illest?*
> *Who's the muthafucka on the microphone about*
> *to kill this?*
> *God damn it, it's me man, it's easy to see man*
> *Breast strokin your girl like I'm lost at sea man*
> *Freestylin, like a skateboard kid*
> *I'm tryin to figure out what I can make more with*
> *Drug dealin, car stealin,*
> *Tires squealing,*
> *Fists flyin, if you tell me that I'm lyin*
> *I'm 90 proof, I set fire to the roof*
> *You lose a tooth showin your teeth to the truth*

I'm the bigger kid, empty out your front pockets
House keys, lunch money, chain and the lockets
Bitch stop cryin! These rules I gotta teach
You get fucked up if you come to Ewa Beach
Am I right? Am I right? Make some noise!
Q and Moon-Dog with the Ewa Beach Boys
and the Sons of Samoa
Act like you didn't know-a
Try to play the role and wind up in
A coma
Fuck who you roll with
I'll take a baseball bat to your whole click
I ain't scared bitch
Tough talk turns to tears and apologies
Sidewalk chalk and years as state property
Or simply show respect when I wreck and bow properly
And tell your girl to come and suck my dick sloppily
Bitch swallow
This a tough act to follow
Tonight house party
Tomorrow The Apollo
Your threats seem hollow
You need to grovel
Or get assed out like you're in a fuckin malo
El Capyton
I'm too tantaran
Forever Ewa Beach
Where the fuck are you from?

#

Moon dog came in and helped me with a new hook for everyone to learn.

#

Can I get a ghetto pass in your hood?
Let me know!
(Yeah fool it's all good)
Cuz if not
Bust a shot
And I'll be elsewhere
I'll disappear like welfare.
But if so
Let me know
And we'll come and do a show
And we'll make you muthafackas
Say "Hell Yeah"
(Hell Yeah)
Dats Dat old school shit!
(Hell yeah)
Let me know dude, shit!

#

I introduced the band, Natural Vibrations, and pulled Moon-Dog out from behind the DJ booth to make sure he wouldn't just start back up again. We pushed through the mass of people who were giving us hand slaps and pounds and hugs out onto the street. There were lowrider cars parked in crazy positions. I couldn't figure out why I was drenched with sweat or how long we had been rockin. Moon-Dog tried to push by me and go back to the party and I bear-hugged him.

"Let me go, Q,!"

"That's it man, we killed it. Let's just enjoy the rest of the party," I said gently.

"No doubt!" he said after thinking about it for a second. "Let me go hear some of this Hawaiian shit."

I let him go and he was smiling ear to ear. He worked his way back up through the crowd and started dancing with D-40. They were laughing and D-40 started trying to get Moon-Dog to do the Kid n' Play kick step. I stood alone for a moment listening to all the conflicting music from people's cars and the band. A kid walked by and passed me a Heineken. I took a sip but

I didn't even want it. I didn't want anything else anymore. Whatever it was that I was feeling I wanted that. I saw Cynthia standing shyly. Finally she saw me the way I wanted her to see me. I was on fire tonight and everyone saw it.

"That shit was crazy right?" I said.

"Everybody really liked it…"

"Everybody?"

She looked around the party searching for something.

"Do you know all these people?"

"Naw, I don't know, I think the word just kinda spread and ya know, people just like to party."

She took a deep breath and then looked me in the eye. The shyness was gone and it was her.

"I didn't like it."

"You know what, I think maybe you just don't like real hip-hop," I said.

I was smiling but it was the smile I used in a fight when I just got my bell rung.

"Maybe, but I like you, so…" She was struggling to figure it out. "I don't know, it feels like, you're just saying whatever pops into your head."

"That's what you're supposed to do. It's called freestyle, so you just grab the first thought and try to tie it to the next one and you know, make it make sense," I mumbled.

I was crushed. The adrenaline was wearing off and I wanted to tell her to go fuck herself.

"Maybe you're just one of those wannabe artists who define themselves by not liking anything," I said. "You sit around critiquing the work of other artists like, 'I don't know what it is but I find Shakespeare's work to be juvenile in its depiction of humans' violent nature. His quatrains have no restraint when compared to Mozart, mah mah mah…' Fuck that, we just killed it!"

"I don't want to fight with you!"

"I don't wanna fight either!"

"Then stop freaking out!"

"Then tell me you like my shit."

"I'm not going to lie!"

"Then don't! Just actually like it!"

"Mozart makes music."

"Mozart's dead."

"Shakespeare was a playwright."

"I know that shit!"

"Please, listen, I'm not saying I didn't like it—"

"Yes you are!"

"No I'm not!"

"That's exactly what you said! 'I didn't like it.' Like, word for word! Fuckin verbatim."

"What I mean is, you can do better or more or maybe you're just starting to figure out what it is you're doing and if you settle for the low-hanging fruit you'll never climb all the way up and see over the top of the tree."

I thought about my rhyme book. I thought about pulling it out and showing her something. Anything. I knew that she would dig some of my new poems. I knew what she was saying and I knew she was right. But fuck her.

"Fuck you!"

Someone put their hand on my shoulder.

"Ahh… young love! It just warms the soul."

The voice sent chills into my stomach.

Kimo.

"Hey, Uncle," said Cynthia, and she jumped on him and hugged him.

"You guys know each other?" my voice cracked.

"I known Twinkie since she was one fat baby!" he said while tickling her. She squealed but didn't try to get away.

"I'm not fat!"

"Not anymore! All your baby fat went to your butt!" he said smacking her right on the ass.

"Shut up!" she yelled, laughing.

"Das why you like popolo guys now yeah, cause they like big butts!"

"Shut up!" She tickled him and he laughed and let go. She slid back down but kept her arms around him and rested her head on his chest. Jealousy pumped through me and I grit my teeth. He had five huge guys with him. He held onto her and tilted his head slightly reading my face. Then he smiled, kissed Cynthia on the head innocently and peeled her off of him.

"Kevin, you s'posed to say something right?" said Kimo.

Kevin came from behind Kimo with his head down and his shoulders slumped. His arm was in a sling and his head was shaved with a bandage on the back of it loosely covered with an old baseball hat. His face was swollen and misshapen. When he began to speak, you could see and hear that all his front teeth were gone.

"I just wanted to say sorry yeah… for always picking fights with you and when we was kids too and even your popolo friends, um… If can, I just like be friends." He mumbled most of it with his head down.

I was horrified.

Kimo rubbed him on the back and whispered "good job" in his ear like he was talking to a little kid… and Kevin looked like a little kid. I realized that I had beaten down a retard. A psycho-killer retard, but a retard nonetheless. The beer and tequila felt like warm ants in my stomach. Kevin held out his good hand and I reached and shook it. He smiled toothlessly and I saw there was no green fire, just a fallen Master Blaster.

I heard some people clapping as we finished our handshake and realized a small group of people had gathered to see if we might fight again.

"Right on!" said Kimo. "If you hold a grudge, ain't nothing else gonna fit in your hands."

He started to leave but then looked me up and down.

"Hey Twinkie, bring your new boyfriend upstairs." His boys parted the ocean of kids and Kevin lagged behind with a goofy smile.

***

The living room was huge and filled with luxurious black leather sofas and chairs that were accented with deep-brown koa wood. There were hardwood floors with some kind of Aladdin rugs all over the place. Incense was burning from more than four places and there were two bongs on a beautiful crystal coffee table. I had never smoked out of a bong and was staring at one that was a glass dragon when I noticed a gun sitting next to it. That wasn't all. My mind slowly recognized things I had never seen in real life before. There were open ziplock sandwich bags filled with cocaine just laying on the table with small piles everywhere. A few lines were drawn out with rolled up dollar bills, silver and gold straws and razor blades. And there was cash. Stacks of cash just sitting on the table. There were almost no teenagers up here except for three other girls besides us. They were younger than me and dressed like Barbie dolls, if Barbie sold a red light district box set. They were huddled together behind the couch where a fat popolo dude with an Aloha shirt and a Jheri curl sat rolling a joint and talking loud in the middle of some story. Standing like a bouncer behind him and the girls was a huge popolo guy who looked like a Jay-Z head on a *Green Mile* dude's body. There were also a couple of old Filipino men, two middle aged Cali surfer dudes, five huge Hawaiians playing pool, six local guys dressed like women and one beautiful Filipino woman glided around the room without touching the floor. She floated over to Kimo and whispered something in his ear and he didn't like it. Then she looked at Cynthia and screamed "Twinkie!"

Cynthia looked at the floor and the woman hugged her and kissed her.

Cynthia didn't like it.

"I'm Marianne."

"Q."

"I know, you're Kimo's little project. He won't shut up about you. You must be special," she said with a coded chuckle.

Her perfume was some kind of flower but it was heavy and musky. It made my skin tingle and my teeth clench. She was a woman. When I was finally able to look away I was confused and overwhelmed. This was over my head. She was over my head. Everything and everyone in this room was over my head. This was me drowning and clawing for air as the giant waves from this morning dragged me down deeper and deeper to a place where the Fireman had told me about.

The place where "the sharks will be waiting…"

I thought about leaving. I searched for an excuse that would get me and Cynthia out of this room. The best I could come up with was patting down my pockets like I dropped or lost something. I grabbed Cynthia's hand and headed back down the stairs. Just as I got halfway down the steps I was stopped by a huge mahu. He was six feet tall. Muscular slim build. His hair was down past his shoulders and he had a huge plumeria flower in it. His makeup was perfect but his face was square and masculine. He was wearing a bright-red sundress with stacked heels, carrying a huge box in one hand and an overstuffed plastic bag in the other. He saw me and immediately shoved the box in my arms.

"Oh, you one sweetheart. I was carrying dis box from all the way. Get so many cars parked outside was like swap meet already."

I turned around and all three of us walked back up the stairs. He took the box back from me and held it up in front of the room.

"First come first served bitches! Hot malasadas! Well, warm malasadas. Was hot before but I had for park way far away!"

Marianne ran up and hugged him and they giggled and squealed like two teenage girls. Marianne glanced over at me as she took the malasada box and whispered something to the man in the sundress who turned and said, "Right! So the knight in shining armor who helped me up the stairs is also Kimo's protege?"

I didn't know what protege meant and I didn't know what was going on. He looked me up and down like he was surveying a construction project. Then he looked at Cynthia and screamed.

"Twinkie!"

Cynthia actually smiled and opened her arms for a hug. The man in the sundress picked her up and spun her around.

"You're breaking my ribs!" laughed Cynthia.

The man put Cynthia down and grabbed the box of malasadas back from Marianne.

"Hello handsome, I am Star!" she said and struck a pose holding the box of Malasadas in one hand and held the other arm high above her head.

"I'm Q," I said.

It was hard to not smile. Not because he-she was a huge, strong man and he-she was wearing a dress. But because he-she was so full of energy and singing half of the things she was saying and just seemed excited and happy. I was about to try to say something to that effect when someone yelled, "Where those Malasadas stay?" and Star was off prancing around the room obliging those who wanted one, convincing those who weren't sure if they wanted one, and forcing those who didn't.

Cynthia and I sat on the couch opposite the fat popolo dude. Cynthia curled up in my flannel under my arm. Kimo sat in one of the huge leather chairs to my right in between the popolo guy and us. The beautiful Filipino woman draped herself over the arm of Kimo's chair. She whispered something in Kimo's ear then leaned forward and picked up one of the golden straws from the table and did a line of cocaine. She passed the straw to

Kimo and he leaned forward and did one. Maryanne took the straw from him and held it out to me. I looked at Kimo. He shrugged and nodded. I took it and leaned forward. As soon as I sniffed it I realized the coke the biker dude had given me wasn't shit compared to this. Everything turned up. Like when your headphone jack isn't pushed all the way in on your walkman and you wiggle it and push it in and boom, surround sound! The fat popolo who had been telling his story to the joint he was rolling now shifted gears as if he had been telling it to us the whole time.

"Dude, it felt like it had been hours. There was no car alarms back then brother. You couldn't just 'churp-churp' you know what i'm sayin? You had to remember where the fuck you parked! But we were *fuuuucked* up! I throw my muthafuckin hands up like 'fuck it! let's just find some bar across the street or somethin' cuz my mouth was all dry and I was at that place where if you keep drinking you're fine but if you stop then you are in a world of hurt. My buddy Keith—we were stationed in Guam together—he starts losing his shit and running through the parking lot. We lose him! Now these girls we picked up are starting to fall apart. I'm like, 'Naw baby dolls we cool, we just playin, we been partying pretty hard. When we find my ride I got some nose candy for you girls. You goan have a good time tonight! Garanfuckinteed! We just gotta find my wheels!' No sooner than I said it, you hear the fucking theme song to *Miami Vice* blasting! Fucking echoing through the whole garage! You hear tires screeching and sliding. You hear this fucking engine roaring around and around."

The fat popolo was into the story now that everyone was listening. He was using his hands to show the car sliding around the garage. I was looking at his hair wondering if Jheri curl juice was gonna fly off like a dog shaking off water. When his hands moved, his super loud Aloha shirt would flap open because all the top buttons were undone. He had a patch of chest hair with baby powder still caught in it. Or was it spilled coke? Baby powder. His gold chain would swing over it. I wondered why some rolly polly fat dude would wear his shirt all open like this and sit in this dangerous as fuck room with so much confidence. He must have been something when he was younger. Some buffed badass black dude. Looking at him for too long was starting to make me sick. Out of the corner of my eye I could see Kimo looking at me. Studying me with a weird look on his face. Like he was waiting for me to catch a joke or something. I was catching nothing but sick. This fat popolo dude was making me sick. I stopped looking at him and focused on the glass skull bong. His voice was like a bad smell. Something disgusting and familiar at the same time. The cocaine wouldn't let me stop long enough to figure out why.

"Keith fuckin skids around the corner and almost slams into all of us in a fucking '72 Ferrari Spyder! And he bumpin the theme song to *Miami Vice*!"

It was obvious he was used to telling this story to a different crowd and was expecting a laugh. The beautiful Filipino woman chuckled politely and the *Green Mile* dude gave a rehearsed "*Whaaat?!* That fuckin crazy!" The fat popolo just pushed ahead.

"So we all pile in that bitch, the muthafucka only got two seats. It's me, Keith and the three bitches. Keith is fuckin power sliding this Ferrari around the garage and I would love to say he was Mario Andretti in this muthafucka! I would love to say that! But we fuckin hit every parked car in that bitch! And as soon as we made it out the parking garage—BAM! We smashed right into a cement sign for the building. Two of the bitches flew out of the car. I jumped out to see if it was gonna be anything more than scraped knees and bruises, and just when I lean down to settle this bitch down—BOOM! I see my car! It was parked on the street! I had parked the muthafucka on the street! I never do that! Not with my sound system. What the fuck?! So we pile in my car! And I'm like 'Keith, let me show how a muthafucka supposed to drive!' So I peel out down the street and fishtail around the next block but, yo! The fucking street was wet and we careen right off the fucking street and into a fucking light pole! BLAW! The bitches is all screaming and crying! I'm like 'Yo Keith, it's your turn to calm these bitches down.' I get out the car and wham! The muthafuckin bar we was looking for in the first place was right across the street! The whole time!"

The Fat Popolo had his arms up by the end of the story. The three Barbie dolls laughed on cue. The *Green Mile* dude put his fist up to his face and said his tag line again. "*Whaat?!* That fuckin crazy!"

The sound of the Fat Popolo's voice was like dumping a bottle of cologne on a fresh pile of shit. It made me sick. Everyone else in the room nodded, laughed, smiled or shook their heads but seemed to be relieved that they no longer had to listen to the story. They quickly sparked up other conversations and random business to ensure they wouldn't be trapped into another story. The fat popolo placed his expertly rolled joint down on the table and grabbed a crystal straw and started sniffing a line of cocaine. The beautiful Filipino woman whispered something in Kimo's ear and he turned towards me with an eyebrow raised and whispered back to her.

Then Marianne and Kimo stood up. The fat popolo hurriedly wiped his nose and stood up to the sound of pool sticks being put down and conversations being halted. Kimo gave me a look to stand up. I stood and turned behind me to see an old man. He looked half Hawaiian–half Filipino. He had an even older Filipino lady with him and two big Samoan men. He was wearing a dark, patterned, fitted Aloha shirt and short slacks. No jewelry at all except for a wedding band and a small gold pinky ring on his right hand. Everyone stepped forward to greet him.

"How's it, Uncle?"

"Hey Uncle, how you?"

"Uncle, good to see you."

"Aloha Uncle."

"Uncle, how's it braddah?"

"How you been, Uncle?"

One of the big Samoans walked with the old lady to a room in the back while another walked Uncle to the lounge chair opposite Kimo. Marianne went over to Uncle and kissed him on the cheek, then sat down on the floor leaning on his legs while he stroked her hair. Kimo had stood but had not said anything to Uncle. He was the last to sit and he did so slowly and gave Uncle the slightest of nods. There was tension in the room and no one spoke.

"This is a nice surprise," said Kimo finally.

"The surprise is you not coming for see me Christmas Day. It's been one whole month!" said Uncle.

"My bad, I was—"

"Brah, don't talk like one popolo to me!" said Uncle.

Uncle then looked at the fat popolo and the *Green Mile* Dude.

"No offense," he said dismissively.

"None taken, Uncle. In my opinion black slang is—" started the fat popolo.

Uncle cut him off and continued speaking to Kimo.

"You go away and come back and all of a sudden you're a popolo?"

"Fifteen years is not all of a sudden," said Kimo softly.

"Humbala… How come you talk to me li'dat, what? What I did?"

Marianne had turned her head and was staring off into nothing. Kimo did the same.

"What Kimo? What I did? I like give you time. I like give you time for be mad. You can be mad at me. What you like me do? You like me go back in time and take your place? You like me for be the one in jail? Then what? What happens to Marianne? What happens to all your cousins. All the little boys and girls we take care of. We would have to close the shelter. We wen talk about this before eh? I'm sorry but I no can let all these kids be homeless? No way I could do that. Fifteen years? How can? Where all the money going come from? Besides that, who wen tell you for do what you wen do? I never told you for do'em like that…"

Uncle was pleading. It was heartfelt and it was private. Everyone in the room had their heads down.

"Maybe we talk about this later, Uncle?" said Kimo.

"Later? When later, when you don't come see me?"

"I will come over tomorrow."

"You will talk to me NOW!" yelled Uncle.

He kicked the table. Marianne reached for a few glasses. The fat popolo grabbed the giant glass skull bong. They both put them down softly, then Marianne began cleaning up a few spills. She looked happy to have something to do.

"Okay, Uncle," said Kimo after a few moments. "What would you like to talk about?"

"Okay…" said Uncle.

He mimed fixing his hair and settling himself. Marianne settled back at his feet. It all looked a little rehearsed. This had happened before. Over and over. It reminded me of when my father would lose his temper and my mother would rush to put things back together. The thought made me feel dizzy.

"Let's just talk story regular kine ah? Maybe you can tell me what the party is for and why this kid's hair looks like one spider on his head and who the fuck this fat popolo is sitting on my couch?"

The fat popolo was about to say something but Kimo stopped him with a look and reached down and grabbed the perfect joint. He lit it and took a long pull. At that point everyone around us went back to whatever it was they were doing before Uncle had come in. Kimo passed the joint to me. I took a small pull and tried to pass it to Cynthia but she was pretending to be asleep. I leaned over and tried to pass it to Uncle, who waved it off. Marianne was still doing something with her feet. I reached over to the fat popolo and for the first time made eye contact.

I recognized him in that moment. The eyes, the tilted head, the puffed out chest. Even if it was now covered in fat. That story. That car. *That voice!*

He was my father.

My mouth fell open and I sank slowly back into the couch. It was him, just fatter and somehow much older. We weren't supposed to have seen each other at the trial since I was only a kid. I was just there to "have a little chat with the judge." Everyone acting like I was a glass house of cards. "Just a little chat, you can be honest… don't worry, he can't hurt you anymore." But somebody had fucked up because when I walked out of the court house, there he was. All dressed up in a business suit. He didn't even see me at first but when he turned his head, I saw his eyes go dark. He gave me the look. The look he gave me the moment before a beating. I didn't look away. I knew he was going to jail for a long time. When he got out I would be big enough to beat the shit out of him.

He was supposed to be in jail. Fifteen years minimum.

He didn't notice me staring at him. Uncle was talking but I hadn't heard a word he'd been saying.

"But before we talk bout all that kine stuffs, I like know how come still yet get a hundred thousand dollars wort of batu sitting in my garage. How come? Kimo?"

Kimo coughed and then cleared his throat.

"The party is for Mr. Spider Head over here and the fat popolo who has been flying a few pounds a week in from the mainland is going to take the ice back to California. He says he can move it faster and get more for it than we could here because people are already hooked on it there, plus it fucks people up and I don't really think we want to sell that shit to—"

"What?! We don't wanna sell it? Why, cuz people get hooked? Brah, it's meth. People been doing meth for since before we was here you lolo!"

Uncle wasn't pleading anymore. He was angry. The words came out fast and his head bobbed back and forth. He pointed at imaginary problems in the air.

"You go to jail and come out all haput. Brah! Operation Green Harvest going rip up all my plants, Fasi going take my ten million for legalize gambling and what? Not yet, not yet, but in the meantime he still yet going shut down my cock fights and my dog fights! Then what?! We get one new haole as the Deputy Director, he like lock me out of Honolulu harbor! And what?! The hotels like push Marianne out! How you not going have nice girls in the hotels?! Brah everywhere I turn around all I get is bad news! And then! What?! You like come outta jail and preach preach preach! You sound like one fuckin preacher why?! I no like hear dat kine! You was reading all kinds of bullshit inside dere and it wen fuck up your head. Bruh!"

The anger was blown out and what was left sounded like genuine concern.

"It makes you look weak! If you look weak, bumbai, I look weak! Dat no can happen! If get blood in da water shark going come! You know dat Kimo! What you tink dis is? You sell what sells! An you take care of all this small kine stuffs. The dog fights. The cock fights. The stolen cars. And the drugs! Simple! KIMO! Simple!! Small kine stuffs. How I can show you the big kine stuffs if you no can handle the small kine stuffs?! Did you even find the kids that stole the pakalolo?"

"I'm, well, sorta. I have a fix for that. It was a kid named Kaipo. His little brother stumbled on it hiking and tried to sell it. They wound up ruining most of it and then Kaipo got popped by the cops before I could get to him."

Kimo motioned towards me.

"This kid was pushing what was left without knowing it was our weed. I figure if it ain't broke… so he works for me now."

I was stunned to hear Kimo spell it all out like that. He knew. He knew the whole time that I had his weed. So why did it feel like Kimo was still dancing around something?

"Us, he works for *us*!" Uncle corrected.

"Us, he works for us… and he got a solid connect on the Big Island. Now he's moving a few pounds a week from his dad over there," said Kimo.

"Your dad is on the Big Island?" asked Marianne all of a sudden.

Now she looked confused as she glanced from my father to me to Kimo. Kimo gave her a look and she put her eyes back on her feet.

"Not Johnny Boy. He's still at Fire Station 11," said Kimo.

There was an awkward pause as she caught on to something that was beyond me.

"Oh, I was gonna say. I thought he was doing good!" she said in relief.

"He is. He remarried. Johnny Boy is his stepdad. This is his stepson," said Kimo motioning to me again.

"Does Johnny Boy know his stepson is sitting in one of my houses?" asked Uncle.

"Not yet, we were gonna to go up and talk to him… we are… soon."

"Well he don't work for *us* until you talk to Johnny Boy. Bumbye he get his head smashed in by the S.O.S.? Then I gotta deal with Johnny Boy. You need to handle those fuckin solays already! You need to handle this Alex punk! Brah! What's all this bullshit I hear about da solays wen make one Meth City?!"

"Crystal City… It's just Alex and some of those S.O.S. kids pushin to the homeless camped out at the bottom of the canal by Pupuole Street… I tried to organize it a little and we take a little off the top… so… I mean…" mumbled Kimo.

"Travis had for cover two bodies!!"

"Three… I know… I gotta tighten that up. I gotta talk to Alex and—"

"Da fact I even know the little fish eye punk's name means da world is upside down! Fuck Alex! This shit is sloppy! Smooth shit out or don't, but do sumting!!" yelled Uncle.

He rubbed his hand over his silver hair and adjusted his gold pinky ring then calmly asked, "Who's da real dad on Big Island? We know him?"

I noticed the talking had stopped and they were all looking at me. Kimo had a strange look on his face.

"Who's your real dad?" asked Kimo.

My ears were ringing and my stomach was burning. I jumped up and ran to the kitchen sink. I threw up tequila and fried noodles. From behind me I heard laughter and teasing. From downstairs I could hear Moon-Dog back on the microphone. I knew he couldn't keep away from it. I thought of grabbing Cynthia's hand and making a run for it. I rinsed my mouth out and went and sat back down.

"Here kid, you gotta get back on that horse," said Kimo handing me a beer.

"Don't do that!" said Marianne promptly jumping up and snatching the beer out of my hand. She went running into the kitchen to get me a glass of water. I couldn't help but look at my dad again.

"He went out with me this morning and got eaten by some monsters at Makaha," said Kimo

"Ho nah, was pumpin today eh?" asked Uncle.

"Pretty much. He got worked. Probably still yet get some ocean in his belly," said Kimo.

"Yep, that's how, take it slow, kid," said Uncle with concern.

"But even though, he learned a lot. Ain't that right, Byron?"

I couldn't say anything.

"Hey kid," said Uncle, "what's your faddah's name?"

I sat still. I couldn't move or talk. I couldn't look away from my Dad's face. He had heard the name Byron and was looking at my face carefully, walking me back to little Byron. I was watching his face change. It was like watching lava slowly fall over a ledge. When he was done, he almost could contain it.

But he did.

And just like that he changed gears.

"Even if you strapped him to a chair and pulled his fingernails out one by one he wouldn't tell you," said my father laughing. "That's loyalty right there! *Eoooowe!* I'm gonna put it like this, like a puppy pitbull. You raise em right in the beginning, they loyal like a muthafucka. Although I'd have to say this one here is more like a German shepherd cuz he smarter than a muthafucka too!"

"Sho'nough," said Green Mile Dude.

Everyone looked at my father.

"He ain't goan tell you cuz I told him 'don't tell no one.' But he ain't know that you, muthafucka, ain't no one. You *some* one. So it's cool, kid. Tell'em."

I was thinking I might throw up again.

Kimo looked disappointed.

"But I'll break it down for y'all: dis here's my boy, I been hidin out on the Big Island for a hot minute and been sendin him back an forth with a little herb so I could kill two birds an he could get a little walkin around money. His momma filled his head with a whole bunch of lies and half truths and he over that now. Done seen a little bit of how shit actually works and I figure I put him up on game, nah I'm sayin?"

The look on Kimo's face was like the final moments of a sun setting into cold darkness. What did he expect? Did he set this up for some twisted truth test or something? To see if I would lie about my dad or what? Point at him like invasion of the body snatchers? I stole the weed! I talked my friends into going that day and I stole the weed and I got Kaipo arrested and Maka hooked on drugs and me kicked out on the street. I lied and said the weed was coming from my dad who I thought was in jail in California. *I lied. I lied. I lied.*

"Dis your boy?" asked Uncle. "Ho nah, I can see'em little bit. His maddah is haole den yeah, that's why he stay light skin li'dat?"

"Word, she was a fox back in the day, *shiiit*, still is last I seen."

"I've seen her den, in fact. Suzy? Suzanna. She wen marry Johnny Boy, den dats her."

Marianne was standing between me and Kimo with a glass of water. Her eyes were daggers shooting into the side of Kimo's face. She knew Kimo was up to something. She looked like she was mad that she wasn't in on it.

"If Johnny Boy is a fireman then we talkin 'bout the same muthafuckas!"

"Den we talkin bout the same muthafucka," said Uncle, imitating my father's accent.

They both laughed and my father gave him a high five.

"I have to apologize for the cloak and dagger shit, Uncle. I didn't know you would be here and I wasn't sure how to meet you. I've just been dealing with your son, Kimo here. And after all the drama went down with a few of my girls down on Hotel Street I thought keeping my son out of this would just be on some safety shit. You know how it is, family first right?" said my father.

It was like watching an artist. What the fuck was he talking about?

"No, no, I get it braddah. Marianne said she was having problems wit some popolo pimps on Hotel Street. I guess at first you didn't know Marianne and Kimo was working together and then the kine ah, working for me, so it's all family ah, like you wen say… I just like make sure you guys is da'kine eh? Understand each odda. Cuz whatever she says about the girls down dere is law. You just gotta follow dat," said Uncle, motioning to Marianne.

She was still staring at Kimo and wouldn't look at my father.

"So maybe we can work it out, my beautiful queen," said my father.

"I'm not your queen. And if these are the girls you're trying to put on Hotel Street, you can go fuck yourself!"

"Oh Marianne, be nice," said Uncle.

"These ain't my girls. I met them the day before yesterday. I told them I was going down to the local side of the island and they wanted to check it out. They ain't been out of the Concrete Rainbow since they got here."

"Uncle, dis sick fucka puts little girls on the strip, den what? They going shut 'em down for how long? An den?"

"Eh, you can not have underage girls," said Uncle to my father.

"No, the traffic on Hotel Street is mine! The girls and the tranies. The high end shit in the Concrete Rainbow we can talk about, but based on what I seen from you," said Marianne, turning to my father, "there is nothing high end about you."

"Eh, look here woman—" My father stopped himself and took a breath and then said, "Time makes all things possible. You don't want me on the strip, but you are willing to see if I can produce some red carpet trim. I read you loud and clear, my not-queen."

"How bout you forget bout Hotel Street and we just focus on the weed from Big Island and the batu in California?" said Uncle, trying to move it along.

"As far as the Big Island goes, me and my son have just been doing our own thing, you know, just sorta makin it happen on the sly cuz these days that's how that shit gotta be," he said.

I was marveling on how he was talking so deliberately and not actually saying anything. He was looking at me though. His look said, 'Jump in here kid, I can't keep this up forever.'

"I'm sure my son didn't tell you much, cuz I put him up on the street shit from back in the day. Oh shit, my mind just blew. I just had a flood of memories just pour into my fuckin head brotha. Oh shit, a conversation for another time, but remind me cuz you will get a fuckin kick out of it, you know what I'm sayin? You gotta raise um right, teach um what's what from the git go, *shiiiiit*, you must know all about that, Uncle! Byron and me, we used to watch *The Godfather* together and and and…" I felt like I was watching him try to roller skate up a frozen waterfall. "…anyway, like I said, I got a friend on the Big Island who hooks me up and—"

"I thought you grow your own shit over there?" said Kimo.

"Well, technically no…" said my father looking at me. "I don't grow it myself, although I water and trim and prune and you know what, fuck it! You could say I grow my own shit cuz my homeboy mos def ain't doing his share of the work. But no, I don't really know how to grow a whole crop myself. Every time Byron has come out though it's like I'm growing it myself."

"Where do you grow it?" asked Kimo.

"In the ground," said my father and laughed. His girls laughed too, and Green Mile Dude gave him five.

Kimo didn't laugh. In fact his eyes never left me.

He whispered to me, "It would be nice to hear the truth."

My father overheard the whisper and for a brief moment, there was a flash of panic. It was gone before anyone else saw it. Like a lost frame in an old movie.

"You hear these kids, Uncle? Truth. No offense, but you youngins have been lied to for so long, you wouldn't know the truth if it was played 24-7 on repeat until your ears bled. Truth could fill up the whole room like that bloody elevator scene in *The Shining* and you wouldn't even notice. It's not your fault. I blame *Star Wars*!"

"What chu tawkin bout?" said Green Mile Dude.

"For real, peep dis shit here," said my father as he started breaking up some weed on the table. "*Star Wars* comes out and the weird beard dude basically was like, 'Yo, I'm a give you producer muthafuckas most of the dough from the film, but I want the dough from like, the toys and shit.' Producers were like, '*Whaat?* Whatever.' Movie comes out. It's dope. Now all the kids find out there's toys for that muthafucka. Movies ain't really go hard on toys and shit before that. That Lucas muthafucka made bank. Not on the movie but on the toys. After that, powers that be done open their eyes to the fact that the kids was the suckas to sell to cuz they is easy to trick. So why make products and commercials to adults who is bustin their asses to make rent? They is like, 'I ain't buyin that shit. I got bills to pay,' but a kid, a kid can talk their parents into buying anything. Sell to the kids. The whole world caught on to that shit. Get'em when they young and you got'em forever. And now you got a whole culture that has grown up believing whatever line they have been fed on T.V. But everything they have been fed has only been to sell them shit. Even the news is telling lies to make shit more ill so they can sell time to commercials who then tell more lies to sell shit."

He pulled out a fresh pack of Zig-Zags. "Now these kids is like the hot chick who thinks she is smart because all the guys tell her she smart. But they just trying to fuck her. Everyone who was under fifteen when *Star Wars* came out is that hot chick. Grown up with a twisted view of how the world looks. How it should talk to them. It should cater to them like a salesperson selling them something because everything in their world has done so thus muthafuckin far. They don't know what truth is because it has been crafted to sell them something. If you gave them some real shit, some real truth! Boy! It would kill them. They can't digest it raw. Their… like… perception is stunted. Their digestion ain't fully formed. Like a trick, a fuckin prostitute, she can't handle real love. She's been lied to and molested and hurt. Her heart gets stunted and it can't handle true love."

He held the overstuffed unrolled joint in one hand and licked it. Then, holding it with his pinky and ring finger, he rolled it without using his thumb. It was a magic trick. "The truth. Truth is like a deer or a bear or a big ass marlin. Someone has to go out in the wild, the dangerous fucking wild. The chaos. And hunt and kill the deer, that monster, that bear, that truth, and bring it back to the world. Then that same someone's gotta gut it, clean it, marinate it, throw some Lawry's seasoning on it and put it on the plate. Everyone else has to eat THAT truth. Or go out into the wilderness and kill it themselves."

My father held up the joint he had been rolling for inspection and smiled. He tilted his head back towards the girls he had brought and said, "You bitches want to go into the wilderness and kill some deer?"

"*Eew!*"

"What?"

"I ate deer once…"

"I said, 'You bitches wanna go to Zippys and grab something to eat?'

"Yes!"

"Yeah."

"I'm starving…"

"Uncle, it was a pleasure to finally meet you in person. I look forward to getting this Cali thing squared away and I will keep my girls off of Hotel Street and outta the Concrete Rainbow."

My father was just about to stand when Kimo asked, almost to himself, "So you make a separate dish for yourself?"

"What was that?" said my dad.

"Do you make a different dish for yourself? Every time you kill a deer, you add in all kinds of shit and cook it up sideways for whoever, but then do you cook it up straight for yourself?"

"It's just a metaphor, young buck…" my dad said, looking flustered.

"I'm probably the same age is you so… yeah… and I'm just trying out your deer recipe."

"Man I'm just talking shit," said my dad.

"Smells like it…" said Kimo calmly.

"The kid's got jokes," my dad said laughing and looking around.

"Do you ever eat the wrong one by mistake?"

"What the fuck man, I'm just breaking it down. Don't get mad at me for breaking down what we all already know," said my dad.

"Some shit don't break down though. It ain't the same thing broken down. You break a car all the way down, it ain't a car. It's rubber and steel and plastic. When you break a song down, it's just notes. There's only twelve notes in every song you've ever heard. When you break down truth it ain't truth. It's just random shit that happens. Any fuckin idiot can break shit down. Who's the muthafucka that can put shit together? That's what truth is. Twelve notes. How do you put together your twelve notes? Cuz you can't just break it down and stack it back up. It won't add back up. Two plus two won't equal four. Sometimes two plus two equals more. Truth is putting shit together the right way. So that it's more than just random facts. It has to be put together and built into something that helps you stay up. Something that helps you float. Something that makes sense."

"Kid, you ain't making no sense," said my dad.

Everyone kind of chuckled or smiled uncomfortably.

But it clicked for me. I thought back to Cynthia singing at her birthday party. A woman's voice, plus a guitar, could equal more if it was put together right.

My dad began patting his pockets and making another show of beginning an exit.

"In prison everyone's looking for the truth," mumbled Kimo.

"Tell me something I don't know," said my dad dismissively.

"The Jheri curl went outta style in 1989," said Kimo.

It took a whole second… then everyone laughed. Green Mile Dude must've short circuited because he said one of his lines for Kimo.

"Oh shit!"

Kimo smiled and decided to keep going.

"Muthafucka look like Ice Cube ate the Stay Puft Marshmallow Man. Look, he still sweats marshmallow!" said Kimo, pointing at the baby powder on my dad's chest. The whole room was rolling. Green Mile Dude was quiet and the girls looked like they were coming out of some kind of spell. My dad was flustered and stood to finally leave.

"I'm just fuckin wit you man. Sit down," said Kimo.

"Naw, it's all good, you got me. That's some funny ass shit but I gotta get these girls some food."

"Naw man, we ain't finished rappin about your little meta—"

"I am. *Shiit*, I'm outta here—"

"SIT THE FUCK DOWN!"

The music downstairs had just stopped a moment before Kimo had said it. In fact, everything had stopped a moment before he had said it. The guys at the pool table stood still. A couple of random conversations in the back of the room had stopped. Everything was quiet.

"Kimo, show some respect…" said Uncle half heartedly.

"Respect? Why? Who the fuck is he? Interrupting me while I'm talking? Who the fuck is he?"

Uncle said nothing, just looked back at my dad as if he had never thought of it that way. In fact, it looked like the whole room seemed to be asking themselves the question now that Kimo had said it.

My dad was many things. Stupid was not one of them. He sensed the change. He sat down fast, leaned forward and said, "Kimo, I'm sorry! I didn't mean to cut you off, that was some rude shit my brotha."

Kimo lightened up immediately, as if he had never raised his voice.

"I'm sayin, I'm getting to a muthafuckin point here. You can talk for twenty minutes about drunk car crashes with underage prostitutes and

Star Wars toys and I can't spend two minutes taking apart your bullshit pimp philosophy?"

"You right!" said my dad.

"I know I'm right! Cuz you're full of shit!"

Everyone chuckled uncomfortably.

"I am! I overindulged on the nose candy and my mouth gets away from me," said my dad to the whole room with his arms out smiling wide. "Please, Kimo, my bad. What were you saying?"

"We were talking about your metaphor, the truth being a bear that you yourself goes and gets for everyone not brave enough or smart enough to go get themselves," said Kimo calmly.

"Right, and you were saying it was wrong," said my dad.

He was leaning forward towards Kimo, submissive and listening so hard and politely that it almost looked sarcastic. Kimo talked slow and quiet like he was describing a picture that was slowly changing.

"Maybe you're right about the truth, actually, I guess, but you're also wrong. Maybe it is like an animal that you have to hunt. But it wouldn't be a bear or a deer or anything like that. It's more like a… like a… it's more like a shark. The real truth is a shark. We all float around on the surface. We scrape together random pieces of whatever facts we come across… kinda, fuckin… like a… life preserver… ya know… and you build, like… your own story out of those facts. The story you tell people. It becomes your truth. The bullshit truth you tell yourself. Your fuckin personal narrative. That's your pieced-together bullshit truth. We use that shit as floaties, or whatever. We use our stories… to float. We use the stories we tell ourselves about oursevles like water-wings to fuckin flop around. We gotta hold them together. The facts that make up our story. Shit is flimsy. Pieces keep floating away or get water logged and don't float anymore. But it's all we got to stay up. To stay us. We call it truth. But it's just facts haphazardly put together, like we was talkin about. The real truth? Because we all know the bullshit we tell ourselves ain't the real truth. The real truth is deep down. The sun can be shining, weather can be sweet and everyone keeps holding their breath and searching the depths to see it. Nobody sees it. But everyone knows it's there. Because everyone knows someone who was eaten by the real truth. Everyone has actually seen someone get torn apart by the real truth. You see the top half of their body bob around like an empty beer bottle in the surf. You hear them scream that scream. You see the water around them turn red and chunky as their insides pop up and float around them. But you don't see the truth. You don't see the shark. You never see the fuckin shark. No matter how much you look. Because the shark is not down there. It's not in the ocean. The truth that rips your guts out and eats you while your still screaming, that truth is already fuckin inside of you. It doesn't come up from the depths of the fuckin ocean. It comes up from the depths of your fuckin soul. That shark is the real truth. It's *your* truth. *The* truth doesn't exist. *Your* truth is what you need to look out for."

Kimo stopped talking and the room stayed quiet. He's eyes were far away like he was scanning the ocean. Finally Moon-Dog's voice came out ridiculously loud over the P.A. system downstairs.

"Okay muthafuckas! We're back! We had some technical difficulties but we ready to go on an on an on! To the break of dawn! When I say 'on an on an on!' you say 'to the break of dawn!' Okay, here we go!"

This snapped the room out of the trance Kimo had put us in. My father laughed and said, "I want a hit of whatever he is smokin!"

Uncle chuckled at the joke but was visibly shaken by what Kimo had said. My dad leaned back and whispered something to the Green Mile Dude, who then started wrangling up the girls. My father stood and faced me.

"I got a new phone yesterday, Son. Here's the number."

He passed me a business card that had nothing on it but a handwritten number.

I stood and was going to shake his hand or something but I got dizzy.

I smelled the salt water and I heard the wind coming off the ocean. I heard it moving through the grass up the mountain. I smelled the salt air. I remembered the billowing curtains and the sound of his voice coming through those tiny speakers. I remembered the door slamming shut.

I reached down and grabbed the glass dragon bong off of the coffee table and smashed it across his face.

I had swung so hard that I fell over the coffee table and on top of my dad. Green Mile Dude pulled out a gun as Kimo leapt over me onto him.

I sat up and began pounding my dad with both hands. There was a gunshot right behind me. It was loud. People were running and screaming and the music stopped again downstairs. I didn't stop punching. Then a louder shot and Uncle was yelling.

"Everyone get the fuck out—party's over!"

Kimo put me in a headlock and pulled me up. Two of the Samoans had Green Mile Dude on his knees with a gun to his head. The girls were crying. They sounded like little kittens.

Kimo let me go and I stood over my dad. He seemed okay. He looked like he had just bumped his head on the counter or something. He wasn't even bleeding. I could hear Kimo whispering something to Uncle. Uncle then collected everyone else in the room besides Kimo, my dad, Marianne, Cynthia and me.

A cop ran up the stairs as Uncle was leaving and said in a hushed apologetic tone, "Uncle, cops going come, brah. Nothing I can do. You gotta hele before—"

"It's okay, Travis, I'm going now," said Uncle as he patted Travis on the shoulder.

Kimo picked up Green Mile Dude's gun and checked the clip and chamber. He came over and put his arm around me and looked down at my dad.

"Look in his eyes," whispered Kimo.

"Son, I'm sorry about how everything went down, I swear. When I saw you tonight I was so happy to see you."

"You didn't even recognize me," I mumbled.

"You're a man now… and you got that fucked up hair…" He tried to laugh at his own joke and then thought better of it.

Kimo passed me the gun.

It was heavy in my hand. Everything slowed down and got muffled except for one question. And then another question. And then another question. Why did he pass me the gun? Did he take the bullets out? Did he want me to bluff? Did he want me to beat him with it? Did he want me to just scare the shit out of my dad? Is Kimo testing me? How can he test me? He doesn't know anything about this muthafucka! He doesn't know that I would do it.

I would fucking do it!

Could I do it?

My heartbeat is loud and drowns out all other questions. I see myself pull the trigger. I see the flash and hear the cracking sound. I see the bullet crawl out of the gun and push into my father's left eye and exit out the back of his head and through the hardwood floor. I see the blood pour out of the hole like red coconut milk out of a fresh coconut at the swap meet. My heart pounds harder and faster until it is no longer a heartbeat. It's a crunching, grinding, breaking sound that is tearing through my chest. Like a metal safe dragging across a concrete floor. The corners bite against my ribs, shattering them. They squeak and pop as this cold sharp gray growth makes its way up to my neck. I can't breathe as it shoves itself up my throat. It's twisting and growing. It's going to rip me apart from the inside. I'm clenching my teeth and my ears are ringing.

I turn once more to look at Kimo. He is looking into me trying to see something. I can feel it. It's swallowing me from the inside. It's chewing and swallowing me from the inside.

My dad starts talking fast but I can't hear him. I see his mouth moving and his eyes widen and I feel the sharp teeth coming out of my skull.

I pointed the gun and pulled the trigger.

Click.

Kimo took the gun out of my hand.

"It's done… get the fuck out here," Kimo said to my dad.

My dad stood up with his stupid Aloha shirt wide open and he was fat and scared and his hair was all fucked up. He spun around looking for a way out and then almost fell down the stairs.

I finally took a breath. I shook all over for a second when I realized I would have done it. The thought almost made me throw up again. I was afraid I might cry so instead I laughed.

I laughed and then Kimo started laughing. Marianne smacked Kimo and then kissed him and laughed also.

Cynthia did not laugh.

CHAPTER 4

STAR AND THE CRYSTAL CITY

"I just wish they could learn how ta fuckin' *tawlk*, you know what I mean? They come halfway around the world and they can't even fuckin' *tawlk*. I said 'no onions' and 'extra mayo'!" he said in disgust.

He was sitting in the backseat to my right. He had his Subway sandwich open in his lap and he was doing surgery on it. He had to be over eighteen because he was a Marine but he looked like he was my age. His head was shaved and beet red from sunburn. There were five of us shoved into this brand new Camaro. It was tight and I was riding bitch. I had made my way onto Kaneohe Marine Base earlier in the day from a girl I had met a few weeks ago. She was stationed there and we had a thing. I went over and spent a little time with her but couldn't bring my car on base. She introduced me to some of her friends and of course I was able to sell everything I had on me. A military base is basically a college dorm with really strict rules.

Kids from all over America.

It could be fun, especially if you love hip hop—this is the place you were gonna find it. Brothas from the East Coast and West Coast and the South all in the same place rapping and making beats and getting together and throwing parties on the base. They would battle each other. It could be pretty fucking epic. It could also be pretty fucking shitty. Not everyone was cool with being mixed in with each other like that. Just like in high school there were groups of people all split up in pockets.

Once I got on base I could go from pocket to pocket seeing if anyone needed anything. Just like in High School I figured I can get along with just about any group of people because I like people. But the group of people I found myself in the car with right now, I did not like. I should've called Kimo and said I wasn't going to make it to Chinatown by sunset. I should've taken my time and found a better ride. Friday night? There's always military dudes going downtown. But the sun was moving fast and making Kimo wait is dumb shit. So instead I was squished between two ignorant redneck racists spilling mayo-covered onions on my brand new Karl Kani jeans.

"I hear ya brother. Ya think if yur gonna go to someone else's fucking country ya should learn the language."

"Damn straight! Then her chink friend doesn't even try. And they start sayin shit behind our backs in their ching-chong shit!"

"She sounded different though. She sounded like 'book book book bungbook.'"

The whole car started laughing at that. I sat there and pretended I didn't hear them. Which wasn't too hard because their southern accent was so strong I almost couldn't understand them. The extra mayo dude balled up all the onions in the wrapper and threw it out the car. Then he stuck all four fingers in his mouth to lick the mayonnaise off his fingers. He caught me staring at him and said, "You should check yur sandwich, buddy. She dun prolly fucked yur shit up, too."

"Naw, my shit is perfect. I'm gonna eat it later when I have enough room to breathe."

"Aye, you lost fair and square."

"Who does one, two, three and then you show?!" I said.

"That's the rules!" said Extra Mayo.

"That's not how we play it here. It's 'jan-ken-po'—boom. It's like one-two-three and on the three is when you show!"

"What the fuck is 'John can-a-pooh?' It's rock, paper, scissors!"

"It's the same fucking thing, we just call it something else! But my point is the count: one, two, show," I said.

"Well, when in Rome," said the huge white dude driving the Camaro.

"We ain't in Rome!" I said.

"That's right! We in America!" said the driver.

"Fuck yeah!" said Extra Mayo.

I didn't say anything. We were almost in town and they were drunk and coked up. I had sold to these guys two times before and both times, they bought all my coke. I shook my head and tried to just look at my brand new Timberland boots. I wished Kimo was here. He would know what to say. He would say, "Naw, bitch, we in Hawai'i. And you are an occupying force. And that chick who made your sandwich was Filipino. The correct racist term for her is book book, not ching chong. That's Chinese. Two languages you don't speak. Not including the Hawaiian language, which is the language of the kingdom you're in right now. Try learning another language and then speaking that second language without a thick American accent. In fact, try speaking the only language you know without a thick American accent. Try. I'll wait. Can't? So who should laugh at who?"

He would say something like that. But I didn't. I was scared. They were older and stronger than me. One of them, the driver, just started up training for special forces. So I sat there staring at my shoes.

We pulled over halfway over the Pali Highway because the G.I. Joe driver wanted to put the top down. As soon as the top was down, I sat up on the trunk and noticed we were exactly across from the place where me and my friends had found the weed. I looked at it until it was out of sight then looked down at the tops of these sunburnt heads. I was glad the wind was so loud that I couldn't hear what they were saying. If I closed my eyes the wind was so loud I couldn't hear what I was thinking. Which was good, because I didn't like what I was thinking. I was thinking about how hard it had been to convince my friends to go somewhere else that day. I was thinking I wish it had been harder. I was thinking I wish I hadn't been able to do it and we just smoked a joint and walked over to the beach that day. Just like we always did. I was thinking I wish I hadn't complained about not ever going anywhere. About how we only did the same thing over and over. How we just smoked weed and surfed in Ewa Beach over and over. I wish I hadn't pushed over and over for us to jump in Bonez' truck and go somewhere, anywhere but Ewa Beach. I had wanted to do something exciting. I had wanted to go on an adventure. I had wanted to see something new. Go to the city. Go to the North Shore. Go to the mountains. Go to the waterfalls. I didn't care what it was. I just wanted something else. I wished I hadn't wanted something else. I wished I had never seen that stupid twisty tie on that tree. I wished I would've let it go. I wished I wasn't so curious. I wished I didn't force my friends to follow me. I wished they hadn't listened to me. I wished I would have gone to school and played football and gotten a cheerleader girlfriend and let her wear my jacket and gone to the school dance and passed all my classes with Cs and Ds. Then my friends wouldn't be in so much trouble. I wouldn't be in so much trouble.

That last thought stopped me.

Am I in trouble?

I didn't know what the question meant. I didn't know who was asking. Trouble with who? With school? With the law? With Kimo? With my mom? With the Fireman? What the fuck are we talking about? Trouble with who? Who has got you spooked? Point them out. Those S.O.S. dudes in Waipahu? Who?

Alex, that's who!

Just the thought of his name made my stomach feel like it was full of ants. Kimo had told me not to hang out with Alex. Some crazy Filipino-Hawaiian kid. Kimo said I wasn't built for the places Alex went. Just like Alex wasn't built for the places I went. Kimo had tried to play it off and say that I was made for the fun places. I knew what he was actually saying though. He was saying I was too soft. I wasn't tough enough. Was I a bitch? Is that what he was saying? I had thought about finding this Alex kid and just beating his ass on general principle. But the thought didn't last long. It died the moment I saw Alex.

***

I was in Waipahu at a small Filipino restaurant called Elena's. I had invited Cynthia's parents to dinner to try to see if we could smooth things out between me and the dad. Cynthia had been talking to her mother since the night she ran away and her mother said that if I could apologize to the dad and show them that I was a good kid, we could maybe start over.

The beginning of the dinner had been brutal. I loved Filipino food and Elena's was the best Filipino food on this side of the island. But my dumb ass didn't figure that if you're Filipino and you cook Filipino food exactly the way you like it seven nights a week, why would you want to go out and then eat Filipino food? Turns out Cynthia's dad's favorite food was Chinese food and if I was trying to be mister big shot and treat her parents to dinner, I should have taken them to Wong Kung Chop Suey.

Cynthia's mom kept asking me questions and then laughing too hard even when I wasn't making a joke. She would repeat everything I said to the dad who just sat there sucking his teeth as if he had food stuck in them. There wasn't. We hadn't even ordered yet. I wanted to grab the tooth picks off of the table and throw them in his face. Then I remembered the scotch. Cynthia said he liked scotch. I had picked it up from across the street right before we came in.

I put it on the table and he stared at it.

I stared at him.

Cynthia's mom leaped at the thought and yelled at the waitress in Tagalog to bring us more glasses.

We had ordered a feast. The table was filled with fish sinigang, pinakbet, bangus, fried chicken, lechon and I was doing my best not to be rude as I demolished the food and nodded in the appropriate pauses. Cynthia's dad was on his third glass and hadn't touched the food.

"*Aagh*, deez kids now, *aagh*, no way dey can even know, too easy das why! Dats why I no like deez kids. I was in Vietnam. Had all the haole guys tinking I'm Veitcong. And only guys dat was nice to me was da popolo guys. I no more problem wit you cuz you stay black! I get problem cuz you wen steal my daughter in da middle of the night and den," said Cynthia's father.

I did my best to sip the nasty old-man drink. He didn't want to hear anything from me. He wanted me to listen. I was wrong and he was right.

That's when I saw him.

Alex.

I had never seen him before. I only had the description from Kimo and the street kids to go off of. Kimo had given me Alex's pager number and I had been paging him for two weeks. I would hear from someone that he was somewhere and I would go straight there. He would be gone. So much so that I was a day or two away from telling Kimo the muthafucker was dodging me. Tonight was the last straw. I had told Siosi and Sleepy, a couple of Kimo's guys that were huge as fuck and Samoan and cool with me and with Alex, that I was going to Elena's in Waipahu. Then after I would need one of them to roll with me to Alex's house and chill spots. If that failed I would give up and tell Kimo.

But now he was here.

He stood by the front of the restaurant where you waited to be seated. Although I wouldn't call it standing. Fiendishly lurking? Concealing aggressively? Like a tornado hiding behind a telephone pole. He paced side to side without moving his feet while trying to stay behind the fake ti-leaf plant between him and the rest of the restaurant. It covered nothing but a piece of his shoulder and a few strands of his matted sun-blonde overgrown mullet. The front was long and hung in his face. He was pale. His dirty sunburned skin looked haole except for the dark circles under his eyes. It looked like the black anti-glare stuff football players put on their faces. And he was skinny. Maybe an inch shorter than me but at least forty pounds lighter. His tank top was stained and dirty and was torn down by the front waist area. He was wearing a pair of denim shorts that were faded and stained from wiping his dirty hands on the pant legs. He was sweaty and dirty. Actual dirt and mud. His legs had dried mud caked all the way up to his knees. He looked like he hadn't showered, slept or eaten in weeks. He was clenching his jaw and staring at me. And he was holding a machete. It was wrapped in a dirty plastic bag that he had obviously pulled out of the trash can in front of the restaurant. The bag was ripped and barely covered the blade.

It was him.

It was Alex.

I wasn't sure what to do. Cynthia's dad was telling a story and the last thing I wanted to do was bring his attention to the fact that I had anything to do with this rabid, sweating creature who was staring at us.

I looked away. I pretended that I didn't see him. I laughed at the punchline at the climax of Cynthia's dad's story. Out of the corner of my eye I could see Alex take my break in eye contact as a physical blow. He stepped back and turned around in a circle and then looked at me again in disbelief. His eyes widened and his brows went up in shock. Then he smacked at the ti-leaf plant. The branch sprang back and hit him in the face. He grabbed the whole tree and yanked it out of the pot. He stood there for a second not sure what to do and then flung it on the floor. People waiting for their table jumped away and one old Filipino lady fell down.

At this point everyone in the restaurant was looking at him.

"You see me now ah, you fucka?!" growled Alex.

His cloudy eyes looked at me. Then he looked around the room, smiled, and adjusted his homeless tank top. Then he looked at the lady who had fallen down.

"Sorry Aunty, let me help you up," said Alex.

She put her hands over her face and Alex started saying sorry to everyone around him while nervously pulling and fixing his hair back away from his face. He gave me one last twitchy glance and then turned and left the restaurant.

"I'm gonna smoke a cigarette, I'll be right back…" was all I could manage.

Cynthia's mom turned to Cynthia with a look of horror while Cynthia's eyes searched my face trying to find an answer. Her dad shook his head and poured himself another drink. I ignored all three of them.

I stepped outside and standing in the parking lot was Alex. Ripped plastic bag in one hand, machete in the other. He held it down and to the side like a Spanish sword fighter. He was smiling. He looked happy and excited. He looked like he was my friend and he had a special surprise for me that he knew I was going to love.

I stopped at the edge of the sidewalk and lit a cigarette, making it a point to not even look at him.

"You was looking for me ah? We go you fucka!" he said, twirling the machete.

"I was paging you and leaving messages for you all over. Looks like maybe you got the wrong one," I said. I was trying to keep my voice even.

"What you mean?"

"I mean I'm just here to get Uncle's money," I said, finally looking him in the eye.

"You Kimo's new guy?" He froze in place when he said Kimo's name.

"Yep."

"But… you not popolo," he said, looking me over.

"Naw… not really."

"Oh… everyone was telling me one big popolo guy like scrap wit me!"

"I ain't that big, I'm not popolo, and you need to give me Uncle's two thousand dollars."

"Oh… you sound popolo," said Alex.

"Hey, put the fuckin sword away before the cops come!" I yelled.

"Hoa… you get one deep voice eh?!" he said. He was laughing and smiling crazy again. He started uncrumpling the plastic bag meticulously.

"I no more the money on me right now. I need for go get'em."

"Naw man, you a fuckin houdini in this muthafucka. You ain't disappearin again."

"Brah, I not disappearing. I stay the same place every night."

"I've been by your apartment every night for two weeks."

"No, I stay working. Crystal City."

"Crystal City…"

"What? Scared?"

"So you sayin that's where your money is?"

"That's where all the money is!"

We could hear sirens from way down the street. People were slowly coming out from the restaurant to see the show. Alex sprinted over to a beat-up moped that was laying on its side and picked it up. He stuck a screwdriver in it and it sounded like an army of twenty thousand weed eaters. He revved it and I could see the muffler was gone. He nodded me over to jump on. I got on the back and put my hand on his boney shoulder. I was afraid to hold it too tight and feel the skin slide off or something.

Cynthia came bursting out of the restaurant running towards me crying and angry. I pulled out a few hundred dollars and held it out to her. She wouldn't take it and was going to say something but the moped was too loud, so I tossed the money at her and it fluttered down to the sidewalk as we sped off.

***

Alex shot right out of the parking lot into oncoming traffic. Going the wrong way into the intersection to make a right onto Pupukahi Street. I looked up to Waikele Towers. I had an apartment up there on the seventh floor. Kimo said it was empty because a friend of his owed and couldn't pay. Kimo had empty houses and apartments all over the island. He said I could keep an eye on Waipahu from this one.

The balcony of my apartment faced Waipahu. I could see Leeward

Drive-Inn, the twenty-four-hour laundry mat, and Star's Lounge. I loved to look down on all the action down there at night. The walkway from the elevator to the front door on the other side of the apartment faced Ewa Beach and Iroquois Point. At first I thought this view was nicer and wished the balcony faced this way because you could see the waterways that fill Pearl Harbor. They broke into little fingers that made a sort of marshy green mirror effect in the morning. But at night there was no looking out to the ocean. There was only looking down on an overturned toy box of broken lego-colored public housing apartment buildings, which was different from some public housing apartment projects on the mainland because it wasn't a project. It wasn't done all at one time. Each building was a one off. Most of them, less than five stories high and five to eight apartments long. All of them, different colors, different building materials and different arrangements. The tallest of them was Waikele Towers at nine stories.

I would stand on the seventh floor waiting for the piss-smelling elevator, looking down on a ghetto filled with things I knew nothing about. I would watch the rain clouds ride the trade winds towards Waipahu and when the showers would cross the swampy ocean fingers, they would rinse the grime and muck from the whole town and then that water would slowly run down past my apartment, down through the trash piles and the abandoned cars and the broken, overturned thrift-store furniture and into the broken meth pipes and plastic bags filled with human shit. Into Crystal City. Then and only then would it slowly return to the marsh to make its way back to the ocean. I never walked down the street in that direction. I knew Crystal City was down there. Down Pupukahi Street. Down past the apartments. Down past the broken-down cars. Down past the dozens of stray cats that darted in and out of the piles of trash that stood taller than me.

Alex made no attempt to dodge the huge rivers of brown street water that flowed down Pupukahi Street. The nasty ass water sprayed up and all over the back of my new shirt. The smell of trash was the baseline. Wet old trash mixed with fresh spam and canned corned beef hash frying from every third apartment. There were almost no real shadows. Along with the street lights, every high wall or pole had flood lights pointing down on every driveway or walkway. Broken glass caught the light and it glimmered like diamonds scattered outward from the trash piles we passed. Preschool-age kids played in the street and Alex swerved and cursed, honking the shrieking moped horn. We came to the bottom of the hill and it looped left, bringing us to the entrance of a small parking lot. It had one of those swinging triangle-shaped steel arms used to gate cars and I could see it led to a basketball court and a small grassy area.

Both of the lights for the basketball courts were smashed and someone had hung a flood light from the pole on one side of the court. You could see the extension cord dangling down the pole and into one of the nearby apartments. A lifted Toyota 4x4 was parked on the grass on the other side, shining its headlights at the court while playing a hip-hop song I didn't recognize. There were thirty or so big Samoans hanging in front of the gate drinking forties. They all had blue bandanas either hanging out of their pockets or tied around their heads. A few girls were hanging around but they looked as scary as the guys.

The gate was closed and I had to get off the moped so Alex could get it up on the sidewalk and go around the gate. I stood by the gate and tried to hide the shear panic that was rising inside of me. My eyes were stuck to the sidewalk. I was using everything I could to lift them and return the looks I was sure were thrown on me by these men. But I couldn't. Alex had brought me down here to have these guys beat my ass. These were the Sons of Samoa, a Crip gang that was started somewhere in Cali but was strong here. Alex rode his moped right onto the basketball court and everyone's attention was on him. He rode around in circles a few times and tried to run a few of them over.

"Pass me the ball!" he shouted.

One of the guys threw him the ball and he rode around in circles dribbling. Everyone was laughing. Then he tried to make a shot. It went way over and the ball disappeared in darkness. Everyone laughed and teased him. He came back over to me. I was about to jump back on when one of the big Samoan guys asked Alex, "Eh sole, you when fuck up dat guy or wut?"

"What guy?" asked Alex.

"The popolo guy who was looking for you?"

"Dis the guy," said Alex motioning to me.

In a split second the Samoan guy grabbed me by my shirt and lifted me off the ground. I could smell Heineken and boiled peanuts on his breath. Three more guys came running over.

Alex was laughing. "Nah, dis Kimo's new guy now."

The gangster put me down.

"Why you no say na ting, sole."

"Where's Kimo?!" said one of the guys who had just made his way over to me.

"Kimo?" said another one looking around.

"Oh… say it again!" said Alex, imitating *The Lion King* movie.

They all laughed and the guy who had picked me up patted me on the chest so hard he knocked the wind out of me.

"We only makin jokes, sole." He turned to Alex. "You guys going down da path?"

"Yep," said Alex.

"You gotta walk cuzin, get choke mud!"

"No wayz you faka, I get jet power! I alwayz revvin bra, alwayz!" yelled Alex and he revved the insanely loud moped. Everyone started laughing and shouting. Then Alex took off into the darkness. He just disappeared beyond the headlights of the truck and into the mud and overgrown keawe trees and brush.

I looked around expecting something. Something bad. Instead everyone seemed to instantly forget I was there. The basketball game started back up. The girls went back to talking and the four guys that were next to me started walking past the gate and back up to the street. I looked down into the darkness that had swallowed Alex.

"Go follow him, sole. Take one right after the fence and go all da way!" said the Samoan that had lifted me off the ground with one arm.

As soon as I was past the truck headlights I was blind. I stood still and closed my eyes waiting for them to adjust. When I opened them I could see a muddy, overgrown road leading into the darkness. The back of the apartment buildings were on my right and the overgrown bushes and keawe trees were on my left. I started walking and instantly found out why Alex's legs were covered in mud. It was unavoidable. The tires grooves were at least two feet deep in some places and you couldn't walk on the grass beside the road for more than ten feet before the trees forced you back to the muddy tire tracks.

I walked like that for a while, focusing on not falling down and not losing my slippers. I could see in most of the windows of the apartments. For a second I tried to imagine what they were talking about. I thought most of the voices that I heard were coming from there but then I realized some of the voices were coming from the trees. As my eyes adjusted fully I saw that there were tents in the keawe trees. I passed Alex's moped. It was on its side stuck in the mud. He had just left it there. To my right, banana trees had begun to separate the back of the apartments from the muddy dirt road. Tents and makeshift shelters were everywhere. There were fires all over the place—in portable Weber grills, trash cans, and one was in an old bathtub. People were darting around, climbing in and out of tents.

I kept pushing forward.

Everyone was muddy and dirty and skinny. Their faces were hollowed out. Their eyes were wide and flittering around like they were following a fly. There were dogs. Stray dogs and kept dogs. Walking, running, playing with the kids. There were kids. Lots of kids. You could tell which ones were working and which ones lived there. The workers were between eight to twelve years old and had on nice football or basketball jerseys. Brand name jeans or cargo shorts. Fake gold chains with huge medallions swung all the way down to their waist. Fake Rolex watches that looked like they would fall off their arms if they made a fist. They walked slow or were sitting in small groups around muddy stolen mopeds. The regular kids were younger and just ran around like normal kids do. They were just so dirty. I saw a toddler trying to keep up with some other kids. She was naked except for a diaper that was so filled with shit it swung side to side as she tried to run.

There were old wooden pallets and pieces of plywood laid down all over the ground as I got deeper in. There was more light here and the apartment buildings and banana trees on my right were gone. The path was blocked by two burned-out cars that I actually had to climb over. On the other side of the cars, warehouses replaced the apartment buildings and I could see extension cords running out of them to a handful of flood lights casting sickening yellow light over a large clearing. As I got closer I realized it was a bridge over a canal. I knew that canal. It ran all the way up past Zippy's and even further past Waipahu Street and Honowai Street up to the freeway. It was lit up like a football game. There were old couches and easy chairs all over the bridge. A wooden antique dining room table and chairs. A fifty-inch television set was sitting in the center of the bridge. The old kind that needed the red and blue lights in front of it to work. It was playing *Rap City* through some house speakers that were set up all over the bridge. As I got closer, I saw Alex sitting in a lazy boy that was lifted up on a stack of pallets right in the center of the bridge. He was facing the T.V., which had its back to the canal. He noticed me as I leaned against the railing next to the T.V. I looked down into the canal and saw even more people hanging out on the beams and pipes down there. I was about to turn and tell Alex to give me the money so I could get the fuck out of his sewage kingdom when I heard *"QUOOOO!"*

I searched the muddy meth heads and saw him.

It was Makalolo.

He was sitting on one of the oil pipes under the bridge talking to two kids and a crusty old grey-bearded haole guy. He looked even worse than when I had last seen him outside The Garden a couple of months earlier. He was wearing cargo pants and a blue and black flannel jacket with no shirt. He was dirty and thin. Thinner than me.

"Q you faka, watchu doin down here?!" he shouted as he scaled up the oil pipes to the top of the bridge. The two kids took off and the crusty old man climbed up with him. He hopped over the railing I was leaning on like he had done it a hundred times.

"I had to talk to Alex," I said.

"Oh you stay working for him now?" he asked.

"No, no, definitely not. We just gotta talk about some shit. You lost alotta weight muthafucka! You're more ripped than me!" I teased.

"I stay on one diet!" he said laughing and looked at crusty beard guy.

"Only one diet?" asked Mr. Crust.

"No, not one. *Bah-two*," said Maka.

They both laughed and high-fived each other. It was obvious they did this routine whenever possible.

"Eh you fakas, try come ova here!" yelled Alex from up on his throne.

Maka and Mr. Crust jumped. Maka jogged over to Alex and Mr. Crust actually ran away. I made a big show of slowly pushing off of the railing and leisurely walking over. Suddenly the sound of automatic gun fire exploded. A kid sitting in a beach chair next to Alex dropped his forty ounce and leaped backwards over his collapsing chair. I dove straight for the ground and knocked the wind out of myself. After about thirty shots the only sound that could be heard was Alex laughing. He sounded like a hyena. After a few seconds some of the dealer kids were laughing too. I stood up and tried dusting whatever dirt would come off hoping to god it was mud and not human shit. I looked up and saw a preteen kid standing next to Alex holding a string of fireworks and a lighter.

"Neh neh, nouf already. We no like Travis for come down and make any kine again," laughed Alex to the kid. "Later we go pop more."

The kid put the fireworks into a backpack and jumped down from the pallets and ran off to meet a meth head that was walking sheepishly up to the bridge. The meth head held out some money and the kid punched him in the gut.

"Not on the bridge you fucken dummy! I told you by the banana tree, lolo!" yelled the kid. He looked back at Alex and shrugged his shoulder like, "I told him." Alex waved him off like, "No worries." The meth head didn't seem to take any offense to a little kid punching him and yelling at him like that.

I walked over to Alex and grabbed the folding chair that the other kid had dove out of. Maka sat down on a piece of pallet that was jutting out.

"Sorry bout your clothes, brah! I never knew you was going dive in the mud," said Alex chuckling again. "Still yet get choke fireworks leftover."

Alex lit a cigarette and offered Maka and me one. We both took them and Alex leaned back and started talking over the music.

"I never was dodging you, brah. I never wen know who was that number paging me. Sometime these fuckin meth heads get my number and never stop till I chang'em. Plus too, I wen tink Kimo was going just come down here, cuz he used to alwayz come hang down here for set everything up. He alwayz used to like for come down here an lecture me on how I fuckin up everyting…"

I didn't say anything. I just looked around trying to imagine Kimo setting any of this up. This place was the bottom of a sewage drain. It actually was. The canal brought it all right here to this very spot. Piled up under the bridge was old broken furniture and rusted shopping carts, a faded yellow and green kiddie pool, soggy couch cushions, a swollen and water logged full-sized kitchen cabinet, and thousands of plastic bottles. After a few seconds though it all became clear. Just like it took my eyes a few moments to adjust to the darkness before. It only took my mind a few moments to see Kimo's fingerprints all over the hell around me.

From where I was sitting I looked up the canal and saw that the chain link fence was cut in strategic places so that the kids could run through easily but a bigger adult person would have a harder time. Looking into the canal I could see wooden platforms every three to five feet tied to the oil pipes to allow the kids to jump down from the bridge to the bottom of the canal and sprint up the canal to Leokane Street. At that point I wouldn't doubt that there were more little slits in the chain link fence, and at that point there were probably stolen mopeds leaning against the dark walls of the empty warehouses. Both sides of the bridge we were on had two burnt, abandoned cars blocking the dirt road to the bridge. Any police in cars or trucks would have to stop and go on foot, allowing time for everyone to hit those escape routes. I wondered how many other things Kimo had put in place that I couldn't see. Not to mention rules about how this was all supposed to be done. Rules that I could guarantee Alex was not following.

How could this be Kimo's creation? It was dirty. It was dirty and cruel. I looked at Maka who was looking at Alex like a hungry pet.

"So what, you going run the rocks for me tonight or what?" Alex asked Maka. "I give you for free if can?"

"Shoots, I like work the Ewa side wit my friend?" said Maka, looking at me.

Alex did his shrieking hyena laugh and looked at me.

"Kimo would fuckin shit if he found out I wen make one of his pretty boys a runner in Cystal City."

Alex stood up and made a big show of stretching. He looked down at me. I couldn't return the look. I looked down and tried to busy myself by getting another cigarette. He chuckled a muted version of his hyena laugh then picked up a flashlight. He pointed it at one of the warehouses about three football fields away on the other side of the chain link fence to the right of the bridge. All of the warehouses were cast in dark shadows compared to how lit up we were. He turned the flashlight on and off three times. A light flashed back three times from the third floor window. Then a small trash bag dropped from the window. I couldn't see it hit the ground or who was waiting for it because my line of sight was blocked by a one-story building that stood between us and the warehouse. Less than a second later a screaming moped engine came to life and echoed through the empty warehouses.

A moped came shooting out of the alleyway between the two warehouses with a small boy dressed in a black Raiders jersey manhandling it. He drove it right up to the fence before jumping off of it. The moped fell over on its side and slid into the fence. The boy hit the ground in a sprint. It looked like he was going to just run smack into the fence but he turned his body sideways at the last second, lifted his left leg, and shoved his left arm out while holding the trash bag in his right arm. The kid did the Heisman to the chain link fence and slid through the small slit without losing a second. He went right over the ledge of the canal and sat on his feet to slide down the slanted concrete to a small wooden platform that stretched across the water like a plank. Once on the other side, the kid tossed the trash bag to another kid who was waiting. This kid was chubby and was wearing a blue bandana on his head. He sprinted in a straight line along the top of the canal and stopped at the oil pipes. He tossed the bag to the fireworks kid, who jogged it up to Alex.

Alex opened the bag and shuffled around inside it. Then he held it open so I could see.

"Dats your two thousand dollars right there," he said.

He jumped down off the pallets and knelt down over the bag.

"Maka, you and your friend take Ewa, and—"

"Eh, Alex! I no like do the townside! Stay all muddy. No can even use moped! I no like fuck up my shoes!" complained the fireworks kid. Alex smacked him in the head.

"Who told you for wear your new shoes down here, eh? You seen was raining all day, lolo!" said Alex like a stern father.

The kid put his head down but he gave Maka a deadly look.

"No give me stink eye, punk! I crack your face."

The kid looked Maka up and down then looked away slow.

Alex started counting out the little gram-sized ziplock baggies. Fireworks Kid shoved them into his backpack and Maka shoved them into his cargo pockets.

"Eh! You kids seen one dog!" came a man's voice.

We all jumped up. Alex grabbed his machete and spun around to a elderly man carrying a leash. The uncle was obviously drunk and probably homeless.

"He's a pit but no be scared. He's a good boy. You kids seen him walking around? He stay hungry dats why," pleaded the old man.

"Uncle, get outta here! You can not be here, brah! How many times I tell you! I no like give you lickens again cuz!" warned Alex. He started to point the machete at the old man but stopped.

"Eh! How dis fucka get in here!" yelled Alex running past the old man to the two burnt cars I had climbed over. I couldn't hear what he was saying over the rap music from the T.V. and the old man describing his dog to Maka but he was definitely yelling at some kids in the darkness on the other side of the cars. He banged the machete on the car a few times and then turned and started walking back towards us. The old man was between us and Alex and had his back to the cars.

"He's a good boy da bugga, he just get scared sometimes you know. I feel bad cuz I no can feed him good all da time—"

Alex came from behind the old man and cracked him in the head with the butt of the machete. The old man crumbled, but before he could fall all the way to the ground, Alex caught him in his arms and squatted down. The old man was out for a second or two but then his eyes widened and he panicked as he came to.

"*Shhhh...* hey uncle!," said Alex in his ear. "No move... no move, uncle. I going cut off your head."

"No! No, wait!" shouted the old man.

Alex was holding the top off the old man's head with his left hand and had the machete to his throat with his right hand. He had now sat all the way down and as the old man squirmed and whimpered, Alex had wrapped his legs around the old man's waist and upper thighs.

"*Shhh...* I just like ask you one ting, uncle—SHUT UP YOU FAKA!" yelled Alex in the old man's ear. The old man shut up.

"How many times you come in here chasing your dog? How many times? I show you respect. I even help you look for him how many times? Brah, it's almost every night now you try sneak in here and get one of the boys for give you sumting for free. What I told you was going happen? HUH! WHAT I TOLD YOU!"

"Please... please... I sorry..."

"I told you if you lose your dog over here again I going chop off his head and bring'em back to you. I told you if you try sneak in here again I going chop off your head. You tink I playing wit you? YOU TINK I PLAYING WIT YOU?!"

"NO... no... *noooooo...* I sorry..."

The music from the T.V. seemed to quiet down to almost nothing. My ears were ringing and everything began to pull away from me. I felt like I was starting to float away. Alex was shifting his body and trying to tilt the old man's head for a better position to pull the blade through his throat. The old man knew this was it and started one last pitiful attempt to get loose.

Then I heard a big voice boom out like it was coming from the T.V. speakers.

"Maybe tonight's not for this, Alex."

Alex stopped and looked up at me.

"Maybe tonight is about getting Kimo's two thousand dollars."

It was me.

I had said it. I blinked a few times trying to get my shit together and keep my mouth shut. Alex looked at me thoughtfully. Then he laid back and the old man shot up, ran and leaped over the hood of the car like the Dukes of Hazard and was gone.

"Brah, I don't need you snitching on me to Kimo like I not running tings down here. You fakas no more the balls for stay down here. You fakas can not even hang for couple hours. Kimo like act all high maka maka. You stand dare all high maka maka. He tell me I not cut out for Downtown. Like I don't know how for talk to all the haole fakas in Concrete Rainbow. Den he like try threaten me for work in Crystal City. I not scared. I run dis shit. I'm the fuckin bunny rabbit."

Alex put a cigarette in his mouth but was still laying on his back in the mud.

"You know da one in the thorn bushes. Dats me. Fuck Kimo if he no like get his shoes muddy!"

He sat up and looked at me.

"And fuck you if you tink you can get his money without coming all the way down, you faka!"

***

As soon as me and Maka hopped over the cars on the Ewa side I instantly felt better.

There was a clearing in the keawe trees at the water line. The soft wind from the ocean found its way through it and up onto the path pushing away the smell of the drainage ditch and the human shit. It was quiet. This side of the bridge wasn't lit up with flood lights. Something about the combination of the trees and the big concrete wall and the canal blocked the light and the rap music from the bridge. The moon was almost full and the natural light seemed cleaner somehow.

I knew the further I got from Alex the better I would feel. Maka seemed to feel the same way.

"Grab one moped, cuz, let's hele," he said, picking up one of the seven or eight mopeds. I picked up the one closest to me and it looked like it was in pretty good condition except for all the wires hanging out by the ignition. I pushed the button to run and kicked the kick starter and nothing. Maka's started right up and he yelled, "Screwdriver!" I looked and there was a screwdriver in the cubby box. I shoved it in and kicked it.

We were off! The path was muddy but nowhere near as bad as the town side of the bridge. I figured out how to turn on my headlight and me and Maka ripped through the overgrown path swerving around holes and big rocks and ducking under low hanging branches. It felt like the speeder bike scene in *Return of the Jedi*.

The faster I went the less I could think about Alex. The less I could think about Kimo and Alex. The less I could think about Kimo having anything to do with any of this. About me having anything to do with any of this. No matter how many ways I flipped this quarter I couldn't get heads. This wasn't selling weed in a college dorm. This wasn't doing coke in a Waikiki hotel room with tourists from Texas who talked funny. This wasn't taking mandies with Japanese girls and talking them into a threesome. This wasn't stealing rented Mustangs and racing them back to the westside for fun. This wasn't fun. This wasn't selling fun to fun people. This was selling misery to the miserable. This was selling pain to poverty. This was feeding on the last bit of life from the festering decomposing victims who had been flushed down to the bottom of the sewer. That's what Kimo had meant. I couldn't handle this. I couldn't swallow the sewage. I wasn't cut out for this. He had known. Just like it was obvious to me that Alex couldn't go where I went. It must be obvious to Alex that I shouldn't be here. Both of us were obvious to Kimo. I felt see-through and I wanted to run. Take the moped and scream it all the way up the path away from Crystal City.

The path opened up again and there were a handful of tents and people milling around. Maka slowed down and circled around. I followed him and stopped a few feet behind him. I didn't stop the moped cause I didn't want to have any problems starting it back up. Maka reached in his pockets and handed a few little baggies to three kids with bandanas and fake gold chains. They handed him an empty Gatorade bottle filled with cash.

"What is dis?!" asked Maka.

"Alex said put'em in one plastic bag," said the youngest kid.

"Dis look like one plastic bag?!" said Maka.

"We no more plastic bag das why," said the older one.

"Dis is stupid! Lolo, still yet can see get money inside!" said Maka holding up the Gatorade bottle.

I thought of Kimo insisting on me putting the cash in an envelope. I guess he settled for plastic bags down here. Maka slapped the older kid in the head and then went to slapping all three of them.

And then we were off again. We came to a fence with a gate but it was cut with a big enough hole that the mopeds could get though. After that the path was paved and we were riding through a manicured bike path. There were no tents in here. Just beautiful rolling grassy hills and well kept coconut trees. We came to a parking lot and Maka did the hand off again. We continued Ewa following the bike path and Maka would stop at a group of kids, drop the baggies and pick up the plastic bags filled with crumbled, wet and dirty one and five dollar bills.

We crossed a metal bridge and then the path looped around a small utility building.

"Try leave the moped. We go rest little bit," said Maka, laying his moped down on its side.

I followed him down the nice grass into the keawe trees. There were four folding beach chairs in the mud right on the edge of the marshy water. It was quiet and the moon was shining down on the water. Maka said nothing but started pulling out one of the baggies and putting a rock into a glass pipe. I looked away, out at the water. There was no wind and it was a perfect mirror of the night sky. Maka took a long pull and the smoke hung right in front of us. It smelled like a burning swimming pool. I turned and looked at him. He smiled and I remembered that smile. He looked like a teddy bear.

"I'm sorry for making us go to the Pali that day," I said.

"What?" he asked, licking his yellow teeth and flaring his nostrils. He looked at the pipe but stopped, forcing himself to listen to me.

"I'm sorry for all of this. Your brother, everything. It's my fault." I whispered because I was afraid my voice would crack. I could feel my eyes filling with water and I didn't want to cry.

"Neh, no worries Dirty Q-tip. Not your fault. We no need worry bout all of dat. Brah, it's just life. It just goes. You no can do nothing. Fuck'em. How you going tell me one wave came and smash us all on the rocks and it's your fault. You no make da waves, you faka. You get one big head if you tink you control any ting. Fuck'em. We hit the rocks."

"We hit the rocks…" I nodded.

"And now I hit the rocks…" he said and took another hit.

"Ha ha ha… I see what you did there. You fucking clown!" I said and poked him in the belly like I used to do in another world. He laughed and held out the pipe to me. I stopped and looked at it.

And then I smoked it.

#

Me and my friend flew through the trees all night.
We laughed and rode a speeder bike
at the speed of light.
We soared under and over the branches.
Around a twisted path where the chance is
that it leads to nowhere
and back again
from nowhere
we laughed again
at the joke.
Knowing it was on us.

Tears pulled out of our eyes that were wide open
to the deep black wind in front of us.
Charging forward
chasing something that was behind us.
Fuck it.
Hands on our nuts,
middle finger in the air.
Fuck it.
I don't care.

#

A honking horn pulled me out of my head. The Camaro I was in was honking at an old Asian lady in a Toyota Corolla in front of us. She was panicking and Extra Mayo was yelling at her. She slowed down even more because she was scared and we revved hard and pulled around her while all the marines gave her the finger.

I looked down at my new boots. For a second I imagined Crystal City mud all over them. For a second I thought I could change the thoughts in my head and stop the next few memories.

The memories of coming down after smoking meth. How I couldn't eat or sleep or fuck for almost four days after. How it called to me for weeks. How it still sometimes calls. How I catch myself imagining the thick white cloud of heavy smoke slowly leaving my lungs and hanging in front of my face like a thought bubble. The taste of sweet burnt plastic. How Alex looked at me when he handed me the nastiest money I had ever touched. How he made a big show of counting it out. How he held up the pitbull's severed head and yelled through the fence as the old man walked slowly across the Honowai Street bridge. How the old man fell down on the ground holding the fence crying. How Alex laughed. The sound of Alex laughing like a hyena.

I took a deep breath.

***

We slowed way down but I didn't sit down. We got into Chinatown and I told them to take me to Hotel Street. I could hear them now and they were laughing at all of the people and the clothes and the food.

"*Quooooooo!* Hey Q, hey sweety! Pull over, pull over, over there!"

It was Star.

All six-foot-three, two-hundred-five pounds of him. He was dressed in a hot-pink mini skirt and a tiny midriff-showing tank top, his huge arms and abs muscles bulging out everywhere. He had on ridiculously high platform sandals. His hair was in a ponytail and he was carrying a huge purse. He was running the best he could in those shoes from the courtyard across the street. The guys in the car all started.

"Oh shit, look at the tranny!"

"What the fuck?!"

"Dude drive! Fucking drive!"

"I can't. It's a red light!"

"Do you know that thing!" Extra Mayo asked me.

I didn't answer and I threw Star a half-assed shaka. He was so excited he almost caused an accident as he tramp-trotted across the street.

"Hey man, don't wave her over!"

"What the fuck brother, don't call that thing over here!"

"If it touches my car, I'm gonna beat the shit out of her!"

"Why don't we just beat the shit out of her anyway!" said Extra Mayo.

They all looked at each other in confirmation just as Star got up to the car.

"Oh my god! Q! I so glad I wen bump into you! We finally wen get Kimo to come Karaoke at Kekai's with us. Maryanne stay coming and Kimo said for her to grab Twinkie."

"Hey Star, let me rap with you a little later…" I said trying to tele-pathically let her know she was in trouble.

She stopped and looked for the first time at who else was in the car and was very quickly putting it together. She didn't miss a beat.

"Hi boys. You guys look like country fried steak just cooking in the sun."

She rubbed Extra Mayo's sunburned head. He slapped her hand and she laughed. The driver yelled, "Get the fuck away from my car, fucking weirdo."

I jumped out of the car just as Star leaned over and kissed Extra Mayo on the head. The driver shut off the car, got out and started to walk around to the other side. The other two marines and Extra Mayo took that as go time. They laughed and the one who was on the passenger side slapped the one who had been on the left of me a high five.

Star backed up and started taking off her shoes fast, threw her purse at me and squared off. The driver rushed and she sidestepped and hit him with a textbook combo. Two jabs and a left hook that knocked him off balance. As he tried to get his balance she laid out Extra Mayo with a Hail Mary haymaker. He fell sideways, half on, half off the curb. His nose was broken and he sounded like he was breathing through a Slurpee. The other two and G.I. Joe all tentatively circled Star. She shuffled her bare feet and moved her hands like a Golden Gloves champion.

"C'mon, you fucka's, you like get dirty lickens ah?" She was talking half under her breath. "Come, you fucka's, I get sumting for you! You like catch cracks cuz, we go!"

Her skirt had ridden up to her stomach and she was wearing a lace G-string. Her dick and balls were easy to see, along with both ass cheeks.

The driver went in again. This time he bum-rushed her and she let his right shoulder go into her stomach as she wrapped her right arm under his neck then splayed her legs out behind her and fell forward onto his back. He was instantly in a choke hold as his head hit the pavement under Star's two-hundred-pound body. The last two standing looked stunned as they stared at their hero getting choked out by what they had considered to be the weakest form of man on the planet.

"Kick the tranny, you bitch!" said one.

"You kick her!" said the other.

"One of you bitches kick me I going knock out your fucken teeth and shove my boto down your throat," yelled Star.

They hesitated. She rode on top of G.I. Joe while he tried to turn his body. He couldn't. She had her legs out wide on either side stopping any twisting he attempted and all her weight on his upper back and shoulders so he couldn't get up either.

The standoff lasted for almost two minutes.

Finally one of the last two kicked Star in the head. I picked up a trash can and threw it at him. It hit him on the head and spilled Chinatown trash all over him. They all looked at me like they were seeing me for the first time. Then they looked down at G.I. Joe as he finally collapsed. As Star was getting off the ground, they looked at each other. Then they did something I had never seen in any of the fights I had ever been in.

They ran away.

Star picked up the trash can and threw it down an empty street.

It was dusk and people had started to gather around the scene. Star pulled her skirt down and started looking for her shoes. One of them was on the ground next to the knocked out G.I. Joe. She picked it up like it was hot and then spit on him. Then she looked at me like she was embarrassed.

"Aye Mary, you could help out small kine yeah?" she said.

The whole thing had lasted less than five minutes, and seeing her now with a full-blown pouty chic lip out, complaining like I could have "helped her up into a truck" or "carried her shopping bags" was too much. I started laughing and couldn't stop.

"You not laughing at me ah? Brah, I going have to give *you* dirty hurts! You fucka!" But she was starting to laugh also.

"No, I'm not laughing at you. I'm fuckin happy!" I managed to get out between fully blown belly laughs. "You beat the shit out of them so fast! And I was standing over here holding your purse! It's fucking funny!"

"I'm gonna kick your ass, you tranny bitch!" said Star in a macho southern accent.

I had to lean against the car to keep from falling down.

She ran around the car and hopped into the driver's seat.

"C'mon, let's steal their car!" she said.

I hopped in the passenger seat and she peeled out like a getaway driver before I could even shut the door. She reached up and adjusted the rear view mirror and grabbed her purse from out of my lap. She drove like a maniac and put on makeup while she talked.

"How come you never wen warn them! I feel bad now! How those poor little boys going know for not fight me?"

"What do you mean?" I had stopped laughing when I realized I might die from her driving.

"These fuckas no like stop an tink just for one second eh? Try tink how many fights I had for be in just for being one mahu in Ewa Beach. Brah ever since hanabata days I gotta fight. Every day pretty much I gotta give someone dirty cracks for calling me one faggot or one mahu and den what? Only had one guy dat fight better than me…"

"Kimo?" I asked.

"Only one. Yep. Brah me and Kimo fuck everybody else up. And Kimo would fight for me wen had choke guys like mob me. Plenty times had me and Kimo against like plenty guys. Kimo always back me up."

"I threw a trash can…" I said with a smile.

"*Aaaahhh*, you so sweet. Oh look in my purse," she said, tossing it back to me. "There… yes. Take one of those pills. You'll love it!"

"Nope. Strictly Mary for me, and the white lady whenever she's in town."

"*Married to Mary with the white chic side wack!*" Sang Star and she gave me a high five. She whipped around the small bridge in front of Honolulu harbor. "Dat's how! More better, stay strong."

"Yep…" I said holding on to the door handle.

"You never wen smoke batu, yeah?" Star asked matter of factly.

"Nope."

The taste of the sweet burnt plastic made me squish my tongue to the roof of my mouth. Flashes of Crystal City flooded my mind again. Alex, Maka, mud, popping fireworks, mopeds, shit-filled plastic bags, soggy money, a half-eaten Big Mac next to a headless dog's body… not ketchup.

"Good. Stay away from dat kine stuffs. Kimo's been trying for find something for sell instead. He said he like try for push dis. They called "ecstasy"! Dat's a great name yeah? Meth, cocaine, heroine, PCP—shatty names. Ecstasy! He said it's more betta cuz it just makes your brain dump the natural feel good stuffs that's already inside into your blood, or I dunno… Kimo wen explain betta, but he wen convince me. You know how he is, yeah, he like try figure everyting out."

"I'm not really into pills…"

"Oh me either honey, but you don't wanna let this pass you by."

She reached and grabbed the little baggy of pills out of my hand and took one. Then grabbed another and held it up on the tip of her middle finger.

Fuck it. I grabbed it and swallowed it.

"No honey, you were supposed to eat it off of my finger…"

"Fuck you," I said laughing.

"Eh, you and your friends is the car guys yeah. What we should do with this one?" she asked.

"We should take it to Freddy's."

"I no like drive all the way to Waianae…"

"Well, we could stash it at the docks for now."

"Shoots."

"Drive towards Zippy's on Nimitz. We'll stash it at the docks until we leave town, then later on we'll use it to get home and take it to the chop shop."

"Roger. Ho, I can't wait for Kimo an Maryanne for sing together. Been so long! Uncle stay all stress cuz people like try start all kine dumb shit for test him so he gotta send Kimo for put down da hammer but den maybe Kimo no like go back jail or something cuz he stay stalling—brah, everybody stay all stress! Tonight will be good!"

It was hard for me to understand what Star was saying. Not just because of her driving. Or because the wind was whipping around her and the car stereo was up full blast bumping a fucking comercial. I could still actually hear her. You can always hear Star. It was what she was saying. I didn't understand. People were starting to test Uncle? Kimo scared to go back to jail? Kimo? scared? Those words didn't go together.

"Kimo doesn't seem like the Karaoke type…" was all I said.

"Oh no, you don't even know. Kimo and Maryanne together is awesome. So much fun. We wen sing every night growing up."

"Are they like… boyfriend-girlfriend?"

"How you sound? So funny, are they boyfriend girlfriend. Are they going steady? Are they k-i-s-s-i-n-g?"

"You know what I mean."

"Why? Cuz you like Maryanne yeah? I seen you giving her the side eye at your birthday party. You like make all sick so she can get you water and rub your head. You like when Maryanne rub your head yeah? Ho, watch I going tell Kimo: 'Kimo your little mini Kimo like Maryanne for rub his little mini head.'"

"Shut the fuck up. She's old as fuck!"

"She still yet look good but eh? You no like puinsi?"

"What?!"

"I said you no like 'put inside'?"

"I know what you said. I said 'what' like, 'What?! No, fuck that!'"

"Right, I gonna tell Maryanne you like fuck that!"

"Don't be starting shit like that!"

"Eh pretty boy, I just fuckin wit you."

We took a left at Zippys and drove up to the security guard at the pier. He shined the flashlight at Star and asked for a Twic card. She pointed at me and I leaned over. I didn't recognize this security guard but he saw my face and waved us in. We parked behind a stack of shipping containers then walked back to Zippys.

Star was talking the whole time on a mobile phone just like the one Kimo had. When we got there I could feel whatever that pill was starting to make my belly warm. The sun was setting and the sepia twilight was losing the fight against the flickering yellow street lamps that hung above the restaurant's parking lot. I could see my new jeans and boots were covered in onions and mayonnaise. I took them off and threw them in the trash. I had a pair of surf shorts underneath and a pair of slippers in my backpack. I could feel the last of the warm south wind retreating into the harbor behind me. It wrapped around my legs as it fled the crisp north breeze that pushed into the city. The hair on my legs stood up and tingled like a thousand wind chimes.

"Order for Byron! Surf Pac!"

I floated over to the counter and picked up my bento. It was warm and the heat rose up my arm like warm water under my skin. I floated over to a table and started eating the fried fish and rice. It was crunchy and juicy and it seemed like there were taste buds in my throat. I would swallow and taste it all the way down to my stomach. I attacked the salty spam. I looked down at the empty bowl confused as to where all the food had gone. I had just decided to order another one when Star yelled into the table area from the parking lot.

"Q, Maryanne is here!"

She pointed over to a huge blacked-out SUV and walked in the other direction to continue her phone call. I got up and floated over to the truck. When I got there the back window rolled down just enough to see Maryann's beautiful black-pearl eyes. She had bangs and her long black hair was pressed straight. She looked like an Egyptian Queen.

"Hey sweety, did you eat yet?" she asked.

"Yeah…"

I was staring at her. I couldn't look away. Her cheekbones were so high. She looked like a huge female cat. She looked like a huge female Siamese cat. If a black panther fucked a Siamese cat and the Siamese cat didn't die in childbirth, that baby Siamese black Panther would grow up and put on some high heels and fake eyelashes and would be staring at me right now.

"I got a surprise for you…" she said.

She rolled the window back up and the door opened just slightly. It took me a second to realize I was supposed to open it myself and just climb in. It was dark inside. Her perfume was musky and filled the whole truck. As my eyes adjusted I saw Cynthia sleeping next to Maryanne. Maryanne had moved all the way over to the passenger side. Cynthia was between us. She was stroking Cynthia's head like she would a pet.

"Hey Twinkie, guess who's here?" Maryanne whispered to Cynthia.

Cynthia peeled her eyes open and saw me. She smiled and her eyelids fought their way back down.

"Hey baby… I missed you…" Cynthia mumbled.

"Maybe me and Twinkie have been having too much fun," said Maryanne.

She giggled. It was a strange sound. It came from deep in her throat and sounded threatening.

"Do you have enough room over there?" Maryanne asked.

I did but she reached over and pulled Cynthia almost up onto her lap so her head was now resting on Maryann's shoulder. Cynthia was wearing a sundress that I had never seen before. It didn't look like something she would normally wear.

"You guys drinking?" My voice came from far away and I was having a hard time keeping my eyes open.

"Kainalu, give us a minute. Why don't you grab yourself something to eat?" said Maryanne to the huge tattooed-up local dude driving the truck.

"Rogah," he mumbled as he left.

After the door shut, it was dark and quiet. Maryanne sat with Cynthia tucked under her arm. She was gently rubbing her and looking at me.

"Do you like the dress I gave her?" she asked in a low voice.

"Yeah, it looks nice. She doesn't normally—"

"No, stop. I don't like your voice."

I didn't say anything. I didn't do anything. I didn't know what to do. Maryanne was playing with the bottom of Cynthia sundress. Every few seconds she would gently rub the back of her fingers up the outside of Cynthia's thigh. Each time she would go a little higher and each time she would look at me. I felt awkward and frozen. Finally she ran her fingers all the way up to Cynthia's right butt cheek and squeezed it hard. She had long dark fingernails and Cynthia squirmed.

"Did that hurt, sweety? I'm sorry…" whispered Maryanne. She was smiling now. It was a twisted smile.

She ran the tips of her fingernails all up and down Cynthia's legs. Then she rubbed them with the palms of her hands.

"She has goosebumps… Feel," she said.

She reached over and grabbed my hand and rubbed it up and down Cynthia's legs. They were warm. They had goosebumps. Still holding my hand, she ran our palms right up Cynthia's legs to her pussy. It was wet and Cynthia moaned. Maryanne pulled out my hand and licked my fingers. Then she grabbed Cynthia's face and kissed her. I reached for Maryanne and she hit my hand away. Then she leaned over and untied my shorts. She grabbed my dick hard and pumped a few times. Whatever pill Star had given me was kicking in full effect. Bursts of light and feelings shot up and down my legs and up into my stomach. She kissed Cynthia again and slid two fingers between her legs. Cynthia moaned as Maryanne rocked her back and forth. I just sat there throbbing not knowing what to do. Every time I reached to do something, Maryanne hit my hand. Finally I leaned forward and started kissing Cynthia on the neck and shoulder. Maryanne reached over and pumped my dick and then went back and fingered Cynthia. Back and forth between us until suddenly Star banged on my window.

"What chu guys doing in there?!" Her voice was muffled from outside the truck. She tried the door. It was locked. She went around the truck and banged on Maryann's window. Maryanne reached over and pulled my shirt down over my dick and fixed Cynthia's skirt. She smiled a surprisingly cute smile and put her finger over her mouth. She rolled down her window.

"What chu guys stay doing?" asked Star again.

I could see her squinting to try to see through the tint.

"Nothing Star, so nīele. Go finish your phone call already!" said Maryanne.

"Eh, no do no stupid kine stuffs with those kids! Kimo wen tell you about Twinkie already!" said Star.

"Fuck Kimo, he not my boss!"

"For real kine, Mary, leave those kids alone!"

"I not doing na'ting. Twinkie when get all sleepy li'dat so den I wen tell her boyfriend for wake her up is all," pleaded Maryanne.

Star hit the door.

"I not playing! Tonight is supposed to be good. I no like Kimo losing his fuckin mind for you doing this kine stuffs! Open the fucking door!"

Star hit the door again.

Maryanne opened the door and Star looked at us with a strange look on her face.

"Try come outside fast kine you guys. I like talk to you."

"She's sleeping," whined Maryanne.

Star reached in the truck and smacked Cynthia on the knee. She opened her eyes and Star was practically pulling her out of the car. I started to climb out but forgot my shorts were still untied. My dick swung out and Star looked at me then looked at Maryanne. Star looked like he wanted to punch Maryanne, who had an innocent "oops" look.

When we were outside the truck I had to hold up Cynthia.

"Where's her real clothes?!" yelled Star.

"If you tell Kimo I will fucking kill you!" snapped Maryanne.

She grabbed Cynthia's jean shorts and tank top and threw them at Star. Then she climbed forward into the driver's seat and pulled out of the parking lot.

Star looked at me. I couldn't read her face but I felt embarrassed. She looked at Cynthia.

"Let's get you changed and get you something to eat," she said softly.

CHAPTER 5

THE DEAD SEA

It was one note.

One chord actually. Played and held on a Roland E-20 keyboard from like 1988 or something. It played loud on a loop and it had me in the Dead Zone. I sat deep in the studio couch with my eyes closed and saw huge trees with dark purple leaves.

They are spread out as far as I can see. On every branch of every tree a dead body is hanging. Men, women, and children. They are dressed in rags. Their mouths are open and the keyboard notes float out of their throats. The unnatural synthesized chord echoes back on itself holding everything in a heavy stillness. It comes from every mouth on every tree as far as I can see. There are purple leaves all over the ground but the ground is moving. It is a calm purple ocean of dead purple leaves. Dorsal fins slowly and quietly move in between the trees.

I opened my eyes slowly, just enough to see the notepad I had open in my lap, and began to write.

#

DOES THE EARTH BREATHE?
IF SO IT MUST CHOKE WITH EVERY BREEZE
IF THE SUN SEES
HOW THE NIGHT BLEEDS

CRYSTAL CITY

It should darken the leaves
On the trees
We were hung from
And the violent seas
We come from
Should wash up red
For the dead
That were thrown over
We've all said it's blown over
But now I'm led with no culture
Like R&B and rap
Is supposed to tell me how to act
And the fact
That we lack
To see the math
We're being asses
While the path
To the past
Is in ashes
And now we're latch kids
With no keys
And the police is no beast
The beast
Is the grief
From the belief
That the relief
Will grow on trees
While the roots hobble our knees
The problem with these
Groveling thieves
Is the bottom degrees
That got them cheese
I'm half slave
Half Master
Drop out, ghetto bastard
But what I'm after

#

All of a sudden the bassline and the drums came in.

The trees and the dead bodies fell over into the water. Then the water swallowed itself up until there was nothing. Nothing but noise and people talking loud over this new beat.

I slammed my notebook shut and Moon-Dog yelled over to me.

"You got something for this one!"

Every Friday night I met Moon-Dog at the studio to record whatever we had written that week. He had big dreams and would talk for hours about how we were gonna be famous. Our mixtape was gonna take off and we were gonna change the world. I just got a kick out of thinking something and then hearing it.

I opened my book back up and flipped through the pages. Most of them were inked out with only a couple phrases even readable. I stopped at one.

#

#

I shook my head no.

Not at all. I couldn't write what I was supposed to be writing.

This new beat was everywhere but I couldn't find it.

It pumped at an insane volume out of four A&L studio speakers mounted on either side of a massive sound board. The studio was dark except for the dancing lights on the mixing table and sound board. Well shit, I thought, the lights can dance to it. My ears could hear it. My body could feel it. I nodded my head to it. But my words? My words couldn't find a place to sit in the beat.

"I gotta get back in the Dead Zone," I mumbled.

"What's the Dead Zone?" said some random chick.

There were three really drunk girls in the studio. I didn't bother to learn their names. I opened my notepad back up and put it in my lap. Then I pulled a golf ball sized bud of Kona Gold out of the ziplock bag and started braking it up in the crease of the book. I was mumbling to myself trying to ride this weird beat.

"That this Hawaiian nigga right here! Straight lost in The Dead Zone! Write your shit muthafucka!" yelled Moon-Dog pointing at me.

He was pacing back and forth swinging his arms like a gorilla. He had on a New York Knicks jersey, a pair of baggy jeans and some Timberland boots. The same outfit I had seen him in two days ago. He had the same philosophy about clothes as me. Wear them till they're dirty then throw them away and buy new ones. Except I hated brand names and expensive clothes. I basically wore surf shorts and tank tops. He liked expensive stuff so he wound up getting a little funky, music or no music. Especially on humid nights like this when it was hot and things weren't going easy. He was yelling over the beat like he was extremely angry at something. He was.

"The world ain't ready Q! They don't even know right now! They don't know what's about to happen. And when it does, they still won't know Q! They still won't know! It's gonna take years to catch our shit! Decades nigga! Niggas goan wake up thirty years from now like 'Oh shit! I get it! I hear it! That's that shit! That's my new shit!' but it's goan be thirty years old! Marinated thirty years until muthafucka stomachs is ready to digest this shit right here! You feel this shit?! This is for the club! The dirty underground after hours spots. Don't gimmie that deep shit Q! None of that emotional 'why are we alive?' shit! 'What does it all mean?' shit! Just flow nigga! Money, cash, hoes! All a nigga knows!"

The girl who was asking questions bounced onto the couch I was sitting on and spilled all the bud I had just broken up. She was a white girl from the military base. Maybe sixteen years old, probably not. She had red hair, freckles, and so much makeup on it was comical. She looked like a ghetto version of Dorothy from *The Wizard of Oz*, but with more make up, riding in the back of Robert Deniro's cab though Hell's Kitchen.

"Are you Dead Zone?" she yelled over the music.

Her breath smelled like a Subway sandwich and skunky Heinaken. I looked at her blankly and pushed her away. I didn't like girls in the studio. Not these kinda girls. I needed to go somewhere in my head. Strippers and hoes are for later, after we finish our four songs.

That was the agreement. We had Monday through Friday to write four songs. Three songs that were for him and I to rock together, one song solo for me. We would split the studio cost and do four hours on Friday evening. One song an hour. Friday was also the re-up, so he had to pay me for that and for the studio. I always came prepared because I always wound up paying for the whole thing myself. Tonight, like most Friday nights, the conversation had gone like this:

"Boom! Yo nigga, I got that shit for you."

"This is—naw… You short…"

"That's twelve hundo right?"

"Yeah, but what about the studio?"

"I'm sayin, you could take the two outta there, right?"

"Actually it's three, that's if we don't go over, which we will… but that's on some other shit. This is separate shit I'm kickin up. You wanna have this conversation with Kimo?"

"Nigga it ain't like that…" Moon-Dog would whine. "I'm sayin, every

Friday, twelve hundo, I ain't short, ain't never goan be again, man. We cool! It's Friday and the money's right there. I owe you for the studio my nigga! And I'ma get you back tonight! Word is bond. I'ma move a pound tonight. That's on the real, son! No doubt, shit won't even touch my palm, *whsssshhhh…* straight into your hand! And! *Aaand!* My nigga, check this out! Bottle service tonight at Pure Platinum on me! Just so you know, I'm grateful for you cuttin me a little slack. I love you! You my nigga! We gonna be famous muthafucka! We gone be HUGE!"

I smiled and playfully punched him. I wanted him to know it was cool. As long as the re-up was straight, it was cool. Drug dealing was not Moon-Dog's strongest talent. Neither was paying for bottle service at strip clubs. Or paying for anything anywhere—plate lunches, beer, cigarettes, gum. He always managed to pay the twelve hundred though. I only had to lean on him once. After that, he always had it. But he was a little weird with me since then. He was shook. It had happened in front of his whole crew and they were a little weird afterwards too. But he had been short. He was short and I had to make a point.

I had watched Kimo make a point a few times. He also had entire chapters in his notebooks about making a point and fixing this type of shit. He said, "If you do a good job of showing someone who you are early on, it's easier than showing them later. Show'em early and it's a few bruises and a smooshed ego. Show'em later and you have to break their legs and smash their teeth. Be honest and show them who you are. Let them see."

I had put my hands around Moon-Dog's throat and squeezed it slow. He was so skinny and so light I could actually pick him up and put him down on the hood of the car. He reached up and grabbed my forearms but he was too scared to fight very hard. He was playfully trying to pull my hands off of his neck. He kept saying, "C'mon Q, quit playin…" even after he had no breath left and it was just his lips mouthing "quit playin… quit playin… Q… Quit playin… for real…"

Suga-C kept mumbling from behind me. "It's all good man, we goan help him get the dough, homey…" but when I turned to look at him, he kept his head down and his eyes on the ground like everyone else.

I leaned on top of Moon-Dog and climbed up onto the bumper and jammed my knee into his nuts and squeezed his throat as hard as I could and looked into his eyes until I could see his pupils open up like slurpee straws. I needed him to see. I needed him to open his eyes all the way. I needed him to see that I would do it. I needed him to feel how close it actually was. I needed him to know that wherever he thought the line was, it wasn't. I needed him and all of them to know.

It took just over a minute for his body to panic. For his legs to start kicking wildly. For his fingernails to start digging into my arms. For Suga-C to start pacing back and forth and begging for his friend. For Moon-Dog to look deep into my eyes and see the flickering light. He saw it, then I let him go. He fell into the gravelly dirt on the side of Ewa Beach Road. He gasped and Suga-C and his crew got quiet, staring at the dirt again.

I turned around and said, "You think we're fuckin friends? On Friday we ain't friends. On Friday we're Biggie and fuckin Tupac! We ain't cool. It ain't cool! On Friday I'm a fuckin shark, you are the muthafuckin fish! PAY ME MUTHAFUCKA! And then!… Then we Tom Saywer and Hulkeberry muthafuckin Finn!"

I reached down and grabbed Moon-Dog's wrist and yanked off his watch. I turned around and walked up to Suga-C. He was taller than me but he slumped down as I got in his face. I put my face right up to his but he kept looking away. I yanked the silver herringbone chain off his neck and got in my car. Just before I drove off, I heard Suga-C ask, "Who the fuck is Tom Saywer?"

I had to turn my head away so they couldn't see me laugh. Suga-C always cracked me up.

The first three weeks at the studio were dope because it was just Moon-Dog, me and the Engineer. We could focus and get shit down. But after we killed it on Hot I-94's Cypher Sundays radio freestyle show, people started showing up at the studio trying to chill and party and shit. I had to bring Siosi and Sleepy to keep people out.

Siosi was one of Kimo's boy who would hang with us and he was cool as fuck. He was a grown-up, twenty-eight years old, but he acted like a kid. A huge almost seven-foot-tall two-hundred-eighty pound Samoan kid. He once smacked a mailbox so hard it ripped out of the concrete. If you don't believe me, then you don't know much about Samoans. Sleepy was his cousin who would come along, too. He was a pimp that worked for Marianne.

But even with them around, it was always hard to keep girls out. We told them the only way they could stay was if they flirted with the engineer because sometimes he'd forget how much we owed him.

I smelled onions and mustard and looked up to see Ghetto Dorothy was back on me again. I pushed her again and she fell back into the couch giggling and flirting way too hard. I stood up.

"Yo! *Yooo!*" I yelled above the music. "Turn the beat off!"

The engineer was a fat haole dude in his fifties. He had thinning dirty-blonde hair and a thick red beard. His t-shirt was too small and it kept rolling up his belly. He looked like a strawberry version of the Stay Puft Marshmallow Man. His face was beet red from all the beer and all the flirting teenage attention from the Italian BMT groupies. He moved one of the Subway girls off his lap, leaned forward and pushed a button. The beat stopped. The silence was heavy.

"Nuff already! This shit is like a hundred and fifty dollars an hour! We need to—"

"Actually it's two hundred an hour after nine p.m.," said the glowing carrot-chin engineer.

"Muthafucka! You havin the time of your life, shut the fuck up!" said Moon-Dog throwing a stack of one-dollar bills in his face. The pudgy red man tried to lean forward to pick up the cash but his gut got in the way. He kept trying but couldn't get forward enough to tip himself over. Each attempt came with the sound of a quarterback calling the hike: "*Huut, huuut, huuuut!*"

The girls started giggling and I started laughing. Cee-Oci and Sleepy, who were sitting on the other couch, started laughing too.

"I ain't trying to bug out or nothin, but let's focus!" I said.

"Word," said Moon-Dog. "Let's do this shit! Bitches, be quiet. I got my shit! Q, you gotta smoke another blunt or somethin man, get in the Zone, man."

"You got your shit already?!" I said.

"Yeah man…" he said.

He started diggin in his bag. I was embarrassed. I always had my shit ready. But lately, every time I sat down to write I couldn't. Or at least I couldn't write what I was supposed to write about. Kimo had put some money in and hooked us up with the radio stations and, soon, someone to shoot a video. We all agreed we should make a dope-ass gangsta dirt-road mixtape. The formula was clear. It wasn't like I needed to do anything but look around to write shit. But my mind would wander off… I would look down at the paper and it would be filled with questions. Some of it wouldn't even be rhymes. It would be long-ass paragraphs about life and the world. It was like some kind of journal or diary entry. Real gay-ass poetry and diary shit and it was getting worse with each new book that Kimo gave me to read. Every time I saw him he handed me two or three books. Revolutionary shit about the Black Panthers, Huey P. Newton, James Baldwin, Marcus Garvey, Iceberg Slim. Weird Russian shit by Fyodor Dostoevsky. Christopher Marlowe and muthafucking Shakespeare! He would always give me at least one of his handwritten notebooks filled with his thoughts on the books he was giving me. He expected me to write about what I was reading like some kinda book report but he wouldn't read my shit. He just looked to see if I wrote something. It was like the more I read, the less I could write. And, the more I knew, the more questions I had.

Moon-Dog leaned over the engineer and put the beat back on soft enough so he could spit a verse.

#

Again we open you, scoopin you down
Knowin God damn well, you feelin us now
And givin us pounds. Sup?
Many daps, like the claps on track ten
Packin the facts like shorty is packin those pants in.
Dancin, how'd she get that ass in
Without payin twice?
No delayin, advancin
Sexually takin all of the chances
Tonight's the night
I'm tryin to get my hands in
Side the box but think outside
Won't think about tomorrow until we collide
Right now we gotta party to rock and numbers to cop
Startin a fire that just won't stop
It's just that hot

And never will freeze
Even if it's iced out below zero degrees
Celius, what is you tellin us
We can't have it?
If we decide to, yo! We grab it!
And let you have it!
Touch it you silly rabbit!
Playin tricks at the bar, beggin for licks!
All you gettin is dis,
Unless you lickin the tip,
Ya get it?
Do you
Feel it?

#

Moon-Dog had been holding his notebook in one hand while his other hand had been moving through the air with the consonants and syllables. He now closed the book, leaned on the mixing table and looked at me. He had done it and he knew it. It was another club song, nothing crazy about that. The stuff he said was cool but not that crazy. It was the cadence that he had figured out. He smiled at me. He could see he had led me to the song. He could see I was now hearing all the possible patterns and words in my head. The beat was still playing softly in the background.

"You want me to roll another blunt?" he asked softly.

"No… roll it in a Zig-Zag… Let's go classic," I whispered.

I was trying not to talk too much and disturb the word structures I was building in my head.

"What…?"

"I said roll it in a Zig-Zag, like classic, smoke it, pass it, we'll take a couple hits and get blasted then I'll write some spastic, jurassic, clubs, hoes and trash shit for the niggas stuck in drug traffic!" I couldn't talk without the flow now. Everything I said fit perfect. Moon-Dog started yelling.

"YO! That's the hook! That's the muthafuckin hook! Say that shit again!" he screamed.

I paused for a second and waited for the beat and then reached behind my eyes looking for words, and then I grabbed them and put them in place before the next bar came.

#

Roll it
Pass it
Smoke it
That's it
Take a couple sips from my flask
Get blasted.
Shorty shake your hips
Like they're hits of acid
Taking me on trips
While I twist
Jurassic
Zig-Zag Classics
Nickel bag addicts
Hit the Cuervo
Until you KO! Ooooooooh...

#

Moon-Dog was dancing around the studio. The stinky girls were dancing too even though they didn't really know what just happened. Sleepy got up and gave me a hug.

"Yo that shit is tight!" he said.

I sat back down and scribbled the rest of the song out in less than ten minutes. I took a shot of Cuervo and swaggered into the vocal booth. It was quiet and dark. I tried to feel around for the music stand to switch on the little desk lamp but I couldn't find it. I didn't need it. The words were swimming around my head and if I relaxed I might say it in a better order than the way I wrote it down. Strawberry Stay Puft came over my headphones. "Okay... let's get a mic check..."

"Check one, two... two, two two... 2pac... too hot... to cop that regular crop... I roll it non-stop... non-stock it's fresh... from the chop-shop makes you sick till your snot rots…"

"Okay… sounds good…" He was laughing.

When the engineer pushed the talk button, I could hear Moon-Dog and the girls and Sleepy's voice all at once with some other music going in the mixing room through my headphones…They were having fun as soon as my grumpy Mr. focus ass was out of the room. I had to reach my arms out and hold myself up to keep from falling as the beat kicked in through my headphones. All the weed and tequila mixed with the pitch dark. I should have brought the bottle into the booth so I could use it as a counter balance.

"Ayo… Pass me the Tequila," I asked into the mic.

"What…?"

"The bottle of Tequila… can you pass it…?"

I could feel the moment coming just as Moon-Dog opened the booth door and handed me the bottle.

#

It's cool
Light it up,
I know the bouncers from High School,
We sold ounces to surfer dudes
Half kona gold, half oregano
Just keep it low
And exhale slow
Into your shirt.
Let's blaze till it hurt
It's amazing
Her skirt
Merely traces her worth
Like the face of the Earth
When your high
Like me
Orbit and fly
Like me
Like Soliloquies

In the breeze
I might be
Killing these
Similes
Till I find my feet
They're the reason
I squeezed in the V.I.P.
And to
Light another one
Until the brother comes
With the MAG light
Telling me to act right.
I'm leaning back like "woah"
That's hydro
I'm gonna need another shot of Cuervo
No lime
No salt
No cryin
Don't stop
Till the bottom of the glass
Ties the past
In a knot
Till we all up outta cash
And I'm askin you not
To be hoggin up my flask
Did we half it or not
I'm sayin
After payin for like six Coronas
The grip I hold is
Lighter than a stripper's
Soul is
Stick to sodas
And splash the fifth
The goal is
Spit till gold is
Coming out my shit

Like boulders
If you know this
Burn with my song
And bounce that ass until they turn the lights on!

***

"Aloha ladies and gentlemen, on behalf of myself and the rest of the crew, we would like to welcome you to Voyager Submarines and Adventures. What you see behind me is a one-hundred-ton shuttle vessel that will take us about two miles out to sea where we then tie up to the world's largest passenger submarine. From there we will ask you to cross a ramp to the deck of the submarine where you will be asked to climb one by one down a ladder through the hatch. While waiting, we ask that you hold on to the handrails on the deck of the submarine. I would just like to point out that there is no smoking on any of our vessels and…"

Kimo shot me a look that said "put that shit out." I took one more pull of the joint I was smoking and checked if Cynthia wanted another hit. She waved it off and popped in a fresh piece of bubble gum.

She had her jet black hair up in a sloppy lopsided ponytail. She was wearing a super tiny wife-beater tank top with a black lace bra and cut-off jean shorts that could double as a bikini. Husbands with their families were doing everything in their power not to look and failing. Wives were giving us looks of disgust. Cynthia was oblivious. I took off my black and blue flannel and told her to wear it.

We were standing on the dock of the Hilton Hawaiian Village. The only dock in Waikiki. Some young blond guy in a white button-down captain's shirt with blue epaulettes and short gray cargo shorts was talking on a microphone about restrooms and life vests to a group of tourists. Kimo had said he wanted to show me something. Every few days he would do something like this. I called it lecture day. It would be us hiking and him lecturing me about life or us surfing and him lecturing me about life or us riding dirt bikes and him lecturing me about life. Just show up out of the blue, standing at the foot of my bed like, "Get dressed. I want to show you something."

This morning had been different though.

"I need you to see something. Get up." Kimo was looking at the wall like it was a math problem he needed to solve.

I reached into a hole I had cut in the mattress, pulled out an envelope with the money from Alex and held it out, trying my best to get ready for his truth probe. I was fully prepared to tell him everything. I wanted to tell him. Tell him how fucked up I thought it was down there. Tell him how crazy Alex was. Tell him I smoked ice. Tell him it was only once and tell him I'll never ever fucking touch it again. Tell him everything.

He stared at the envelope and I stared at my bedsheet.

"Where are you guys going today?" asked Cynthia half asleep. She was peeking out from under the sheets.

"Shut up," I said and put the pillow over her head. She started whining.

"I wanna go. You guys always go do stuff and I just—"

"Go spend my money—"

"Fuck you!"

"Fuck you—"

"You can come, Twinkie. Just hurry up," said Kimo.

That shut us both up. Cynthia always asked if she could come and he always said no. She jumped out of bed naked and ran to the shower. Kimo's eyes followed her all the way to the bathroom. Then he looked back at me and grabbed the envelope with one eyebrow raised. "Damn, she grew up…"

He put the envelope in his pocket and that was the end of it. He didn't ask.

***

It was a little jarring to see the Concrete Rainbow during the day. We had been coming to town earlier now to sell weed and coke at the college dorms but we never got to Waikiki before sunset. There were people from all over the world carrying towels and floaty toys. So much sunburn and farmer's tans. So many fat people. Kids who didn't know how to walk in flip flops. So much laughter and cheerful conversation. I thought about getting a drink but knew Kimo wouldn't approve because it was still morning. Maybe I could get away with smoking the rest of my joint once we got on the boat.

Cynthia and I waited by the ticketing booth while Kimo went up into the wheelhouse of the huge shuttle boat to talk to the captain. There were three ticketing girls behind us and we could hear them talking to each other.

"His name is Kimo. He's like, someone."

"Totally, like a badass."

"He's like, a real local guy. He's like, I think he's, like, native or something. Like, nobody can fuck with him. Everyone knows about him…"

"I have a cousin in California who sells drugs."

"You mean Toby?"

"Yeah, Toby is kinda big time."

"No disrespect but like, totally not the same thing! Kimo is like, there's like Hawaiian like organized crime, you guys don't even know, like for real, they are like tied in with like the Yakuza or some shit, like for real"

"Isn't that Japanese?"

"What ever, Tammy."

"But he's so hot!"

"Shut up!"

"But he is."

Cynthia was rolling her eyes and snapping her gum as if it would drown out the girls' talking. Kimo motioned us up into the boat. He told us to hang out on the upper deck while he talked to the captain. The boat backed out of the dock, turned around and headed out towards Diamond Head crater. It was beautiful. I never surfed in Waikiki or even went to the beaches. My only time in town had been at night. Seeing Waikiki in the morning from a boat off shore was epic. It was like a tourism commercial for Hawaii. The trade winds rushed across the water blowing salty fresh air. It whipped Cynthia's hair around and she smiled. I had bought her a little disposable camera from the ABC store and she was snapping away like a tourist. The haole kid came over the microphone and pointed at dolphins swimming with the boat. Cynthia screamed and ran over to take a picture.

Suddenly Kimo's voice came over the P.A. system.

Now if you take a look down towards Waikiki you can see what all the fuss is about. It truly is breathtaking. Voted number four of the top twenty most beautiful beaches in the world. It's not real, but it is beautiful. In Hawaiian "wai" means water and "kiki" means spouting. Waikiki was where we grew kalo. It was wetlands. After the land was stolen, the hotels needed sand for the tourists to have a place to put their umbrellas, so they brought sand in on barges from all over the world and dumped it along the shoreline. The outgoing current takes that sand off of the beach and it kills all of the surrounding coral. The devastation is without measure. But it's better for tourists, who only sit on the beach and wade in the water anyway. Now I can see by the looks on your faces you are concerned. Don't worry, it's okay. The Hawaiians don't own any of it anymore anyway. It's yours to destroy now. But if you do feel bad about it, make sure you leave a big tip next time you see one of us cleaning up after you. Enjoy the rest of your stay here. Mahalo!

Kimo walked past me with a grin on his face and went back inside the wheelhouse. I stood there thinking about what a tourist sees when they come here. A tour guide tells them about how Hawaiians are a welcoming people and that the word "aloha" means love. They go to a luau staged especially for them and eat some poi and go home thinking and feeling that they have connected with something ancient and exotic. But in reality, all they experienced was this shimmery commercial layer of the island designed to take their money and give them that feeling. Like how in commercials they use shoe polish to make the burgers look good or pour engine oil on pancakes. Waikiki was an ad from the glossy pages of a magazine. It's not real.

The boat turned and pulled up to a huge submarine. We tied alongside it and a ramp lowered down. Kimo told Cynthia to go on the submarine and Kimo and I went across the submarine to a small inflatable speed boat that the crew used to get around between the shuttle boat, the submarines and a small tugboat that was anchored close by.

Cynthia seemed excited waving goodbye to us as she headed down into the sub and I kinda wished I was going down with her to see what that was about. But instead me and Kimo and two crew members motored slowly over to the tugboat where another crew member talked into a handheld radio.

"Voyager Nine, hatches are confirmed closed, skiff's away from the side. Control, you have the con."

"Voyager Nine, this is control. You are clear to begin dive sequence."

"Control, this is Voyager Nine, hatches are confirmed closed, ballast set at eight thoushand pounds, request permission to submerge."

"Voyager Nine, Control, clear to dive at 0-8."

"0-8 DIVE, DIVE, DIVE!!!"

I jumped from the speedboat to the tugboat and looked back at the submarine that Cynthia was on. Puffs of spray popped up from the side of the submarine as it slowly began to disappear underwater. I watched it until it was completely gone. Then I heard Kimo arguing with one of the captains in the wheelhouse of the tugboat. The other crew members were eating or sleeping on the deck.

"Kimo, I can't let you just disappear with the speedboat," said the captain softly with his head down.

"Where's the maintenance speedboat?" asked Kimo.

"It's still at Pier forty, so…"

"Well, have them bring it out here. We can wait around for a few minutes," said Kimo.

"Brah, I can not do dat," said the captain, finally lifting his head. He was trying to speak Pidgin, maybe outta respect, but it was horrible and sounded like he was making fun of the way locals talk. Kimo ignored it and spoke slowly and clearly like he was talking to a child.

"Why can't you do that? You're thinking you're gonna get in trouble?" pushed Kimo.

The captain picked up the radio.

"Pier forty, this is Control."

"Control, go ahead."

"Yeah hey, we uh, we gotta do a little black ops, missing vertical cover, but I think I know where it is. Can you have one of the guys bring the maintenance skiff out here?"

"It's gonna be a few minutes but we'll have Joey bring it out."

"Roger that, thanks."

Kimo walked out to the deck and was gonna say something but stopped and looked at the scuba gear that was kept against the smoke stack. He looked back at me with a grin.

"You know how to scuba dive?" he asked.

"Oh yeah, in California I—" I stopped talking.

He waited with his eyebrows raised.

"No," I said.

"Well, if you don't know how, then I can teach you."

Kimo started grabbing the scuba tanks and regulators and BCs and fins. The captain came out of the wheelhouse and started talking to Kimo while he was setting up. He had stopped trying to sound local.

"Kimo, I can't let you dive right now! I got two subs in the water and Marcy's driving one of them. You know how she is."

"You can't let me go scuba diving with my nephew?"

"Well because—"

"Is that what you said?"

"No it's just—"

"Do you have twenty grand?"

"No. It's just—"

"Do you even have this week's vig?'

"No, it's Wednesday—"

"No. It's whatever the fuck day I say it is. But I'm letting you come to work. I'm letting you have some room to breathe because I know you're good for it. It's a favor, Bob. A big favor. Now I come out here, and I wanna scuba dive and drive a speedboat around a little and show off to my little nephew and you can't *let* me? Is that the conversation we are having right now?"

Bob was sweating. He was a skinny unhealthy white guy that managed to look pale in spite of the haole forever sunburn. He didn't look at Kimo and Kimo had never looked up from the dive gear. In fact, Kimo never raised his voice. He was sincerely asking the question, slowly and clearly. Like asking a five year old does he really want to spend his allowance on that bullshit key chain. Kid, you don't even own keys.

"Try not to get too close to the subs and try to come up inshore and Diamond Head. With a big bubble, please!" said Bob, sounding like a captain again.

Kimo had everything all set up. He put on his own gear and helped me put on mine.

"Aight kid. This ain't a big deal unless you freak out. It just takes a second to get used to it. It's just like snorkeling except you have to pull a little on every breath. Just pretend you're taking a hit off a joint every breath except don't hold it in. Breathe slow—that's the main thing. I'll be right next to you the whole time so if there is a problem, you let me know. This means no air."

He made a hand signal like cutting your throat.

"This means go fuck yourself."

He gave me two middle fingers. Some of the crew members were watching us now. They chuckled.

"This button fills your BC with air. This lets the air out. You wanna find the sweet spot so you're floating perfect. Don't come up without me. We have to come up real slow and chill at around twenty feet after we're finished so we don't die from air bubbles in our blood. So stay with me, no Icarus shit."

"What's Icarus?" I said.

One of the crew members laughed and said, "You didn't learn that in school?"

"No, but I just learned this."

I used both hands and gave him two middle fingers. Everyone laughed.

"This kid learns fast," said Kimo proudly and everyone laughed again.

"Shit dude, I should've gotten certified with you. Cut out all the bullshit and just dive!" said another crew member and they all laughed some more.

Kimo said to the captain, "If we come up after the first sub, send the hot Asian chick in the daisy dukes over here to the tug to wait for us."

We stepped off the tugboat and I immediately started sinking. I had been spear fishing with Kimo a lot and he was right. This wasn't that far from it. As I sank to the bottom, I rushed to clear my ears. I turned over head first and was happy I already knew how to clear them without using my hands. I searched my whole body looking for the button to let the air out. I didn't find it until I was already crumpled up, upside down on the ocean floor. I was right next to the anchor that was holding the tugboat.

Kimo floated near by watching, making sure I wasn't freaking out. I thought I was fine once I straightened out, but he swam over anyway and started motioning me to slow down my breathing. He grabbed my gages and pointed at the numbers on it: 2800 lbs. He made me breathe with him. Slowly in, slowly out. He motioned taking a hit from a joint. I smiled and water went in my mouth. Once we started swimming, it took all my willpower not to freak out. I never felt like I could relax. I was used to coming down around sixty feet but I would be holding my breath. To breathe down here took an insane amount of trust in this tank and hose strapped to my back.

I followed Kimo and he was following something I couldn't see. Maybe a rock or a brick or a coral head. Every two minutes or so he would stop and look around and then point with his whole hand and we would change course slightly, usually to the left. We came upon a huge field filled with giant cement columns and metal pipes and pieces of PVC pipe. There were plenty of fish swimming around here. Trigger fish, butterfly fish and puffer fish. I wanted to spear some.

Kimo swam up to me and checked my air. He shook his head disapprovingly and made the slow down motion again. He turned and we continued offshore. He picked up the pace and this was actually easier. I could time my breaths with the kicks. Breathe in, kick, kick, kick, breathe out, kick, kick, kick.

I could feel myself relaxing into the rhythm. I stretched each breath to last through the kicks and in between I could hear the ocean. The sound of the sand and rocks and little pieces of dead coral rolling around the ocean floor. I could feel the energy of each swell as it pushed me and the fish around me. I could read it with the hair on my arms and legs. The water was all around me. It was in my ears and my mouth and my nose. I could smell and taste the sand and the rocks and the coral. The ripples on the surface made sunlight dance on the ocean floor in colors that were strange.

The ocean floor began to drop off but Kimo stayed at about seventy feet. He pointed down to the right. It was a giant southern stingray slowly gliding in our direction. It must have seen us too because it turned around and slowly started swimming the other way. Kimo motioned for us to keep going to the left and we swam on. My legs were starting to burn and it was getting harder not to just gulp air. My heart was pounding but I kept my breathing timed with my kicks, with only the occasional four or five seconds of freaked-out panic breathing.

It appeared suddenly, as if it had always been visible. The huge shadow that had been just outside our vision morphed all at once into a giant sunken ship. It was massive. It's bow was directly in front of us. It became harder to kick as we approached it. The current was bouncing off the ship and pushing us away. I struggled to make it the last twenty feet while Kimo hung on to the bow egging me on.

When I finally reached him, he grabbed my arm and put my hand on the edge of the bow. He checked my regulator and motioned me to slow down my breathing. It was almost impossible. My ears were ringing and my head was pounding. After almost two whole minutes I was able to get a hold of myself and look around.

Right in front of me was a young Hawaiian green sea turtle resting on the bow. It looked at me less than three feet from my face. It blinked slowly and I swear to god it was smiling. Kimo nudged me awake and motioned for me to follow him. He swam through a hole in the deck of the ship and we went inside. There were two more turtles sleeping in there. We swam right out the other side, and when Kimo swam away to the right of the ship, I almost motioned him back until I realized he was swimming towards an even larger sunken ship. This one must have been military because it had gun turrets and a super narrow hull. I was just starting to kick over when I heard what sounded like a huge fart. A huge slapping, grinding fart. I looked to the left and saw the submarine coming right for me. Kimo saw it too. He swam back toward me like he was Aquaman or something—so fast. He was motioning me towards the on coming submarine. I hesitated, trying to figure out what he wanted and why he was swimming into a death collision with a giant submarine. He stopped right in front of it and waved me over once more. Then he faced the pilot's glass-bubble view port and grabbed his nuts with one hand and stuck up a middle finger with his other. At the very last second, he kicked up over the pilot's dome and grabbed the railing of the upper deck.

In that second, I finally figured out why he was motioning me over. He wanted us to ride the submarine. I kicked with everything I had towards the sub that was now passing me by. The electric motors made a high-pitched whirring sound that got louder and louder as I got closer. It was like those old train robbery movies where the bad guys are trying to run with the train fast enough to jump on except we were ninety feet under the mutherfucking ocean. I reached out for the railing somewhere in the middle of the sub and grabbed on. I was not ready for how fast it was going. It yanked my arm so hard I thought my shoulder dislocated. My mask was ripped off my face and I bobbled back and forth banging my scuba tank into the handrails. My regulator almost came out of my mouth but I managed to bite down hard on the edge of the mouth piece at the last second. It was still too far out of my mouth to get a clean breath so each inhale came with a full glass of fresh salt water. I wasn't sure what to do so I just hung there. I was choking and gagging on the water and any second I would lose the mouthpiece.

Kimo always said, "If you're going down, go down swinging."

I wrapped my legs around the railing to keep myself from thrashing around. Then I grabbed the railing with both hands and used my legs and arms to pull myself closer to the T portion of the rail. I put my arm through it and hooked my elbow. This freed up my left hand. I put the mouthpiece all the way back in and breathed a full breath… then gagged and vomited for a few seconds… then breathed again. The mask had luckily been pulled down around my neck. I took another deep breath then took out my mouth piece and untangled the hose from the mask strap and put the mask on. When I cleared my mask, I saw Kimo's smiling eyes right in front of my face. He had been making his way back from the front of the sub to help me. He had a proud look on his face. I had figured it out without help.

He started signaling me that we would let go together and float through the gap in the rear sail of the submarine. Now that I knew how fast the sub was going I figured he was just joking. The sail on the sub was a super hard eight-by-six-foot fiberglass square above the rear hatch well. Letting go of the railing and floating through while the sub was going full ahead was fucking insane. What if we missed and hit the sail, or worse, hit the solid steel hatch, smashing against it, scuba tanks and all?! Kimo must have read my eyes because he shrugged his shoulders and let go of the railing. He crossed his straightened legs and folded his arms making himself thinner, like jumping off a super high cliff into the water. He went right through the sail.

I let go.

I started to drift left and I skidded across the inside of the sail with my hands and flippers then immediately had to kick away to avoid getting hit by the rear handrails. Kimo put his hands up and cheered. I could actually hear him yelling underwater.

We swam away from the ships and gradually got more shallow. At twenty feet Kimo motioned that we would chill there for a while. He floated away from me slowly as we both waited. He reached and grabbed his fins with his hands and pulled himself forward. He was stretching. I copied him and realized how tight my back had gotten, then I saw him with his legs crossed like he was sitting Indian style floating. I tried it and kept flipping over. He was maybe forty feet from me, floating like a picture of Buddha from one of his sketches in his notebooks. Suddenly a shit ton of fish started swimming around him. The sun was shining through the water behind him casting a single ray of light over him. I didn't have a way to think about or to understand what I was looking at. It was a feeling. The feeling of remembering you had a dream but not remembering the dream. A tickle in the back of your mind that you can't touch. It moves further and further away the more you try to think it. I smiled and was about to cheer or yell something to him about how cool he looked, but then I took my last breath.

***

"Hey boys, fancy meeting you here," said Cynthia in her weird, flirty 1950's T.V. debutant imitation. She was leaning over the side of the inflatable pontoon with a huge smile on her sunburned cheeks. Kimo and I had popped up together. In fact, we were holding on to each other sharing his air. Cynthia tilted her head sideways with a puzzled look.

"Is there something I should know about you two? I mean I'm not judging! It's the 90s. Express yourself, but I will never be able to satisfy you that way, babe..."

Kimo took off his mask and threw it at Cynthia.

"God damn, you grew up with a mouth!" said Kimo.

"Apparently the mouth is not what my boyfriend wants," she snapped back.

"I ran out of air," I said.

"Maybe you were blowing too hard," she said.

Kimo started cracking up. I knew better than to say anything else.

"Bob let you drive the speedboat?" asked Kimo.

"Yeah, he's a super sweet guy. He said anytime I want to go on a boat he'll take me and literally show me the ropes," said Cynthia excitedly.

"Yeah, I'm sure he'll show his rope. Probably more like a string," said Kimo. "Very gently come ahead and then put it in neutral. We'll swim alongside you. And drape those two small yellow ropes over the side so we can climb up in."

We climbed in and took off the gear. Then Kimo took the helm and started driving super fast away from the tug boats and the submarine dive site. He was headed west, back towards Ewa Beach and Waianae. I laid down in the front of the skiff and tried to breathe and let my head stop pounding. Cynthia sat on the fiberglass box in front of the control panel with a huge smile on her face. Her hair was flapping in the wind and she had her arms spread out wide like she was flying. She caught me looking at her and yelled down to me, "I got a badass picture of you. Underwater from inside. You look sexy as fuck!" she said. She pinched both of her nipples and blew me a kiss. I grinned and closed my eyes.

When I woke up we were stopped, rocking gently in the swell. I sat up and saw the west edge of the island way off in the distance. Some time had passed. It was well into the afternoon. Cynthia was curled up next to me fast asleep. I stood and looked at Kimo. He was not smiling. He was looking at the island, leaning against the back railing with his arms crossed. His eyes were far away and he didn't even acknowledge me. I stared in the same direction, waiting to see if he would come out of it on his own.

"Grab your mask. I want to show you something," he finally said.

He started the motors and nudged the boat slowly this way and that. He was lining it up with some sort of landmarks on the shore. After a while he said, "Stick your head in and look for a buoy."

I saw it right away. We were right on top of it.

"I see it," I said.

"Kay, dive in and follow the line down about thirty feet. You should see some chains attached to it with more line. I need to know if there are at least three separate lines with three separate chains. Tug on everything and check the knots."

I jumped in and it was cold now. I was tired and hungry and cold. My head was still pounding. I took a few long slow breaths on the surface then dove down to the bouy. I grabbed it then suddenly wished I had put some gloves on. The line for the buoy was old and covered with sharp barnacles and growth. I walked it down about thirty feet and saw another rope tied to the main line, then another about five feet under the first, then another five feet deeper. Each line then had a length of chain attached to it with a ten pound plate. The line then ran back up and was tied to the buoy line with a simple half hitch. At this depth I could see the main buoy line go all the way down more than a hundred feet to an anchor on the bottom. It was just like the anchor the tugboat was moored to.

I waited a moment to make sure I remembered to check and double check everything he asked then swam back up to the surface.

"How's it look?" he asked. He wasn't looking at me. He was still staring off somewhere.

"It looks good. Everything you said was there and the knots and the lines look good."

He leaned down on the inflatable pontoon onto his elbows so his face was right in front of mine. I was still in the water holding on to the thin piece of yellow nylon rope used to climb in and out of the skiff.

"I'm going to help you do something. Something that you really need to do. I don't think you can do it by yourself. Once it's done you can be a whole new person. Cuz right now you're trapped. Me too. I need you to help me with the same thing. We can help each other. Whatcha think, can we help each other?" asked Kimo sincerely.

I didn't know what he was talking about.

I didn't know what to say.

I was cold and he was scaring me.

"I don't know what to say, Kimo." I was shivering.

"My bad, I must sound crazy as fuck," he said and smiled wide. He reached out his hand and pulled me into the boat.

CHAPTER 6

DOG EAT PUSSY WORLD

I LOOKED AT MY pack of Kools. Every morning I would roll ten ciga-rette-sized joints and put them in with my cigarettes. It was dark. I was about a hundred yards away from the lights of the farm. Far enough so that the noise and the smells were dimmed down. There was a chill in the air. I could tell it would rain soon. It was between fights and all of the chickens were being loaded up into various beat-up Toyota trucks. An older sinewy Filipino man was yelling in Tagalog at two younger men who were obviously his sons. You could tell they won. The two young men were drunk and laughing and the old man was concerned about the cages being tied down right. If the chicken fights were done, the dogs would be fighting soon.

The cock fights were fun. Sometimes local bands would come and jam. Sometimes it was just old uncles and aunties who used to perform in Waikiki before the hotels got rid of the lounge shows. Guitars and ukuleles and whole families blending their voices together in crazy harmonies sing-ing songs that held memories of things that were gone. I didn't understand most of it but I loved to try. And the food. They always had at least three or four roasted pigs all done in different styles. One would be chicharon. Roasted perfect so that the skin was super crispy and the meat was juicy and salty. It would be laid out on a table and you just take a clever to it and take the pieces you want. Another one would be kalua pig. Buried in an imu right there on the farm and dug up just as the fights started, roasted so long that it shreds itself like string cheese. Trays and trays of lumpia and pancit. And the fights were fun to watch. They put blades on the ankles of the birds and put them in the center of a ten-by-ten-foot square. They would go at it! It was a flurry of feathers and then one would drop. There usually wasn't that much blood and it was a fucking bird, so who cares?

The dogs though, that was something different. No matter how many fights I had been to, no matter how drunk or how high, I had to puff myself up to look at the dogs before the fights. When I walked by the trucks beforehand, I could easily tell that they all knew what was about to happen. I could see them handling it in different ways. Some were mean and aggressive, barking and showing teeth to anyone who came too close. Some were slumped in the back of their cages, crying and whimpering. Then there were the smart ones. They didn't bark or cry. They would stand in the center of the cage looking at me carefully, thoughtfully. They would be tense and ready, showing a little teeth and an almost quiet, low growl as I got close, but they were thinking. The aggressive ones and the bitch ones couldn't shake me, but the smart ones—I would always feel fucked up about the smart ones. For them it was lose-lose. If they lose, then they get fucked up and probably put down. If they win, they get fucked up and they have to fight a bigger dog next because they were smart and figured out a way to beat bigger, more aggressive dogs. But eventually the bigger dogs win. That's just the way it goes.

In fact, they all lose. It's just a matter of time. I wondered if the smarter dogs could see the cage. If they could see that their only hope was to run away. To bite the hand that feeds them. To look for an opening and run. Run to somewhere else. Maybe a little boy would find the beat-up dog and bring him to a little family with two and a half kids and a little yard. Would the dog be happy there, or would it have fucking post traumatic stress disorder and bite the little boy? Then get sent to the pound and put down.

Lose-lose.

I could find him, though. If he bit me, I would understand. He'd had a fucked up life. His first owner fucked up his head. He had trusted his first owner and his first owner took that trust and twisted it…

I held out the pack of cigarettes and I was able to catch some moonlight. There were four joints left and six cigarettes. I wanted to smoke a joint but I took a cigarette. I needed to think. My mind kept running off on stupid excursions and when I forced it to stay put, it would be cloudy.

It wasn't just me—Kimo was acting strange. When he talked he would ramble, which was fine when I first met him because him rambling would usually be fucking hilarious and end with some kind of button—some kind of rule that I could follow to make more money or not get arrested or killed. Street shit. But over the last few weeks it would drift into some sort of slow-moving swamp. Almost doubt. He would waver back and forth on what he was saying until even he couldn't get it to make sense. He would stop because all of it led to the same place over and over again. It led to a place that was not here. Not stealing cars. Not selling meth. Not beating and threatening people. Not taking people's entire paycheck. Not breaking girls and pimping them out on Hotel Street. It led to a place that I could not see.

He had seen it.

He said he would walk around the place when he was in solitary confinement. He said he would take his time building the place first. He would start with his favorite beach. Then he would take his favorite mountain and his favorite valley and he would put them right next to each other and put a small cabin right in the middle. Then he would take all the people he loved and all of their problems and he would wash them in the white wash until all those problems were gone. Just roll them back and forth in the sand. He would wash himself too, he said. Then he would surf and fish and plant kalo and pick mountain apples all day. Smoke weed and drink kava and laugh all night with his washed people.

He said sometimes he would fall asleep while he was building it and it would build itself. It would be different though. Him and Maryanne would have a kid and they would live in a small apartment on the top of the mountain. They had regular jobs and got into fights about regular stuff. They would make love and cook and fold clothes. At night he would take out the trash and look up at the stars and while he was walking back he could see Maryanne in through the kitchen window singing and doing dishes. In the afternoon he would walk down the street to go pick up his son from kindergarten. Him and his son would walk home holding hands and talk about how a centipede was in one of his friend's shoes at school. Then they would laugh about the time Mommy got bitten by a centipede and was super dramatic about it.

When they would open the cell door to let Kimo out, he wouldn't want to come out because he wanted to live in the other place on the mountain. He would punch and kick and bite the guards until they let him stay there and he would curl up and punch his head to try to get back to that place.

Is this what Star had meant when she said Kimo was scared of going back to jail? Or was it something else? It was something else. It wasn't scared. Kimo was not scared. Kimo wasn't scared and Uncle was not stressed. Uncle was scared. Kimo was something else. Uncle was scared because he needed Kimo and Kimo was… something else.

"You gonna stay out here or what?" asked Lehua.

She was half black, half Hawaiian. Tall and beautiful. Super thick, long, curly black hair and bright green eyes. So bright I could see them in the moonlight.

"Naw, I'm just smoking a cigarette," I said.

"The old Filipino guy who was staring at us wen leave."

"Oh yeah? Just now?"

"Yeah, pretty much. I wen follow him out to his car and then he wen go."

I thought it was funny that she was speaking such thick Pidgin to me alone in the dark. She never did when we were alone. Neither did I. We spoke black, but because the fights were super local both of us went super mok.

"Was he buggin?" I asked, stopping the Pidgin.

"Yeah, he didn't even bet on the last cock fight and he fuckin peeled out when he left," she said.

She seemed excited by the whole thing. She thought this was some gangsta shit going on and she loved it. She loved being a part of it. Unfortunately for both of us, this wasn't gangsta shit. It was trifling shit.

I had spotted Cynthia's dad from across the room. He had spotted me at the exact same time. My hope had been that he wouldn't recognize me because my hair wasn't braided like it was the last time he saw me at dinner. That was stupid. How many half-black drug dealers are there in Ewa Beach? I couldn't leave though. Tonight was the night Kimo was finally going to "take care of this whole Alex thing." When he had asked me to come with him he didn't look me in the eye.

If he had he would have seen the wave wash over me. Just hearing Alex's name made my hands and feet feel prickly like a hundred ant bites.

Then another fear, like the second wave in a set. Did Kimo know I had spent the whole night in Crystal City with Alex. Did he know about me smoking ice? Is that why he was acting strange? What did "take care of" mean? What is "this whole Alex thing"? Why am I a part of the "whole Alex thing"? Does he mean "whole thing" like Alex and all the S.O.S.? I couldn't see anyone, not even Kimo, going down to Pupuole Street and "taking care of" the S.O.S. No way. Ain't nobody doing the old school strong arm to those muthafuckers. Did he mean the dealer kids? Did he mean shutting down Crystal City? That would be like wiping the Devil's ass.

I took a deep breath and settled on Kimo having something up his sleeve. He probably just wanted to show me how to fix a problem. He's the teacher, I'm the student. If he knew about my night down there and had a problem with me, I would know by now.

My problem right now was my girlfriend's dad who had just been staring at me with my arm around a girl who was not his daughter. And now he was gone.

"Aight, good work keepin an eye on him. Let's just see how it all plays out. Let's go back inside."

"Wait," she said.

She put her hands on my shoulders and stopped me from walking back in. I could feel a light rain starting as the breeze rustled the kiawe trees.

"Kiss me," she said bluntly.

I looked at her and watched her green eyes searching my face. She was almost as tall as me so we were pretty much to eye to eye. I kissed her. She had huge thick lips. Nothing stirred inside of me. She wrapped her arms around the back of my neck and pulled me in. She was feeling something. She pulled away and was breathing hard. She read my face and then slapped me.

"Who's Cindy," she said.

It wasn't a question.

"Why?"

"You're fuckin around behind my back?!" She was raising her voice.

"I'm not behind your back."

"Are you guys living together?!" She was yelling now.

"Keep your voice down," I said firmly.

She lowered her voice to a seething whisper.

"Are you *living* with a girl named *Cindy*?!"

"You've been to my house…"

"I've been to one of your apartments in Waipahu! You have another apartment in Mililani and a fucking house in Kapolei!" she yelled.

She had her finger all in my face.

"What the fuck you think this is!" I was starting to yell. "I'm a fucking drug dealer—I'm out here fucking hustlin. You think I'm going to have a fucking girlfriend?! What we gonna do, hold hands and I let you wear my fuckin football jacket?! You gonna be my ride or die chick? Why? Because you sucked my dick in the parking lot outside the strip club?"

"*Fuck you!*" she screamed.

"No, FUCK YOU!" I yelled.

A few guys from inside the farm started laughing and yelling "no, fuck you," "*fuck* you!!" and "fuck both of you!"

I grabbed her hands to keep her from hitting me and I pinned them behind her. We were inches from each other. Breathing.

"Calm down!" I growled at her.

"Fuck you!"

"Calm the fuck down, please!" I said.

Her eyes were going back and forth from my eyes to my mouth. She stopped struggling. Then she leaned in and kissed me. My chest caught on fire. I let her arms go and reached up behind her and grabbed her hair. She bit my lip and I had to yank her head back to make her let my lip go before it popped. I grabbed her hand and we ran to my car. It was raining now and it took a minute to find my car because I had just bought it and I couldn't remember what kind of car it was. I had bought it for one thousand dollars cash from some old dude. It was a 1976 Ford Gran Torino.

The old dude had been like, "It's the exact car from Starsky and Hutch!" and I was like, "Dude, I don't know what you're talking about. All I see is an old ass faded yellow car. Plus, you said the electricity is broken?"

"The alternator. It will drive just fine but you only have electricity if you're givin it gas, so you know, headlights, radio—"

"Whatever, I'm just driving it home, so how about one thousand dollars?"

"Sounds good, here's the keys…"

As soon as I opened the door, Lehua pulled the front seat forward and leaped in the back. She laid back and was rushing to peel off her jeans. I stood in the rain for a second. This was stupid. I was here to back up Kimo. I should be inside looking for Alex.

She finally got her jeans off and pulled her g-string to the side and slid two fingers into her pussy. Then she got up on her knees and reached her arm out to me. She grabbed my face and shoved the two fingers into my mouth. I got in the car and shut the door.

***

The rain was coming down hard. It was loud all around the car. I didn't even notice it until we finished. The windows were completely steamed up and both of us laid naked half-on, half-off the back seats trying to catch our breath. I found my cigarettes but couldn't find my lighter. I leaned forward to push in the cigarette lighter. Then I remembered what the old dude had said about the car and went back to looking for the lighter in my pocket. Then I decided to put my pants on first, then look for the lighter. The whole time Lehua watched me, smiling.

"You're all over the place," she giggled.

"Yeah, you got a lighter?" I whispered.

"Yeah, but at least roll down the window?"

She reached in her purse and passed me a lighter as I put on my clothes. I tried to roll down the window but the rain was coming down so hard it splashed all inside the car.

"Hey I gotta check on Kimo anyway. Why don't you just chill here for a while and I'll be right back?"

"You can smoke in here. It's cool." she said softly.

"Naw, I'll be right back"

"Chill for a second..."

She wrapped her arms around me and put those big fat lips gently on my forehead. I relaxed a little.

"I've been bumpin your mixtape. That shit is bangin!"

"For real?!"

"Yeah..." She laughed. "Like you didn't know."

"Naw, I mean, I think it's pretty good but I don't know," I said in an almost whisper. "I'm from Ewa Beach, so what do I know about hip-hop?"

"You're a trip," she said and kissed me again.

"That's really cool that you dig my music."

"My shit is the "Heartbeat" joint! I like when you say all that other shit about, I don't know, real life an shit."

"For real? Nobody likes that song. That's actually the song everyone was trying to get me to take off the tape."

"You hanging with the wrong people, boy! Some of your other shit is like, kinda like, regular brag street shit, stupid shit, but when you step outside of that, you say shit I ain't ever heard before, but ya know, it's like real."

"Dang, you sound like a friend of mine…"

She kissed me again and I kissed her back. She bit my lip softly and made a playful grunting sound and then leaned back and looked at me. Then she grabbed my hand and put it against her chest.

"Can you feel my heartbeat?" she whispered.

I nodded yes. It was beating fast and seemed to match the sound of the heavier raindrops falling from the trees and banging onto the metal of the old car.

"This is what the song feels like to me," she said so soft I almost couldn't hear her.

"What do you mean?"

"This is what it means, right?"

"Heartbeat?"

"It means heaven is in these moments when your heart beats like this, right? Everyone is searching for heaven but it's actually inside of you but… you have to find it in the moment. Right?"

She was searching my eyes.

"Can you say that shit?" she asked.

"What, the song?"

"Yeah…"

"Well… I don't have the instrumental or nothin…"

"Nah, acapella."

"I'm not sure if I remember the whole thing cuz… like… I didn't think anyone was feelin that one…"

"I can help… cuz I memorized it…" She laughed shyly.

"No shit!"

"For real! I told you that's my joint!"

"Okay… well shit… Just …um… say the hook and let me see if it comes back…"

She looked out the window and was whispering my song. It sounded so deep and poetic coming out of her. Her voice was deep and husky but still felt feminine. Like dirt. Rich light fluffy dark dirt. The kind of dirt that will grow things. She was making my words grow. I had planted a seed in her and I was hearing it grow into a tree. I tried to match her voice and not overpower it and we both whispered it to the rhythm of the rain and the wind.

#

No bread just crumbs
Misled victims
Chasing waterfalls in late night sitcoms.
It comes, it goes
That's the path we choose
But there's mad zeros
In our graph.
Heros that we have
Steer those on the Ave
Near holes on the path
Cuz their goals are strictly just cash.
In my notepad
I scribble over negativity with harsh pen strokes
Cuz the dark bends hope.
On a park bench wrote
Only songs of revolution
for the children on the merry-go-round
Cuz it's confusing.
Do the ends justify?
If it bends does it lie?
If the rules take the food out of your mouth
Do they apply?
When we die,

Explain to me again how it is
Cuz I've been sounding like an Idiot
When telling these kids
That God ain't got no pity on your felony sins
And even the city is shitty
Ain't no heaven for them

#

That's just bullshit
Cuz heaven is in your heartbeat
It's the sound of the Earth through your souls on the palms of your feet
It's the taste of the wind when you speak
It's the sun on your skin when you're weak
And now you're warm

#

Go ahead and pray for many blessings
But what I'm telling you is
The only way out of oppression
Is intelligent kids.
I travel on the bus with both hands in empty pockets
Hearing all the babble about grams and pretty rocks
It ain't our fault
The cheese, the trap, we got bought
They diseased the rap we call art
Memories go back, we all start
From centuries of Black hearts
Passed on the breeze to back lots with thieves.
I play my part
But my soul's got holes
Like old socks.
In the dark I compose
My prose with no spark.
It's a paradox.

A box that locks
With no keys.
We bury thoughts
And we're taught with glocks
From O.G.'s
And the police
Shots go off…
What am I sayin?
When we hold these blocks with rocks
What are we sayin?
That there's no choice?
The system talks with no voice
Only long ass sentences.
Look at the percentages.
But our leverage is
Whenever there is music then we have hope.
Put your headphones up to your ears
Like it's a coat
I know it's cold

#

But Heaven's in your heartbeat
It's the sound of the earth through your souls on the palms of your feet
It's the taste of the wind when you speak
It's the sun on your skin when you're weak
And now you're warm

#

I don't know how long we sat there after that. I thought I understood what I had written, but hearing it like that let me know that it wasn't mine anymore. It was hers. Maybe it never was mine. Maybe I had just heard it and was lucky enough to write it down before it was gone. Maybe I was just how it got here. It passed through me to get to her. It was special to her. So special. She was looking at me like I was special too. Like I had something to do with it. Like I had thought it up. When all I had done was make my head real quiet until I could hear it and then write it down. I didn't even know what it meant! She did! It's hers. I wanted to tell her it was hers.

"Where did you get the tape from? I thought that shit was just floating around Ewa Beach? We only made a hundred of them."

"Naw, your shit is banging all over the island, boy! Me and my cousin bought it at the swap meet. They got that shit on C.D. Everyone is bumpin your shit!"

"Wow, I guess I've just been busy hustlin…"

"You should focus on another tape while this shit is still hot, maybe make something they can play on the radio."

"You mean like a love song," I said jokingly.

"Shit, why not? You be like the Hawaiian L.L.," she said, teasing me.

I grabbed her arms and pinned her to the seat.

#

Capital Q is hards like pohaku,
Battle anybody leave'em assed out like a malo…

#

She started laughing hard.

#

When I'm alone on the beach
Sometimes I stare at my hands,
And in the back of my mind
I am a lonely man.

#

She screamed and laughed, trying to break free.

"Oh god! No, it's horrible. You're stupid—"

I gave her another kiss and then finished putting on my clothes.

"I'll be right back. I gotta handle something."

I got out fast and started to head toward the farm.

"Babe," came a voice about thirty feet from the car.

It was Cynthia.

"Oh shit, it's pouring out here! Let's go inside," I said, trying to get her away from the car.

"Who is she?" asked Cynthia so softly I almost couldn't hear her over the rain.

Just then Kimo walked up and pushed me back against the car.

"Where the fuck were you?!" he yelled.

"My bad I was—"

"Yeah, where were you, babe!" yelled Cynthia.

Kimo looked back and saw Cynthia for the first time. Then he looked at me, then he looked at my car. Almost as if on cue, Lehua wiped some of the steam away from inside the car window.

"Oh shit!" said Kimo, almost laughing.

"*Who the fuck is she?!*" screamed Cynthia.

You could see the car moving a little as Lehua rushed to get dressed.

"Yo! Twinkie fucking chill! You two can work this shit out later. In Fact"—Kimo shoved his finger in my chest—"your stupid ass can take Twinkie home right now and meet me at Siosi's apartment in Waipahu in forty-five minutes. Don't fuck this up! Look at your watch. Sparks flying in forty-five minutes! Twinkie! Get in the fucking car and go home!"

"Fuck you, Kimo!" screamed Cynthia.

"It's raining. How you gonna get home?" asked Kimo.

"You take me home, muthafucker!" yelled Cynthia.

"I can't. I gotta handle something! Get in the fucking car!"

"Fuck you! I'll walk!"

"You're not walking through the back road at one in the morning in the fucking rain!"

"I'm not getting in that car with that fuckin skank!"

Kimo turned and looked at me. I opened the car door, leaned in and looked at Lehua.

"Hey listen I'm sorry—"

"You *are* sorry. You a sorry ass muthafucka."

"Yeah, you gotta go."

"Go where?"

"Out of the car."

"Muthafucka, I'm not walking down the back roads in the rain at one in the morning either. She the one who said it's cool with her. Let that bitch do it."

"Fuck you, bitch."

"Fuck you, bitch!"

"Fuck you! You fuckin skank."

"It's not my fault you got played, bitch."

Kimo picked up Cynthia and tossed her into the car. She rolled across the front seat and smacked into the passenger door. Lehua was in the backseat and they instantly started punching and slapping each other. Kimo smacked me so hard in the head it rang like a dog whistle and my eyes watered. Then he punched me in the stomach and pushed me into the car. I started it and the engine roared. The tape player came on full blast playing N.W.A.'s "Fuck the Police." I peeled out of the farm, spaying rocks and gravel in all directions. The girls were yelling and pulling each other's hair.

I got on to the old road toward Kapolei before I discovered the real problem. As soon as I took my foot off the gas nothing worked. No headlights, no music, and worst of all no windshield wipers. It was dark and the rain was coming down in sheets. The old road had no street lights. Pitch black. I had one hand going back and forth between both girls and the other on the steering wheel with my head out the window trying to see through the rain. I pushed my foot on the gas until I was going eighty or so until I would start to hydroplane, then I would take my foot off and it would all go black and the music would stop. Then I could only hear the girls panting and slapping and screaming. Every few minutes a car would come in the opposite direction and I could just aim for the right hand side of their left headlight. I kind of got a rhythm going until the girls figured out that fighting with each other was stupid and they should be taking their hate out on me.

Lehua started punching me in the back of the head and Cynthia leaned back against the passenger-side door and started mule kicking me in the head. I reached back and grabbed Lehua's wrist and twisted it back hard until I heard her make a squeaking sound. I let go just as I saw headlights in front of me but I couldn't really see anything through the rain on the windshield. I started to stick my head back out the window when one of Cynthia's kicks caught me square.

My foot came off the gas and everything fell silent except for the ringing in my head. I blinked, shook it off, and got my foot back on the gas and my head back out the window just in time to see we were head on with the car in front of us. I pulled the steering wheel left and we missed the car and swerved off the road so I pulled back right but overcorrected and we spun across the pavement sideways into a telephone pole. The pole crashed down around us, but the car didn't stop sliding until we hit an embankment and it rolled over on its side.

***

The rain woke me up before anything else. I was laying on my back and it was raining so hard it was pouring up my nose and into my open mouth. As soon as I woke up I saw Cynthia sitting over me with my jacket over her head smoking a cigarette.

"We call it even and I love you forever on one condition. We leave the skank in the car and walk away."

The car was upside-down underneath a broken telephone pole. I couldn't tell whether it was the car or the telephone pole but something was on fire. Baby flames were licking the bottom of the car and the pole.

I stood and for the first few steps thought I had broken both legs. When the feeling came back it was nothing but pain. Lehua was still in the car and she was banging on the back window. It had spiderwebbed but had not broken. Both doors were crushed and the back window was the only way out. There were cables tangled all over the car. I reached out to move some of the cables and Cynthia shouted.

"You'll get electrocuted!"

"I think it's just phone cables…"

"You *think*?"

I reached again and then looked down the road just as sparks danced in the rain from one of the torn cables. I looked back at Cynthia.

"A rock," I said. "A big rock!"

We both started looking around. I found a huge boulder and yelled to Lehua," "Move back!"

"What?!" came her muffled voice from inside the burning car.

"Move back! I'm gonna smash the window!"

I tossed the boulder and didn't smash the window, but the whole web of glass folded inward. I crawled through a tangled net of cables feet first and kicked it in enough for her to crawl out. Even in the rain I could tell she was bleeding, and she was holding her arm crying.

I grabbed both of the girls and started jogging and dragging them as fast as they could go. We got about a hundred feet away from the car and I turned back, waiting for the action-movie explosion.

It never came.

The girls were holding each other shivering and crying as I stood waiting. The fire spread through the car and when the gas tank finally went, the flames just got a little bigger.

"Shit, that's funny..." I mumbled after a few seconds.

Cynthia wiped the tears and hair out of her eyes so she could cut them at me.

"You're both into all that universal planet alignment shit, right?"

Lehua lifted her head to look at me. Her eyes were wide and empty as she blinked through the huge raindrops.

"I'm just sayin, maybe the car didn't have like... a big explosion cuz I forgot to get gas, and so we can conclude that my procrastination was part of the universe's divine plan to keep me a badass muthafuckin hustla."

For a second when they didn't respond I thought they didn't hear me, then a huge flash of lighting showed me Cynthia's face all scrunched up as her mind tried to digest her absolute disgust. The sky returned to darkness as she took a deep breath to scream at me, but whatever she said was covered by the thunder.

CHAPTER 8

A BITCH OF CIRCUMSTANCE

I T WAS ALMOST DAWN.

I tried to run up the stairs to the second floor where Siosi's apartment was but had to stop. Both of my thighs were so black and blue they looked like I had poured paint all over them, and some of my ribs were definitely broken. Cynthia and I had been thrown from the car when it rolled over. My legs had gotten slammed against the steering wheel and my ribs had hit the door. Lehua had a broken arm. Cynthia was taking her to the hospital in my other car. I had grabbed my truck and raced over to Aniani Place in Waipahu to meet Kimo.

Aniani Place was a third world country tucked in a swamp next to an irrigation canal. A lot of the kids that worked in Crystal City lived in here. I had learned my lesson about coming to these places without Kimo. The Sons of Samoa controlled this area as well. Even though Alex was not Samoan, not by a long shot—he was Filipino and Portuguese—he had grown up here and he was considered family. Siosi grew up with him and was the only thing keeping this situation from boiling over.

As I rested in the stairwell I wondered if the pills I took were gonna kick in soon or if they already had and that's just how fucked up I was. I used the handrail to make it the rest of the way up. At the top of the stairs there were two huge Samoans. They were obviously there for us. Gangstas don't just hang out in stairwells at five-thirty in the morning.

"Hoy, sole! Where you tink you going?!"

It was the same Samoan dude that had picked me up by my shirt at the basketball courts outside of Crystal City.

"I'm here with Kimo. Alex told us to come through and chill," I said, trying not to sound shaky.

Whatever the pills were supposed to do, they weren't. What they were doing was giving me chills. I felt like I had to hug myself to keep from trembling.

They both looked down and turned their shoulders slightly for me to get by but I had to squeeze through. There was another one by the door. He had to be six-five, three hundred plus. He must have seen me before because he nodded, then knocked two and then three times, then opened the door for me.

The apartment was tiny.

The door opened into an area that was meant to be a dinning-slash-living space. It was maybe ten by ten. The room smelled like burnt spam, weed and cigarettes, two day old McDonalds and Taco Bell, spilled beer, dried shit and vomit. In that order. The walls were cement with peeling paint that had been white many years ago. The laminate floor was peeling badly exposing the dirty cement underneath. Not that I could see much of the floor because it was completely filled with a cheap round plastic folding table. The door wouldn't even open all the way. Off to the right was a kitchen area separated by a peninsula countertop and hanging cupboards. Siosi was standing by the door as I walked in and he shook my hand. Travis was standing next to him. He wasn't in his uniform but his badge was hanging from a thick gold chain around his neck. Kimo was sitting on a folding chair to the left and Alex was across from him on the right. They were playing poker. There were three other big dudes at the table and another standing in the kitchen. I sat down to the left of Kimo and tried to stop trembling. Luckily the back of my chair was right up against the wall so I could prop myself up.

"Ho! Dirty Q-Tip! Someone wen give you dirty lickens!!" said Alex laughing.

"Naw, I got in a car accident," I said quietly.

"Another one, just now?" asked Kimo.

"Yeah, Twinkie's alright. The other girl broke her arm. Twinkie's taking her to the hospital right now," I said while slowly shifting my body trying to find a comfortable position.

"Twinkie is taking the girl she caught you fuckin to the hospital?" asked Kimo in his direct way.

"Oh shit, that's dirty!" said Alex, laughing again. "I guess that's how wen you one pretty boy eh!"

His high-pitched hyena cackle rattled in my head. It instantly got under my skin and I wanted to shove the leg of the chair I was sitting on through his eye socket. Just to stop that sound.

"That's not cool, man," said Kimo. "You gonna have to sort that shit out later. Twinkie don't deserve that shit."

I looked down at the table to avoid his disappointment and that's when I noticed Kimo had almost no chips in front of him. Alex, on the other hand, had almost all the chips that were on the table stacked in front of him and he was caressing them like an evil cat in a James Bond movie.

"Is it too late for me to play a few hands," I said.

I reached for my money and realized I didn't bring any. I also realized I was shaking and was past the point of doing anything about it.

The guy in the kitchen said something in Samoan to Alex and everyone laughed and looked at me and Kimo.

Kimo smiled and said, "Yeah Q, it's a little late in the game. We about finished here—"

"Shoots brah, let the little boy play if he like play! No more such ting as too much money, eh!" said Alex motioning to his stack.

All the Samoans laughed.

Kimo and Travis did not.

Two or three of them had that same hyena laugh. I gritted my teeth. Alex was only a few years older than me calling me little boy. He knew I was scared of him. He knew it that night in Crystal City and he knew it now. Kimo looked at me and was reading my face.

Then Kimo's eyes flashed something I had never seen in them before. They flashed fear.

And then it was gone.

It was just the four of us in this ghetto apartment with eight killers who did not care about the legend of Kimo nor did they have old school respect for Uncle. This was the opposite of what I had thought I was coming down here for. This is what my stepdad had warned me about. These were the sharks.

"Actually there is such a thing as too much money," said Kimo reaching into a small backpack on the floor.

"Mo money mo problems," I said trying to make a reference and get a chuckle, but the room was tense.

Kimo started stacking bundles of cash on the table two and three at a time. Each time he bent over to grab more stacks, it seemed like everyone in the room was about to tackle the table. But they didn't. They watched like trained dogs salivating and licking their sharp hungry teeth.

Kimo let the room wait as he made a big show of counting and checking if he had it all on the table. Then he leaned back in his chair and looked Alex in the eye. Alex stared back, his eyes menacing and empty.

There is a condition a person can get from being out in the sun too much. Surfers and lifeguards get it all the time. It's called pterygium. It's scarred tissue that grows on your actual eyeball. Alex had it bad. It covered all the white of his eyes and he already had light eyes to begin with. I thought I was imagining it in Crystal City. But here in this junkyard porta potty, under the single exposed bulb protruding from what was left of the broken ceiling fixture, casting everyone in its tooth tartar glow, I prayed he did not turn his gaze to me. In my condition those zombie eyes would cause me to piss all over this cheap folding chair.

"So what, you like lose some more money or you just out for show us your boto because—"

"Let me say something," Kimo said quietly. He had been waiting for Alex to speak just so he could cut him off.

Once the silence had been broken there was air in the room again. Everyone shuffled a bit.

"I know that shit changes. I understand how it is. You muthafuckas gotta make your own mark and make your own rules for your shit. For the world that you live in. You look around and you make a few choices, make a few decisions, and that's how you make a fuckin name for yourself. You start wondering about the names that have already been made. You start feeling like, 'Who the fuck are those names?' Time heals all wounds. It also erases all deeds. The muthafuckas I came up with, there ain't too many to try to tell you nothin. Uncle has rules. But who says those rules need to be followed? My brother Travis isn't really a people person. Maybe a few miscommunications with him speeds up the growth of some of these thoughts. Maybe all you muthafuckas start feeling like, 'Fuck Travis,' like, 'Who the fuck is Travis?' and, at a certain point, 'Who the fuck is Uncle?' I get it. Now, I get out of jail and shit has fuckin changed. It's like I time traveled, or traveled to some twilight zone shit, some other dimension. It's a place that's familiar like a fuckin… like a memory, but not quite how your remember it. Everything is the same, and bang, there's one crazy thing. Like for real, all the men are walking around with their asses hanging out? Their pants are falling down. Muthafuckas walk around with their pants hanging down showing their ass. They have to hold them up with their hands. Do you know what that means in Jail? If your ass is showing? And there's a million little things. Some of them I can't put my finger on. It's too subtle. It doesn't go into words well. It's like, the perception—it's like the group perception is slightly off or changed. The consensus. The whole 'We agree this is the way shit is,' ya know? That's the shit that's slightly off. There's some lies in there. Little ones. Everyone is lying, just a little bit. But everyone is doing it because everyone is doing it, and it's so little that it ain't fucking shit up enough for anyone to notice. You only notice if you come here from some other fuckin dimension. Everything is built on how we see shit. If we lie about how we see shit, then what we build is off. It's wrong and—"

"Brah," interrupted Alex with his hyena laugh, "what the fuck you talking about?!" He looked around as he said it but no one else wanted to directly laugh at Kimo.

"I'm talking about how you see shit, dumbass! I'm talking about you being from a place that maybe I don't see right. A place where it's okay to make promises that you don't keep. A place where you shake hands and give your word and it might not mean shit. Who knows? Your word is just another word. It can't be broken cuz it was never fixed to anything. And it's all good, cuz the same is true for everyone everywhere I fuckin go! So instead of listening to your bullshit words, I gotta speed read through your fuckin soul! So these last few months, you leaving us voicemails and using words like, 'No, Travis, I get no problem wit you guys, I just trying for do what we wen say,' or, 'Sorry yeah, I never wen meet up wit you guys, I had one family emergency,' and when you *are* set up to actually meet Uncle and talk the shit out, you're not answering my calls, and you dodge us when we come through, selling shit in places you ain't supposed to sell, and now, not kicking up what you owe. Your words say you're sorry, you wanna do business and you don't want your arms and legs broken. But what does your soul say?"

Kimo leaned forward and his chair made a slow squeaking sound. He looked into Alex's cloudy shark eyes.

"Your soul says, 'Who the fuck is Uncle?'" Kimo whispered then leaned back in his chair.

"Who the fuck is Uncle?" whispered Alex.

"See, just rolls off the tongue. If you haven't actually said it out loud before, I bet it feels good to finally say it," said Kimo with a sales-pitch smile.

Alex looked down at the table. He looked unsure or lost. He actually started to dig his long dirty fingernails into the cheap folding table. Maybe I was just sick. Maybe Kimo had this whole thing under control. Alex's boys started shuffling again. The next words out of Alex's mouth would be apologies.

"Tafa'i, count that money," said Alex to the huge Samoan to his left.

"DON'T FUCKING TOUCH THE MONEY!" boomed Kimo.

Kimo's voice froze the room and the big Samoan snapped back to his post.

"My poker game, my apartment, my town, my money," said Alex in almost a whisper. He was looking into Kimo's eyes.

Pushing and checking.

Pushing and checking.

Take a chance and go in close with a jab. Then gauge the speed and power of the response. Kimo was in it now. Kimo looked into the blood-shot clouds of Alex's eyes. Then Alex leaned back.

"I know who Uncle is," he said.

"You really believe that? You do. That's some Orwellian shit. How you hold both of those ideas in your head at the same time. 'I know who Uncle is' and 'This is my town.' That is an incredible brain pretzel—"

"*FUUUUUUUUUUUUUUUUUCK!*"

Alex let out a sound that was primal. He was holding the table with both hands while he shouted, almost using it as a way to anchor the sound that bellowed from deep in his gut. I had jumped back but was pinned by the table and the wall behind me so I just wound up banging my head into the wall.

Then all was silent again.

Until Siosi leaned over to Kimo and said in a hushed whisper, "Brah, I so sorry braddah, I gotta take my daughter to school lidat, eh, I gotta go"

"Eh, no worries. Tell her I said to get more focused or no CD player!" said Kimo with a smile.

Siosi practically ran out of the apartment.

Kimo turned to Alex without missing a beat.

"Where were we? Oh yeah, '*fuuuuuuuuuuuuuuck!*'"

A few guys chuckled and I laughed.

"Listen Alex, I'm sitting here for one reason and one reason only. I'm trying to make this right for everyone. I don't want to see this go sideways. You just don't really know how sideways this shit can go. What are you, nineteen? Twenty? Let me help you get your shit together—"

"I know who Uncle is," whispered Alex again.

He was looking at the table, picking at a small tear in the plastic.

"We gonna go around again?" said Kimo. He was still smiling but it looked forced.

"It's twenty grand," said the huge Samoan leaning in to Alex.

"Brah, I tell you the real question, if you like make your brain one pretzel. Da real question is, do *you* know who uncle is?"

"Okay…" said Kimo.

He made a show of leaning back and folding his hands behind his head.

The thing I had been dreading since I sat down finally happened. Alex's cold dead eyes fixed on mine.

"Do you know who Uncle is?" he said to me.

"I met him once," I said and then pretended to look at my pager.

"I met him twice," said Alex.

He turned back to Kimo. "Back in hanabata days you guy's main house was five blocks from us. That's where had all the cool toys and games and all the kids use to wen go over dere. My maddah when tell me, 'Boy! I ever catch you going over dere I going give you dirty hurts!' Still yet, I when sneak over there couple times. I seen you too, you know. Kimo! You and da'kine, training on the heavy bag in the carport. Marianne would be sitting watching you train and brushing her hair or painting her nails. Whoa! All the boys had the meanest crush on Marianne. My uncle Donald was you guy's age so den he would like try mack with her when

Kimo wasn't looking. I tink so they never wen smash but just kiss little bit, whatevas, but then my uncle was goin for fight you in the 'No Holds Barred' competition in Waianae. I tink so he had one chance. Kimo dis, Kimo dat, but then my uncle Donny had some fuckin skills. Had one party at Hau Bush two weeks before the fight.

"Had choke people, plus had like three hundred kids there. Was afta da football game, Campbell High School versus Kaiser High School. Bumbye we lost but I guess had some players was cool with each other cause they wen invite the rich kids down to our side of the island. That would explain the school bus I wen see cuz even some coaches came eh? Everyting was cool at first.

"Me and my cuzin was too young for go but den we wen sneak in the back of my braddah's truck. Had bonfires, had all kine different music. Everyone was telling Uncle Donny for give you cracks. Everyone! Everyone like see you finally get what you deserve. "Brah, dis Kimo guy like make all big body! Donny Boy goin give'em cracks!"

Alex looked at me with a smile on his face.

"Brah, wen Kimo went to jail, had all kine bullshit stories about who he wen lick and who he wen gave cracks, brah! Like Kimo is one fucking God of War or sumting! He not! He was one fuckin punk! Brah Kimo used to make all any kine, like he can do whateva an everyone make all scared around him. Uncle Donny wasn't scared. Not one bit. Brah, Uncle Donny Boy was half german, half Samoan! Bigger, stronger, faster! Jus one better fighter, plus had better guys training him. Everyone knew was going be time for Kimo to fuckin eat shyit! Brah I was following Uncle Donny like one puppy. Everyone like give Uncle one beer cuz it's a party, eh? Uncle was gettin all bus lidat. Uncle started talking too much. Uncle started talking about how he was sneaking with Maryanne on the sly. Too much people was hearing. Boom, outta nowhere, choke trucks pull up to the beach. Kimo jumps out and brah, was one epic fight. I wen see the whole ting! Kimo looked like a little kid standing in front of Donny Boy. Plus too, they was in the sand so Kimo can't do his dance around bullshit. Kimo was taking cracks."

Alex turned back to Kimo.

"Then you was scared so you wen try for take him down. But Uncle Donny get the Gracie Jiu Jitsu skills, yeah?! Boom, they stay rollin, rollin until Uncle Donny wen da'kine! Hit his head on one rock or sumting cuz his head was bleeding. Brah you got lucky and den you was choking him out. Everyone was mad! They no like see you win. They start yelling 'Up and up!'"

Alex looked at me again.

"Everybody starts pushing and spitting and chrowing sand at first but then they wen start chrowing rocks! They no like see Donny Boy lose! Then one guy jumps in and kicks Kimo in the head. Brah, the whole beach exploded! Everyone was scrapping everyone. Everyone was throwing rocks. All Kimo's boys had baseball bats and they looked like muthafuckin Jedi nights. They was all around Kimo. Protecting him. I was so little but I no like for leave Uncle Donny by himself so I wen run in for go, I don't know—try for hit Kimo wit one rock or sumting. When I get there, I see Kimo smash my uncle's head wit one rock, and den he wen kneel down next to him and put his arm on top his leg and snap Uncle Donny's arm. Boom. He walked around and snapped Uncle Donny's leg. Boom. He walked around, took the other hand and smashed 'um with a rock over and over until one of his friends wen finally stop him. I never wen do nahting! Was too scared."

Alex was peeling the table again.

The guy in the kitchen said, "Eh, that was da'kine eh! When the Campbell High School kids wen flip over the Kaiser school bus?! Was all on the news, yeah?"

The guy directly across from me answered. "Yep, they wen change'em on the news! Uncle wen make it so the police never do nahting. Uncle had power back den!"

"My uncle Donny Boy would never walk or use his left hand again. His dad wen go talk with your uncle. The Uncle! He came home so white he looked haole. Then, tree weeks later no one can even find his dad. His wife no can make enough money for rent, for food, for regular kine stuffs, so what? Uncle Donny Boy just like sit in the house and drink. Then his sister, my aunty Maili, gotta start stripping in Waikiki and den what? Uncle Donny Boy O.D.'s. And what? Nobody say nahting!"

And nobody was saying anything now.

Kimo looked crushed. Almost like he was going to cry.

He cleared his throat a few times and then tried to say something.

"I'm sorry… I'm sorry I did that to your uncle. I hurt a lot of people back then. I know me sitting here saying sorry doesn't change anything, but I am."

Alex didn't say anything. His eyes were on fire but everything else about him looked dead.

Kimo looked around the room and turned his palms up.

"So what do you wanna do now?"

"I like you for fuckin leave me *the fuck alone*!" shouted Alex.

"Like I said, 'Then you don't know Uncle.'"

"I know your uncle. I wen go see my aunty who wen she become one stripper then was working for your Maryanne. I wen tell her just get me close to Uncle, I going get these muthafucka's back! I going make them pay! She wen sit me down and hold me and she wen cry and tell me, 'No Alex… no do that Alex.' She was crying and she wen tell me I should let all you faka's live cuz how you live is more worse then if I wen kill you. She said when you guys was all little boys, all you guys! Travis, Kimo, your mahu braddahs Keone and Star, all you guys! She says Maryanne wen tell her when she was drunk that when the little boys come to the shelter, Uncle locks all the boys in one room and fucks them up the ass. He make the softest ones wear dresses and lipstick. That's why I was never allowed for come your guys' house. That's why all the boys come out Uncle's youth home either mahu or killers. So what? Your two braddahs is mahu and you two is the killas?!"

Alex was shaking.

I was shaking.

I grinded my teeth to keep them from making any noise and grabbed handfuls of my shorts to keep my hands still.

Kimo was a stone.

Everyone in the room was locked on him.

"This game is boring," Kimo finally said, matter of factly. "Wanna play a different game? Let's play some ill M.A.D., Nash-equilibrium shit. This is twenty-three grand. How much do you have in front of you?" Kimo spoke slowly.

"Brah, I not goin."

"COUNT YOUR MUTHAFUCKIN CHIPS!" Kimo's voice was so loud and so deep that my ears started ringing. You could feel it in your chest. It had actual force to it. Everyone in the room reacted like a bomb had gone off and needed a second to get their cool back. Alex reflexively reached for his chips and then realized what he was doing and pulled his hand back. Tafa'i leaned over and whispered, "Sole, you get about fifteen grand right dere"

Alex motioned for him to shut the fuck up.

"Okay, here's what is going to happen," said Kimo.

His voice was the authority.

"You're going to leave that on the table. I'm going to leave this on the table. It's all on the next hand, cards up. You win, you take the cash. Me and the kid walk out of here and whatever unresolved childhood traumas you have with me, you take that up with Uncle. I'm gone. You never see me again. Unfortunately, you're a few grand short. So if I win, I take your stack and whatever you have parked down stairs and whatever you have in the top right cabinet above the refrigerator and you suck my dick."

The last phrase hung in the air like dust. Everyone was frozen waiting to see what Alex would say. He didn't say anything. He just stared at Kimo and Kimo just stared at Alex.

Alex finally looked away first. He stared again at the torn table. Then he shook his head like he had just got a twisted joke and started laughing hard. Kimo started laughing and everyone started laughing. It sounded like a den of hyenas except for Kimo's big thunderous laugh. It was almost an entire minute before it died back down. Everyone was smiling and it looked like there might be a way out of this alive.

"You going leave the money and leave Waipahu?" asked Alex.

"Leave Hawaii," said Kimo.

"And what about Travis?"

"I ain't going nowhere. Whatever deals you two muthafuckas is making is between you guys. I'm not a part of this and Uncle is not a part of this," said Travis with his head down. He had his arms crossed so that his right hand was resting on his gun.

"I lose, you take the stash, fifteen grand and my truck?" asked Alex.

He had a smile on his face now and he was toying with his chips.

"And you suck my dick," repeated Kimo.

Everyone started laughing again but it wasn't the same laugh.

"Oh yeah, rajah," said Alex halfheartedly.

The room came to stillness once more as Alex and Kimo faced off again and the smile on Alex's face slowly turned hard.

"And it has to be pretty much right after the hand. Before I leave," said Kimo. "I don't want to meet up somewhere later and you suck my dick when we're alone. You suck my dick here, now, in front of everyone. We'll move this table out of the way and you'll kneel down here on the floor. I'll pull my pants down and spread my legs nice and wide so you can cup my balls and everything. I won't drag it out, fifteen minutes tops. I've been busy lately so I ain't fucked in a couple of days."

Alex's face was so skinny you could see his jaw muscles work as he grinded his teeth.

"I'm sorry, was that disrespectful?" said Kimo mockingly.

He turned to Travis. "Was that disrespectful? It's hard to tell, right?"

Travis put his head down.

Kimo turned back to Alex.

"What's up, Alex? Are you a bitch or are you a bitch? Cuz a bitch would be too scared to play everything on one hand. If you ain't a bitch, you should play the hand. If you are a bitch, take your little fifteen grand, I'll go tell Uncle you told him to go fuck himself, and let nature play itself out. It's the only sure way to win. But it's the bitch way. Smart bitch, but a bitch nonetheless. Cuz if you lose the hand and let my pubic hair tickle your nose? Well, that definitely means you're a bitch. You lose everything and you have to suck my dick? That's a dumb bitch. Which bitch are you? Smart bitch? Dumb bitch? A bitch of circumstance?"

"Brah, if I win the hand then you the dumb bitch, bitch!" yelled Alex.

"Now you M.A.D.!" Kimo looked at Travis. "Deal the hand so we can get the fuck out of here. Smells like a fucking dumpster."

Travis scooped up the cards, shuffled fast and put the deck in front of Alex to cut. Alex cut the deck without breaking eye contact with Kimo.

Travis picked it back up and dealt both hands face up.

Alex got an ace of spades and a queen of hearts.

Kimo got a ten of clubs and a nine of spades.

"You guys is all sick. You guys isn't even one family. You just fuckin stray dogs running in one pack. You make other families sick. You steal all of us's food. Uncle dis, Uncle dat… How's he one uncle? He no more one braddah. You guys ain't even real braddahs…"

Alex continued to talk shit. Kimo nodded at Travis for the flop.

Ace of clubs. Two of diamonds. Eight of hearts.

Tafa'i slapped Alex in the arm and Alex gave him a pound. The mood in the room started to lighten and the guy in the kitchen said something in Samoan. Alex answered back in English.

"Yep, c'mon baby! No jacks, no pairs, no sevens! C'MON!"

His boys started clapping their hands and smacking each other on the back.

Travis stared hard at the side of Kimo's face but Kimo sat quietly.

"Brah! Put down the turn card!" demanded Alex.

Travis looked at Alex, and when he turned back to Kimo, Travis couldn't hide his fear. Kimo nodded and Travis put the card down slow.

Six of diamonds.

Alex and his boys erupted in cheers. I stood up. I thought for a second I was going to throw up. I turned to see if I should rush to the bathroom but then I imagined that leaning over the toilet in this apartment would be worse than just throwing up on the table. Plus maybe it would stop the game. Then I realized nothing would stop these two men from seeing this through.

Through the cheers, the guy in the kitchen was yelling something. Alex started to calm everyone down and then turned to the kitchen and asked the guy something in Samoan.

Kimo answered before the kitchen dude could.

"He said I could still get a seven…"

They all saw it at the same time and the mood changed. Alex sat back down and put his shark mask back on.

Then Tafa'i laughed.

"Hey sole, what's the odds ah dat?"

Kimo nodded at Travis and Travis put down the river card.

Seven of spades.

Everyone made the quiet sound of getting hit with an invisible sucker punch. Kimo stuffed his twenty-three grand back into his small backpack and passed it to Travis. He whispered in Travis's ear and Travis went straight to the kitchen. The kitchen dude didn't try to stop him as he opened the cupboard above the refrigerator. Travis stuffed ziplock bags of meth into his duffle bag then came back and held the bag open to Tafa'i, who looked at Alex. Alex nodded. Tafa'i opened a large dirty cooler that was on the floor behind him and shoved the rubber-banded rolls of cash into the backpack Travis was holding.

Alex was digging at the hole in the table.

Travis zipped the bag and whispered to Kimo, "Let's go…"

Kimo didn't move. He was staring at Alex. I didn't need an invitation. I stood up but realized Kimo would have to scoot forward for me to pass behind him. If I went around the other way, Alex would have to scoot forward.

"Kimo, time for hele," whispered Travis again. "Now, braddah…"

Kimo's nod to Travis was so small I would've missed it if not for the look on Travis's face. The look of unwanted knowledge. Travis looked at me, nodded and left. Two of Alex's friends started to walk out. They stopped next to Alex to shake his hand and Alex didn't even look up.

Now it was me, Kimo, Alex, Tafa'i and the kitchen dude.

I opened my mouth to say I'm out but Kimo leaned forward and put his hand under the table. He lifted it up with one hand and was messing with the folding legs. Suddenly it dropped flat on the floor. It was loud and chips scattered all over the place. Alex wouldn't even have noticed except the little hole in the table he was lost in disappeared. He slowly looked around and then his cloudy psycho eyes found Kimo.

Kimo was sitting back in his chair with his legs wide open rubbing his dick over his shorts.

"I know it was part of the bet but I'm not really feeling it. Maybe you could dance a little. Or whisper some sweet nothings in my ear?"

Alex was shivering. I stood with my back against the wall. I was trying to sink into the cement.

"Your uncle's sister, you said Maili," Kimo went on. "Your aunty, I remember her. Her name was Alissa though, right?"

"Alicia…" Alex's voice cracked. Without the table to hold on to he was rubbing his hands up and down his shorts.

"Alicia, right! Alicia was her middle name. Maili was her first name. We called her Alley. Actually we called her Alley Cat. Like a cute nickname. Her and Maryanne were tight. She would do anything for Maryanne. She was hot enough to dance at Totally Titanium but she would always get into fights. Finally, Maryanne had to put her in Chinatown. That's how she got her nickname, Alley Cat, from suckin dicks in the alley way on Hotel Street. Actually, more like Merchant and Bethel, right down at the end of Fort Street Mall. There's a little, like, plaza area. When she hit the street, she was fuckin hot. Maryanne used to always like to watch me fuck her. She would have these crazy rolling orgasms. I would fuck her and she would come and come and come, and then I would fuck Maryanne until she was done. We would lay there all fuckin burnt and Alley Cat would be ready for more. Maryanne would fuck her with a dildo for a little while just to try to knock her out. I would hold her face and look in her eyes and she was somewhere else. Moaning and chasing the feeling. Or maybe running from another feeling. Maybe running from something else. Maybe running from someone. Maryanne would help her. Maryanne would talk to her for hours. Hours of tears, but Alley Cat was too scared to tell her who she was running from. Finally Marianne told her she wasn't alone. Maryanne shared some secrets and Alley Cat shared some secrets. She said maybe she was running from someone called Uncle Bobby. Who's Uncle Bobby? Alex! Who's Uncle Bobby? Wouldn't that be your dad? He's Robert Tolentino, isn't he? Wow, is that a coincidence! Well dang, Uncle Robert taught Alley Cat how to suck a good dick. Did he teach you that too? I guess I'm about to find out!"

That was it.

Alex jumped out of the chair at Kimo. I tackled him before I knew what I was doing but my body was not doing what it was supposed to. It was all jelly and aches. Alex rolled me over fast and sat down on my legs and started pounding me with right hands. I would've blacked out but somehow the kitchen dude went flying through the air and landed on top of me and Alex. Alex fell backwards off of my legs and got tangled for just a moment with the kitchen dude. I was not in fighting shape. I saw a broken piece of folding-chair leg and I grabbed it. Just as Kitchen Dude turned to face me I shoved the broken chair into his side. It slid right in so easy I thought he didn't even feel it.

But he did.

He screamed loud as fuck and looked down at his side in disbelief.

So did I.

I was trying to get to my feet when I heard the first gunshot. It was so loud I instinctively curled up for a second. Then I saw Kimo and Tafa'i fighting over a gun. Where was Alex? Alex walked back into the room with a fucking shotgun and pointed it at Kimo. I jumped and tackled Alex. The gun went off right next to my head and everything went quiet. We fought over the gun. I was on top of him, bleeding and screaming and punching and pulling in pure silence. He grabbed my face and tried to dig my eyes out. I shook my head violently and his fingers went in my mouth. I bit down with everything and the fingers broke like biting off some buffalo wings. There was blood everywhere. Alex let go of the gun and I took it and cocked it. I tried to point it down at Alex but I was too close. I stood up and fell backwards into the frame of the hallway. Just as I got my balance, Kitchen Dude half tackled, half fell into me. We fell down together and the shotgun went off again. I tried to hang on to it while Kitchen Dude choked me with all his strength. I was pinned. There was no way to move under this massive, rabid human being. The piece of chair stuck out of his side like a kickstand and there was blood spraying out of his mouth with each frantic exhalation. I began to black out. It was already quiet. Now the picture was fading and I watched it slowly close on black.

Then the hands around my neck went limp. I gasped as air rushed into my lungs. Kitchen Dude's face came clearly into view just before he collapsed down on top of me. All the air rushed back out of me. A moment later, his body rolled off of me and Kimo was standing above me holding a bloody pistol. He grabbed me by my shirt and lifted me off the ground. I saw him ask, "You good?" I pointed at my ears. He let me go and I sat down. I was trying to catch my breath and trying to make my ears work. They started ringing and muffled yells were coming through. Tafa'i was on the floor crying. His arms were wrapped around his stomach like he was holding a baby. They were filled with blood that was running down both elbows like cheap syrup.

Kimo was holding Alex up off of the ground by his neck. He had him by the neck with his left hand and his right hand was holding the gun to Alex's eyeball. He was shoving it into the socket.

"*Who the fuck is Kimo?!*"

I stood back up and used the wall to hold me. I leaned there and looked out the door that was now open. The sun was up. From the second floor I could see the orange of the morning. The leaves on the top of the trees rustled as the morning breeze worked its way west. A super weak squall left over from the night before was trickling down over Pearl City a few miles away and it made a rainbow with the morning sun rays.

Then Alex's limp body went flying out the door and over the balcony. My ears were working well enough to hear his body land on top of a parked car below. The sound of crunching sheet metal and shattering glass had become all too familiar this past year.

Kimo swaggered out the door and jumped up onto the ledge, paused for a moment, and then stepped off and disappeared like Batman.

I drunkenly limped out the door and over to the waist-high brick ledge. The morning breeze hit me and I could smell fresh blooming gardenias and white ginger. I looked down to see Kimo standing on the hood of the smashed car yelling to the sky. People were standing outside of their apartments all around us.

"WHO THE FUCK IS KIMO?!" he boomed.

He reached down and grabbed Alex's right arm. He squatted and leveraged the arm with his leg and broke it. Alex screamed in blackout pain.

"WHO THE FUCK IS KIMO?!"

He reached down and grabbed his other arm. I stumbled down the stairway and almost fell. When I came out of the stairwell, I saw Kimo deciding he couldn't break Alex's left arm from that angle. He stood back up and looked at the people who were now gathered around the parking lot. Some were regular people. Moms and grandmothers. Kids getting ready for school. Most of them were going back inside and closing their doors once their curiosity was over. All the dudes wearing jerseys and gold chains and beanies stayed though.

"This muthafucka is nobody. Nobody! He is nobody and nobody knows who the fuck he is! Nobody talks to him! Nobody even fucking looks at him!"

Kimo stuck the gun in Alex's mouth and yelled again.

"*Who the fuck am I?*"

It sounded like an actual question. Like Kimo desperately wanted to know who he was. But how would Alex—even if he was conscious, which he wasn't—how was he going to answer with that gun in his mouth?

"WHO THE FUCK AM I?!"

This time it was clear. Kimo was going to blow Alex's head open in broad daylight in front of all these people.

"Kimo…" I said, just loud enough for him to hear me.

Kimo didn't move. His head was cocked to the side waiting for Alex to answer.

"Kimo!" I said a little louder. I saw Siosi across from me on the balcony.

"*KEEEMOOOO!*" said Siosi in a loud, clear, deep voice. He sounded like Ice Cube yelling "*Weeest Syyide!*"

A couple other dudes yelled it back.

"*KEEEMOOO!*"

They were saying it for the same reason I was. To stop Kimo from shooting Alex.

Kimo took the gun out of Alex's mouth and stood up straight. He scanned the parking lot and found my eyes. I was shook to the core. It was a different man. This man I was looking at right now was a killer. He did not even see me. His gaze went straight through me.

He tilted his head and took a breath and closed his eyes.

Then he was back.

He opened his eyes and saw me and it was him.

The dude I had spent hours and hours talking with. The patient teacher. He leaned forward and dug through Alex's pockets and pulled out some car keys. He pushed a button and a beautiful Toyota Tacoma chirped. He motioned me over and we walked slowly and confidently to the truck. He tossed me the keys and I was about to tell him I was in no condition to drive when I noticed he had been shot at least twice. His stomach was bleeding bad. I walked around the passenger side and almost had to lift him into the truck. I looked back at the building. A few more guys had shown up and were pushing closer and closer to us. I saw at least two were holding pistols and three or four were holding bats. I climbed in the driver's side and locked the doors.

"Call Travis and tell him you're taking me to the hospital. I'm gonna black out…" Kimo mumbled.

And he did.

CHAPTER 9

SUNSHINE COCKTAIL

THERE WAS A BUZZING sound. Not a continuous buzz. More like a series of short buzzes and then nothing. My pager was always on vibrate. I wanted nothing to do with anyone or anything those buzzes could be about. I opened my eyes to see a fly slamming itself into the screen. That's good. That's a problem I can solve. I was lying on the floor in the living room of my Waipahu apartment.

Travis had called Maryanne and she met me outside the hospital, where a doctor met us in the parking lot. The doctor was upset. He kept saying, "You didn't say there were gunshot wounds, God dammit!"

I took the truck, which was full of blood, all the way to Waianae to drop off at Kimo's cousin's auto shop. That's where we dropped all of the cars we pulled normally but it was too early so I had to wait. I was still covered in dried, caked blood so I sat in the tinted truck on the side of the auto shop until I got the idea to jump in the ocean and get clean. But then I thought that was dumb because the truck was so bloody that once I was clean I would have nowhere to sit. It turned out the pills I had taken earlier had worked very well and now they were gone. My head and my body were screaming and I couldn't hold a thought in my mind for more than a few seconds before I had to scrunch my face and focus only on breathing. Time would pass, but I couldn't tell how much, and then I would get a reprieve and try to make a decision before the next wave would come. Kimo's cousin finally came and knocked on the window. Travis had called ahead. He helped me to the beach and gave me the shirt off his back. He also lent me a beat-up Honda Accord to get home. I made it to my apartment, took a few swings of tequila and passed out on the floor in the living room.

I had left the front door open so the trade winds would blow through the apartment. The buzzing, vibrating fly had come in the front door and was trying to go through the screen of the balcony door. It was partially open but the dumbass fly couldn't see that. I tried to reach up and push the screen door all the way open. I collapsed back down hoping I could pass back out.

Buzz-buzz.

I looked back up and didn't see the fly.

Buzz-buzz.

This time it was my pager. I sat up and looked at it. I didn't recognize the number but there was 911 after it. I crawled over to the phone and dialed the number.

"Yo."

"You page me?"

"Yo! Q muthafucka, you home?! Turn on the radio right now! I-94! Now nigga, now!"

I crawled over to the stereo and pushed power. The radio came on and it was our song. I sat back and tried to figure out what was going on. I double checked to see if it was the tape player. It was the radio. They really were playing it. It was at the end when I turned it on and the DJ started talking while the song ended.

"There it is, the most requested song for a week straight. That's Dark Side, couple of local boys from Ewa Beach. They are performing tonight at The Rhythm House downtown. Check 'em out! Eighteen and over to party, twenty-one to drink, doors open at 7:30, party ends at 4 a.m. Stick around, we got more of today's hottest R&B and hip hop! Hawaii's only Hot I-94!"

There were sounds of explosions and laser beams and then a serious woman started talking about all the things the Bank of Hawaii has helped her family with over the years.

I sat there on the floor leaning against the coffee table. The phone was on the floor and I could hear Moon-Dog's voice yelling.

"Yo! We made it, nigga! We got a show tonight, muthafucka!"

I sat there a moment, unsure of what to say or do. Unsure of what to think. It didn't feel good. It felt bad. It was supposed to feel good. But how could it? There was no way that it could feel good after everything.

I hung up the phone and I pulled it out of the wall.

***

"God dammit! What he needs is sleep. Sleep and food. Real food. And then more sleep and then more food. Period. Nothing else."

"See, so you're making my point! He's fine. Give him the sunshine cocktail and a bag of cocaine! It won't kill him. He can do the show, then he'll come in, get some x-rays and, ya know, all the clinical testing and shit you wanna run, and he'll rest here at the hospital with me."

"Kimo! This is a kid! I am not giving a kid a fucking morphine cocktail and a bag of cocaine!"

"Hey, he's not a kid! He's a fucking badass. And he works for me. And he's a fucking rockstar, or at least he's gonna be in a few hours if you stop acting like a little bitch! Maryanne?! Hey, Maryanne!"

"I'm here…"

"Call Doctor Moral's wife and tell her how much of a good man he is for not administering drugs to a drug dealer, please!"

"Both of you need to calm the fuck down," said Maryanne.

"Yo! Is this some shit that we can do in the car?!" said Moon-Dog.

"Go back in the room," said Maryanne.

"I'm just sayin, the show is in like two fuckin hours and it's all the way downtown!"

Moon-Dog was all dressed up in brand new Karl Kani shit and was pacing back and forth around the living room. I could hear all of the Pearl City crew and god knows who else in my bedroom. D-40 and Suga-C were arguing with Moon-Dog.

"I'm just saying we can leave right quick at some point, steal the car, drop it off at Q's chop shop and be right back!" pleaded D-40.

"No, no and hell no!" Moon-Dog shot back. "Why you gotta take Q? I don't need him distracted with some stupid shit ya'll is tryin to do!"

"Cuz we can't just drop a stolen car at the shop, Dog. That's Kimo's people. We ain't cool like that. Q gotta be there," said Suga-C.

"It's an insurance scam, Dog! We get money on both sides! We'll give you a taste!"

"Shut the fuck up!" screamed Moon-Dog. "Give me a taste?! You ain't gansta! Fuckin dough boy!"

I tried to open my eyes and the light shot through my head, hard and hot. I closed them fast but the damage was done. My head started throbbing in time with a newly discovered ringing in my ears.

"He's waking up," said Maryanne in a stern aunty voice. "All of you go down and wait in the parking lot, now! He'll be down in about ten minutes and you guys can go do your little talent show or whatever it is Kimo thinks is *so* fucking important."

"Dis ain't no talent show, woman! This is our concert! This is us, man! We doin it big! After tonight—watch, you goan see! We about to blow the fuck up!" Moon-Dog was freaking out.

All the boys were coming out of the bedroom, and standing next to Maryanne was the most out of place white dude I had ever seen. The kinda guy you see coming out of those secret airport lounges. He was almost hiding behind Maryanne.

"Get out, c'mon, all of you wait downstairs. Go, now!" she was repeating as she playfully smacked all of them.

"Hey so if you ain't doin nothin after the show maybe I come back through on this side and we could grab a drink or something…" said Suga-C to Maryanne.

She stopped for a second and seemed to be sizing him up. I thought she would slap him but she tilted her head and put her hand on his chest.

"This ride is only for grown men, little boy," said Maryanne.

She leaned into him and he retreated a little against the wall. He didn't expect her to put her body on his.

"Oh, I'm grown up…" said Suga-C sounding flustered.

"Oh yeah? Really? Let me see…" Maryanne gently squeezed him between his legs. "Aww… that's cute… But I hope you're gonna grow a little more."

The whole Pearl City crew exploded in laughter and she smacked him in the face and sent them on their way.

Then she turned and I saw her beautiful face. She was fucking stunning, even as fucked up as I was, I could feel my stomach tighten up and get warm.

I was sitting in a beach chair. Which I thought was odd because I was still in my apartment and I didn't own a beach chair. Then I noticed that my arms and legs were duct taped to the chair. I didn't freak out because Maryanne kneeled in front of me and gently rubbed my head and the back of my neck while she talked to the old white dude in a tacky sports coat and slacks.

"Sam, listen…" she started.

"Call him Doctor Morals! That's his new name now!" shouted Kimo over the speaker phone. Someone must've plugged it back in. I should've thrown it off the Lanai.

"Fuck you, Kimo," said the Doctor in the most non threatening way possible.

"You da one!" said Kimo half laughing.

"Kimo, shut the fuck up!" said Maryanne. "Sam, listen, I know this seems outside of the box—"

"Outside of the box?! Honey, this is an entirely different box all together. We had a deal for a few prescriptions and some off-the-books abortions, not gunshot wounds and turning minors into heroin addicts!" cried Sam.

Even though I didn't know this guy I could tell this fit he was throwing was a well worn script that he had been performing with Maryanne for a while. I tried to say something and noticed my mouth was like sandpaper but I wasn't thirsty. Then I saw an IV bag was hanging from a clothes hanger dangling from my living room lamp above my head.

Maryanne turned and hugged Sam. She put her hands around his face and was whispering to him. She grabbed his arms and wrapped them around her. He didn't stand a chance. His words turned into unrecognizable vocalizations of complaint. She consoled those sounds with tighter squeezes while saying, "I know, I know baby, I know this isn't what you signed up for. Kimo is my brother. He's family. I didn't know who else to turn to. I didn't know who else could help me. I know I'm trouble. I know. I told you I was bad news. I tried to warn you. I tried to not get you wrapped up in all of this. I tried but… I can't think about what that means… That means I can't ever see you again. That's the only way to get you out of all of this. It's what's best for you. I'm so sorry. I'll talk to Kimo—"

"*No!* I knew what I was getting into with you, and I can help, but I have to know that you want my help. This life you live… it doesn't have to be this way. I can help you. Like really help you. Help you out of this, but you have to want it!"

"I do want it. I want you. Please help us!"

"Okay, but you need to step away Maryanne. I know it will take some time but—"

"Jesus fucking christ! You two are going to make me throw up! Give the kid the drugs and get the fuck out of there!" yelled Kimo over the phone.

"Baby, I just want to know that my brother and my nephew will be okay. Alright? And then we maybe try this for real. But you have to figure out what you're gonna say to your wife. Maybe we wait a little, until after Tammy finishes this school year. You know the divorce is gonna hit her hard… she's such a gentle little girl…"

Marianne turned back to me as she trailed off and grinned. Her eyes sparkled. Sam's eyes were glazed over as if he was in some kind of spell. He was thinking about leaving his wife and throwing his daughter into chaos to live with Maryanne. And she was encouraging him.

"Okay… okay…" Sam was mumbling to himself.

He pulled out a syringe and put it into the IV line close to the inside of my elbow.

I felt a cold burning slowly crawl up my arm and into my chest. When it reached my heart, the world exploded in sunshine.

***

My heartbeat was loud. Strong and loud.

Thump, Thump, Thump, Thump.

Like a techno bass drum.

Thump, Thump, Thump, Thump.

A bright light would flash and white out my world. The image that returned would be a different moment.

Thump, Thump, Thump,

Flash,

Thump,

Flash,

thumpthumpthump,

Flash,

thumpthumpthump,

Flash.

I'm above myself, watching myself perform with Moon-Dog in a tiny crowded nightclub with everyone shouting the words from Kimo's notebook and words I had written down as scribbles in my rhyme book.

Thumpthumpthump,

Flash!

I'm pulling D-40 away from a raging car fire.

He's on fire!

His Hornets jersey sparkles as the flames stream up and around his body.

I'm rolling on top of him and throwing sand and dirt on him! He's screaming—a blood-curdling scream.

Thumpthumpthump,

Flash!

The girls in the front row are reaching for me. Trying to touch me. All the brothers from all over the island are up front reaching their hands out to give me a pound while I yell my rhymes into the microphone.

Thump, Thump, Thump,

Flash!

Cynthia is outside the nightclub. She's crying. She is trying to give me some kind of scrapbook she made filled with pictures and poems. She says she's leaving to go to a military school on the mainland. Her dad's paying for it. To help get her away from me.

"Fuck your dad!" I yell too loud. People are looking.

"He's right! I'm sorry."

"What do you mean he's right?!"

"You don't love me!"

"What are you talking about?!"

"I don't know, everyone around you is fucked up! You're drowning and everyone is pulling you down. Maryanne is evil! Kimo is fucking evil! That whole family is evil! They're feeding off of you and you're bringing me into it. I thought you were different but you're gonna drown me too. I have to take care of myself!"

I look down at the scrapbook. On the cover is the photo she took from inside the submarine of me scuba diving. Around the photo she has drawn a bleeding heart with knives violently plunging through it. She has written "You'll always be my Badass" with skulls where the letter a's are supposed to be. The memory of the day tries to bust through all the noise in my head and in my chest.

"I LOVE YOU! You know I love you!"

"You can't! You can't love me!"

"What the FUCK are you talking about!"

"You can't love anyone! You're broken! I can't fix you!"

"You're broken, bitch! You're fucking crazy!"

"Stop! Please, you're so fucked up right now. I can see it! You need to go to the hospital."

"You gonna listen to your dad? After everything?! First I gotta save you from him and now he's gonna save you from me? Then some military dude gonna save you… Ha! An actual captain! Literally, Captain Save-a-Hoe!"

"You didn't save me! Fuck You! I left because I love you and I thought we could be something together… Fuck you! My dad ain't saving me! I'm saving me! I don't want—"

"Fuck what you want! You just think you're too good for me cuz I'm a fucken criminal—whatever. What? You think I'm a loser?! What makes you think you ain't broken, huh?!"

"Baby, stop! Please, I'm going."

"Go then, bitch! Ain't nobody stopping you! I don't give a fuck about you! Never did! You was just a clingy-ass Monday bitch! A place for me to rest and wash my fucking clothes! You see my name on the fucking marquee?! Look at all these bitches! Get to steppin! You gone!"

Thump, Thump, Thump,

Flash!

I'm standing in the parking lot of my Waipahu apartment and Alex is holding a gun to my head with his left hand. His right arm is in a cast and sling. All his boys are around me with baseball bats. One is holding a steel pipe from a broken chain link fence.

Thumpthumpthump,

Flash!

I'm in a stolen souped up Honda Civic with all four tires off of the ground. We land hard two lanes over from where we went airborne and the carriage hits the pavement. The racing bucket seats do their job and I remain in my seat able to keep control. Police sirens are screaming behind us. D-40 is laughing uncontrollably.

Thumpthumpthump,

Flash!

I sniff cocaine through a cocktail straw right out of the baggy in the dirty bathroom stall of the night club. There are two girls with me. One white and one Latina. They are military housewives. The white one is rubbing my dick while I hold the Latina one's hair and help her with the straw.

Thump, Thump, Thump,

Flash!

"I wen tell you Waipahu is mine!" Alex turns and limps away.

The bats come up and I charge the one with the pipe. He swings but it's so big it's easy to time. I crack him dead in the nose and he goes down. A bat hits me from behind. I turn and catch a fist in the mouth. Then a bat to my legs. Then I'm down. I cover up the best I can as they start stomping.

Thumpthumpthump,

Flash!

We lose the cops twice but the chop shop is abandoned. We double back and pull up slow in Hau Bush. It's my idea to use the car cover. We stuff it into the gas tank and drape it over the side of the car and stuff the rest under the hood. We soak it and douse the rest of the car in gasoline.

"Let's light this bitch and get back," I say as I look for a stick or a branch to light and toss onto the car.

D-40 has a lighter.

Wind rushes towards me as the fire that's about to erupt sucks all the air out of the surrounding area. Then it growls and booms as heat comes from behind me and pushes me over. My shirt and my jeans are on fire. I roll around frantically to put it out when I hear the screams.

Thump, Thump, Thump,

Flash!

Cynthia's mom is driving their beat up old Toyota and it putters away from the nightclub. I can see the back of Cynthia's head and wait for her to turn and look back so I can give her the finger. She doesn't and as the car makes a left turn onto Nimitz Highway I almost run after it. My legs start to move. I take two steps and look at my legs. I throw the scrapbook at the car but it flaps open like a dying bird and flutters its insides into the air.

"Fuck her," I say out loud.

Pictures and hand written poems and love letters all over the dirty broken pavement. I see the picture but I think of her excited face inside the submarine snapping it and giving me the middle finger playfully. My guts churn and I feel all the drugs and energy fade away. I feel every broken rib and bruised bone and—

Thumpthumpthump,

Flash!

I'm curled up in the fetal position and for a few seconds surprised by how well it works. I have never been down like a bitch before and I think, "Oh shit, not a bad move for worst-case shit." Until someone's boot gets through my arms.

Flash!

An old Samoan lady yelling, "You guys going kill'em! *Nooooo,* go home! Go, home!" She is swinging a broom at the boys.

Flash!

I am collapsed on the floor in the elevator of my building but my leg is blocking the door so it keeps opening and closing on my leg. I can hear the old lady yelling.

Flash!

The elevator door closes. I am alone. I'm bleeding all over the floor. I can't see at all out of my left eye. My right eye is cloudy. I can't make out what floor I am on and I can't get up.

Thump, Thump, Thump,

Flash!

"You gotta take me to a hospital, *ooooooooeeeeeeee.* You gotta, *ooo eee,* it hurts, it hurts…"

D-40 is crying like a five-year-old. I'm driving. I can see Hau Bush and the fire is growing. The whole place will burn in the next hour. There is too much underbush. I yell back to D-40.

"Stop being such a bitch. My ass caught fire too… and that shit hurt but you don't hear me crying like a little bitch. We'll get back to my place and figure it out from there."

"*Pleeeeeeaaase* Q, it *huuuuurts,* please… Hospital… *pleeease.*"

Just then police cars race by us on their way to the soon-to-be-out-of-control brush fire.

"Dog! If we drop you at the hospital for burns right down the street from a fucking bush fire, we are all going to jail!"

"Word," says Suga-C, "you know his ass is gonna sing."

We both laugh.

"*Pleeeeease*, Q, it hurts!!"

I shake my head and reach for the inside cabin light so I can take a look at him.

"Look, it's not that bad. We both just lost our eye lashes, for real."

The light comes on and I adjust the rearview so I can see him.

His face has melted completely off and the skin is hanging off his chin like burnt chicken skin dangling off a BBQ chicken thigh. The flesh is exposed. It is different shades of pink and red with big gobs of puss and goop strung in between.

I look over at Suga-C and he has seen the same thing.

"We gotta do something, Q."

Thumpthumpthumpthump,

Flash!

Thumpthumpthumpthump,

Flash!

Thumbthumpthumpthump,

Flash!

Thump, Thump, Thump,

Flash!

***

The flashing red and blue lights were all I could see. Everything hurt. It hurt to try to see more and so I didn't try, but I could hear. The sound of a big truck idling. Sirens from far away getting closer, closer, and then stopping somewhere nearby. A man was talking. He was talking to me.

"Can you open your eyes?"

"No…" I tried to say.

"Subject is responsive…"

I heard walkie talkies chirping back and forth. I was starting to feel something around my neck. It was a neckbrace. I saw a bright light out of my right eye.

"Good! Good job, kid!" said the man.

"That shit is bright man!" I said.

"Okay," said the man and the light stopped. I could see him. At first I panicked. It was a fireman. But then I could tell it wasn't *the* Fireman.

"Can you tell me your name?" he said patiently.

"Yeah…"

"What's your name?"

"Oh yeah… it's… um… shit…"

"That's okay… Can you tell me what happened?"

The old lady started yelling from somewhere that I couldn't see.

"The hoodlum boys was trying for kill him! That's why! I was screaming at them and—"

"Ma'am, Ma'am! Thank you, but we need to ask him questions to see if he's okay. You can tell that officer over there and he will take your statement."

"Aunty! Thank you for saving me with your broom!" I said.

"You lucky I wen save you! You almost as bad as them, that's why! I know you! Now you like act all any kine. I only wen save you so you no die in front of me! You punk! No act all nice nice now!" I saw her face for a second and her eyes were wild and I thought she might slap me. If she did, I knew I would die from it.

She disappeared and the questions continued.

"Can you tell me what happened?"

"Yeah, I got my ass beat."

"Say that again," said the firemen. He chuckled and I could hear another fireman in the background laughing.

"Do you know what year it is?"

"Yeah…" I couldn't remember. "Shit…"

"That's okay. Do you know who the president is?"

"Yeah… shit…"

"That's okay…"

"Wait… yeah… shit… The guy who smokes weed."

The firemen chuckled again.

I passed out.

Thump, Thump, Thump,

Flash!

CHAPTER 10

DADDY'S LITTLE GIRL

THERE WAS A SHAFT of light.

It ran down the wall and onto the floor. It was coming from a window behind me. It would have sharp edges and then slowly transform into a soft glow and then back to a bright, well-defined beam. It must be clouds passing in front of the sun. I couldn't turn my head to see the window. In fact, I couldn't even open my left eye. If I thought about it I could feel throbbing, but it was far away. If I let it go, it would soften and then I would wake up again and wonder the same things until I could feel the pain begin to sharpen like the beam of light. I tracked its movement down the wall. I started to look forward to waking back up and seeing if it would be all the way onto the floor. I was disappointed when I woke up and saw that I had missed it. It was gone.

It was dark now but there was still light coming from behind me. A lamp or something. It wasn't very bright but it gave enough of a glow for me to see a chair and an end table with a phone on it. Next to the end table was a hospital tray with a jug of water and some plastic cups. There was a door in my line of sight. It was open but my view was blocked by a plain curtain divider. I could hear voices outside the door but they were too far for me to make out what they were saying.

I tried to move and lighting bolts of pain surged through me. I couldn't even tell where the pain was coming from. I laid there completely still, hoping that I wouldn't black out. I didn't want to go back to the nothing.

I slowed down my breath and tried to bite my lip. I couldn't get my lip into my mouth to bite down on it. It was too swollen. I tried to breathe through my nose and was happy to find that one nostril was open enough to slowly inhale. I smelled a cigarette. The craving hit hard. It gave me the strength to slowly turn my head.

Kimo was leaning on the windowsill smoking a cigarette. I had never seen Kimo smoke a cigarette before. He was wearing a hospital gown and had an IV on a roller attached to him.

"Wanna a cigarette?" he mumbled.

"Yeah…"

"Can you hold it?"

"What?"

"You want me to hold it for you?"

"Huh…?"

"Do your arms work? They got you on some pretty heavy shit. Can you move your arms?"

I tried to lift my arm up to reach for the cigarette and it felt like moving through the ocean against the current. And it hurt.

Kimo took a drag and then held it up to me to take a drag. The smoke filled my lungs and I felt better.

"You still got your teeth?" he asked.

He was talking so soft and mumbling.

"Huh?"

"Teeth… did they kick out your teeth?" He tried to speak louder and held his side.

"Oh, no, I mean… I don't know?"

I opened my mouth and he looked at my teeth. He seemed relieved.

"Good. I thought maybe, because what I did to his uncle… I went through a smashing people's teeth phase," he mumbled matter of factly.

He gently put the lit cigarette into my hand and I struggled to bring it to my mouth but eventually was able to take another drag. He held his stomach while he limped around the bed and carefully sat in the chair. He put his pack of cigarettes and lighter on the end table.

"You got shot," I said.

"Yeah, went through a few ribs and some guts. Sam said I gotta be here on this antibiotics IV bag so I don't… 'go septic' is the term he used.

Then the other one went through my thigh. Didn't hit the bone though, so there's that."

"That's cool."

"Yeah."

He lit a cigarette for himself.

"You're more fucked up then me," he said.

"Dude you got shot—"

"Yeah but—"

"Twice!"

"You got stomped."

"You got shot!"

"You got stomped after being in a fucking car accident!"

"You got shot!"

We both started chuckling.

"You have brain swelling. Sam is real worried about that. They been bringing you in and out of the big ass head x-ray tube thing…"

"MRI?"

"Right, and your skull is cracked around your left eye, and that shit looks fucking grotesque. Sam is saying he might have to do some surgery to cut your eye and let some of the fluid out, but he's worried you'll lose your vision in that eye. You broke three ribs on your left side and there's some fluid in your lungs. He's worried about that… Next time if you get jumped, try to grab one of them when you're going down and pull him on top of you. His boys will have a harder time kicking you. Grab his hair with one hand and his ear with the other. It's super easy to rip off an ear. It pops right off. Show it to him and yell, 'Look at your fucking ear!' He'll usually stop and freak out. Jam your thumb in his eye and get the fuck back up. Sometimes that will get a few of them a little shook. His boys will—"

His voice cracked and I figured his ribs were bothering him.

"I should've thought of that," I said.

"The eyeball stuff though… Sam is worried about your eye because—" Then his voice cracked again and he wiped his eyes and I saw that he was crying. He didn't make a sound. He just sat there quiet for a moment. I didn't know what to do. I didn't look at him.

"I'm sorry," he finally mumbled.

I looked at my cigarette with my good eye. I wished I didn't see him.

I wished I had something to say. Something that would erase this. I closed my eyes and felt a stinging warm tear slide down my face.

Then the voices outside the door got very loud and Maryanne came bursting through the curtain. She flipped on the main fluorescent lights and walked right to the window. Her perfume filled the room. She was talking loud and right behind was Travis in regular clothes and Star. She was dressed in surf shorts and a t-shirt but she had a headband pushing her hair back like a girl would wear.

"This is the time! I don't want to hear any of this bitch-ass complaining!" said Maryanne.

"Homballah bitch! Travis is speaking his mind yeah! You need for listen instead of da'kine!" said Star.

"Listening to bitch shit is what got us here in the first place," said Maryanne.

"Aye Mary! He's awake!" Star shrieked. "I'm glad you're feeling better. I would've brought you a lei or some shit but Maryanne is on the rag *sooooo* you have to settle for a kiss."

Star leaned forward and kissed me on the side of my face that felt less swollen.

Maryanne stopped and looked at me then looked at Kimo. She saw that we were crying and looked disgusted. She stomped away from the window and around the bed. She reached in her purse and pulled out a travel-size packet of tissues and tossed them dismissively at Kimo.

"Clean your fucking face," she whispered through her teeth. "Uncle will be here any minute…"

She turned to me and put on the most loving, caring face I had ever seen.

"How you feeling, sweetie? Do you need some water?"

She reached for the hospital tray and poured me a cup of water. She held it to my lips and gently gave me a sip. I wanted to curl up into her arms and go to sleep. Feel her skin and smell her perfume and drift away.

"Let me see your teeth, sweetheart," she asked. I showed her the best I could and she smiled.

"That's good!" she said like she was speaking to a toddler. "You still have that beautiful smile!"

She turned to Kimo.

"What the fuck is wrong with you?!"

Kimo put his cigarette out on the arm of the chair and frowned. He wouldn't make eye contact with Maryanne.

"You come out of jail and you're a little fucking pussy? Who the fuck are you?! I let it slide for a while cuz I figured that much time gotta make even you a little weird, but what the fuck?! Sell some fucking drugs! Steal some fucking cars! Beat the shit out of some people! It's fuckin easy!!"

She leaned forward and smacked Kimo. Star made a sound and turned her back to the room and Travis stepped forward.

"Maryanne, take it easy. Let's just talk about it for a minute… please," finished Travis sheepishly.

"Talk about what?! What the fuck is there to talk about?! All we fucking do is talk! You wanna go to jail? Uncle is weak. Old and weak. It's only a matter of time. There is blood in the fucking water Travis! This is the only way! Now! Tonight! No talking. No bitching."

She leaned over Kimo like she was scolding a child.

"No fucking philosophizing! No fucking self help bullshit! No fucking Oprah Winfrey shit. You little fucking bitch. I need you now! Uncle will be here and I need you to man the fuck up now!"

She put her finger in his face and was poking it on his forehead and cheek with every word.

"I swear to fucking God! Kimo, don't lose your shit right now! You weren't the only one! And you know it! You wanna find divinity or God or some shit?! You do that on your own time. You owe me! You promised! You promised all of us! This is on you!"

Kimo was quiet. Maryanne had finished her rant and was leaning over him with her head tilted waiting for a response. When she didn't get one, she slapped him.

Nothing happened.

Kimo didn't even look up.

She slapped him again.

Kimo gently and slowly slid a cigarette out of his pack and lit it.

Maryanne slapped the cigarette out of his mouth.

Kimo reached up and grabbed her by the throat with his right hand. He squeezed hard. Travis ran up but Kimo's voice was too much.

"BACK THE FUCK UP!!!"

Travis retreated. Star started crying at the wall like a kid in time out. Kimo lifted Maryanne off of the ground and laid her on her back on the bed right over my legs. Pain shot through my body but I didn't dare make a sound. Kimo leaned over her and put his face inches from hers. He was growling and veins were popping out of his forehead. He didn't yell. His voice was a low grovely rumble.

"What world is this? Huh? In what world can you talk to me like that? I will fucking kill you! I will squeeze my hand and fucking kill you! Like this."

Kimo squeezed and Maryanne made horrible sounds.

"Can you feel it? You're dying?! I can feel it! I can feel you dying in my hand!"

Star was whimpering. It was above the other sounds. The room was a symphony of pain. Kimo was breathing. Maryanne was choking to death. And above those sounds was Star's mahu whimpering in long, soft, drawn out notes. The notes became words.

"Keeeeemooooo…pleeeeease…kimo…pleeeeeease…doooooooooon't… pleeease…keeeeeeemoooo…you sound like hiiiiiiim…keeemooooo…"

Recognition slowly filled Kimo's eyes. His hand released. He collapsed in the chair. Maryanne gulped air and put her hands around her throat. Star ran to her and hugged her. Travis stepped out of the room.

"I'm okay… I'm okay… stop," said Maryanne to Star.

Travis rushed back in.

"They're here," he said.

Maryanne stood up and straightened her dress.

She looked at Travis.

"Good," she said.

Then she cut her eyes at Kimo and said, "Good, that's who I need you to be, baby."

She took a deep breath and transformed right in front of us just as Uncle entered the room. She gave Uncle a huge hug and said that this was how to turn tragedy into opportunity. She stepped in front of my dad as he walked in and held his hand and then turned and walked him to my bed. She casually slid her hand under my blanket and laid it gently on my calf.

"Now listen, you two can be mad at each other, that's fine, but after I found out how long it's been since you saw each other and how much he misses you and how sorry he is for leaving you and your mother, I think that maybe, just maybe, a few hours of real time can at least give you two a chance to say what you need to say. Then after that, if you need to go your separate ways, so be it. But you could have died out there and what if the last time you two spoke was that debacle of a birthday party?" She was gently rubbing my leg and speaking in the most soothing and caring way. My father had his head down and he was holding her hand. She was rubbing her thumb back and forth across the back of his hand.

I couldn't look at him hunched over like that. I looked at Kimo. He shrugged and gave me a look that said to just let her play her game. I nodded okay to Maryanne.

She lit up in a show of joy that was so over the top I cringed. If I hadn't seen her just a moment before, I would have taken her as the sweetest thing. I would have said whatever she wanted me to say and wondered why such an angel was helping me. Instead her duplicity was horrifying. She pulled my dad forward and rubbed his shoulder while he began his performance.

"Son, I was trying to help. I didn't know you were back and when I saw you, all of these memories, all this shit that I had buried, just came up. You can hate me and you have every right to, but I just want you to know that—"he was even able to manufacture a few tears—"I love you son! I love you so much. Just know that… and maybe we can rebuild some kind of relationship. You're hanging out with Uncle's kids, and him and I are doin big things, man. We can all hang. We can get to know each other as, ya know, who we are now…"

I wanted it to stop.

I closed my good eye and tried to go into the morphine haze until I was lost. I felt the hairs on my calf get suddenly ripped out of my leg. Maryanne was standing there with that sweet look on her face. She tilted her head and raised her eyebrows in a question. I was about to try to say go fuck yourself when Kimo spoke up.

"Hey, cut the kid some slack. His brain is swelling up against his skull and he's pumped full of morphine and whatever the fuck else Sam's got in these IVs."

"Right, hey little man, hang in there," said my dad.

Travis was wheeling in some wheelchairs and extra hospital trays.

"I couldn't find any more regular chairs," said Travis.

"I ordered some small kine grinds," said Uncle.

Star was hanging fabric all over the room.

"What are we doing here, Uncle?" said Kimo.

"You know what we're doing," said Maryanne. "We are being a fucking family again. You and your 'new little brother' are hurt. You are patients in Sam's clinic. We are trying to be here for you. So how bout you stop acting so stink, yeah?!"

"Hey sweety, take it easy. He jus wen get shot couple times. Okay, yeah? If he like act little bit stink, eh?" said Uncle playfully.

"He always stink!" said Star, plugging in the boombox.

Sam came rushing into the room. He had on a lab coat and scrubs. He was rolling in four IV stands.

"Okay, that was my last patient. I have a few presents for you, Uncle. This my special sunshine cocktail."

"Yeah, shoots, but first I say sumting. Star, stop buzzing around for one second. I like make one toast," said Uncle.

Star and Maryanne rushed to get drinks in everyone's hands. Star set a drink for me on the table. Kimo gave me a look and I didn't even try to pick it up.

"I just like for say, brah, times like this you neva know. Anything can happen and then, what? All we get is right now! All we get is each oddah. Kimo, we jus wen get you back. We not even back regula from the last time you wen leave. I jus wanna… I jus want you to be happy again, Kimo. We miss you. I miss you. I like be one family again for whateva time we get left…"

My dad raised his glass and said, "Hell yeah!"

Star and Maryanne hugged each other. "We love you, Kimo," they said in unison.

My dad laughed and so did Sam.

Kimo raised his glass slightly and acknowledged the toast, and Maryanne kneeled in front of him, whispered something in his ear and kissed him on the forehead.

Star pushed play on the boombox and Madonna's "Celebrate" started blasting in the room.

***

"What world is this?" mumbled Kimo for about the twelfth time.

I had drifted off and it took me a second to remember where I was. The room was dark. The only light came from a flashlight that was on the floor propped up to point at a styrofoam disco ball that Star had hung from the ceiling. My father was laying on the floor of the hospital room. He was laughing uncontrollably. Uncle was sitting in one of the wheelchairs—Maryanne was sitting on his lap—telling a story about something that I couldn't keep track of because he kept stopping every few words to laugh or make a weird squealing pig noise.

"So, den, Kimo wen try for run up and put da pig in one choke hold," laughed Uncle. "Brah, da bugga stay bigger den him! Maryanne get one princess costume on and da bugga stay all dirty!" Uncle giggled. "Maryanne stay all butt hurt, brah, she's pissed. The pig stay dragging Kimo all around the yard, braddah, all chu the mud li'dat. Kimo just stay holding on!" He could barely get the words out he was laughing so much. "Kimo was yellin, 'I sorry, Maryanne, I neva mean'um. I no like get your dress dirty. I going wash'em, promise!'" Uncle looked at Kimo and was almost choking he was laughing so hard. "Marianne was all salty li'dat. She neva like hear one apology. She jus like give'em cracks, so she stay trying for hit'em wit the shovel, but then she so small she couldn't even pick'em up and run at the same time, so den"—he was gasping by this point and his eyes were watering—"she run in front of where she tink the pig going go and bring up the shovel and wait for the pig to run by, but the pig one smart bugga too. The pig no like get hit by one shovel! So den, when da pig see the shovel go up, she turn, but Maryanne no follow eh, so den they both go in separate directions tinkin what the other one going do! Both of them spinning, spinning, running and spinning, and poor Kimo just crying and apologizing, hanging on to the pig who stay squealing, *squealing! Hahahahahahaaaaahahahaaa!*"

"*Sqeeeeeeeeee!*" screamed my father from the floor, holding his belly. Uncle was leaning to the side laughing like the king of the Hyenas at my dad who was on his back on the floor squealing like a pig. Maryanne was sitting on Uncle's lap and he my father both had IV bags in their arms. Sam was sitting on the windowsill. He also had an IV bag. His head was laid back against the window. His eyes were open and so was his mouth. The boombox had been set up in the corner and there was a huge briefcase on the floor filled with tapes. Two more hospital trays had been brought in and one had some take-out trays with roast pig and poke. The other had two bottles of Crown Royal and two bottles of vodka. On the floor was a cooler filled with beer. Travis kept giving Kimo nervous looks. Maryanne kept laughing and petting the back of Uncle's head. And she kept refilling my father and Uncle's cups every time they took a sip. Star was buzzing around the room making small plates of food and throwing away trash. She was in full drag, swinging a flower-print shawl around like a cape. She was also playing DJ, switching tapes. The boombox was huge and it had two tape decks so you could play one tape while fast forwarding or rewinding another. Star jumped on top of my father and started tickling and slapping him. It was loud. It was weird. It got even more weird when the music stopped.

Star jumped and ran over to the tape deck.

"Maryanne! You going help, yeah?! Just trust, yeah?! You going re-member!" yelled Star.

"Don't you fucking dare! Star! NO!" yelled Maryanne playfully.

My dad got up off of the floor in stages. First he sat up. Then rolled over to his knees. Then got one leg up. Then Pulled on his IV stand and haphazardly stood.

The Stylistics' song "You're a Big Girl Now" started and Maryanne giggled, rolled her eyes, and screamed, "*Nooooo!*" like an embarrassed little girl.

Uncle was laughing, pushing her to stand up. Star ran over and started pulling her up. My dad was swaying back and forth trying to keep his balance but he was smiling and clapping.

"Wait!" yelled Star over the music. "Wait, okay! I'm gonna start it over! Maryanne you need a scarf!" Star threw her scarf at Maryanne and grabbed another scarf that was hanging over the window, then she kneeled down and rewound the tape to the top of the song and stood up next to Maryanne. Maryanne got all serious and stood with the scarf in her left hand over her head.

"Star! Put your arm up!" Maryanne whispered.

"Aye no! It's the right arm!" Star whispered back.

Then they both laughed and switched places so that the arms they had up matched up.

The room was quiet for a moment and you could hear the hiss of the tape between the music. My dad was now standing right next to Star.

"Eh baboose, sit down and watch!" Star pushed him playfully and he fell back into his wheelchair. Uncle laughed. Star reached up and spun the disco ball.

The song started again. Maryanne and Star stood still and moved only their arms with the scarves. Then they slid side to side together. The movements were choreographed. The singing started and they acted out the lyrics.

You're a big girl now
No more Daddy's little girl…

Star went behind Maryanne and held her hair in ponytails.

No more pigtails in your hair
No more silly looks with a childish glare…

Then Maryanne slid behind Star and reached her hands up and smooshed a silly expression onto Star's face with her hands. Uncle and my father were having the time of their lives. Maryanne put her hand out and helped Uncle stand. Star reached out and practically lifted my dad back out of the chair. They all started slow dancing together. They were laughing and cracking jokes.

The disco ball was spinning slowly. They slowly turned and swayed. Maryanne had her head on Uncle's chest and Uncle was rubbing her head. Star was basically holding my dad up. It was dark. Tiny freckles of colored light moved around and around.

You can love, girl, if you must
You can kiss, girl, if you must…

Maryanne lifted her head and started kissing Uncle. They turned and I thought for a second I was seeing things. They turned back and it was happening. Uncle and Maryanne were kissing. I turned to Kimo. He sat still in his chair. He was looking at them, too. My dad finally collapsed in his chair. Travis appeared and walked over to my dad and stuck a needle in his arm. Then he wheeled his chair out of the room. Uncle noticed and looked back at Maryanne. She gently pushed him back into his chair.

You're a big girl now
Yes, you are…

He had a blank expression on his face. She knelt down in front of him and opened his legs.

You're my happiness
Shining STAR...

Then she stuck a needle in his thigh and he blacked out.

The lights came on and it was too bright. I had to close my eyes. The music stopped and I could hear Maryanne stomp over to Kimo.

"You're up," she said.

I could hear her heels as she stomped all the way down the hall. I opened my eyes and saw Kimo putting something into my IV. His eyes were all red and he looked tired. His face was hollowed out and there was a deep space behind his eyes. He looked empty.

"I was so sure about this for so long... I came all the way back for this... but now..." He took a long breath.

"Did you guys just kill Uncle and my dad?" I managed.

He looked at me for a while.

"Are you killing me?"

"You said you would help me. You promised. We promised to help each other."

CHAPTER 11

AND THEN THERE WAS NOTHING

THE OCEAN WAS GLASS.

The sun was just beginning to come over the horizon. The sky was bright orange and yellow. The air was crisp and fresh. The morning breeze was already warming as it gently glided across the top of the water barely making any ripples. I sat on the floor in the back of the inflatable speed boat right by Kimo's feet. I had on a pair of his surf shorts and one of his big camouflage-print rain jackets. It was huge and made for much colder weather but I needed it. Whatever he put in my IV was not as fun as the sunshine cocktail. This felt like maybe just a little more morphine and a shit ton of speed. I was nauseous and sick. My head hurt so bad. Every small bump or jerk set off lightning bolts of pain.

No amount of drugs or pain or lying to myself could hide what we were doing. We were going to kill these two men. I didn't know how we were going to do it. I didn't want to think about why. But I knew we were going to do it.

I could see them in the front of the boat. They were passed out. They each had a pair of handcuffs attached to one of their ankles. I closed my good eye and noticed that I was crying. That helped. I was crying because I didn't want to kill anyone. *I don't want to kill anyone. I don't know what I'm doing here and...*

"I don't want to kill anyone."

I had said it out loud. The sound of the boat and the wind had covered it, but I had said it. I had said it and I had meant it. Pulling the trigger at my birthday party was a spark. I thought I had wanted to kill him that night. The spark of wanting to kill him felt just like the sound of the hammer coming down on the empty chamber of the gun I was holding. *Click.* Just a little spark. A little click. Somewhere deep down inside my gut. *Click.* And a spark. I thought it meant I wanted him dead. But the fire never came. The chamber was empty. The spark didn't catch. It never started the fire that I needed. The raging hell fire that would dry my tears and burn away the pain and stand me up in front of him so I could look him in the eyes and kill him. The inferno of hate that I needed to melt him would have to be so big, it would have to be so hot, that the flames would swallow what was left of this fragile little boy shivering in this oversized rain jacket. I didn't want to murder him that night. I just didn't want to see him. I didn't want to remember… I didn't want to kill him. I just wanted to kill what he did to me.

I took a breath deep enough to make my head swim and yelled it above the sound of the twin motors.

"I don't want to kill anyone!"

Kimo slowed the boat to a stop.

"What?"

"I don't want to kill anyone," I said.

I was really crying now. It was flooding out of me and I sounded like a little baby.

"I know, I know… hey… hey, it's okay," said Kimo.

He knelt down and rubbed my head gently. He held me until it slowed down and then he stood up and continued driving.

That was it. That was all the protest I could give. I had nothing left in me. I had no fight for anything or anyone.

The boat slowed and Kimo was looking at the mountains and trees, trying to line up the boat to the same spot we had come to before. The day that I had scuba dived down to those sunken ships and rode a submarine underwater and my beautiful girlfriend had stood on the bow and flew across the ocean and laughed and screamed with joy. That day was another life. This day was horror.

"Kay, little man, you gotta stand up for a second and keep the boat here while I go get the line."

I stood and held on to the rail above the control panel. I was close to passing out. I thought maybe I could just pass out and I would wake up somewhere else.

Kimo jumped in the water and disappeared. I looked at the two men. From here I could see that their hands were duct taped. They were sleeping. My dad was smiling and mumbling something. Even in his sleep he wouldn't shut up.

Kimo popped back up and I saw that I had drifted a little way from him. I slowly motored back over.

"Come all stop and grab these lines."

I came all stop and stepped over the sleeping men and grabbed the ropes that Kimo was handing me.

"Tie them on the forward post," he said.

I did.

Kimo climbed back into the boat. I half sat, half collapsed down right next to my dad. Kimo was busy tying ropes. My dad had a mustache. I could see it was going grey and that he was dying it. I looked at his hair and noticed the same thing.

Kimo ran a separate rope through the empty hand cuff on each man's leg. He was connecting the ropes using huge zip ties. Then he cut the duct tape off of their hands. He propped them up so that they were laying on their bellies on the edge of the left pontoon. This took forever and it looked like Kimo was hurting. He was breathing hard and grunting. He kept stopping and holding his side and catching his breath. When he was finished, their arms were dangling in the water.

Kimo reached in his bag and pulled out a needle and syringe. He stuck it in each of their asses and put it back in his bag. Then he walked back to the controls and stood there.

The sun was climbing fast. It was warm now but I kept the coat on.

"What the fuck!" said my dad.

Kimo slammed the boat ahead full and turned the right side. The men were ripped off of the boat. They flipped into the water pulled by the ropes that were connected to the handcuffs on their legs.

I was happy at first. That meant this nightmare would soon be over. They would sink to the bottom and we would be done.

They both popped up fast and were treading water. I had seen the chains and the weights before when I had dived down myself. Why were they floating?

"Kimo! What are you doin?!"

"Byron, hey, Son, what's going on?!"

Kimo didn't answer. Neither did I. They both yelled and asked and cursed and we just looked at them. The weights were not there to drown them. They were there to make treading water just a little harder. Even if they dove down they couldn't untie or unhook anything. Everything was either chains or ropes with industrial zip ties. The rope that was holding our boat in place was much longer than the ropes that were holding the men. It also had a weight on it so that it hung far beneath them.

We were going to watch them tread water until they got too tired. Then they would slowly drown as they fought to their last breath.

The yelling and shouting and questioning didn't last very long. They very shortly figured they needed to focus their energy on treading water. My dad had been a really good swimmer when he was young. He started trying to float on his back. The weight was a little too much for that, so he would float on his stomach with his head down and rest for a few seconds, the weights would pull him down, and then he would swim up and take a few breaths and repeat that. Uncle wasn't doing so well. He was older and he was trying to just find a rhythm treading and breathing.

Kimo sat on the side of the boat and lit a joint. He smoked it slow and never took his eyes off of Uncle. There were four cement bricks sitting in the bow with me. I pushed one to the side of the boat so I could see what Kimo was seeing. It was quiet. Just the sounds of heavy breathing with an occasional splash.

***

The sun was slowly making its trek across the sky.

Kimo had a cooler with water and beer and some sandwiches. We sat on bricks and ate the sandwiches. We didn't talk. We would both look over at the men every few minutes. After the first hour my dad had held his breath and swam down to the buoy to take a look at the rig. He did it three or four times. At first I was concerned he would figure something out but Kimo didn't even flinch. My dad popped back up after the last time defeated and exhausted. After another hour he swam down and brought up the five pound weight that was holding his line down and put it on his chest. He then back floated and was able to rest that way.

"Uncle…" said my dad through heavy breaths

"No talk to me you fucka!" gasped Uncle.

"Uncle… swim down and grab… your weight! You can… float like this… and rest!"

"For what stupid?! You still going die!"

Kimo started laughing.

It was a chuckle at first then it slowly turned into a bellowing laughing fit. He was holding his side but he wouldn't stop laughing.

"You still going die!" whispered Kimo, laughing. "You still going DIE!" Kimo stood up in the boat and faced Uncle and started yelling, "YOU STILL GOING DIE! YOU STILL GOING DIE!"

"I sorry, Kimo, I'm sorry. What I did?! I love you, Kimo! What I did?!" screamed Uncle between full blown sobs and cries. Kimo was crying now too.

"YOU KNOW WHAT YOU DID!"

"I neva wen do nahting. I just love you as all, Kimo!"

"FUCK YOU! FUCK YOU FUCK YOU FUCK YOU!"

Kimo picked up a brick and threw it down onto Uncle's head. It made a muffled crunching sound and a pop. Kimo picked up another brick and threw it down but it missed completely. He threw another one just as Uncle's lifeless body rolled up to the surface and it hit Uncle somewhere on the back. The water filled with blood. Uncle's body slowly sank down to about ten feet and just floated there. There was a trail of blood floating away from us into the slight westerly current.

Kimo stood there in the boat breathing and looking at Uncle float beneath the surface. Every couple of seconds between the ripples in the water you could see Uncle's ghastly broken-open face.

Kimo sat back down in the boat and cried. His hands were over his face and he cried. He wept. He choked and held his side and gasped for air and he wept. I couldn't look at him. I was embarrassed. I looked at my dad floating on his back with the weight on his chest. He could be floating in a resort pool with a plate of chicken wings on his chest. That's what it looked like. How long could he do that?

"I should have just beat your ass and dropped you off at Johnny Boy's house when I first saw you. You're not my problem. Not my responsibility. You're Johnny's problem," said Kimo. He wiped his eyes and blew his nose into his hands. Snot filled his hands and he leaned over and washed his hands and face in the water.

"But I knew what he would say if you actually told him what happened to you. If you told him what your father did. I knew because I told Johnny what happened to me and Maryanne and Star and Travis and he... he turned his back on us. I knew he couldn't understand... Johnny Boy can't kill it for you. He doesn't... he can't understand this... I tried to tell him... I did..." He sat back down in the boat. Tears were running down his face. He didn't sound like Kimo. He sounded like a little boy. A four-year-old little boy who had fallen down outside and was bravely explaining how he got hurt through gasps and sniffles.

"I knew when I met you... in the rain... you were gonna kill Kevin. I knew why. Someone had already killed you... like Uncle had already killed me. I could see it in your eyes... They're sick... what they did to us... to kids... they're so sick... they kill the best part... the real part... the human part... What's left grows up to be a monster... I saw you and I knew... You were me... I thought if I helped you... it would help me... like Marty Mcfly going back and changing shit... I would wake up and everything would be changed. Me and Maryanne would have a kid... would live... on the top of the mountain... with regular jobs... fight about regular stuff... make love and cook and fold clothes. At night I take out the trash and look up at the stars... I could see Maryanne through the kitchen window singing and doing dishes... but... I can't see anything now... I think... I think... I was wrong..."

He started crying into his hands again but then sucked it back up and took a long slow breath.

"Oh shit..." laughed Kimo, "I'm fucking losing it, huh?! I'm losing my fucking mind. Pass me my bag?"

I did. He pulled out another needle and syringe and stuck himself in the leg.

"I'm gonna take a fucking nap."

He sat in the boat and looked out at Uncle. Kimo looked like he was calming down. His eyelids got droopy and his breathing slowed down.

Then he looked at me. His speech was slow and slurred.

"I'm not losing my mind. I'm in my mind. My mind is like this fucking boat, ya know? Except, it's all smashed up and old. My mind, my fucking… psyche… my muthafuckin emotional apparatus… is a seventy-year-old fishing boat. It's all old and smashed up. It's been pulled out of the water like thirty times and put back together…"

Kimo laid his head back and closed his eyes. He mumbled in a whisper that I could just barely make out.

"It's to the point where it's leaking in like, a hundred places, and being held together with old moldy ropes and flakey old duct tape. The motor… the motor is all fucked up. It roars and chokes in a death-defying symphony with every passing wave and swell. The fucking thing overheats and dies a thousand times but it starts back up again. Grinding and growling its last words. I'm alone… in my mind. In my boat. I'm so alone in this boat. I'm alone and I'm up to my waist in cold salty water that's rushing through the rusted steel walls. I'm alone and I'm watching a storm coming on the horizon. I'm alone and I'm laughing…"

Kimo laughed quietly and then passed out.

Now I was alone.

I started crying again. I would hold my breath and let it out slowly so my dad wouldn't hear me. After I was done I laid down the best I could and tried to pass out too.

***

"Byron! Byron! Please! Hey! *Pleeeeease!*"

My dad was screaming.

I was trying to get up when something knocked into the boat. I fell down and pain froze me. My head was ringing so loud I couldn't think.

"*Heeeeeelp! Heeeeeeeeeeelp!*"

My dad was screaming. It was the scream of death and desperation. The sun was setting and it was hard to see the water but the dorsal fins were unmistakable. Uncle's blood had called the sharks. At least four giant tiger sharks were swimming around us. The biggest one had bumped the boat. I went to the controls and started the engine. The sharks disappeared for a moment and I pulled in closer to my dad. He was screaming and trying to swim to the boat but the rope wouldn't let him.

I stopped about five feet from him. I gently rubbed my numb hands back and forth across the engine levers and watched. He was panicking. He flailed his arms. His eyes were wide and his hair was wild. It was good. I did not pull in closer to help him. I wanted to see him like that. I wanted to see him helpless.

"I want to see the sharks eat you," I whispered.

He was suddenly yanked under water violently and it was quiet. Then he popped back up with a horrible scream. The water turned red in the fading sunset. A tiger shark's head appeared above the surface for a brief moment and I saw its dark black eye close slowly as it bit down on my dad's chest and stomach. His screams turned into a gurgling sound as blood shot from his mouth. The tiger shark rolled over and he was gone. The water bubbled and churned violently for a few moments as the sharks tore at him under the surface.

Then there was nothing.

I sat down in the boat and watched the last of the sunset.

CHAPTER 12

A FLY WENT BY

HOW LONG HAD IT been?

It must've been at least twenty-four hours. More maybe. It was morning. The next morning? The one after? I was sleeping in my own filth. Vomit, piss and shit. I was in my apartment in Waipahu. There was an IV bag hanging from my television stand. It was empty. There was a fly banging violently into the sliding screen door. I closed my eyes and drifted off again…

***

I see Travis from the backseat of his truck talking on a mobile phone.

"I don't know, Sam, the kid doesn't look good. I know, I know, but Kimo is kinda… I don't think Kimo is gonna be taking care of anyone for a while. Uncle is gone. We don't know if he's ever gonna come back. It's for his own good. For all of us actually. This is a good thing, Sam. It's time to put your money where your mouth is. Do you really love my sister or is she just a side thing. The time is now, Sam! Listen, I'm gonna see if I can get a hold of the kid's girlfriend and see if she can keep an eye on him. You go by his place and get him on some drugs… I don't know! Whatever—morphine, antibiotics, anti-inflammatories for the fucking swelling! I don't know! You're the fucking doctor!"

***

I see my car crashing and rolling and Cynthia flying out of the car and then the car rolling to a stop right on top of her. The metal sliding through her stomach.

I see me holding a broken chair leg and sliding the metal right through Cynthia's stomach.

***

I see Maryanne standing on the shore as I drive the speed boat up onto the sand. She doesn't even look at me. She walks up to the boat and slaps Kimo.

"Is he dead?" she asks Kimo.

Kimo doesn't wake up and Travis comes to grab him. Maryanne looks at me and asks, "Well… is Uncle dead?"

I nod yes.

She closes her eyes and tilts her head back. Her hands clutch at her chest like she's holding her heart. She takes a deep breath and smiles at the night sky. It's almost a full moon and the white sand is glowing. The white wash from the small shore break runs up to her legs with glowing white bubbles and swirls around her flowing sundress. The white moonlight lays gently on the dark skin of her shoulders and cheeks. For a moment, it is the most beautiful thing. For a moment the sound of her breathing and the sound of the waves and the sound of the light breeze through the dry beach grass mix together as one thing. One beautiful thing. For a moment she looks real. She looks like she is about to dance or sing or laugh and spin around stretching her arms out. Round and around until collapsing onto Kimo's chest giggling. For a moment…

She opens her eyes and looks around puzzled.

Her head tilts slightly as she asks herself something and then sarcastically chuckles at the answer. The coldness slowly pours back over her face like poisoned honey.

Then she looks at me.

"Your dear old dad?" she says in a pouty voice with her bottom lip out feigning sadness.

I see my dad screaming with the shark's head above water. The shark's black eyes looking at me. I squeeze my eyes shut and cover my face with my hands.

She gets real close to me and gently puts her hand on my head. Her breath smells like whiskey and toothpaste.

"I don't like you. You are a very fragile, weak little boy. I don't ever want to see you again," she whispers and pushes her thumb into my swollen eye. The pain swallows me. I scream out. She lets go and uses her other hand to open my good eye and says:

"Make sure I never see you again!"

***

I see my dad's eyes wide.

I see the shark, now tripled in size, coming up and crunching into his chest. Then it is me. The shark is triple in size and it is crunching into my chest and ripping a huge chunk out of me. My ribs are cracking and breaking. My organs are shredding and tearing. A huge part of me is gone.

***

Buzz, buzz, buzz.

***

I woke up and my arm had been pinched under me against my broken ribs.
Buzz, buzz, buzz.

The same fly. I opened the sliding screen. It was afternoon now. The breeze was pushing against the fly. It couldn't get out. It kept jamming itself into the screen. It could see the world on the other side. I closed my eyes and drifted off.

***

I see the shark. Now four times its size. In my living room thrashing back and forth. Its jaws snapping at the air. I can't move. It swings my way and it clamps down on my head. Slowly my head starts to crack open. It makes a high-pitched squeaking sound like when a super thick branch is about to break on a tree. Finally it busts open and blood and chunks of meat and brain spill out onto the floor. I fall out of the shark's mouth and he snaps at the air looking for me. I sit up and try to pick up the chunks of meat from my head. They shouldn't touch the floor. As I grab at them I can see they are pictures. Blood and meat cover pictures that are moving. They are memories. They are memories of me and my dad. Memories of us together playing. Swimming. Memories of me riding on his back underwater. Memories of him smoking a joint listening to records in the living room. Memories of laughing with him. Memories of him letting me steer the car while he pedals. Driving. Memories of looking at the curtains. Memories of the light breeze coming in through the window and easing them slowly up the wall. Brown, sheer, billowing curtains. Memories of me being afraid they would get caught in the ceiling fan. Memories of the bedroom door slowly being pushed by the wind. Memories of him laying down in his bed naked. Memories of me crying. Memories of me saying it hurts. Memories of him saying relax. Memories of us in his bed together. Suddenly, the shark comes up out of his bed and clamps down on his chest and his bed turns into the bloody ocean. I sit in the corner of the room holding chunks of my own bloody brain in my tiny hands. I am little. I am a little boy. I am a little boy screaming and crying and bleeding with chunks of my brain in my little hands.

The shark lifts its head and swallows the last of my father. I can see its body bulge and constrict as what's left of him makes its way through the shark's body. The shark eases back down and floats on top of the stagnant pool of blood my living room floor has become. It is still for a moment. I try to push back further into the wall. The blood ripples as it swims toward me. It turns its head to the side and stares at me through one black eye the size of a dinner plate. It doesn't blink. I stand up and yell at the shark. No words. My little boy's voice cracking and shrieking. The shark opens its mouth and swings back to face me. It bites down on my legs and lifts me into the air. I reach down and pull back the rough skin covering its black eye and shove my whole hand straight in. My arm slides in all the way up to my elbow. The shark's mouth opens immediately and splashes me onto the floor. I stand up and yell at the shark again. This time my voice is bigger. I am bigger. The shark opens its mouth once more and I yell down its throat. Blood shoots out of its gills. It snaps down on me again but I catch its mouth and hold it open with both hands. Its teeth rip open my palms but I don't stop stretching its mouth open. I yell again and more blood sprays out of its gills and all over the wall. The shark tries to pull away but now it's smaller. It's smaller and I'm bigger, I'm stronger. I yank its mouth open until it tears on both sides and then I let go. The shark scurries off into the corner and tries to hide. It stares at me timidly through its one good eye. I yell once more and my voice is loud and strong and echoes off the walls.

***

I woke up yelling with tears streaming down my face.

I couldn't see.

It was dark.

I felt my hands and legs for gaping teeth holes.

There were none.

The neighbor's balcony light was on.

"Eh, braddah?! You okay over there?!" he asked, concerned.

"Yeah, yeah sorry… bad dream."

I sat up and was almost sick from my own smells. I would crawl to the shower and deal with this mess after. That was my plan. I would pull myself together and figure shit out from there. I just needed some time. I just needed some sleep. The thought of going back to sleep and seeing those things again made me start shivering until the shivers turned to full blown body contractions. I started to dry heave and didn't stop for a solid five minutes. When I finally got control of myself I was back on the ground next to the sliding glass door. I saw the fly. It was dead. It had banged its head against the screen door until it died.

I started to get mad at the stupid fucking fly. At any point throughout the day it could have turned around and flown back and gone out any of the open doors. I had left them open with the stupid fuckin fly in mind. But, it didn't. It didn't because it couldn't. It couldn't see the whole living room. It couldn't see all the doors that were open. It couldn't see it that way. It was a stupid fucking fly.

I was that fly.

I had banged my head against the screen door and now I'm dying on the floor.

I lied to myself to believe what my mouth told me
And I was high enough to believe the clouds hold me...

I crawled backwards towards the kitchen. Reached up and pulled the phone by its cord onto the floor. I stared at the numbers until the dial tone turned to a busy signal. I hung it up and tried again. I couldn't remember my mom's phone number. I couldn't remember the number to my home. I left the phone on the floor and slowly got to my feet. Hung the phone back up and took a deep breath. I looked around my apartment expecting to see chunks of my brain on the floor. There wasn't. Just piss and stomach bile reflecting the evening sun on the couch and part of the floor.

I picked up the phone and looked at the numbers and dialed 672-4286.

It rang forever. I was just about to hang up when I heard my mom's voice.

"Hi, you've reached Suzanna. I'm not home right now but leave a message and I'll call back as soon as I can."

There was a long pause and you could hear her fumbling with the recorder until it beeped.

I hadn't thought of leaving a message. I hadn't even thought of talking.

"Hey... um... hey so... how's the new house? Um... this is Byron... by the way. I guess... so call me back at... I forgot the number here... um... page me at... shit... I lost my pager... or I'll call again. I was thinking of stopping by... just to you know, talk and stuff. If that would be cool... aight... so... love you, bye."

I walked to the doorway of the apartment and looked down on the underside of Waipahu.

The setting sun had turned the sky orange and the shadows were growing on the low-rent apartments. The flood lights would turn on soon. The zombies would start to make their nightly trek to Crystal City.

I lifted my eyes further and looked past Pearl Harbor and out over the ocean. Something was different. My head throbbed and the nausea threatened to ring me out again but I would not look away. I saw something. Something above the ocean that I had never been there before. Something of mine. It was a thought. It wavered over the horizon. I struggled to shape it, pulling at it gently, afraid it would disappear. The smells of trash and the sounds of fighting and the meles of conflicting music tried to pull my eyes and thoughts down into the swamp of sadness that led to Crystal City. I fought it. I focused on the mirage that danced on the very edge of my vision. It tumbled in an evening breeze that carried echoes of an unfamiliar future. A future that had always been there. Just over the ocean. Just behind the rising sun. I had never seen it. Shielding my eyes from what was behind me had blocked out what was in front of me.

I smiled wide enough to pull the stitches in my head.

Now I could see it. I could swim across that ocean and wrap my hands around it. Then use it to scoop up the rising sun. I could ride it back and forth across any sky.

"I can fuckin fly…" I said out loud.

"Damn nigga they fucked you up!" said an eight-year-old boy. He was coming out of the elevator with two of his friends. They all started laughing.

I nodded and gave an embarrassed smile. I stepped back into my apartment and shut the door.

Maybe I would clean up first and get some sleep. Then I'll fly.

EPILOGUE

"You have one new message. First new message."

"Ayo, I don't know if this is the right number. I'm trying to reach a rapper called Q. We got your mixtape from… Ayo, what's that chick's name…?"

"Lilly!"

"Nah man, it was some Hawaiian shit. Lileena or some shit, right!? Anyway my boy was out in Hawaii and got your tape and this shit is bangin man for real! You be sayin some shit. I ain't gonna front like we some big label or nothin but we got a couple joints bangin around New York right now and you know, we building! We looking for some different shit that ain't nobody heard yet so you know we wonderin if you wanna come out here an make a mixtape with us. We'll put that shit out on the streets and see what's happenin. First and foremost we put that acapella shit you spit, that 'Forever Beach'shit, over that new Biggie joint—"

"Hell yeah! Niggas ain't ready!"

"That's wassup. You know what! Let me just play this shit for you so you ain't gotta feel no way about it. Yo Mega, just play that shit…"

#

Honestly it's so far back
It's hard to remember, in hindsight on trees of youth,
The truth hangs

Like frames from still photos
We called Police popos
and hid in tall grass on our ass
until the sun rose
Frozen searchlights,
the first fights were lost
on Ewa Beach Road,
like 9 years old.
But my real pops always told me,
"The only way for you to lose…
Is to not fight back,
now you go right back
and kick and spit, talk shit until the end.
It don't matter if you win. He ain't fighting you again!"
So, bruised up, tooth chipped, blood soaked and crying
I went back to crack his fucking head with a brick.
I moved up to high school
the same rules apply,
except I was six feet.
Now who the fuck want beef?
I kept my profit
in my left pocket,
and what I owe below my nutsack
right next to my ass crack.
The drug game is shitty, gritty, it's a pity it's all we know.
I braided my fro
And Dated a hoe
And the first time I busted in like… under a minute
Fuck it I admit it
Just happy to finally get it.
Now I'm seduced by the induced euphoria
Of ass and thighs
In class I'm high
Asking girls why
Don't we cut and fuck and be right back
In my Mazda GLC hatchback

\#

Hard times and pain
often fade into something vague
What color was the paint on that Chevrolet?
What was that silly girl's name in the lingerie?
And all her silly friends
And all those weekends
Stolen tire smoke billows
Into dark black pillows
Up and down what street?
Who's that kid we beat?
Where's that silly old man that helped us dry 50 pounds?
Does the city sounds mix
With our lost innocence?
Forever beach
4 ewa out of reach
For ever
4 Ewa Beach

\#

Too much fucking, fighting, drinking and drug dealing
With Old E as my best friend
In school I'm left back again.
Fuck this bullshit. I drop out.
Now my mom's out
On the corner in her night shirt
At one in the morning
Screaming
Rain pouring
I'm leaving
Ignoring
Her voice as she cries in my rearview mirror.
I hear her though
And it echoes in the giggles of coked up hoes

And sometimes when the wind blows
I can hear what I'm supposed
To be
But mostly
I cheat life and she cheats me back.
I got a Rivy
Dropped
Intri provoc
With crushed velvet
And I stop on the corner of every block.
I let 'em all see
I'm O.C.
Mostly
Grossly encrusted by the demons so don't provoke me.
I get high all day
Drink all night
I cuss, drink, fuck and fight.
I'm right. In the wrong way.
Fuck arraignments, district attorneys, judge, jury and the plaintiff.
Bail has become a monthly expense,
I make payments.
I have the veil of can't-fail cuz I expect to be famous
I lied to myself to believe what my mouth told me
And I was high enough to believe the clouds hold me…

#

Hard times and pain
often fade into something vague
What color was the paint on that Chevrolet?
What was that silly girl's name in the lingerie?
And all her silly friends
And all those weekends
Stolen tire smoke billows
Into dark black pillows
Up and down what street?

Who's that kid we beat?
Where's that silly old man that helped us dry 50 pounds?
Does the city sounds mix
With our lost innocence?
Forever beach
4 ewa out of reach
For ever
4 Ewa Beach

END

ACKNOWLEDGMENTS

Lee Cataluna. Had it not been for how gracious she was with her time and counsel, I doubt this novel would have seen the light of day. Also a big thank you for recommending Eleanor Svaton as an editor.

Eleanor Svaton. Patience, creativity, vision and encouragement. Above all else, I sincerely appreciated her true respect for my artistic process.

Markell Parker. Thank you brother. There were a lot of phone calls.

My wife, Angelica. How many times have you heard …. "But babe!!!… Listen to this sentence!!!"

Lawrence Perrone. Yeah, we did say we would help each other all those years ago. Thank you for helping take the ball over the finish line.

The entire Hawaii Theater and Indie film community. It is here that I began to hone my storytelling craft. No matter where in the world I go or what medium I use, I carry the style, flavor, and swagger that comes from walking barefoot on a sandy gravel road. We all do.

Thank you to the ghosts of Forever Beach, Crystal City, and the Concrete Rainbow. You can rest now. I love you, but hopefully I won't be talking to you any time soon.

ABOUT THE AUTHOR

JASON QUINN has committed his life to the spoken and written word. He is a writer, producer, director, and professional actor who spent more than twenty years honing his craft on and behind local, national, and international stages and screens in New York, Los Angeles, and Honolulu.

A cinematic storyteller, Quinn performs and writes brutal truths with grit, subtlety, and nuance. He dropped an acclaimed hip hop album that had a song featured in *Grand Theft Auto*. His short film, *The Trickle Down Effect*, won best short film in the San Francisco Black Film Festival and the New York Underground Film Festival. In 2020, he starred in the movie *Waikiki*, which won best film at the Hawaii Film Festival, and he's also appeared in shows such as Marvel's *Inhumans*, *Magnum P.I.*, *Hawaii Five-O*, and *NCIS: Hawaii*.

However, Quinn's greatest professional achievement is publishing *Concrete Rainbow* and recording and self-narrating the audio book. The audio book serves as a culmination and synthesis of all of Quinn's talents. It's a must listen.

Quinn lives in Honolulu with his wife, Angelica, and son, Ziya.

9 789898 672280